THE CAPRICORN
QUADRANT

THE CAPRICORN
QUADRANT

CHARLES RYAN

NAL BOOKS

NAL BOOKS
Published by the Penguin Group
Penguin Books USA Inc., 375 Hudson Street,
New York, New York 10014, U.S.A.
Penguin Books Ltd, 27 Wrights Lane,
London W8 5TZ, England
Penguin Books Australia Ltd, Ringwood,
Victoria, Australia
Penguin Books Canada Ltd, 2801 John Street,
Markham, Ontario, Canada L3R 1B4
Penguin Books (N.Z.) Ltd, 182-190 Wairau Road,
Auckland 10, New Zealand

Penguin Books Ltd, Registered Offices:
Harmondsworth, Middlesex, England

First published by NAL Books, an imprint of New American Library, a division of
Penguin Books USA Inc.

First Printing, August, 1990
10   9   8   7   6   5   4   3   2   1

 REGISTERED TRADEMARK—MARCA REGISTRADA

Library of Congress Cataloging-in-Publication Data:

Ryan, Charles, 1937–
    The capricorn quadrant / by Charles Ryan.
        p.   cm.
    ISBN 0-453-00737-6
    I. Title.
    PS3568.Y265C36   1990
    813'.54—dc20   90-5749
                                                         CIP

PRINTED IN THE UNITED STATES OF AMERICA
Set in Primer
Designed by Leonard Telesca

PUBLISHER'S NOTE
This is a work of fiction. Names, characters, places, and incidents either are the product of the
author's imagination or are used fictitiously, and any resemblance to actual persons, living or dead,
events, or locales is entirely coincidental.

To my father, Thomas Ryan,
who showed me the value and
power of the written word.

Beware the Latitudes of Capricorn and the Great South Equatorial, for there the *Kraken* waits in silence . . .

  —from the journal of Captain Jeremiah Pollard,
  Master of the whaler Prudent Mary,
  1854

THE CAPRICORN
QUADRANT

Prologue

Sary Shagan Missile Research Center
Tulun, Irkutsk Oblast
Time: 11:02 P.M.

Colonel Valery Tukhvalin liked the rain, for in his native Kazakh it was a symbol of good fortune. As he watched the tiny droplets glimmer on the windows of the ICF-1 Project's operations room, he nodded in satisfaction. Yes, he thought, the coming test flight would run smoothly.

Tukhvalin was fifty years old but looked much younger. His hair was thick and black, and his dark eyes held the cool placidity some men get when they've spent their lives in a dangerous business. The colonel's was testing experimental aircraft, and he was considered the best of the breed in the Russian air force.

His electronics officer, Captain Second Vil Pyadshev, appeared from the upstairs ready section. Like the colonel, he wore a tight-fitting black flight suit for high-altitude flying. Together the men went out through a small tunnel that connected the OP room with an adjacent hangar.

The immense hangar was ablaze with lights for the ground crews and design technicians busily working on a strange-looking aircraft. Totally black, it had no fuselage as such, but was one continuous wing curved like a boomerang. It spread 188 feet, and the tips nearly touched the walls of the hangar. Astern of the

1

root frame, two vertical stabilizers towered thirty-five feet into the air.

The most prominent aspect of the huge spy plane, though, was a brooding aura of menace. Its outer surface reflected no light, and the twin slit windshields, glowing softly from the cockpit panels within, looked like the watchful, evil eyes of a night creature.

It was called the Saber.

Production schedules called for operational deployment of an entire squadron of Sabers within the next four years. Cruising at altitudes of over sixty miles, they would form a temporary suborbital defense screen against American Star Wars satellites. By the late 1990s they would then be replaced by the main Soviet missile defense network of orbiting antisatellite (ASAT) vehicles, code-named Cosmos, some of which were already in orbit in a shut-down state so enemy radar sweeps would show them as merely space debris.

For now, though, it was the Saber's mission to stand guard and it was well suited for that. Its technology was the result of years of secret Soviet research, primarily in the fields of stealth aerodynamics, artificial-intelligence electronics, and cold-fusion ordnance.

In flight the aircraft was nearly invisible to radar probes. Frames and struts were made of reinforced carbon-carbon material welded to a graphite epoxy matrix. The surface skin was made of high-tensile ceramics and cyanamid-based plastic checkered with radar-absorbent wedges that channeled and dissipated radar impulses. Its three Lyul'ka FL 30P turbofan engines were fitted with meshed intakes, serpentine baffle ducts, and recooling, high-aspect ratio afterflows that left nearly zero detectable thermal wash.

The aircraft's electronic component was composed of two separate computer systems relay-linked for emergency backup. The first controlled all flight and avionics functions; the second, all weapon targeting, guidance and memory data. This second system was centered around a Kamov-T-VAC fourth-generation computer linked to a low-arc artificial-intelligence subunit. Possessing a memory bank of astounding complexity and content, it worked off an external network of active/passive radar and infrared sensors.

The weapons module represented a level of technology years ahead of any other country's. Utilizing cold fusion, it was comprised of a miniature particle chamber made of lidium-tin, which contained heavy water and a reaction core of radioactive polonium. In its "hot" state, it could produce a high-pulse, phased beam of fusion energy, fired through a barrel located in a ball turret aft the cockpit. Except for a six-degree arc directly astern, the barrel could be homed to any target above or below the aircraft. Within the Kamov's memory bank was a countermeasure response grid consisting of five category modes in ascending orders of power.

Category Five was designated to retaliate against enemy nuclear weaponry.

At last, everything was go. The pilots and technicians gathered under the nose of the aircraft for a ritual *na pososhok*, a toast of vodka flavored with cinnamon. Then Tukhvalin and Pyadshev climbed aboard and the canopy was slid back and sealed. They sat one behind the other in the cramped cockpit, and all around them were screens and monitor-tracking displays, engine grids, computer video consoles, graphic screens, and digital key panels. The air smelled oddly of lemons from hydraulic packing.

As external power conduits were reenergized, the panel instruments instantly came alive. Tukhvalin began running through preflight checklists and Pyadshev droned responses. A field dolly with a power carriage hooked up to the nose wheel strut and pulled the huge aircraft out into the rain.

With checks completed, the colonel turned his full attention to the little red sleeve of light from the ground chief's flashlight. When it twirled, Tukhvalin started flicking switches and hit the starter buttons. There was the whine of blowers and then the three Lyul'kas came up into power. The aircraft trembled and the sound roared off into the night as he threw a moment of full military thrust and then backed off, the echoes dying into a rushing rumble.

Cleared, he began taxiing down the centerline of the runway. Twirling his frequency dials, he listened in to Sary Shagan Flight Control for updated recon reports of air and sea traffic east of Vladivostok. Meanwhile, Pyadshev linked to the Tulun Meteorological Station and began feeding into the avionics system a tape of the latest weather information from the EURO-SOV network via transmission stations in Moscow and Tzetvosk.

At the end of the runway, Tukhvalin swung around. Before him the periphery of the runway was faintly illuminated by blue lights. He hit engine power for a second, then dropped back, and keyed his intercom: "Vil, have you completed weather link?"

"Yes, Comrade Colonel. All systems are showing go."

"Give me primary course."

"At one-five level, maintain standard climb and hold one-point-one turn to the left to course zero-nine-nine degrees."

Tukhvalin repeated the numbers. He checked his panel chronometer which, like all Soviet military units, was fixed to Moscow Standard Time. "Mark TO roll and log: one-eight-zero-two hours."

"I have it, sir."

A minute later, the Saber lifted into the rain.

Tukhvalin leveled at 280,000 feet and began cruising on a southeast heading at five hundred knots, slightly under Mach 1. He would remain at this altitude for the next thirteen hours. Then, eight thousand miles from his starting point in central Russia, he'd descend to fifty thousand feet for a rendezvous with helicopter tankers from the Soviet carrier group HC-3 for refueling. The *skadra*, with its carrier flagship, the *Minsk*, was already holding a position eight hundred miles south of Tahiti at coordinates 30:30 S/140:30 E. The actual linkup had to be precisely timed so it would occur during an eight-minute shadow period when American surveillance satellites were out of range of the refueling site.

As he eased into his seat, he glanced below. Fifty-two miles down, the dark world was punctuated by tiny clusters of lights that marked cities. They drifted past imperceptibly. Above, the stars were like stark, icy jewels.

Moving in silence—the rumble of its engines was left behind in the thin atmosphere of this altitude—the Saber's flight track would take her first across Manchuria, then over the Sea of Japan and Honshu Island, and finally out above the vast reaches of the Pacific. Her radios would remain mute except for thirty-minute position reports given in pure code encapsulated in short three-second bursts.

Running against the sun, time would become distorted to the pilots. They would pass through a speeded-up dawn and a day and then into night again before they reached the Tahiti rendezvous.

*   *   *

Seven hours after takeoff, when they were two hundred miles south of Wake Island, Tukhvalin set up a new heading of one-four-one degrees. And two hours later, near evening, they sighted a large flotilla of warships off the Kingman Reef. Intelligence reports identified the ships as elements of a U.S. task group out of Pearl Harbor with the carrier *Coral Sea* as flagship. They took high-resolution photos of the group's strength and deployment patterns, and coded the sighting to Cam Ranh Bay headquarters, which was now their vector control.

Tukhvalin, finding his calculations indicated they were running one minute, forty seconds ahead of schedule, powered back slightly to eat up some time. Within four hours they would be passing over the Tuamotu and Society archipelagoes of French Polynesia, where he would begin his gradual descent to meet the tankers.

Night came at them, fusing up with an indigo wash out of the curved eastern horizon. With it came a nearly full moon that sat in the heavens like a molten plate. Soon afterward, they began picking up the navigational radar signal from Faaa Airport, located three miles south of the capital city of Tahiti, Papeete. Down there it was now 11:47 P.M. Pyadshev made the fix, logged the time, and advised Tukhvalin to initiate his descent angle.

Six minutes later, something went violently wrong.

The Saber's primary avionics/control system suddenly experienced wild malfunctions. Warning lights began blowing all over the cockpit panels. Tukhvalin, jolted by the sudden profusion of emergency signals, was immobilized for a second. Then, hands flying, he began bellowing orders to Pyadshev: "Shut down, shut down! I'm going manual."

It was too late. Key PAC subsystems were already deteriorating, and the first to go completely were the human-survival and engine-power circuits. Oxygen pressure within the tank lines instantly dropped to a catastrophic level. Air already in the feed conduits to the pilots' helmets was sucked back. This caused an imbalance gorge at the intersections from the main tanks, and automatic lock-down switches, designed to prevent contamination, immediately activated.

Tukhvalin, hearing the switches go, slammed his hand onto the emergency system button. It was dead. He whirled around and glanced back at Pyadshev. The man's face was wide with shock and he suddenly arched backward, as if some terrible force had just struck him in the small of the back. He began clawing frantically at his helmet straps as his body became starved of oxygen.

Tukhvalin's mind was whirling, yet he was aware that he was moving with unbearable slowness. He watched his hand cross in front of him, headed for the emergency ejection master panel. The visual infeed of it had also slowed. It seemed to come at him in blocks of individual, colorless frames.

His throat muscles began convulsing in spasms. Then his chest. He opened his mouth, distinctly heard himself gagging. But that, too, came as if from a tape slowed down to a near stop. Even as he tried to tear off his helmet, he blinked once and blacked out.

The PAC continued disintegrating. Internally, its main emergency core unit, the attack/damage subsystem, was becoming flooded with interjects. Respond surges began shorting tiny circuit links, and automatic shutdown switches were activating all over as the system neared total collapse.

Within the weapons bay, the Kamov-T-Vac, which had been monitoring the PAC's fatal electronic plunge, now activated itself and assumed control. Running through its trillionth-of-a-second grid panels, it instantly ran tracer probes through the less dense PAC circuitry. Electrons were hurled out and came back carrying bytes of data like homing bees. The Kamov analyzed the probes and drew up the artificial-intelligence subunit for a response:

STATUS: PAC DISINTEGRATION
REASON: INVADING NUMERICAL SEQUENCE INTERJECT
DANGER ASSESSMENT: EXTREME
CMR: SIDE SHUNT AND DESTROY

Within nanoseconds the Kamov located the invading sequence and set up a pre-circuit pathway into a dead end. There the sequence was broken down and annihilated. But now, fuel-starved, the Lyul'kas flamed out and the Saber began losing thrust momentum and dipping into a right spin. The Kamov shot out countermeasure commands to the now subservient PAC system. With power vectors at zero, it set up the aircraft's controls for an emergency landing, power-off glide. As it went, it repaired the downed circuits of the primary system by creating bypasses and inserting override memory input. Instrument lines were recharged, gyros spun up. Remaining fuel cells were blown empty to decrease weight and prevent impact explosion.

Momentary glide stability was achieved.

Gradually, then faster and faster, it began to dissipate. The weight of the engines, with combustion components forward of the span line, were beginning to pull the nose of the aircraft down despite maximum aileron deflection. If not stopped, the Saber would pitch down, its own momentum carrying it into a fatal inverted spin.

The Kamov instantly reacted. It extended the roll/lift-dump spoilers, located inboard the trailing wing edges, and adjusted the flaperons that would act as airbrakes. Abruptly the aircraft slowed, nosing up. The computer stabilized it again.

But it was still a delicate business; it was imperative that the weight-to-lift component be redistributed. The Kamov began scanning all internal systems and masses to find superfluous weight. By using circuit boards for ID and the cockpit-environment sensors for nonintegrated mass, it catalogued each piece of gear and assigned it a priority base.

Almost immediately it fixed on the inert bodies of Tukhvalin and Pyadshev. For a moment it was puzzled. If these objects had been outside the aircraft, its fine-tuned external sensor system could have given a complete analysis of matter density, temperature, even internal components and, thus, an identification. But the cockpit sensors were inadequate, giving only general parameters of mass weight.

The Kamov went to the AI unit for appraisal. The AI pondered a moment, then came back:

```
SUPPOSITIONAL STATUS: HUMAN BODIES
COMBINED MASS: 153.93 KILOS (ADJ.)
ASSESSMENT: UNNECESSARY AVIONICS FUNCTION
CMR: JETTISON
```

The Kamov activated the ejection-firing procedure. Instantly the flush canopy slid forward. The airstream roared above it, yet the aerodynamic curve of the aircraft had been so finely calculated, it passed without causing inboard-suction turbulence. A moment later, the bases of both seats exploded. With Tukhvalin and Pyadshev still strapped in, the seats went rocketing out into space. Instantly the flush canopy slid back and was resealed.

Now the Kamov began sealing all other external cavities: air intakes, refueling vents, antennae sleeves, shield locks inside the after-exhaust tunnels. And the Saber continued its controlled plunge toward the ocean, dropping twenty thousand feet a minute.

Altitude: 120,000 feet . . .

100,000 . . .

80,000 . . .

The external sensors and active radar pulses were now "feeling" the impact zone. The data was analyzed and instantly displayed on overhead screens for the pilots no longer there. Ident:

STATUS: OCEANIC PLAIN
TOPOGRAPHY: UNDULATED/CREST-TO-TROUGH MAX: 1.7 METERS
TEMPERATURE: 24.8 DEGREES CELSIUS
WIND: 8 KNOTS AT 187 DEGREES
BAROMETRIC PRESSURE: 101,300 N (PER SQ. METER)
ALTIMETER SETTING: 29.92

Down she came into thickening air, black and silent.

20,000 . . .

10,000 . . .

At two thousand feet, the Kamov began easing the aircraft out of its steep descent angle: full up nose, everything hard up deflection. She glided, dropping slower, easing to the sea.

The after underbelly struck first with a thunderous impact. The aircraft richocheted off the surface, flew for another hundred yards, and then struck again, once more lifted like a skipping stone. The third time the leading edges of the wings plowed into the water, hurling back a fuming cascade that shimmered in the blue-white light of the moon. On she went, blowing through swells, losing momentum. At last she skewered to a stop and lay still on the ocean. Like a feeding bat, she pitched slightly, light pulsing through the slit windshields.

Deep within her, the Kamov was bristling as sensors scanned the environment and ran integrity status reports. Data shot back: the luminosity rating of moon glow, the density of adjacent water, chemical analysis of the wind. All of it went into the computer's memory banks.

Out of the plethora of information, the Kamov detected an energy pulse from the southwest. Instantly it homed to it, fixing range and bearing, frequency, and pulse vector. It explored the avionics memory tapes and found Pyadshev's log of the Faaa Airport navigational-beacon coordinates. The AI gave parameters:

STATUS: ELECTROMAGNETIC PULSES (RADAR BAND)
WAVELENGTH: 6.8 MM (20,000MHZ)
BEARING: 193.7 DEGREES (RELATIVE)
DANGER ASSESSMENT: POTENTIAL MILITARY A/D VECTORING SYSTEM
ELEVATION: BELOW LINE OF SIGHT
CMR: CATEGORY ONE STRIKE FOR CLOUD VECTOR BOUNCE TRAJECTORY/
    ELEVATION: 3 DEGREES SPAN AH

The Kamov fixed the firing solution. It activated the fusion chamber and fed it in. A bright, pulsing red glow fused from the ball dome. There was the soft hum of electric motors and gear chains as the firing barrel came up into trajectory angle lock-on.

Firing command was hurled.

There was a hushed expulsion of energy that threw proton thermoluminescence in a beam no larger than a copper wire. One one-thousandths of a second later, the "enemy" vectoring pulses disappeared.

The Kamov scanned the now quiescent horizon. Then it clicked itself into watch state as the sensor matrix continued probing the environment. In the silence of open ocean, the Saber rocked and pitched, the passing swells creating sucking sounds under her. Inexorably she was being nudged by a three-knot current toward the outer atoll fields of the Tuamotu Archipelago forty miles to the south.

1

Scripps Research Station 3
Mataiva Atoll, Tuamotu Archipelago

Shortly after midnight, Tahiti time, a large albatross crashed through the window of the station's operations Quonset. Amid flying glass, the mortally wounded bird then slammed onto a work table containing microscopes and specimen jars. All of them were swept off the table and shattered on the floor.

Six feet away, marine biologist Cas Bonner sat bolt upright in his bunk. He had been deep in a dream—something to do with a woman's mouth, a long, slanting wave front—and still caught up in it, he rolled to the floor, his left hand sweeping a spear gun from a wall rack. Trying to clear his head, he crouched beside the bunk near a pool of moonlight.

The bird, a shapeless shadow on the floor, thrashed convulsively. Both its wings had been broken by the impact, and now it savagely pounded the severed joints against the planking. It hissed in terror like a roused snake and the sound merged with a shrill screeching coming from outside the Quonset.

Cas spied a movement across the room. His diving partner, Skip Cowell, was inching his way toward the window. Cas heard the sudden metallic *chunk* of a carbine bolt ramming home and then Skip whispered, "Cas?"

"Yeah."

"What the fuck is that thing?"

At that moment the animal went still. Bonner eased over to it and touched it gently. The feathers were sticky with warm blood, and he could feel the body quivering. "It's an albatross."

Skip flicked on a flashlight and came over. The bird had left a Rorschach pattern of blood on the floor. Its neck was broken and one eye, bulging grotesquely, glistened in the light like a dark marble. Cowell looked up. "Damn, listen to that. Sounds like a whole—"

A heavy thump! against the outside of the prefab shelter cut off the rest of his sentence. Both men jumped. A second later, they heard another heavy collision followed by the rustling sound of something sliding down the wall.

"Kill that light," Cas snapped. Scurrying to the window, all the while feeling glass shards under his bare feet, he peered out. What he saw jarred him. There were downed albatross all over the compound, thrashing on the ground. Above them, others skimmed low over the sand, their great outspread wings throwing shadows.

Cowell crawled up beside him. He watched for a moment, then cursed loudly. "Son of a bitch, they're gonna demolish my chopper." He and Cas headed for the door, flung it open, and lunged out. Skip raced for the cement landing pad where the station helicopter, a two-man LT-2, was chained down.

Cas headed for one of the downed birds and dropped to his knees beside it. He smelled the tangy scent of excrement and fear emanating from it. Hearing Cowell shout a warning, he glanced up. Three huge albatross were sweeping directly toward him. In reflex, he dropped to the ground. The movement caused the birds to lift slightly, but almost instantly the one on the right smashed head-on into the compound flagpole. Its neck snapped with the cracking sound of a small whip.

The remaining two veered, one pulling into a climb, the other passing directly over him. He felt the downwash of its wings and heard the soft sough of air through its feathers. Like an aerobatic pilot going into a snap roll, the animal turned upside down and instantly rammed itself viciously into the ground.

"Fire into the air," Cas bellowed. "Drive 'em off. They're disoriented."

Cowell opened up with the carbine, rapping the rounds out in three quick bursts. As the explosions bounced off the Quonset and echoed out over the ocean, they seemed to cause a shock wave in the albatross skein. In a unified swerve they wheeled away. Then, bunching and flaring and bunching again as they rose, the skein crossed the narrow atoll. The birds headed toward the east, their cries slowly fading into the night.

Bonner got up and wandered among the fallen birds. There were at least thirty down, most of them dead. The wounded continued to struggle, hissing and trying to strike at him. Skip jogged back across the compound, holding the butt of the carbine braced against his hip. "Jesus H. Christ," he said in wonderment. "You ever seen anything like that?"

"How's the chopper?"

"I think it's all right. One smacked into the glass, though. Got blood and shit all over the place." He looked up at the sky. "Man, what in hell made them do this?"

Cas shook his head. "I don't know." The whole thing was weird. He knew that seabirds—particularly this species, *Pholebritias sootie*—avoided flying over land masses, especially at night. They were able to use their cries like radar probes to pinpoint exposed ground. Obviously something had radically disoriented these creatures. But what? And how?

For the next twenty minutes, they wandered all over the small atoll, searching for wounded birds. Those merely stunned were left alone, and the others with more massive wounds were humanely dispatched. They carried the carcasses down to the beach and left them for the outgoing tide to take out to sea.

Bonner saved three bodies, including the one in the Quonset, and put them into the food locker so he could perform an autopsy on them in daylight. Still, even a quick examination had already shown a bizarre wound pattern. All three had feather and body-tissue burns in straight lines. And the eyes bulged grotesquely, as if they had been exposed to a sudden drop of atmospheric pressure.

The evidence triggered an idea in his mind, and he didn't like what it was telling him. Although a full autopsy would have to wait until he could get the body tissues back to Papeete, he decided to do the preliminary work now rather than wait for morning. He chose the Quonset bird and took it to the small station lab in the rear of the maintenance shop.

He went over every inch of it: felt the texture of bone structures with his fingers, studied feather roots, tracked the burn
lines across filoplumes and lores muscles below the left eye. The
intensity of the heat source had literally melted the beak cartilage
like wax. He gazed through a magnifying glass into the imploded
depths of the dead eyes and saw that the back of the retinas had
turned to phosphorescent powder.

Then he dissected the bird. Several internal organs were shattered, particularly the liver and brain, and others showed burn
damage. In particular, the lungs were seared black. Meticulously
he sliced tissue samples and packed them in labeled solution
bottles. He and Skip were scheduled to run several station specimen panels back to the military lab in Papeete tomorrow. With
the better gear there, he'd be able to study these in depth at the
same time.

Cowell had already cleaned up the mess on the Quonset floor
when Cas returned and was now reassembling their radio transceiver. Inexplicably it had blown circuits during or after the bird
strike. He had it working again, though, and rock music from
station WKIH, Auckland, was coming softly through the speaker.

Skip glanced over the top of the radio. "Well?"

Bonner poured himself a cup of coffee before answering. He
was a big man, six-three, with the shoulders of a weightlifter
developed from years of underwater work. His hair was bleached
by the sun and his skin had the smooth, rich tone of burnished
copper. His deep brown eyes usually held a mischievous, be-
mused twinkle, but at the moment they were hard.

"Those birds were struck by an energy beam," he said.

"A what?"

"A beam. With one hellish amount of heat in it." He explained
what he'd found.

"Jesus!" Skip said when he finished. "Where the hell could—"
Then he stopped, gave Cas a sidelong look. "It was that secret
Frenchie platform, wasn't it?"

"You got it," Bonner snapped.

Shortly after one, two divers reached the underwater northeast
main induction vents of the French experimental platform located one hundred thirty miles northeast of Mataiva. Both wore
wet suits and self-contained, refiltering breathing gear that cre-

ated no exhaust bubbles. Each carried a shielded crimson dive light, invisible from the surface, which gave objects a gray, pallid distortion. They were also equipped with a knife strapped to one calf, a small P-6 pistol holstered on the other, a compact butt bag of tools, and a short bang stick armed with a twelve-gauge shotgun shell to ward off sharks. They had come under the platform's radar screen on a swift native twin-hulled sailing canoe called a *natarua*, which was now riding a small sea anchor a half mile to the west.

One of the divers signaled to the other, who quickly lifted away and disappeared into the darkness. The first diver studied the nearest vertical vent. Three in all, these huge shafts drew in seawater for the massive cooling ducts that maintained a constant temperature in the platform's main power transformers and the network of above-surface transfer units. Tendrils of *lemu* seaweed grew along the edges of the vents, waving gently in the slight suction current from the induction pumps.

The diver's name was Kiri Valjean, and she was the leader of a two-man KGB covert unit based in Papeete. After a moment she slipped into the vent. Several yards in, it narrowed and curved upward. Within a minute she reached a heavy mesh screen. Here the current was stronger, and bits of debris and dead fish were stuck against the wire.

Using a small underwater aerosol cutting torch, she quickly carved a hole in the mesh, slipped through, and continued up the vent. Now it went straight up, narrowing even more. Twenty feet beyond the mesh there was a cluster of individual conduits in the center of the tube. The suction was powerful around the ends of the conduits, and it pulled at her as she skimmed past.

The vent was now only about four feet wide and she had to squeeze between the wall and the conduit cluster. She reached a ladder made of U bars bolted to the wall and there were plimson depth marks beside each step. A moment later, she reached the surface. It had little whirlpools and made a sucking sound that went hollowly up the tube. She was now somewhere between sea level and the bottom of the platform, since capillary action was holding the inside water above the ocean surface. The air in the vent was hot and thick.

At the zero plimson mark was an inspection hatch. The door had metal chits in a circular pattern with a small wheel handle.

She pulled off her breathing mask and tucked it into a pouch in her filter pack. Brushing back her hood, she listened at the hatch a moment, then whirled the wheel, pulled the door open, and climbed through.

She entered a small room filled with electrical wall panels and two low-voltage auxiliary pumps. On a small work desk standing on tall legs was an empty coffee maker, a journal filled with schematic displays, and a pornographic magazine opened to a picture of two women cavorting in a bathtub. Scanning the rest of the room quickly, she noticed a larger hatch door to her right.

Kiri slipped out of her fins and looped the ends through her weight belt. For several minutes she studied the journal, mentally absorbing each of the schematic displays. Then she moved to the larger hatchway, again listened, and opened it slowly. The next room was huge, brilliantly lit, full of hum. It looked like the control room of a gigantic dam's main power station. There were numerous banks of monitoring dials, transfer exchangers, and panels of switching grids.

Once more Kiri scanned all around, her dark green eyes flashing. With the hood pulled back and her rich brown hair plastered against her skull, the sculpted, stunningly beautiful features of her face were set in relief. She had high cheekbones that drew in and down to full lips. Her skin was the soft color of maple, and her eyes, carrying a faint Oriental narrowing at their edges, gave her glances the sharp, sultry look of an angered feline.

As she studied the equipment, she shook her head, impressed. Tremendous power was being handled through this room, much more than she had anticipated. But there was something missing. Although everything was running on automatic, there should have been an operator here. Where the hell was he?

Taking advantage of her momentary luck, she scurried to the main door. It opened onto a corridor that led deeper into the platform complex. The hall was painted a soft green and there were overhead conduits of brightly polished brass.

She paused, considering. From the snippets of information she had managed to gather in Papeete, she knew that the primary project-control room was somewhere on this floor. Her goal was to actually see what monitors and panels it contained. If she could do that, she'd know precisely what the platform's main experiment was and, more important, how far it had already progressed.

She was about to step into the hall when she felt a tiny wisp of ocean air touch her face. She drew back. At the far end of the hall was a fire door. The sea breeze had moved it slightly. She tried to see what was beyond it, but it was too dark. Dammit! she thought. Had the door merely been left open or was somebody out there?

She looked up the hall the other way. It was about seventy feet to where the corridor formed a corner: too far to risk being spotted by someone between her and retreat. She'd have to check it. She paused a moment, then darted to the fire door and hugged the wall, listening. All she heard were the sounds of the ocean sixty feet down, the soft slaps of wavelets against the platform's foundation pilings.

Gently she eased the door farther open and listened again. Still nothing. Her body relaxed, but just as her hand reached up to pull the door shut, it was jerked fully open and a man in bright orange coveralls was standing there staring at her.

For a split second neither moved. Then the man opened his mouth to yell. To stop him, Kiri hurled herself forward, planting the top of her head directly in his chest. Her momentum carried them both out and down onto a small landing. There was a string of tiny red lights along its edge and up the frame of a metal stairway.

Instantly rolling away, Kiri caught the smell of the man's outburst of breath. It held the sharp acetate odor of methamphetamine. Obviously, this was the missing power room operator who had slipped out here to fire some recreational crank.

And then he was on her, his weight driving her to the deck. She felt his fist just miss her head and slam into the landing. He gave a strangled groan and started another swing. But the momentary pause in his attack gave her enough time to twist and bring up her dive knife. She slashed it across, aiming for his throat. But it was a clumsy thrust. The blade nicked his cheek instead and then banged against the edge of the stairway. The impact broke her hold and the knife went skittering across the landing and over.

The man cursed wildly, and with tremendous strength he grabbed her body and rose, pulling her completely off the deck. Growling, he started to whirl her around, building momentum to smash her into the bulkhead. Before he got completely turned, she lifted her knee and rammed it into his groin. The pressure of the contact shoved back the safety sleeve of the shark stick and the twelve-gauge round exploded in a muffled *whomp*. The operator was instantly hurled up and back, still holding her. Locked together, they went hurtling over the edge of the landing and dropped the sixty feet to the ocean.

The man's body took most of the shuddering impact when they hit. Still, Kiri was momentarily shaken. She floundered, aware that he was floating close by, feeling the warmth of his blood in the water around her. High above, the massive, dark underside of the platform was silhouetted against its brilliant top lights, which cast shapeless shadows down onto the surface.

She tried to clear her head as the body drifted away, sinking slowly. Gradually, even though her ears were still ringing from the hard, wild pounds of her heart, her equilibrium returned. She stared up at the landing from which they'd fallen, then scanned right and left. No one appeared nor was there any sound of alarm.

Quickly she put on her mask and fins, somersaulted, and dove for the induction vents, going full out to escape the blood cloud. Sharks would already be homing to it, she knew. By morning there would be nothing left of the operator's body.

When she reached the vents, she began tapping on one of the outer rims. Within a few minutes her partner loomed out of the darkness, his red light floating toward her.

With hand gestures she explained what had happened. Through his mask she could see him grinning, his skin like a ghost's. His name was Valentin Katevayo, an ex-Spetsnaz swimmer commando. He had been surveying the foundation pilings for future demolition charges.

Kiri rapped her fists together, indicating abort of mission. Katevayo shook his head, his contempt clear in his face. He jacked his light up twice, held out five fingers, and sliced the back of his hand across his throat. *We go back and kill us five more Frenchmen.*

Kiri shook her head angrily, rapped her fists together again, then swam away from him, headed for the *natarua* going full out, putting her frustration into the movements of her body.

The whole mission run had gone up in the smoke of a shotgun shell. Rotten, shitty luck. Still, that excuse was unacceptable to her; only inept people depended on luck. No, she'd simply screwed up. And Katevayo's imbecilic suggestion for more blood-letting only deepened her indictment of herself.

In his office in the Council of Ministers building, Yuri Markisov, General Secretary of the Soviet Union, was meeting with an agricultural minister and deputy from Tashkent. Early afternoon sunlight flooded through a large window overlooking the east Kremlin wall and the Lenin Mausoleum. The furnishings were spare and functional: a large desk with several white telephones, a wall mirror, and twin beech credenzas containing history books in Russian, German, and English.

The minister's name was Puriesky, a plump, nervous man who shuffled papers and talked with a high, rapid chatter. He was complaining about food shortages in his province. Next to him, his deputy sat in utter silence, overwhelmed at being in the presence of the most powerful man in Russia.

Markisov paced about the room, outwardly showing interest, yet he was barely listening. He was mentally replaying an acrimonious meeting he'd had with the chairman of the Council of Ministers earlier in the day. The chairman's name was Ivan Bardeshevsky, dubbed the "Lion of Leningrad" in World War II and now leader of the reactionary Old Guard faction within the Politboro.

Others present had been Supreme Marshal Sergei Petrov, Chief of the General Staff, and council ministers Brulov, Rybinin, and Bardeshevsky's yes-man, Kandalov. The subject under discussion was the recent outbreak of ethnic rioting in the Uzbekistan republic. Bardeshevsky was more outraged than usual. "This—this insurrection must be stopped," he boomed. "If it isn't, it'll spread like a disease."

"What more would you have me do?" Markisov asked. "Troops have already been sent in to control it."

"Don't control it, destroy it."

"No, comrade, I disagree. If too much force is used too quickly, we merely create martyrs."

"Then give the bloody swine martyrs." Bardeshevsky threw out a huge fist and began opening fingers as he ticked off the locations of other nationalistic unrest within the USSR. "Lithuania,

Latvia, Turkeniya, the Ukraine: My God, our Motherland is deteriorating and you do nothing to stop it!"

Markisov eyed him calmly. "We are not doing nothing."

"Your reactions are too passive."

"Slaughtering people is not the answer, comrade. There's been too much slaughter already."

Bardeshevsky snorted with disgust and rolled his eyes toward the ceiling. They contained fire, the same fire that had burned when he hurled his tank corps against the Nazi Tiger Panzers.

Kandalov coughed softly. "But Comrade Secretary, you must admit that things are getting foreboding. Coal strikes in the north, food lines everywhere. Discontent is deepening rapidly. When will it stop?"

"I've already warned you that there would be dark times until our national transition has been completed."

"Transition?" Bardeshevsky blurted. "*Perestroika? Glasnost?* These are foolish words that mean nothing. Yet they're being used by fanatic scum to destroy this nation."

Minister Brulov quickly interjected, trying to head off the old general before things got out of hand. "Come now, Comrade Bardeshevsky, recriminations do us no good. I think that—"

The Lion of Leningrad would have none of it. "I don't give a damn for what you think," he snarled. "We all know where *you* stand." Then he turned his hot gaze on Rybinin. "And you." Then Marshal Petrov. "And even you, a soldier. Yet you shy from the thought of spilling blood."

Petrov's eyes narrowed. "What moronic talk."

The red flush on Bardeshevsky's face deepened as he thrust himself toward the marshal. "You call me moronic?"

Markisov's hand slammed on the table. "Stop this!"

Bardeshevsky turned and stared wildly at him.

"Sit down, comrade," Markisov said quietly.

"No, I will not sit down. *You're* responsible for this."

Everyone around the table gasped, and even Kandalov looked jolted. At the door, the two KGB guards stiffened. Bardeshevsky, undeterred, raved on: "If Comrade Stalin were still alive, this sacrilege would never have happened. We Russians were kings then. Now you and your idiotic *perestroika* have turned us into emasculated peasants."

Petrov burst to his feet, shoving his finger at the general. "How dare you? You overstep your bounds, Minister."

Kandalov had also risen and hurried around the table, anxious to calm Bardeshevsky. "Please, comrade," he pleaded, "you go too far."

The old general shoved him aside with a growl and continued glaring at the general secretary.

Markisov did not flinch. And when he finally spoke, his low voice carried the forceful timbre of menace: "Sit down, Bardeshevsky."

The room was absolutely still.

"Now!"

For a moment Bardeshevsky's eyes widened slightly. Then confusion came up into them. He turned and looked dumbly at Kandalov. Then he dropped heavily back into his seat. Casting his head down, he mumbled, "Forgive me, Comrade Secretary. My words were inexcusable."

Markisov felt his heart racing and his hands faintly trembled as Kandalov returned to his chair. Gradually, the tension seeped out of the air, but everyone remained extremely uncomfortable.

At last Markisov looked away from Bardeshevsky and scanned the faces of the others. "This meeting is adjourned," he said simply.

Instantly everyone except Marshal Petrov rose and wordlessly headed for the door. Bardeshevsky did not look at anyone when he stood. Brooding, he followed the others out.

Markisov turned to Petrov. "So?"

"Watch out for that man, comrade," Petrov said. "You have humiliated him. Now he will be dangerous."

The mental image faded as someone knocked on the office door, interrupting the ceaseless flow of Puriesky's complaints. Standing before the window, Markisov turned. "Yes?"

His personal secretary, Erien Trofimov, came in. "I'm sorry to interrupt, sir. But Admiral Ivan Kralkaya and a Professor Andrik Titov are begging to speak with you. The admiral says it is most urgent."

"All right, have them wait a moment." Mumbling apologies, he quickly ushered Puriesky and his deputy out. Then he returned to his desk and buzzed Trofimov to bring the others in.

Kralkaya, Chief Military Liaison for Research, snapped to attention before the desk. He was fat and had a haughty air. "Thank you for seeing us, Comrade Secretary," he said stiffly.

Titov, in sharp contrast, was a thin, almost emaciated man who creeped furtively into the room as if anguished by sudden attention. He wore a shabby gray suit and garish yellow necktie.

Markisov leaned back in his chair. "So, Kralkaya, what's so urgent?"

"We have lost the Yak-ICF-1 aircraft, sir."

Markisov's eyebrows lowered. "What the hell do you mean, you've lost it?"

"It disappeared somewhere over the South Pacific."

"Dammit! When?"

"Over two hours ago."

"And you tell me now?"

For the first time anxiety showed on the admiral's face. "We have been trying to find it, sir. We're running reconnaissance bombers out of Cam Ranh Bay and have ordered the refueling *skadra* force south of Tahiti to search its sector."

Markisov felt a kernel of rage form like a fist in his stomach. The Saber! The loss of that aircraft would be disastrous once the Old Guard got wind of it. Then a new thought struck him: What if the pilots had defected? Were they at that very moment landing at an Allied airfield? That possibility made him freeze.

"How did this happen? Why did it happen?"

"We're not positive yet. But it seems a massive malfunction occurred aboard."

"What kind of malfunction?"

Kralkaya turned slightly, passing the question to Titov.

Markisov swung his gaze to the old man. "Well?"

Titov brushed a bony finger over his mouth before speaking. "We believe the aircraft's ASPC computer was invaded by a virus."

"What? How could such a thing happen?"

Titov blinked rapidly, as if he were facing an arctic wind. "Evidence indicates it was injected during a weather-data infeed just before takeoff. It must have been on a time trigger. Once activated, it could have destroyed the integrity of the aircraft's control system. Linked stations all along the network experienced virus-originated malfunction at the same instant."

Unable to contain his rage and confusion, Markisov lunged

from his chair and moved distractedly around the room. Finally he stopped directly in front of Titov. "Are you telling me that our secure circuits have been breached?"

"No, sir. It must have entered the aircraft through the one circuit that was not secure: the transmissions from the EURO-SOV weather-information network. They are always given open channel lines."

Markisov thought about that a moment. "But that still means our security net over the Saber's been penetrated."

"Not necessarily, Comrade Secretary," Titov said hurriedly. "I believe it was a computer hacker who didn't even realize what he was doing."

"What the hell is a computer hacker?"

"An amateur computer operator. They're called hackers. They try to penetrate international computer systems and inject virus codes to disrupt the network."

"For what purpose?"

"Simply to see if they can do it. Our trace isn't complete yet, but it points to Stockholm University. There are many of these hacker clubs there."

Markisov turned away, then whirled right around again. "Is this political sabotage?"

"It could be, sir, but I doubt it. The virus was put primarily into the western European weather network. It isn't very likely that this person could have known these data would be fed to the Saber at that precise moment."

Markisov turned on Kralkaya. "I want the KGB all-out on this trace immediately. We must know if the Saber's security curtain was penetrated."

"Yes, sir," the admiral said. He hesitated. "Do you wish me to do it now, Comrade Secretary?"

"Yes, now. Notify Petrov, he'll handle it."

Kralkaya braced, departed.

Markisov returned to Titov and studied his face for a long moment. It seemed sickly and pale, coated with a veneer of perspiration. The man's eyes would not meet his, but darted like those of a schoolboy caught in a lie. Finally Markisov asked softly, "You haven't told me everything, have you?"

Titov's eyes quivered in fright. "No, sir," he mumbled.

"What else is there?"

"It's only my conjecture, Comrade Secretary. Perhaps there—"

"*Tell* me."

Titov shifted anxiously from foot to foot. "If the Saber is still intact, it's possible her weapons system has been activated."

Markisov jerked back, startled. "How can that be? The weapons bay was to remain inert on this flight."

"In a deteriorating state the ASPC computer might have passed command to the Kamov-T-Vac unit."

Markisov felt an icy chill ripple down his back. "No, that's not possible. If the plane crashed, it couldn't be intact."

"But we're not sure it did crash, sir. It's conceivable the pilots were able to bring it down safely in some remote location. Perhaps on the sea. It's completely sealed and would remain afloat."

"Then the pilots would shut the unit down."

"They can't. Without interject codes from Sary Shagan Command, the Kamov will continue operating automatically. They wouldn't even be able to enter the unit physically without proper instruments."

Markisov stared at Titov's cadaverous, distressed face. And he glimpsed something awful there, more horrible than a lost plane. He gripped the professor's fragile shoulders. "What are you holding back, damn you?"

"The category logs," Titov whispered.

A guttural sound of pure shock escaped the general secretary's lips.

"They were infed before takeoff."

Markisov recoiled. "No, that can't be! Those logs were not programmed yet."

"Sary Shagan Command chose to simulate full operational conditions and transferred the tapes."

Markisov spun away, rushed to the window, and gazed out, unseeing. His mind was roiling. He looked at the sunshine, at two soldiers talking beside the entrance to Red Square. Gradually the fury of his thoughts began to subside into coherent plans.

He marched to the intercom. "Erien, send a coded order to the commandant of the KGB garrison at the Sary Shagan missile complex. He is to take complete charge of the command structure there. No radio transmissions in or out except those from this office."

"Yes, sir."

"Go through KGB headquarters for this. Don't use the normal military circuits."

"Yes, sir."

He glanced at Titov. "How much does Kralkaya's division know?"

"Only that the aircraft is lost."

Markisov's mind was awhirl now, evaluating danger parameters, considering options. He tried not to think of the horror that lay beyond them. "I want you here, Professor. I'll have quarters prepared for you in the room next door."

"Yes, Comrade Secretary."

Markisov studied his hands and slowly, reluctantly, let the horror take full shape in his consciousness. It wore a number: five. Category Five, the last and most powerful firing mode of the Saber, the one that instructed the Kamov to detonate nuclear weapons.

Without looking up, he murmured, "Is it possible the computer could reach Category Five mode?"

The answer was a whispered hiss:

"Yes."

2

Cas Bonner had one leg locked onto the starboard strut of the LC-2 chopper as he scanned the ocean two hundred feet below. It was now mid morning, and for the past two hours they'd been working a five-square-mile area west of Mataiva, criss-crossing in proper search procedure. So far they'd found nothing.

Just before dawn, a radio call had come into the field station from Scottie McKenzie, fisheries officer for the northern Tuamotus. "Aye, Bonner," his raspy voice boomed. "Had a bit of a worry up your way last night. Thought you swinkies might take that whirlybird of yours and go have a look-see for me."

"What's the problem?"

"Some of my fisherboys claim they saw something fall out of the bleedin' sky."

"What?"

"Don't bloody know. The boys thought it was the ghost of a departed relative, scared the runny shits right out of 'em. They swear it had a ruddy blue light that kept blinkin' even after it went into the water. It's got my curious up."

"What's the fix?"

"Nothing definite, but it's up in the Taaramu Shallows. Just

27

keep a keen for net floats. The silly buggers run off so fast they left their bleedin' gear behind."

"Okay, we're scheduled for a specimen run to Papeete anyway. We'll veer over and check it out."

"Thank ya, mate. I'll shout you a few next time you're in the Burmese Garden. Just tell that luscious bird of yours, Kiri, to lay 'em on my tipple sheet till you and Cowell are shit-o."

Bonner chuckled. "That's gonna be expensive." Then he sobered. "By the way, Scottie, we had something peculiar ourselves last night."

"Ah?"

Cas explained about the birds. Scottie was startled. "Aye, that *is* a brummy, all right. I've heard of the buggers runnin' into a ship's mast at night, but not a whole bloody swoop of 'em. And you think it was that ruddy platform?"

"Right. What do you know about that thing?"

"Not much. AlPaci Command's keepin' a tight arse on it. No rumors, even."

"Well, I think I'll jerk a few chains."

Scottie laughed. "Go it, mate. But be watchful, those military types don' like foreigners nosing in."

"Will do. See ya."

Now Cas glanced at Cowell and yelled over the sound of the engine: "So, what do you think? We just dickin' off out here?"

"Yeah, let's head for Papeete." He grinned. "I'm working up an unholy thirst."

"Give it ten more minutes."

"Okay." Skip dipped the little craft into a hard ninety-degree turn, and Cas went back to squinting down at the harsh sun reflections on the swells below them. The Taaramu Shallows formed a vast field of coral heads and sandy channels submerged about sixty feet, yet the water was so clear, the bottom seemed to lie just below the surface.

He was still raging inwardly over the albatross. The more he thought about it, the more he was convinced the French experimental platform was responsible. One of the few things he really valued was the ocean and its environment. Ever since his boyhood in California, the sea had constituted a solidity in his life. It was a boundless laboratory that fascinated him, a retreat from the absurdities he encountered above the surface, and a place of balanced order he could understand. When somebody screwed with it, he saw red.

At forty, Cas Bonner was considered by anybody in the know as one of the finest marine scientists in the world. Unfortunately, he didn't act like one. To begin with, he lacked proper subservience to established scientific protocol, and his research methods always set off apoplexy in the mildewed atmosphere of oceanic academia. That was because he had a hell-raiser streak a mile wide, which seemed to gleefully enjoy blowing accepted theories and theorists out of the water with infuriating regularity. To cap injury with insult, his project results were invariably innovative and brilliant.

But eventually his disrespectful attitude had pissed off those holding the money and research grants, and they had turned the screws. For three years he had been locked out of research, forced to run a fishing boat out of Honolulu's Kewalo basin. It was only through the intercession of a classmate from Scripps that he was allowed back in, first as the main biologist on a field operation at French Frigate Shoals, and then as American liaison director for this, the Tiare III project.

The T-III was a joint marine operation between the Scripps Institute of Oceanography and the French Societe des Etudes Oceaniennes (SEO). The main project headquarters was on the island of Ruruta in the Austrul Group, five hundred miles south of Tahiti, and scattered among the islands of the Marquesas, Tuamotu, Society, Austrul, and Gambier archipelagoes—which make up French Polynesia—were twelve field stations. Mission goals covered a wide spectrum of oceanic research, from commercial recovery of copper modules from the sea floor to the use of the secretions from the anal gland of a tiny mollusk called Amphineura Type 6 as a serum against human shock syndrome. Bonner was the overall head of biological research and had been given use of the small laboratory at the old armory at Papeete's AlPaci Command headquarters, the main base of the French military in Polynesia.

Suddenly, Cas spotted three lines of net floats about a half mile to the north. He signaled Skip and pointed. Cowell swung over and they descended until the small helicopter was skimming twenty feet above the ocean. A moment later, they flashed past the first string of floats, tiny glass balls spaced six feet apart.

Bonner leaned out over the starboard strut a moment, then pulled back, grinning. "I'll be a son of a bitch. There *is* a blue light down there."

"What the hell is it?"

"I can't tell. Bring her around. It's about a hundred yards this side of the first net line."

They swung back, slowing, and finally hovered over the position. The wash of the rotor blades whipped the surface into opaqueness, but even through it, the tiny flashing light was clear. Judging it submerged in about a hundred feet of water, Cas tossed out his tanks, pulled a mask onto his head, and slipped on flippers and a weight belt. He already had a large dive knife strapped to his right calf. He climbed out onto the strut, and holding the mask, he dropped off.

The ocean was warm and crystal clear. A hundred yards out, the clarity fused into green shadows pierced by dancing beams of sunlight. He shouldered into the tank harness and as he started down, the rumble of the chopper's engine faded.

The light was flashing directly below him. He timed it: one thousand-one, one thousand-two. It was running on a ten-second sequence. Squinting harder at it, he felt the hackles on the back of his neck rise. It seemed to be coming from a black body sitting on the bottom.

Because a current was running toward the south and pulling him away from his drop line, he angled slightly against it to reach bottom above the light. He landed fifty feet up current from it and squatted, holding onto rocks to maintain his position. It *was* a body, a man in a black flight suit, strapped into what looked like an aircraft seat. His arms were floating level to his shoulders. It made him look grotesque, like a seated crucifix.

Cas skimmed toward the corpse. As he approached, a small school of *manini* fish darted away from the man's face and scurried into crevices. Cas pulled up directly in front of the body and gripped its legs to steady himself against the current. The fish had been feeding, leaving hundreds of tiny pits where they had nipped out bits of flesh. The man's eyes were wide open, and his black hair waved gently in the water. The blue light was coming from a small brass cannister hooked to the seat strap. A locater blinker, Cas realized.

He examined the skin-tight suit, but he couldn't find any

insignia or nameplate. He pulled himself around to the back and studied the seat base. The cushion was made of gray leather and there were hydraulic coupling nozzles in the under plate. A manufacturer's mark was stamped into the metal. It looked like Russian script.

Once more in front, he unsheathed his knife and cut the seat harness. Freed, the corpse lunged upward at him, and its arms wrapped around his shoulders. Recoiling, Cas dropped slightly and swung the body around, then grabbed the suit collar, and headed for the surface.

He and Cowell had a bitch of a time getting the corpse up onto the chopper's port strut. It hung disjointedly, dead weight. The chopper's downwash kept sucking moisture off it, water mixed with a white mucal liquid from the facial wounds that turned to spray and coated them.

They finally got it tied down. Cas closed the staring eyes and Skip dropped a marker buoy. Then, with Cas riding the starboard strut to balance the weight, they eased around and headed for Papeete.

Michel Cotuse, Director of Operations for the French Marque Acceleration Quantique (MAQ) platform, knew he couldn't save his beloved wildflowers. He had watched them dying for weeks, slowly and inexorably. Frantically he tried everything he could think of to stop the deterioration: a tiny drip system, new combinations of fertilizer, even growth boosters and infrared lights at night. Nothing had worked.

Filled with sorrow, he squatted forlornly beside his little patch of Soison soil in the lee of one of the platform's main generators. These bits of color that had once flourished so gaily against the backdrop of drab gray girders and bulkheads had represented something fundamental and continuing to him, a flux field of smooth transition from windblown seed to blossom. Their withering seemed to be an ominous sign.

Cotuse was the world's most renowned research theorist in the field of subatomic physics. At seventy-two, he had at one time been a protégé of the great Giotto of Italy and had since been hailed as the new Einstein. The MAQ was to be the apex of his career. The heart of the gigantic, open-ocean project was a super-collider, every inch of which had first evolved in his mind. Inside the submerged collider rings he intended to do what no other man had ever done: create a proton mass collision at quantum-O velocity, the speed of light.

Everything had gone smoothly until three months before. Then doubts began assailing him. They haunted his sleep, caused him to repeat procedures, mount endless check runs. Once so certain of his theories, he now found himself questioning everything. Had his years of solitary thought and calculation been adequate? Or would the slightest error, a mere item unthought of, bring chaos?

The voice of his second-in-command, Pierre Savon, interrupted his reverie. "Michel, Frenier's helicopter has been sighted. It'll be landing in a few minutes."

"Ah, yes." Cotuse replaced a withered bluebell stalk and rose from his crouch. As he and Savon walked up the ladderway to the chopper pad on the main deck, Cotuse asked, "Any news of Chapon?" Leonid Chapon, one of the low-echelon technicians on the MAQ, had disappeared sometime during the night.

"Nothing. Some of the men think he fell off the platform and drowned." Savon shrugged. "As I told you, Michel, I suspected he was using drugs."

Cotuse shook his head sadly. Another bad omen.

Together the two men stood in the bright morning sunlight as the dark brown shape of a naval Dauphin helicopter hove into view. His visitor was the French minister of defense, Louis Frenier, stopping in after a series of meetings on New Caledonia for a short conference before returning to Paris.

Frenier greeted Cotuse formally, and for the next hour he was given a tour of the platform. He walked about with his hands behind his back, nodding silently like a somber schoolmaster inspecting toilet facilities. Cotuse considered telling him that one of his technicians had disappeared sometime in the night, but he chose not to. After all, he secretly believed the disappearance was a suicide. The man had been recently despondent over his wife's demand for a divorce.

After the tour, the two men retired to Cotuse's office for a private session. With a glass of wine in his hand, the minister planted himself before a large window overlooking the sea. "A most impressive view," he said quietly. He turned. "Such expansiveness must surely draw one's mind into lassitude?"

Michel smiled. "Yes, it does have that effect at times."

Frenier's face hardened. "Unfortunately, that isn't the state of mind we wish you to have, monsieur."

Cotuse looked away, studied a pencil on his desk. "Yes, of course. I know Paris must be growing impatient with the repeated delays. But there have been so many unforeseen things that—"

Frenier held up his finger. "No, no. I didn't come here for explanations. Rather for . . . understanding."

"But you must realize the difficulties, Minister. A project as complex and as potentially explosive as this necessitates the most extreme precautions."

"Indeed." Frenier sipped his wine and then eyed Cotuse over the rim. "I think the problem is that *you* do not realize the true significance of what you're doing."

Cotuse was shocked. "Monsieur, how can you say that?"

"Because it seems to be true," Frenier snapped. "From a political and military point of view." He smiled coldly. "You scientists always consider such aspects mundane, don't you? Too crass to include in your pure world of science. Yet without the enormous funding our military has allotted to you, there would be no MAQ project. Is that not true?"

Cotuse felt himself flush, but he said nothing.

"Mm?"

"Yes."

Frenier studied him for a moment before he went on, "You're a great man, Cotuse, a great mind. What you can give to France is incalculable. The technology, the power all this"—he swept his wineglass, indicating the platform—"will bring could make us militarily and economically preeminent in the world. Literally, a new France, as majestic as it once was."

"I understand."

"Do you?"

"Of course."

Frenier's voice bristled with ice. "Then why in hell hasn't your quantum run been carried out yet?"

"I've told you. There have been numerous problems."

"Problems are solvable."

"They will be solved. Eventually."

"That's not good enough. We want them solved now."

"To rush could be disastrous."

"To wait too long could also be disastrous. For you."

Cotuse stiffened. "What are you saying?"

Frenier again eyed him for a long moment. "I repeat, you are a great man. Unfortunately, great men are sometimes disabled by their own greatness. At such times it becomes necessary for ordinary men to carry on."

That went into Cotuse like an electrical shock. Stunned, he stared dumbly at the minister. Frenier turned slowly and once more gazed out the window. A seagull suddenly appeared, skimming the surface. He watched it a moment, then held up his glass. "What wine is this?"

Confused, Cotuse mumbled something.

"What wine is this?" Frenier repeated.

"Franjeur du Campagne from Algeria."

"The tropical heat has tainted it."

"I'm sorry."

"Don't be sorry. Merely expedite its consumption before all your supply is ruined." Frenier glanced over his shoulder. "*C'est juste?*"

New Zealand Airlines Flight 130 was still out at the end of runway 21 of Papeete's Faaa Airport. Headed for Los Angeles, it had been waiting for over an hour for takeoff clearance. Sometime after midnight, the Faaa control tower had lost vectoring capacity. A sudden power surge through their scanning radar beacon had blown back through the main transformers, threw everything black, and completely screwed up control panels. Nobody could figure out what had created the surge.

For an hour it had been touch and go with incoming pilots confusedly wandering around hot airspace. The harried controllers finally got things sorted out by using old-fashioned hand light signals from the tower. By three in the morning, technicians had managed to get the system partially functioning. The western sectors checked out, but a hundred degrees of the eastern grid were still giving problems. Frequency-filtering processors kept feeding cluttered data.

On the flight deck of NZA 130, Captain Nat Karroll was getting damned tired of watching heat waves fume off the tarmac. For the twentieth time he keyed his mike: "Faaa Control, NZA One-Three-Zero. What is departure status?"

The Faaa controller came right back. In a thick French accent he stated, "One-Three-Zero, we are still on hold."

"Dammit, I can't stay out here forever."

"Sorry for the delay. You should be cleared within ten minutes."

"Roger that." Jesus, ten more minutes, he cursed silently.

There was a soft knock on the door and his chief stewardess, Stacey Voight, came in. She leaned between the command seats, spreading a hint of gardenia perfume. "Do we have a solid TO time yet, Captain?"

"Ten minutes."

"They're getting very restless back there, sir. Downright testy."

"Keep charming 'em, Stacey."

"Yes, Captain." She turned away, giving the copilot, Jack Hollenbech, a furtive wink.

Karroll caught it and winced in irritation. He'd heard the lounge rumors about Hollenbech and Voight sharing the sheets. That Hollenbech was married didn't bother Karroll. He just didn't like members of his crew cracking fat; inevitably, it created problems in the air. He was about to retire after thirty-eight years of commercial flying, and this flight was his second-to-last run. The last thing he needed was emotional fireworks screwing up his departure.

The radio crackled. "New Zealand Air One-Three-Zero, Faaa Control. You are cleared for takeoff on runway two-one after touchdown of Convairbus now on approach. Wind four knots zero-one-zero. Altimeter two-niner-four. Traffic one-seven-oh-seven on downwind. Departure frequency is one-two-two-point-eight. Sorry for the delay, gentlemen. Have a good flight."

Four minutes later, Flight 130 lifted off and turned east.

As the huge 747 climbed to its assigned flight level of thirty thousand feet, Faaa control vectored it to a heading of zero-four-one, slightly north of normal departure track. An airman's advisory had just come in, reporting stepped-up military air traffic in the corridors north of the French naval airbase on Hoa Island in the Tuamotus.

As flight level was achieved, Faaa came back with a request. They wanted to check their eastern sector approach/departure vectors. Would NZA 130 execute a few emergency locate maneuvers for sequence-position fixes?

"Goddamm it," Karroll said. EL maneuvers were standard, one-minute-timed ninety-degree turns used to locate an aircraft without radio capacity. He keyed: "Faaa DC, we copy your request. Will initiate ELs in sixty seconds. And mates, you owe me one."

Far below, the Saber's sensors tripped a warning relay to the Kamov computer. They had been tracking NAZ 130 for the last eight minutes, but now the aircraft's unusual movements clicked the units into focus intensity. The Kamov ingested the click-on and began isolating the aircraft target from peripheral read.

The spy plane had by now drifted to the outer fringes of a vast field of small atolls and *motus*, bits of vegetation-covered coral reef that protruded above the water. In the silence of the empty cockpit, electronic burbles riffled. The uphead instrument display came on as the Kamov scanned through its memory-indent banks. Words began flashing:

> BOEING: E-A—US NAVY
> CREW: 4 FLIGHT/6 MISSION
> ENGINES: 4 GE SNECMA CFM-56-2A2 TURBOJETS
> WEIGHT (MASS): 155, 130 KILOGRAMS
> RADAR: APS-133 RECON/SIDE BAND
> MISSION: AWACS (AIRBORNE WARNING AND CONTROL SURVEILLANCE)

Three lights on the up display began flashing rapidly. Within the AI subunit's threat recognition and countermeasure track, a priority status was assigned the target. The aircraft's unusual maneuvers were perceived as electronic mapping turns.

> COUNTERMEASURE RESPONSE: C-1 MODE.

The Kamov activated the weapons chamber. More numbers flashed: calculated convergence point, corrected trajectory azimuth. Gimbal motors swung the firing barrel to the designated fix.

In the lidium-tin weapon chamber, the "hot" command started the firing sequence. The internal fusion-generating box activated. This was a small sphere of clear, high-density plastic that enclosed a solution of heavy water under extreme pressure. Around the core was a lidium-tin cylinder with movable slats and magnetic baffles. These in turn were enclosed within a dense matrix of hollow, microscopic filaments of carbon that held a radioactive solution of polonium. Between the matrix and the cylinder was a double shield containing thousands of minute openings formed in chaotic array.

A moment later, the Kamov sent a fire-on command. Instantly the cylinder slats were canted to the degree determined by the category-mode input. For a hundredth of a second the polonium radiation was allowed to focus on the core. The instantaneous heat hurled the hydrogen atoms of the heavy water into a frenzy and coil fusion. There was a nanosecond of "dirty" throw-out of low radioactive and electromagnetic energy. Funneled by the magnetic baffles into the firing barrel, it went out into the air in a needle-thin beam . . .

The first indication of trouble aboard NZA 130 was a sudden, wild swing of the standby magnetic compass. As it began jumping crazily, Karroll noted it and frowned in puzzlement. A second later, Faaa control's transmission trailed off in a violent blow of static and went dead. Then the cockpit instruments began going berserk. The radar altimeter directly in front of the captain's control yoke dropped to stop level, fluttered, and began to rise slowly. Warning lights were popping everywhere.

Hollenbech gave a yell: "Jesus Christ, we're on collision course!"

Karroll's eyes shot to the air-traffic transponder. It was flashing red. Blood exploded in his temples as he frantically searched the sky ahead. There was nothing out there but sky.

The control yoke began to shake under his hands. He could hear the engines straining, the chilling whine that precedes fuel starvation. He reached out and rammed the four thruster levers full up. Instantly he felt their power surge.

For one terrifying moment he froze. Things were happening too rapidly, all crazy and out of sequence. Then his instincts broke through and he began hurling commands. He grabbed the yoke with his arms and braced against the surges coming up through the wheel. Hollenbech was slamming switches.

Slowly, fighting it, they began to regain flight control.

*   *   *

As chief stewardess, Stacey Voight was always the last to buckle herself in whenever the captain informed the crew they would be executing unusual maneuvers. This time it was those damned ELs. Lordy, she thought, another shitty delay. She had already deployed her girls on cocktail service and had to call them back. The bloody passengers would really get bitchy now.

Her seat was against the after bulkhead of the main galley module, facing the business-class section. For the last three minutes she'd been getting glares from everybody. She gave back full teeth. The aircraft was just starting a fourth bank when she heard a sharp sizzle from the galley, followed by a muffled pop. Another. Then the aircraft started trembling. The stewardess seated beside her shot a glance: What's going on?

Maintaining her smile, Stacey twisted against her belt and pulled the galley door open. Good God! There was coffee all over the place. Streams cascaded off the prepared food racks from the two huge metal percolators bolted to the shelf. They'd blown open. Shaken, she could only stare.

Then she quickly pulled the door shut just as the aircraft began leveling. She leaned close to the other stewardess. "Dolly, I'm going forward."

"What's happened?"

"It's nothing. Just keep smiling."

As her fingers touched the belt buckle, the 747 began trembling again, a solid shake of the fuselage that came right up through her backrest. The first tendrils of panic began icing her insides.

She unbuckled and stood up. Opening the galley door just enough to pass through, she slipped into the module compartment. It was filled with coffee-smelling steam. She started to reach for the forward door when there was a small explosion, then a powerful hissing, as if a steam line had just parted. One heartbeat later, the module shook as a violent ripping sound blew back through the aircraft. She felt the 747 yaw sharply to the left.

"Oh my God!" she cried in horror.

Air was sucking loudly through the forward door seals. Her head felt suddenly huge, painful. She grabbed the door latch and pushed at it. Instantly the door itself was wrenched from her hand.

She screamed. She was staring at open sky! A huge section of the starboard fuselage, as large as a cement truck, had been totally ripped away. With it had gone frame ribs, hull sheeting, seats, luggage—and passengers.

Nine seconds before, Captain Karroll had started getting a grip on himself. His instincts, his years of training and execution, were powerfully reasserting themselves. He had already started backing off power. Instruments were slowly nearing normal read, save for an unusual temperature gradient in the ship's hydraulic lines.

He ordered Hollenbech to reestablish communications with Faaa and declare an emergency. Mentally, he began running through crisis procedures. The aircraft began trembling again in quick, sharp jolts. After a pause, another jolt erupted, escalating into a full-out shaking. A loud hissing began to come through the door seams of the after hatchway. An explosion cracked viciously and the control yoke was nearly torn from his hands as the 747 yawed violently to the left. He fought it, his body lifting against the seat harness.

"We've been breached!" he bellowed.

Groaning with the strain, he scanned the instruments and fixed on the exhaust-gas temperature gauge for engine number three. It was way past the red line. Before he could react, the engine went dead. He locked his arms harder on the wheel as thrust imbalance pulled the plane to the right.

He could feel a horrendous pressure building inside his head, as if his brain tissues were enlarging rapidly against his skull. He freed his right hand long enough to pull down his oxygen mask. On the other side of the control console, Hollenbech was yelling into his mike, "Faaa DC, this is NZA 130. Mayday! Mayday! Squawking on 7700."

Karroll took a deep pull on the mask, but nothing came out. The oxygen lines had obviously been ruptured. He tore it off and hurled it aside. Dammit! he cursed. He had to get this plane down to where he could breathe again, and goddamned fast. Putting his full body weight against the yoke, he pushed the nose down, shouting to Hollenbech to start coming off power settings. Over his shoulder he hollered to his third officer, Al Lucinda, "Get aft. I want a damage report."

As Lucinda headed for the hatchway, a fire-warning light from number four engine began flashing and a Klaxon blasted. Automatic extinguishing vents in the engine cowling were instantly triggered, blowing retardant. The warning signals continued, indicating an uncontrolled fire. "Shut her down," Karroll cried to Hollenbech. The copilot obeyed, and three seconds later, the warning signals ceased.

Now they had only two functioning engines, both on the port wing. The offset thrust became hellish as the aircraft surged to the right. Karroll fought it with all the strength in his body, thighs trembling as he rode the rudders. The altimeter showed 26,000 feet.

Faaa started coming back, their frantic questions periodically interrupted by furious static. Hollenbech did his best to feed status in jerky, breathless phrases. The third officer returned, wide-eyed.

"It's gone," he croaked. "The whole goddamned starboard side of the fuselage at the main lounge level."

Karroll's head snapped around. "Oh, Jesus! What about the passengers?"

"They're gone. They're all gone."

Karroll and Hollenbech exchanged one fleeting, tormented look. Lucinda was still leaning, staring at nothing. Karroll shook himself free of the shock. "Get your ass aft," he shrieked at the third officer. "Seal that goddamned area." Lucinda, still dazed, withdrew.

Altimeter: 23,000 feet . . .

Focus, Karroll told himself, you've got to focus. First priority: Get this damned ship down so we can breathe. With oxygen lines gone, people back there would start going into hypoxia. He could already feel his own heart beginning that warning spiral as cabin air depleted. But if he put the 747 into a power dive, he knew that it might tear apart.

Altimeter: 20,000 feet . . .

His thoughts now probed ahead, to the approach to Faaa. A new problem flared. He was still carrying nearly full fuel tanks. If he went in like that, his landing gears would be overstressed. If *they* went, the aircraft and everything in it would disappear in one big ball of flame. He ordered Hollenbech to start dumping fuel.

Fourteen seconds later, Karroll felt a jolt of pure adrenaline hurtle through him. Hydraulic oil was dripping from the back of the yoke. And to the right, on the central console, it was seeping from the aileron and rudder trim switches. Flight-control system integrity was going!

Altimeter: 17,500 feet . . .

He could feel heavier air crossing the wing surfaces. Immediately the plane's instability increased. His hands were getting numb on the wheel. Still, they could now breathe at least. One hurdle had been passed.

They were now crossing over the channel between Tetiaroa and Huahine, islands to the north of Tahiti. Faaa lay sixty miles away. To Karroll it seemed like an eternity. He wanted to pour on full power and streak. But once more his instincts countered. Heavy throttle could sunder the already wounded aircraft. He'd have to take it slowly, right on the edge of stall.

But what the hell *was* stall speed now? With half the fuselage blown out and two engines down, it could be anywhere. If he dropped below it, he might never recover.

Altimeter: 10,000 feet . . .

He checked fuel gauges. Hollenbech had dumped 300,000 pounds; there was still 240,000 pounds in the tanks. They'd never be able to dump enough to achieve safe landing weight. He'd have to circle.

No, he decided. They were going straight in.

Altimeter: 4,800 feet . . .

He began bringing the 747 out of its descent. She was unbelievably sluggish, like an eighteen-wheeler with flat tires. Powerful buffets, tricky, jolting yaws kept pulling him this way and that.

Twelve miles out, he ordered flaps lowered. After a few moments Hollenbech cursed. With the hydraulics fading, all he could get was ten degrees of flap. Twenty was minimum for deceleration on a two-engine landing. They'd have to go in hot, at least two hundred knots. At that speed they'd eat up runway damned fast and possibly blow tires from the friction.

Karroll brought down the landing gears, holding his breath as he watched the down-and-locked indicator lights. The plane rocked as the huge struts hit the airstream. Agonizing seconds passed, as ponderous as funeral marchers. At last the indicator lights flashed green.

Far to the left, the peaks of Mount Orochona moved past, and for no good reason Karroll eyed the wisps of mist still clinging to the upper valleys. Seven miles ahead, he could see the landing strip on the edge of the ocean. All perimeter lights were turned on and the approach arrow markers flashed their rapid strobe bursts.

On they hurtled. Papeete slid under the port wing. He saw a freighter with a rust-streaked hull standing off the entry channel, then a glimpse of morning traffic on Pomare Boulevard.

Down, down, much too fast . . .

They shot over a stretch of emerald green water that seemed close enough to touch the wheels. Then they reached land again: palms strung in neat rows. All of it began to blur with speed distortion as they neared the ground. The runway threshold fled under the nose. Its tarmac was slashed with dark tire marks.

Fifty feet . . . twenty . . .

The wheels touched, lifted slightly, touched again. They screeched sharply as they took hold. Karroll hauled back on the wheel and jammed all his body weight against the brakes. Hollenbech cut the throttles. The thunderous whine of the engines dropped instantly. Dead ahead, the ocean hurtled toward them.

Thirty-seven seconds later, NZA 130 rolled to a rocking stop in soft sand two hundred feet beyond the edge of the runway. Karroll took his hands off the wheel. A droplet of sweat slipped into his eye with a pleasant sting. Outside, rescue vehicles raced into view, their red lights flashing.

3

Kiri Valjean, wearing shorts and a T-shirt, paced frustratedly under the steaming tin roof of a tiny shed on the island of Takaroa in the northern Tuamotus. The shed was the island's flight terminal for the Starburst Air-Ferry service out of Papeete. Every day Starburst sent its ancient twin-engine Corsair SP-110 seaplanes transiting through the archipelagoes.

The shed consisted of a single wooden bench, a coral yard scattered with empty beer and wine bottles, and a dialless telephone nailed to a post. If a passenger wanted a Corsair to land, all that was necessary was to lift the phone, wait for a tone, and hang it up. The incoming aircraft, however, might arrive in one hour or twelve.

Kiri had been waiting since sunup after Katevayo had deposited her on Takaroa and headed away in the *natarua* for his own base on Tikahao. Sweat cascaded between her braless breasts and her temper challenged the heat. Adjacent to the shed was an old rock quay with tires lined on each side and mudflats near the pierhead that stank of sour alkalai and dead fish. It reminded her of a drunken man's vomit.

For the twentieth time she dropped onto the bench and sat

there, staring furiously out at the western sky and distractedly twirling a large pigeon's blood ruby ring on her little finger. It was a beautiful eight-carat natural stone she had purchased in a bazaar in New Delhi. It was the single thing she possessed that she would never part with.

Her real name was Ilya Vashkin. She was thirty years old, a physicist specializing in subatomic research, and had been a KGB operative for four years, doing mostly low-level covert diplomatic/scientific operations in Europe, India, and Australia. She was half Russian and half Burmese; her father, a military attaché once stationed in Singapore, had married an Atua concubine from Burma.

Through the shimmering heat waves, she drew up the images of last night's run on the French platform. A total bust. She pictured the face of that moronic French doper who had screwed it up, seeing again the violent shock in his face when the twelve-gauge charge blew a hole in him the size of a plate. The memory sent a chill up her spine. He was the first man she'd ever killed.

Then her anger shifted, settling on Valentin Katevayo, the animal she had been strapped with for this mission. She despised the man, a savage with a gleeful psychosis in his gray eyes. And his insolence was intolerable, his contempt like a spray of acid to the face. He had been that way ever since their first meeting, in a sidewalk café in Sydney:

He had made her wait a full hour, smoldering at a tiny glass table and sipping white wine. When he did arrive, he approached with a predatory rapidity, like a cat rushing its prey. He slid into the opposite chair, smiling his icy, crazy grin. He wore filthy seaman's clothes.

"You're the one," he said in Russian. It wasn't a question, just a statement.

"Katevayo?"

"Who else?" He had a narrow face and brows that slanted down, reminding her of the intent stare of a serpent. He watched her for a long moment, then withdrew a pack of cigarettes rolled up in his shirtsleeve. He lit up and expelled a cloud of smoke at her. "You have Asiatic blood," he said.

"Yes."

"Thai? Sumatran?"

"Burmese."

He grunted and blew another coiling burst of smoke at her. Again he studied her closely. "You ever kill anybody, Burmese?"

"What?"

"You ever kill anybody?"

"No."

"Could you?"

"I think so. I know how."

A scornful grin spread across his face. "But there would be shit in your underpants, mm?"

Rage welled up in her. To calm it, she turned and watched a cruise ship entering the harbor past the soaring peaks of the Sydney Opera House. When she turned back, she saw that Katevayo had rolled up his sweatshirt to bare his chest. There was a vicious scar under his left pectoral muscle. It was at least ten inches long, shaped like a scimitar, and the scar tissue was shiny and waxy-looking.

She studied it calmly.

"You see that?" he snapped. "You know what it means? Before you can kill, you first have to die."

"Is that right?"

"It arouses you." Again not a question.

"Go to hell."

Valentin chuckled maliciously as he slowly lowered his shirt. "All cunts are aroused by the sight of sliced flesh."

That's it, she thought. She set her elbows on the table, tented her fingers, and stared fixedly into his mad gray eyes. "Listen, you arrogant prick. First, I don't give a shit for your opinions on female sexual responses. Second, a cunt I may be, but I'm also command agent on this mission. As such, when I speak to you, you'll keep your vulgar obscenities to yourself. And when I tell you to jump, you jump." She probed the canescent depths of his eyes, seeking his core. "Or I'll kill you."

Katevayo grinned, and she felt the enormity of his lethalness washing over her. Then he shrugged with casual disdain. "But of course, Burmese," he said, and blew another cloud of smoke into her face.

The remembered scene propelled her to her feet. She walked out from under the shed roof into blinding sunlight. Down in the mudflats, crabs scurried as she walked out onto the quay and stood watching infuriatedly for the little glint of sunlight in the sky that would mark the approach of the seaplane. "Come on, you assholes," she hissed.

Time was driving hot needles into her. She *had* to get back to Papeete, sound the waters, find out what was coming in from the platform. Had they found any trace of the crewman? Were they now on all-out alert?

Like most addicts, Del January despised his need for caffeine. It was now noon in Washington and he had already put away over a dozen cups of coffee since arriving at the Joint Analysis Directorate of the National Command Center in the Pentagon at eight. As cochairman of the JAD, he had spent the morning overseeing a simulated war-game exercise of a Cuban invasion of the Canal Zone.

He was still at it when a call came down from Captain Tony Peck, a senior officer on the staff of the chief of naval operations. "Del," Peck said, "I need your smarts. Can you pull free for a few minutes?"

In his primary capacity as director of naval research at Alexandria, Virginia, January was often called in by the CNO for ideas. "Sure, what's up?"

"The Russkies are showing antsy in Polynesia."

"Okay, I'll be right up."

Peck's office was located on the second floor of the Pentagon's DS wing, and January found him huddled with a navy commander when he arrived. The two officers were studying a map of the South Pacific. The commander's name was Kirkpatrick, from naval intelligence.

"Over the last three hours," Peck began, "we've been getting reports of unusual Soviet surveillance activity in and around Tahiti. Badger-D recon aircraft from Cam Ranh vectored out of normal patrol track, and some pretty heavy Top Sail radar scans from the forward elements of a Russkie carrier force south of the Tuamotus. There's even been an unconfirmed report that a Delta-class attack sub was seen on the surface."

"Whoa! A Russian AB exposing itself? What the hell's going on down there?"

"We don't know yet. But there's more. Latest NAVSAT photos seem to indicate there's launch activity on the Soviet flag carrier. It's the *Minsk*."

Del searched around the room until he found Peck's coffee urn. He strode over and poured himself a cup. "Sounds to me like the Russians have lost something they want back. Real bad."

"But what? The bastards wouldn't go this heavy for a downed Badger. Maybe one of their intelligence-gathering ships, but no AGIs have been seen in the area for the past six months."

Del was surprised at that news. "You're kidding. What about that French experimental platform? I'd think that'd draw AGIs in force."

"Yeah, you'd think so, but apparently the Russkies are steering clear of it. I guess they don't want another touchy incident with the Frenchies." A year before, a French frigate had been rammed by a Soviet patrol boat in the Black Sea. The affair had caused a stink in Paris before it finally blew over.

January sucked his lips thoughtfully. "What's your SSOS showing?" The SSOS was a vast network of undersea sensors spread across known Russian submarine patrol corridors.

"Nothing unusual so far."

"What about that Delta?"

Peck shrugged. "Nothing but that unconfirmed report." At that moment his telephone buzzed. He lifted the receiver, listened for a moment, then replaced it. "Well, there's another click on the wheel. The *Minsk* launched fighters ten minutes ago. And her forward frigates have already entered French territorial waters in the south Marquesas Channel."

January and Kirkpatrick exchanged glances. "This is beginning to look like it could get very dicey," Del said.

Peck pushed himself up from the conference table. "I've got a meeting with the CNO in twenty minutes. I'd appreciate some ideas on this, soon as you can come up with something."

"Let me give it some thought. I should have an OA to you in, say, two hours?"

"Fine."

"How do I keep in the link?"

"You can go through Kirkpatrick's facilities."

"Right." He glanced at the commander in time to see a frown on the man's brow. Apparently he resented being strapped with a civilian. "Where's your site?" he asked.

"Level One, 414."

January gulped down the last of his coffee and headed for the door.

*   *   *

Admiral Viktor Turesky, flag commander of the battle *skadra* HC-3, was infuriated as he watched six of his Forger interceptors lift off the deck of the *Minsk* for low-level search operations up the Marquesas Channel. He considered his order to search for a downed aircraft in the northern Tuamotus foolishly provocative, one which left his force, now steaming on the southern fringes of the latitude quadrant called the Capricorn, in a highly vulnerable position.

Moreover, it would mean a complicated operation: two in-air refuelings for the Forgers and an extended eighteen-hundred-mile flight *without weapons*. His interceptors, updated T1-D models, were capable of armed mission range of only four hundred and fifty kilometers, and to carry out the order, they'd had to exchange missiles for fuel tanks. Still, Cam Ranh had said the order had come in the general secretary's personal code.

His wing commander, Captain First Class Toomas Koik, had, as was his manner, said nothing when told of the mission. Yet Turesky knew what he was thinking. Koik was a short, muscular officer with narrow, icy black eyes known to his men as "Bullcat." Also, as usual, he had asked permission to lead the mission.

Together they had gone over the task plot with the *Minsk*'s skipper, Captain First Vitaly Akhromeyev. "You'll be running the entire length of the Marquesas Channel," Turesky said. "The key is obviously to avoid detection as best you can. It won't be easy. We can assume the French naval airbase at Hoa—right here— will be on the alert, looking for anything coming up that channel."

Koik nodded.

"When you reach your search coordinates, be very careful to avoid that French open-ocean platform. Surveillance reports say there are several frigates patrolling its zone. One other thing, there's a large American carrier task group up north, near the Kingman Reef. That's fifteen hundred miles off, but just be aware that the Americans have satellite surveillance in this area."

He paused as the distant roar of engines signaled the takeoff of the J-3T Hormone helicopter tankers heading out to take up refueling positions for the Forgers. After a moment he went on, giving Koik chopper link coordinates and time sequences. Then he turned to Akhromeyev. "You have anything to add, Vitaly?"

The *Minsk* skipper studied the illuminated mission map. "Perhaps we might alter our heading fifteen degrees north, Admiral. That could give both the tankers and Comrade Koik a better approach up the channel."

"I agree. See to it." Turning back to Koik, he said, "Choose your best low-level men, Toomas. With those heavy tanks you'll have precious little margin for error since your refueling will be so close to the deck."

"Yes, sir."

"And when you reach your search area, be extremely alert to your magnetic rebounds. Remember, this aircraft you're looking for is supposed to be nearly invisible to radar probes. You and your people will have to spot minute ocean anomalies to find the damned thing."

"Yes, Comrade Admiral."

Turesky leaned away from the map table. "Have a good flight, Toomas."

"Thank you, sir." Koik saluted and departed the bridge.

An hour and a half later, Koik and his wingman were skimming fifteen feet above the ocean in the southern approaches to the Marquesas Channel. The two other pairs of Forgers were spaced four and six minutes behind them.

The first refueling had gone perfectly, despite the whipping lines from the two Hormone helicopter tankers as turbulence came off the ocean. The ocean seemed calm, yet there was a slight feathering on the surface that indicated a fifteen-to-twenty-knot wind from the south.

As Koik glanced to the right, he could just make out the banks of low clouds that marked the peaks of Tahuata and Motane islands in the Marquesas chain. He swung around and looked in the opposite direction. Only the empty blue sea stretched away, for the flat atolls of the Tuamotus were hidden in the ocean haze.

He scanned his instruments. He was holding a steady five hundred knots. For a moment he studied the chart on his knee board, mentally calculating. They would be passing due east of the Hoa naval base in four and a half minutes. He turned and made a wide circle with his arm to his wingman: Keep a sharp lookout. The other pilot nodded.

Koik returned his attention to the sea. It flashed under him in a blurred sweep of deep blue, and only when he lifted his eyes could he see the sunlit undulations of the surface. He smiled, enjoying the sensation of tremendous speed. He always preferred flying close to the earth, for it gave him visual reference of his speed. Up high, in contrast, only his instruments and the sensations of his body told him of the velocity of his aircraft.

Koik's first flying had been close to the ground, in the rich wheat country of his native Krasnoyarsk in central Russia. His father, a World War II fighter pilot, had taught him to fly when he was only thirteen, and within two years he'd become a full-fledged crop duster, flying an old bi-winged Shkirov 33, patterned after the American Stearman. It was a good plane, simple, quick on the controls. He loved it. Seat of the pants flying, *real* flying.

Now he scanned the sky again, left to right. It vaulted above him, bisected only by the curve of his cockpit's forward strut. It was all a faded blue, washed and misty with sea evaporation. He thought about his mission. Invading French waters to find a single downed aircraft was, of course, foolhardy. Whatever was aboard that plane—including its crewmen—was certainly not sufficient reason to commit the carrier group to the vulnerability this mission would garner. He relished confrontation, but only when it made tactical or strategic sense.

They passed Hoa without being spotted.

One hour later, at coordinates 15:30 S/146:10 E, Koik changed to heading three-five-zero in preparation for the search run. The operational plan called for a slight flaring maneuver of the three sequenced flights in order to cover as wide an area as possible. Koik's sector was the most northern.

Sixty seconds after changing his heading, he noticed his electronics recognition meter flashing. Something had just picked him up on radar. The probes were weak, intermittent. He descended slightly, until the Forger was nearly touching the ocean. His wingman followed. The ERM light went off.

Ninety seconds later, the huge French platform loomed up from the sea dead ahead.

Twenty-one miles to the southeast, the French missile frigate *D'Estienne D'Vois* was running picket station when suddenly one of the radar men in the command information center shouted into his microphone: "I have two airborne targets. Low and moving fast. Bearing two-six-eight degrees, range ninety kilometers."

The operations officer, an ensign named Pierre Cantineau, hurried to a ship's phone and rang up the officers' wardroom. "Request captain to the bridge immediately."

A minute later, Lieutenant Vaisseau Cogne hurried through the starboard hatchway. He was a slim officer with thick, jet-black hair and startlingly soft, almost feminine blue eyes. He was munching on a half-eaten cookie.

"We've got two airborne blips, sir," Cantineau said. "On the deck, bearing two-six-eight."

"Ours?"

"We're still analyzing. But I don't think they're from Hoa. There's been no T-and-A transmissions from them over the last three hours."

Cogne strode toward the panel man seated in front of the Sperry SYS-2(V)2 automatic-tracking-systems screen. Part of the after bridge the CIC was slightly darkened, and the screens and computer modules formed a half ring against the after bulkhead.

The SYS man called out: "Target ID clean and updated. Russian Forger Yak-38. Holding speed five-zero-zero knots. No incoming radio or radar signals."

Cogne exchanged a shocked glance with Cantineau. A Soviet fighter here? And running silent? A cold sliver of excitement crept up his spine. "Go to general quarters," he snapped.

Cantineau echoed the command and hurried away.

"Helmsman, bring me to bearing two-six-eight."

The helmsman repeated the order. Bells rang and there was the sudden, raucous clang of a Klaxon.

"Go to flank speed as soon as we clear fifteen degrees on new course."

"Flank speed on fifteen degrees of new heading, aye."

The deck of the frigate heeled sharply to the right as she came around. Cogne moved to the bridge window and as he lightly put his hands on the coaming, he felt the delicate pulse of his blood in his fingertips. What do I do now? he wondered.

Newly graduated from the frigate school at the Fleet Training Center in Toulon, the *D'Estienne D'Vois* was his first command. Fighting off the sense of his own inadequacy, he struggled to remember his options of duty. Earlier reports from AlPaci Command had told him of a course change by the Soviet carrier force south of Tahiti. But now it had actually sent aircraft over French waters. Worse, they had bypassed both the huge nuclear test center on Mururoa and the naval base at Hoa, the likeliest targets for reconnaissance or strike. Why were the fighters this far north? The answer struck him like a blow to the pit of his stomach. They were after the MAQ platform!

He whirled. "What's target position relative to the platform?"

A few seconds later, the SYS man shouted, "Targets have passed directly over it. Now executing a hard-climbing one-eighty. Present separation from MAQ is fifteen kilometers."

"Transmit on open and ITF frequencies. Warn the swine off."

Cantineau returned to report, "General quarters in effect, sir. All stations ready."

The frigate tore through the sea. Part of an inter-Allied exchange, she was an American-designed Brooke class. Her armament included the Mk 92 fire-control system, which was adaptable to various missile profiles. During French refit, twin Exocet MM-38 launch tubes had been installed aft her main stack.

"Are you raising anything?" Cogne bellowed.

"Negative, sir."

Feeling the jarring power of the frigate's twin LM-2500 gas turbine engines driving her through the water, Cogne squinted, trying to pick up the occulated flashes of the powerful strobe light located on the three-hundred-foot tower atop the MAQ platform. Finding that salt mist blurred his view, he wheeled about and returned to the CIC. The SPS-10F digital radar-enhancement console was now running a picture: blue grid lines with a column of changing position data to the right. The platform was a tiny blue circle, the frigate marked as the outline of a toy ship. The Forgers were two moving dots of white light.

Another panel man called out, "I'm getting radar probes, sir. Low band, narrow spread."

Cogne's gaze settled on the two white dots. He pictured the aircraft they signified, driving like missiles toward the platform. The blips passed through the blue circle, broke to the right, and swung back for another sweep. He nodded. The bastards were making surveillance photo runs.

Or were they?

Twenty minutes earlier, the Saber had finally grounded on a long stretch of half-submerged coral heads a hundred yards from a string of atolls. The current was swift here. Twice she had touched, moved on. Now she was fast, her nose facing west.

The Kamov began "feeling" its immediate environment. The sensors picked up scattered sounds and movements: the chatter of marine life, the boom and hiss of surf, and the delicate, riffling swirls of fish schools. Twice they had picked up the sinuous undulations and heart pulses of moving bodies far beyond the edge of the reef.

The computer scanned everything, analyzing and pigeonholing data. Some of it was confusing, not on the Kamov's memory tapes. Then, suddenly, the quick flash of a radar return was registered. The Kamov processed. Initial identification was a low-flying aircraft toward the east-northeast. Before it could map parameters, the pulse faded. The computer went into alert watch.

Two and a half minutes later, the pulse rebound came again. The target was changing altitude. Speed: five hundred knots . . . six hundred knots . . . It was in a steep climb. The Kamov went to the AI, which immediately made the engine-wash resonance:

```
SOVIET: 1 LYUL'KA AL-21 TURBOJET
    2 KOLESOV TURBOJETS (LIFT/CANT)
AIRCRAFT: YAK-38 MP/MOD-1
TRC ASSESSMENT: FRIENDLY
```

A heavy burst of radio signals followed, ranging through frequencies. Voice: English/French. Analysis showed signal strength secondary. They were bouncing off a large ferrous object NE. The Kamov scanned previous track tape and fixed onto the coordinates of a light tower it had picked up the night before.

A sharp flurry of higher frequency bursts came in. They were faint but increasing, indicating that the source was approaching from beyond the horizon. In the cockpit, the ERM began flashing brightly.

AI unit identified:

```
SIGNAL SOURCE: MK 92 MOD-4 FIRE CONTROL SYSTEM
SHIP (PROBABLE): PERRY-BROOKE-CLASS MISSILE FRIGATE
ARMAMENT: TARTAR SAM (US); EXOCET MM-38 (FRENCH); NARVIK 35T
    NORWEGIAN)
TRC ASSESSMENT: SHIP IN ATTACK POSTURE
RESPONSE RECOMMENDATION: C-2 MODE ON DEFLECTION
```

The Kamov activated the fusion chamber and began feeding in firing coordinates for a bounce shot off the weather tower to the incoming frigate's fire-control system.

The instant Captain Koik saw the French platform, he knew he had made a slight navigational error. His OF vector should have put him west of its position. As he hauled back into a climb, he watched it flash past.

Huge, covered with lights even in the day, it reminded him of Russian oil rigs in the Black Sea. A narrow radio/weather tower with a flashing red light projected high above it. As the platform fell astern, he put the Forger into a hard bank with his wingman right behind him.

Well, he thought calmly, now they know we're here. He considered. Getting back would now be difficult, for the air over the Marquesas Channel would be swarming with French Entendards. He wondered idly whether or not the fighters would actually engage him. He doubted it.

He leveled at eight thousand feet and quickly scanned the sea below. Where were the frigates? He saw nothing. Then his ERM began flashing incoming radar probes. Since the sea was empty, he assumed they were coming from the platform. He glanced back at it and thought: Since their cover was already blown, why not turn an error into a plus and take a few photos of the rig for the carrier's air intelligence? He signaled his wingman for camera run, raising three fingers to indicate three passes.

They swung around in a long one-eighty, dropping swiftly. His radio began crackling through frequencies, and he caught garbled splurges of English and French. Again he figured it was the platform warning him off. He swung his dial and shut off the signals. Then, checking himself, he again looked all around. No, there were no ships to be seen.

They neared the ocean again, running eighty meters above the surface. He flicked on his nose camera and powered back until his air-speed indicator showed three hundred and fifty knots. The platform rushed toward him. On the screen just below the windshield, he could see the digital picture of it: a white dot that sat between cross hairs. The dot shifted slightly and then disappeared completely as he pulled up into a steep, banking turn.

On the second pass, he switched on his downview radar. It

would give a peripheral view of any construction outside his camera's viewfield. This time as he pulled up, his ERM began flashing red in quarter-second bursts. He stared at it, shocked. He was under a fire-control probe.

How could that be? Was the platform armed with missiles?

He jerked his head around, scanned the eastern ocean. There it was, a ship's wake! He cursed himself. How had he missed it? He leveled, glanced at his wingman, and pointed west. The wingman nodded.

Koik considered his options. They could turn northwest and outrun the incoming ship. But that would compromise the search mission. By the time they got realigned, their fuel state would force them to head back into the Marquesas Channel. No, that was unacceptable.

He heeled over and headed back toward the platform, dropping toward the sea. They'd angle past it to the right, then veer due west to begin the search. The fucking French *babushkas* wouldn't fire on a Russian, anyway.

Cogne moved around the command center like a man on roller skates, pausing now to glare at screens, then to listen to incoming deck-force status reports. The pressure of making a decision made his forehead ache. He wavered momentarily when he thought of the consequences of an actual missile launch, but then again, the MAQ was sitting out there completely helpless. What if the Russians were not merely taking pictures? What if they were at this very moment starting their attack run?

He swung around to Cantineau. "Arm the Exocets."

The ensign's head snapped up, eyes wide.

"Arm them, dammit. And hold."

"Yes, sir."

The console men shot furtive glances at one another as Canteneau began shouting into his DIM phone. His voice seemed to weave a sharp, punching sound into the general clatter and pings of the CIC.

A moment later, the loudspeaker blared: "Number one launch tube armed and on standby sequence, Captain."

As Cogne clenched his teeth, he felt a remnant of peanut from the cookie wedged against his gum. It seemed as large as a stone.

"Number two launch tube armed and on standby sequence, Captain."

Cogne breathed in, wondering if the Russians might force him to give the next command. In that same moment he was startled by a sharp cry from one of the console men. He whirled about. The CIC screens were going crazy with electronic flush lines, brilliant bursts of light. The soft, steady hum of computer banks suddenly accelerated into a whirring.

"Malfunction," someone shouted. "We have malfunction."

Cogne bellowed, "Trace and isolate."

Two seconds passed.

"All circuits receiving solid data on trace."

Another man shouted, "Captain, we're losing tracking integrity." An instant later, one of the display screens blew out, hurling bits of smoking glass into the operator's face. Cogne's heart jarred. Two men ran to the injured man, who was holding his hands over his face, blood oozing between the fingers. Other panels were now smoking and the air was suddenly filled with the odor of burned electrical wiring.

"What the hell's happening?" Cantineau cried.

Cogne felt everyone's eyes on him, waiting for him to do something. It was obvious the Russian aircraft were disrupting his electronics. That meant they *were* attacking! Panic came up into his throat, brought the taste of copper to his mouth. What should he do? He watched the escalating chaos in his CIC and realized that if he didn't react, the entire system would disintegrate. Then he'd be helpless.

He found his voice. "Go for primary lock-on starboard missile," he bellowed.

"Going for primary lock-on starboard missile." Three seconds later: "Lock-on achieved."

"Fire on command."

"IF status clean. Holding for firing command."

"Fire starboard missile."

"Fire missile."

An instant later, a huge billow of smoke and a flash blew back across the bridge window. A hissing, rushing sound like a train speeding through a tunnel filled the bridge. As it receded, a voice shouted, "Starboard missile away and tracking clean."

"Go for secondary target lock-on port missile."

The sequence was repeated. There was another blowback of smoke and fire. Cogne stood perfectly still and listened to the fading sound of his missiles.

Mon Dieu, he whispered softly. *Mon Dieu.*

At the same instant Koik saw the burst of smoke and light come off the frigate, his ERM registered an incoming missile. They did it! he thought wildly. The bastards actually did it!

Yet even as his mind absorbed this, his body was already reacting. His hands flew, his feet shoved as he rolled the Forger violently into a left wingover. The horizon went reeling across his cockpit. Upside down, he stopped the roll. The ocean lay directly over his head, two thousand feet away. He drove for it, bellowing to his wingman: "Missile! Break right, break right."

The surface rocketed toward him, but he held the aircraft to it. Two seconds and then another hard over: the Forger came out of the dive only feet from the water. He hauled back into a spiraling climb, blowing afterburners. Sea and sky spun around him in a blur.

At eight thousand feet, he leveled, then snapped into another wingover. For a fleeting moment he caught sight of two smoke trails laced against the sky. And then he was plunging straight at the ocean again.

As the water rushed toward him, his ERM tone speeded up drastically. A red circle appeared with smaller flashing circles within it. The guidance system of one of the missiles had just locked onto him. He pulled up, coming out of his dive so near the water he could actually feel the rebound of his own pressure wave tremble across his after surfaces. Once more he spiraled into the sky.

One second later, the first Exocet exploded in the sea right below him. Up he hurled, Gs pulling at him. He crossed through the sonic barrier with a small tremble and swiveled his head, searching for his wingman. He finally spotted him just as the second missile struck his tail pipe.

Koik watched the Forger come apart as if in slow motion. The forward section, afire, whirled and spun, shards of it caroming away, wreathed in smoke. His hand went limp on the control stick. He stared at the debris as it began its lazy drift toward the ocean.

Then it was gone, out of sight. He looked at his altimeter. He was at eighteen thousand feet, still in steep-climb configuration. He held optimum power and reached for the sky, angling slightly southward toward the Marquesas Channel and home.

*　　*　　*

Two miles west of the MAQ platform, the Russian Alfa-class attack submarine *Troikiska* steamed slowly at periscope depth. Her skipper, Captain Third Class Ivan Garesemov, had been watching the distant combat with mounting fury. For the last four hours the sub had been prowling the waters north of the Polynesians. Pulled from her normal patrol sector by a high-code order during a scheduled plot report off the Soviet Mish-4T satellite west of Fiji, she had since been scanning the area for a downed aircraft.

Garesemov jerked from the periscope's padded viewing mount, eyes blazing. He stared at his executive officer, Lieutenant Stefan Korotich who squatted on the rim of the scope pit. "They just shot down a Forger," he bellowed. "The French pig-fuckers just shot down a Russian."

Heads around the control space jerked up. Garesemov pulled himself out of the pit and began pacing, cutting loose with a steady stream of obscenities. The *Troikiska*'s hardass skipper was hot-tempered and heavy on his crew. He always wore a black turtleneck sweater and floppy officer's cap. It made him look like a Nazi raider, which he fancied.

Korotich was scoping as Garesemov returned to the pit. "What's happening?"

"The downed Forger is still burning."

"Where's the other prick?"

"I've lost him. No, wait, there he is. He's heading south, high up."

"South! He's running?"

"Apparently, sir."

"Get out of the pit." Korotich scrambled up onto the rim and the captain dropped down. Draping his arms over the conning swivels, he swung the periscope a quarter turn. The platform loomed into view.

He studied the huge gray pilings, the main decks washed in sunlight, the men launching Zodiac boats from a small floating dock. The scum is going out to pick at the entrails, he thought fiercely. Enraged, he whirled. "Sonar, give me hard bearing to platform."

Everybody snapped to as the order echoed. Korotich took up his position beside the main attack console. Garesemov set his thick forearms on the pit edge.

"Control, Sonar. Platform bearing one-seven-two degrees. Range three-point-two kilometers."

"Helm, bring us to one-seven-two degrees. Torpedo room, prepare torpedoes one and three for free firing."

Again orders cracked across the control room, and the *Troikiska* heeled slightly as she came about. "Helm, coming up to one-seven-two degrees . . . we have it."

"Give me three knots and set up for firing. Where the fuck is the frigate?"

"Control, Sonar. Screws on outer range, moving slowly now. Heading two-nine-seven degrees, bearing one-eight-seven degrees. Range eight-three kilometers."

The torpedo room came on: "Control, Torpedo. Number one and three in slot and set up."

Garesemov pressed his face against the scope's rubber buffers. The platform sat out there as large as a carrier, defiant as a goddamned Zuzino Prospeckt whore. He watched it with malevolence, envisioning what his torpodoes would do to it.

Then, cursing, he pulled away from the viewer. "Torpedo room, stand down. Helm, give me a new heading of two-eight-five, go to one third."

The submarine heeled again, moving to the right.

"Down periscope." Garesemov slammed the conning swivels and pulled himself out of the pit. "Planes man, take us to two hundred feet."

He strode to his pedestal chair and flopped into it. Nobody met his eyes. Fucking French sodomizers, he thought viciously. Not this time, assholes, but we will meet again. Count on it.

4

Oh, yeah, Cas Bonner thought.

He leaned away from his microscope, took a pull on his beer, and scowled down at the line of slides spread out on the work-table. The situation was much worse than he'd thought.

He was in the AlPaci Armory lab, an old room with brown walls and wainscot and tin workbenches standing on pipes. Louis Pasteur would have felt at home in this place, Cas reflected.

Two hours before, he and Skip had deposited their corpse at the small base infirmary, landing right out in the parking lot with the body hanging down. Seamen came out and carried it through a side entrance while officers watched curiously from the windows of the AlPaci headquarters building across the quadrangle.

Soon after, they were questioned by a French captain of intelligence. His name was Coude Plasque, a very precise man with a narrow red face and intense dark eyes. They told him what they knew. Plasque studied them through squinted lids, as if he didn't believe a word. He chain-smoked native *ku'ai* cigarettes, as slender as marijuana joints and smelling like watermelon. He requested they remain in Papeete for a few days in case he had further questions.

But Cowell was scheduled to fly down to the SEO main office on Rurutu to drop off the previous month's analysis reports and pick up supplies. After two quick beers at the base commissary, Skip took off. Cas would remain at the lab until the following day when he got back.

Before starting on his regular work, Cas had run microscopic and chemical analysis on the tissue samples from the dead albatross. The examination shocked him. Every one showed deeper cellular disintegration than he'd first suspected. And there was clear eschar, the layer flaking indicating exposure to tremendous heat. Fat, muscle, even bone fragments displayed the same decomposition. The albatross's body had internally exploded due to the instantaneous heat expansion of liquid components within inner cavities. The only logical answer was that the beam had been thermal. But what could create such a thin stream with that much energy? Could it have been a nuclear power source?

He dug through the cabinets until he found Cowell's old field Geiger counter and ran it over the samples. The read was very low, almost nonexistent. Confounded, he got himself another beer out of the specimen cooler and approached the problem from a different angle.

Not all the birds had been struck, yet the entire skein had become disoriented. Why? He knew that seabirds used, in addition to sound probes, the earth's magnetic field to navigate over long stretches of ocean. Their ability to detect anomalies was phenomenal, even to the smallest fluctuations around atolls and *motus*. It also helped them maintain spatial orientation. So it was possible the beam had knocked out that ability. Or—a far scarier thought struck him—had it actually distorted the earth's magnetic field?

Such a wild supposition was hard to swallow. He lit a cigarette, mulling it over some more. But he continued to be stumped by what might have caused such a thing. These were questions for a physicist, not a marine biologist. Still, there seemed one sure conclusion. However the fine points were drawn, the beam source had to be the French experimental platform. And the correlation to that was the obvious, stunning question: If it could do this to a flock of birds, what could it do to the ocean environment? To people?

Someone tapped lightly on the door of the lab, and Cas turned to see the shy, impish grin of Lieutenant Georges Bourgerie, the base medical officer. "Hey, Georgie," he called affectionately. "Come on in, you little fart. How the hell are you?"

"You busy?'"

"Not really. Grab a beer and have a seat."

"Have you heard?" Georges asked as he hurried to the cooler. "It's a terrible thing."

"What?"

Bourgerie's eyes danced with excitement behind their yellow lenses. "One of our frigates shot down a Russian fighter this morning."

"No shit! Where?"

"Up north, near the experimental platform."

"The platform?" Bonner's eyes narrowed. "Were they attacking the damned thing?"

"I don't know. Everybody's keeping very mum about it." He snapped open the beer and took a long pull. "All forces are on heavy alert. Will there be war over this, do you think?"

"Hell no. This sort of thing happens all the time. The politicians will squeal for a while and then everybody'll forget about it." Cas frowned. "But what the hell was a Russian fighter doing in this area?"

"Oh, I don't know, I don't know," Bourgerie sighed anxiously. "I think I'm very nervous about this." He wandered over to the lab table and absently glanced at Cas's slides. "What are you working on?"

"Something that's bothering the hell out of me."

"Ah?"

Cas liked Georges a great deal. Quite often they had gotten roaring drunk together. The little doctor with thinning hair and a short beard was high-strung and faintly effeminate, yet he possessed a self-deprecating sense of humor and had an endless repertoire of bawdy Parisian café songs.

Cas hiked up onto the edge of the lab table and fixed Bourgerie with a solemn stare. "Georgie, what are you people doing out on that platform?"

Bourgerie hesitated a moment, glanced at the door, then whispered dramatically, "I think it's a super-collider. But please, don't tell anybody I told you that. The whole thing is very top-secret. That imbecile Plasque would get very intense with me if he found out."

Cas grunted in satisfaction. He didn't know much about colliders, but didn't they have something to do with splitting atoms and all that nuclear shit? That certainly fit what he had seen, didn't it? Feeling his hunch confirmed, he decided not to press Georgie any further about it and changed the subject.

"So, what's the word on that body we brought?" In mentioning that, it struck him that the seat markings had looked Russian. Now here was a Russian fighter in a shoot-out with a frigate. A connection? "You people find out anything about him?"

Bourgerie was thoughtfully silent for a moment, then he gave him a sly look. "Have you a free moment?"

"Sure."

"I want to show you something startling." He bent closer and held up a finger. "But this is strictly confidential. Promise?"

"You got it."

They left the armory and walked across a small boat ramp area with cement benches and stunted Samoan coconut trees with trunks painted white. Bourgerie's office was on the second floor of the infirmary overlooking the Taunoa Channel bridge.

Once he had closed the door behind them, Georges hurriedly pulled a personal journal from a drawer and opened it on his desk. "These are my notes on that cadaver. It's been put into cold storage until Paris decides what to do with it. I wanted to perform an autopsy, but Command forbade it." His eyes blinked rapidly. "But, you see, there were certain exterior signs on the corpse which intrigued me. So I took some sample tissues. Hands, facial, tongue, septum membrane, and two slices from the testicular corridor."

Cas grinned at him. "That was sneaky, Georges."

Bourgerie giggled. "I know."

"And?"

"Read it. Particularly page 143."

Cas scanned the page of small, neat handwriting. Examination of the corpse's tissues showed that all samples exhibited advanced cellular cyanosis, or oxygen starvation. There was also a marked degree of hematomic crystallization and low levels of blood lymphocytes. The facial and hand tissues showed freeze burn. Georges's notes suggested these had been caused by sudden "tunnel blast" exposure to temperatures of at least eighty degrees or more below zero Celsius.

Bonner glanced up. "Jesus! You sure about those temperature parameters?"

"Yes."

"But that would mean this joker ejected at a hell of an altitude."

"Exactly. I've already checked altitude charts. Temperatures like that occur only above fifty miles. But that's not all, read on."

Cas continued, but paused on the very next entry. The freeze degeneration of exterior skin had apparently taken place *after* onset of cyanotic coma. "You're saying he was unconscious when he left the aircraft?"

"Yes. Moreover, the pressure residue locked inside the suit's conduits was at atmospheric level."

Bonner shook his head, trying to imagine the scene. Obviously the pilot had been ejected automatically, way the hell and gone up there, and then fell through cold that could split steel.

"It's very strange, isn't it?" Bourgerie said, watching him closely.

"You got that right."

"What should I do with this?"

"Tell your people."

"I can't. If they—"

"What is this man doing here?" a man asked sharply from the doorway. Georges jumped as the intelligence officer, Plasque, strode into the room. "I want to know what this man is doing here?"

Georges looked stricken. "Ah, *capitaine*, he is with the SEO—"

"I know who he is. But why is he here?"

Bonner watched Plasque with a slight grin. "Georgie and I were just discussing plans to bomb Paris."

Plasque shot him a searing look, then glanced down at the journal. "What is this?"

"That's the map where all the whorehouses are," Cas snapped. He was still smiling, but it was only on his lips now. "Sure as hell wouldn't want to bomb them, right?"

Aghast, Bourgerie blurted, "They are merely medical notes."

Plasque turned a few pages, but obviously didn't comprehend what he was reading. After a moment he lifted his head and eyed Georges. "It is a breach of both military and ethical rules to allow this man to see these data."

"Oh, for chrissakes, Plasque," Cas said.

The captain turned slowly toward him. "Monsieur?"

"We're just two scientists discussing science. You got a problem with that?"

Plasque stared for a moment longer, then returned to Bourgerie. "I wish to speak with you. Alone."

"Yes, of course, *capitaine*." As Bourgerie looked beseechingly at Cas, the latter shrugged and made for the door.

"One thing more, Monsieur Bonner," Plasque said. "A quarantine has been placed on this facility. You are to remain here until further notice."

Bonner stopped. "What did you say?"

"You will not leave Command premises until I say you can."

"Bullshit."

"You will be arrested if you attempt to."

Cas advanced until he stood chin to chin with Plasque. "Listen up, Frenchie. I'm an American citizen under contract to the SEO. You fuck me over, and I'll see to it your commander nails your balls to the barn door."

The captain's face went stiff, eyes blazing. But he said nothing.

Bonner grinned icily at him. He was, of course, bluffing. Since he was a foreigner, Plasque would be well within his rights to detain him, particularly since the base was on a high alert. But he'd already tagged the captain as a petty asshole who'd freeze at the mere mention of higher-ups.

He put a finger two inches from Plasque's nose. "While we're at it, maybe you'd like to tell me what's going on out on that goddamned platform of yours."

"That is no concern of yours," the captain snapped.

"The hell it isn't. Your scientists are damaging the environment out there. I know, I've seen the results."

"We are merely conducting experiments within our sovereign waters."

"Fuck your sovereign waters."

That hit Plasque like a fist to the stomach. He blanched, then swung away, striding to the window and looking out. His body was so tense he was trembling.

Bourgerie, looking absolutely forlorn, wrung his hands. Cas gave him a wink. "Hang in, Georgie," he said, and left.

Cas was right about Plasque. Fifteen minutes later, nobody stopped him as he rode his motorcycle, which he kept at the lab, through the main gate of AlPaci Command and headed for town to hunt up a boat.

*   *   *

The President of the United States found Secretary of Defense Woodrow Lauderdale waiting in the Oval Office when he returned from lunch. He'd spent a few hours with several All-Pro players from the National Football League, sharing laughs and locker-room camaraderie. Carrying a presentation football they had given him, he was still glowing until he saw Lauderdale's face. He stopped short. "What?"

"There's been a serious incident in French Polynesia, sir."

"What happened?"

"Apparently two Russian fighters penetrated deep into French territory. One was shot down by an AlPaci frigate."

"Oh, shit." He laid the football onto his desk and sat on the edge, arms folded. "What in the hell was a Soviet warplane doing over French territory?"

"We don't know. Apparently there's been some pretty heavy Soviet surveillance activity in that sector for the past few hours."

"Why?"

"We don't know the reason for that, either. But there's a sizable Red fleet carrier force about a thousand miles south of the Polynesians. From our intelligence reports, it was supposedly headed for a goodwill tour of South America. But that's apparently changed. It's gone into a holding pattern and some of its forward elements have actually turned north. Obviously, the fighters were from it."

"What do the French say?"

"Nothing. We've tried making contact with AlPaci Command, but they're playing it close to the vest. No details. And Paris is silent, too."

"What about Moscow?"

"Not a word."

"Then how'd we find out about it?"

"Our NAVSAT satellite photographed the whole thing. Enhancement just got passed through from our tracking-and-monitor station on Phoenix Island."

The President moved around to his chair and sat down disgustedly. Toying thoughtfully with his upper lip, he asked, "What's our deployment in the area?"

"Normal missile and attack sub patrols. There's also the *Coral Sea* task group supporting Marine assault exercises on the Kingman Reef."

"Where the hell is that?"

"About a thousand miles north of the Capricorn."

"The what?"

"The Capricorn latitudes, sir. They cover French Polynesia."

"Do Hubbel and his people have a slant on this thing yet?" he said, alluding to Admiral Jack Hubbel, Chairman of the Joint Chiefs of Staff.

"Nothing solid. He's already had naval intelligence run some computer scenarios. They think it was an accident. Maybe a panicky frigate skipper."

"That makes sense. But it still doesn't explain why the Russians were there in the first place."

"Hubbel feels it has something to do with the increased radar activity. They're looking for something. Apparently, it must be damned important to them."

"A ship down?"

Lauderdale shrugged. "We just don't know. The CNO staff has also got people from the NCC on it. No report yet."

"What are JCS's recommendations at this point?"

"Well, Hubbel's more worried about French reaction than Russian. As you know, Vasillon's government has been sore as a boil since that thing in the Black Sea. They could get stiff-backed. In fact, there's some indications they're pulling a carrier group out of the Indian Ocean to support AlPaci."

The President snorted, "Oh, terrific. That's all we need right now, hysterical 'Vive le France' shit."

"Hubbel suggests we shove some power down into the area, too. Show our displeasure on the chance this thing escalates. Deploy the *Coral Sea* force south and maybe sortie some elements out of Pearl."

The President nodded. "All right, that sounds good. But, goddammit, you make sure the *Coral Sea* stays out of French waters. I don't want us drawn into anything."

"Yes, sir."

The President began unconsciously squeezing the skin on his forehead. After a moment he looked up. "I want some diplomatic notes sent to both Paris and Moscow. Make it plain we don't like this sort of crap in our ocean and want it smoothed out now."

"Yes, sir."

"All right, get on it. Keep me apprised."

As Lauderdale departed, the President sighed and looked at his football. A good afternoon could sure get screwed up fast, he thought.

Del January had remained in Commander Kirkpatrick's office most of the afternoon, monitoring incoming updates on the heavy surveillance activity in the Capricorn. Most of it was standard CNO staff memo and a few NI "scatter" reports, all low-classification stuff.

Kirkpatrick turned out to be a pain in the ass, insisting on seeing everything before passing it to a civilian. Despite that Del had managed to work up a supposition analysis for Captain Peck by two. It didn't have much content except to indicate that it was the platform that was causing all the radar traffic.

The other possibilities—a downed aircraft, a surface ship in trouble, even a sunken sub—hadn't grabbed him for the simple reason that if it had been any of these, intelligence sources would have tumbled to it by now: radio intercepts, intelligence leaks, something. Besides, the Russians never seemed to give a tinker's damn about their personnel. No, they were interested in some *thing*, and the platform was the only logical answer.

Still, he was bothered by the analysis report. He didn't like sending up conclusions based on meager facts and shaky assumptions. For a while he even thought Kirkpatrick might have been withholding classified data just to make him look bad.

Then word of the Polynesian firefight came down. That shocked even Kirkpatrick. "Jesus Christ," he said, leaning over the computer relay from CNO. "Look at *this*."

January walked over and read the message. He instantly picked up a phone and rang Peck's office.

"Yeah, it's true," Peck said. "Apparently some of the *Minsk*'s Forgers were sent right up the Marquesas Channel."

"Who fired first?"

"The French."

"Were the Russians actually attacking the platform?"

"We don't know. NI thinks it was an accident."

January thought, a Russian intrusion into French airspace? My God, they were acting frantic. An attack or even a reconnaissance on the platform now made no sense. There was something else down there they wanted to find. But what?

For the next hour, he haunted Kirkpatrick's NI transmission room, trying to glean info. A lot of it was coming in: filings of U.S. response moves, in-fleet command relays from Pacific sectors, and some CIA dispatches from field stations giving world reactions. But it was all backlogged material, nothing less than two hours old. Obviously Kirkpatrick was a low priority link. Del'd have to get more pertinent news. He tried to raise Peck again, but the captain was in a staff meeting with the CNO. Rather than try running other higher-up contacts upstairs, he stuck with Kirkpatrick, downing coffee and devouring every item flashing on the screens.

By five in the afternoon, his stomach was queasy with gas. Cramping slightly, he walked up the hall to the small cafeteria near the officers' lounge for something to eat. He chose a dried-out hamburger and a glass of milk and found a table.

Two minutes later, a fat, sweaty man came in, spotted him, and ambled over. He gave him a slap on the shoulder with a meaty hand. "Del, baby, how the hell you been?" His name was Tom Burkhalst, a weather expert attached to the astrophysics division of CCN. "Haven't seen you in a month of Sundays."

"Hello, Tom."

Burkhalst lowered himself heavily into a chair. "How's Alexandria?"

"Same as always. How come you're still here? I heard you got transferred."

"Nope." As Burkhalst put his elbows on the table, Del noticed the huge perspiration rings under his arms that smelled faintly of beer yeast. "I'm still trying to study the heavens through the military bullshit." His eyes narrowed mischievously. "What're you doin' in Washington?"

"I had some JAD runs."

"Ah, yes, the ultimate Monopoly game." Smiling, he watched Del chew a mouthful of hamburger. "What do you think of that little set-to down under?"

"What's that?" January said disingenuously.

"Oh, shit, January, the seepage is coming out of the walls. Everybody knows." His grin widened. "Hell, boy, we got a crisis again. You know, I once worked it out. Every two thousand, one hundred sixty hours, it's crisis time. That's right. Somebody sets it up that way. It's designed to prevent the military testicles from getting musty."

January swallowed, shook his head.

Burkhalst studied him slyly. "You're liaisoned with this Polynesian thing, aren't you?"

Del glanced up. "Where in hell do you get all your information?"

"I stroke, Del, my man. I stroke."

"You should have been a spy."

"Too fat."

January returned to his burger. Two secretaries working the evening shift came in, moved past the counter. Burkhalst eyed their long legs lasciviously before turning back. "You want to know why, don't you?" he asked.

"Why what?"

"*I* know why."

January stopped chewing and looked up.

Burkhalst nodded at the hamburger. "Finish that damned thing, will you?"

Del dropped it onto his plate. "I'm finished. Tasted like wood pulp, anyway."

"It is wood pulp." Burkhalst stood up and crooked a finger at him. "Come with me, my man. I got something to show you."

The photograph was as clean as a portrait, showing a black, angulated shape that looked like a bat in flight. Behind it was a solid light source. Del studied it a moment, then turned to Burkhalst in puzzlement.

"There's your why," the astronomer said gleefully.

"I don't understand."

"I just got that from the Socorro Radio Astronomy Observatory. It was relayed from a coast guard weather ship running sequential shots of Mars from a fix station in the mid-Pacific. That's Martian backlighting, boy." He poked a finger at the bat shape. "And *that* is a fucking airplane."

Del's mouth dropped open in surprise.

"I ran estimated coordinate fixes from the ship's position and Mars," Burkhalst went on. "That sucker was right over French Polynesia. Sixty goddamned miles over it."

"Sixty miles?" Del gasped. The aircraft's technology would have to be phenomenal, far beyond what the U.S. had, to reach that level.

"That's right," Tom said. "The Russkies have a high-performance aircraft down in that area. My calculations show it was in steep descent when this picture was taken."

Del came out of his shock. "Who else knows about this?"

"Just my division. We haven't sent it upstairs yet." He grinned. "Wouldn't make any difference anyway. Those dudes upstairs never look at what we send up. They think all we do is watch stars and jack off."

"I want this photo."

Burkhalst chuckled. "I thought you would."

Ten minutes later, January was in Peck's office, showing him the photo. "There it is. That's what they're looking for."

The captain, grunting occasionally, studied the picture while Del explained. He concluded with: "That's why they're so desperate, Tony. It's that plane they want."

Peck nodded.

"And they sure as hell don't want us or the French finding it first."

"Okay, I'll take this right up to the CNO. I'd appreciate your updated OA as soon—"

January interrupted, "Tony, let another analyst handle that. I want down there."

"Down where?"

"French Polynesia. I want to find that thing or what's left of it before the Russians do."

"A full-out search operation? In that area? No way, Del. The place is too unstable."

"Look, you've got the *Coral Sea* moving south, right?"

"Yeah."

"Put me on her with some orders. All I'll need is one of her helos."

Peck thought a moment. "You think it's that important?"

"The Russians obviously do."

The captain sighed. "All right. I'll radio a note to Admiral Passmore and scan out a transit jet for you."

"Thanks, Tony."

Peck smiled ruefully. "You better prepare yourself for a hardass, Del. That Passmore's a flinty old boy."

"I'll convince him."

"Good luck. Keep me posted."

"Right."

Forty-five minutes later, Del January took off from Andrews Air Force Base aboard a Navy A-6 Intruder trainer for a twelve-hour flight to the *Coral Sea.*

Earlier, Rotuf Parunin, Yuri Markisov's security chief, had eased aside the curtain of the general secretary's box in the Bolshoi Theatre and bent to whisper, "Sir, Marshal Petrov is here and wishes to speak with you."

Markisov and his wife, Altynal, were attending a performance of the Kirov Ballet Company's *Swan Lake.* He snapped around and looked at Parunin. Petrov here? His first thought was: the Saber. He murmured an hasty apology to his wife, then rose and followed Parunin.

The marshal was in a small anteroom, pacing agitatedly. He waited until the security man returned to the outer hall before speaking: "The French just shot down one of Turesky's fighters."

Despite the gravity of the news, Markisov felt a shiver of relief. At least not the Saber. But he became grim as Petrov gave the details he had. "What is Turesky doing?" Markisov asked when the marshal finished.

"He's reformed the elements of the *skadra* and is holding station until the search aircraft return."

"Have there been any other attacks?"

"No, sir."

Markisov walked slowly around the room. The French frigate commander's aggressiveness shocked him. But worse, it now placed him in a diabolically delicate situation. To continue search operations for the Saber could create a full-out shooting war in the South Pacific, with the Russians perceived as the aggressors. Yet to break off the search meant—

He turned to Petrov. "Order Turesky to continue search operations."

"But, comrade, that would be extremely dangerous now. The French would—"

Markisov cut him off sharply: "You need not point out the obvious, Petrov. Unfortunately, we have little choice but to continue."

The marshal sighed. "As you say, sir."

Markisov studied him closely for a moment. "How much do you know about the Saber project?"

"Merely that the aircraft has disappeared over the South Pacific."

"No, I mean about what it's capable of doing."

"I've studied some memos on it. As I understand, it contains some sort of fusion weapon."

Again Markisov eyed him carefully. He liked Petrov, but more important, he trusted him. The marshal had repeatedly shown his loyalty by defending the new ideas of *perestroika* and *glasnost* against the powerful reactionary elements of the Old Guard. "I'm going to tell you something, Sergei," he said slowly. "It must not leave this room."

"Of course, sir."

Markisov related what Titov had said, explained the full significance of it. Petrov's eyes widened with shock. "Is this possible?"

"Yes. If this aircraft is still intact, it could trigger chaos in the South Pacific."

Petrov's features registered deep disgust. "How could those fools at Sary Shagan have done this?"

"That's no longer important. We must find that aircraft and either disarm it or destroy it."

"Yes, sir." Petrov hesitated. "But what do I tell Turesky to do if his people are attacked again?"

Markisov thought a moment. "What is French strength in Polynesia?"

"Their AlPaci Command is a small force, mostly patrol vessels. There's a naval airbase in the Tuamotu Archipelago, but our intelligence puts less than a squadron of fighters there."

"Then Turesky's *skadra* could easily handle them?"

"For now, yes. But the French presently have a large carrier force conducting exercises in the Indian Ocean. They could conceivably send it through the Strait of Malacca to support AlPaci. Also, a powerful American carrier task group is less than a thousand miles north of the Polynesians."

Once more Markisov ambled slowly around the room, thinking. Would the French openly challenge with full force? He doubted it. More significant, the Americans wouldn't allow it. The South Pacific was their domain; they'd never tolerate a shooting war started by either Russian intrusions or French rashness.

That accepted, he still had to have a plausible justification for sending his aircraft over national boundaires. He paused, glimpsing sight of an idea. He turned it over and over. Island chains, by the very fact that they were separated by wide expanses of ocean, presented unusual aspects of sovereignty. If he were to issue an immediate note to Paris demanding an apology for the Forger downing based on the challenge to French rights of preventing passage on or over these open ocean waterways, the shooting situation might, just might, temporarily be held in abeyance. Further, he could insist the question be thrown to the World Maritime Commission for a decision. Compliance with the subsequent decision would even save face all around. But the essential thing would be that he would gain time to continue the search for the Saber.

When he told Petrov of the plan, the marshal looked doubtful. "If I may say so, sir, it seems like an obvious ploy."

"Of course it is. But it does give us time. Right now, that's more important than anything else."

"And if Turesky is fired on?"

"He is to defend himself."

"Yes, sir."

"I'm returning to my office immediately. I want constant updates on the situation."

"I'll see to it." Petrov paused. "Sir, there's one other thing."

"What?"

"Bardeshevsky. He'll use this French incident to attack you. And if he learns about the Saber—which he undoubtedly will eventually—the damage to you could be severe."

"I'll handle Bardeshevsky."

Petrov looked uncomfortable. "Will you at least increase your personal security?"

Markisov scrutinized him narrowly. "Surely, you don't think he's that foolish?"

"It's difficult to know, sir. The man's a fanatic and he was badly humiliated this morning. This French thing could make him and his people think it an opportune time to openly challenge your power. Or, worse, they could even strike directly at you."

Markisov thought about that a moment, then waved it off. "No, I think you overestimate friend Bardeshevsky's threat."

"Just be careful, Comrade Secretary." Petrov braced and departed.

Ten minutes later, Markisov's black Zil limo pulled up to the rear entrance of the Council of Ministers building. The Kremlin grounds at this hour were empty but flooded with lights. Markisov hurried to his office on the third floor. Erian Trofimov was at his desk, in shirtsleeves. Markisov spoke briefly with his aide, then entered the room where he had installed Titov.

The professor was sipping a cup of tea and studying a printout from one of the teletype machines that had been installed for him. All around the room were other consoles and computer terminals. On Markisov's direct order, Titov had been given total access to all high-priority reports coming into KGB, Supreme Military Command, and Politburo facilities.

Titov turned at the sound of the opening door. "Oh, Comrade Secretary, I'm glad you've come."

"You know of the situation in Polynesia?"

"Yes, I was just following it. That's what I wanted to speak with you about."

Markisov fixed the old man with dark, steady eyes. "You think the Saber was responsible?"

"It is possible."

"Dammit!" Markisov swore, pounding a fist into his other palm. "How?"

"The ship's low-category modes are able to spoof an enemy's fire-control system."

"What is this 'spoof'?"

"The beam can create dysfunction within a fire-control system by causing shortages and aborting circuits. It can actually induce false data and even bring complete breakdown."

"Did this happen aboard the French frigate?"

"I can't be sure, sir. There are so many unanswered—"

"Did it?" Markisov shouted.

Titov nervously scratched his thin jaw. "Yes, I think so."

Markisov cursed again, whirled, and wrenched the door open.

"Comrade Secretary?"

He paused, glancing back over his shoulder.

"If the Saber did this, it not only means she is intact, it also means she's moving up through category modes."

Three miles away, near the gay lights and music of a carnival in Gorky Park, a young man was sitting alone on a bench, gazing fixedly into the dark waters of the Moska River. His name was Latif Gankin, a student from Latvia who had arrived in the city that morning. Three days before, he had buried his only brother—his twin brother—killed by Russian troops during a violent protest march in the Latvian port city of Riga.

Finally, Gankin rose from his bench and headed toward Leninskij Prospeckt, the broad boulevard that leads across Trinity Bridge to the main gate of the Kremlin. He walked quickly, hands deep in his coat, his shoulder-length hair riffling in the slight breeze.

Once across the bridge, he skirted the river side of the Kremlin wall until he reached its south corner. There he paused to read several newspapers tacked to a small kiosk. There were copies of *Izvestiva* and the Red Army newspaper, *Srezda*. Both were filled with information about the parade commemorating Russia's victory over the Nazis, which was scheduled for the following morning. The parade route was inked in green on a map of Red Square.

After a few moments he walked to St. Basil's Cathedral, located on the southern end of the square. The building's striped onion domes were brightly lit with yellow light. Deeper in Red Square he could see construction lights and men working on a scaffold near the permanent reviewing stand from which Politburo dignitaries would watch the parade. Before turning away, he visually measured the distance to the stand.

Ten minutes later, Gankin entered the lobby of the shabby students' hostelry where he had rented a room on the top floor. From his single window he could see across the Kremlin wall to the Bell Tower of Ivan the Terrible, drenched in red light.

He stood at the window for a long time, then turned and moved to his bed. From beneath it he pulled a worn black suitcase and opened it. Inside were several metal tubes with screw ends, a heavy, round base plate, and a calibrated windage gauge. Between the tubes lay a single Czechoslovakian 7.62 MG mortar round.

He lifted it from the case. It was heavy with a compact lethality, the metal ice cold against his palms. He could almost feel the death locked inside. It made him quiver with a dark, viperous fear. Soon, he told himself, soon those responsible for Alexander's dying would taste its terror.

5

Kiri slammed down her radio mike and paced furiously around the small stockroom of her restaurant, the Burmese Garden. She had just talked with Katevayo, and, as always, the man's barbarian intellect inflamed her. She always felt dirtied after speaking with him, as if she had just been witness to a particularly brutal torture.

She was in a grim mood anyway, having just returned from Takaroa, after the Corsair finally appeared in the late morning. She snorted as she thought of her seat partner, a very fat Tahitian woman with a mouth stained with betel nut who had apprised her of the status of an endless collection of relatives.

To top off an awful morning, the French pilots informed the passengers that there had been a rumor of a confrontation between French naval forces and Russian aircraft up north. They were so scared they skimmed above the ocean all the way back to Papeete, down where the turbulence was most hellish.

The rumor had turned out to be true. But what the hell were Russian aircraft doing here? she wondered. She knew nothing of the Soviet carrier group farther south. But the upshot of the situation was that now her position had worsened. French security around the platform could now be impossible to penetrate. Particularly if they also found enough of the man she'd killed to start putting things together.

When she had told Katevayo, he hadn't believed it. The fucking pig-dicked French would never dare attack a Russian airplane, he shouted. He wanted to get on with their mission and get it over with. She told him they would have to wait, feel things out before moving again. He let loose with a string of obscenities. She had swung her dial and cut him off.

At last, she reached up and shut the radio down, sat there a moment to settle herself, then went out smiling into the lounge. Her restaurant, located on Cruiser Wharf in the inner edge of Papeete harbor, had been purchased with KGB funds filtered through a bank in Hong Kong. It had also quickly become the favorite watering hole for the French colonial aristocracy along with a scattering of officers and technicians from AlPaci and the research facilities of the nuclear-testing center on Mururoa and the MAQ platform. From these last, in their moments of drunken talk, she had managed to collect a fair amount of classified information.

She found a boisterous group of American tourists at the bar, all attired in outrageous aloha shirts and muumuus. At the end of the bar, though, was a lone man, nursing a beer. Kiri smiled the moment she saw him, aware that a soft, sensuous wash of warmth instantly flooded through her body. She walked over and ran a fingernail across the man's back.

"It's about time you showed up," she said into his ear.

Cas Bonner turned and flashed her a wide grin. "Hi, love."

As Kiri slid onto the stool beside him, Cas noticed how stunning she looked in her blue jumper and slim white slacks, her long hair in a single braid down her back.

"It's been too long," she said. "How've you been?"

"Surviving. You?"

"Lonely."

"You don't look lonely."

"My hostess face." She signaled the red-jacketed Filipino barman to refill his glass. "You hear about the shooting incident?"

"Yeah."

"Could it get dangerous?"

"No."

She turned and watched one of the tourists laboriously trying to dance the Tahitian *tamure*. "How long can you stay this time?"

"Till tomorrow."

"Lovely." Poking a finger into his arm, she ordered him not to leave and headed for the kitchen. On the way, she bought the group of tourists a round of drinks on the house.

She had met Cas four months earlier, when he and Georges Bourgerie had come into the Garden one evening singing drunkenly. She had spotted him the moment they walked through the front door: a big, shockingly handsome man in a filthy T-shirt and shorts. Even drunk, he moved with a smooth grace, the casual power of a leopard at ease. When Georges introduced them, Bonner stood and took her hand, grinning down at her, his eyes dancing. Even in remembering the moment, Kiri winced in confusion. For the first time in her life, the mere touch of a man had triggered a delicate electricity in the secret places of her body.

She next saw him, unexpectedly, three nights later. As she was leaving the Burmese Garden long after closing, she heard the thudding, grunting sounds of fighting men coming from the alley beside the restaurant. At first she ignored them and started to get into her car. But then her curiosity got the better of her.

She discovered Bonner fighting with two French sailors against a backdrop of garbage cans and cardboard boxes. He'd already knocked down one of the sailors, who was crawling around, trying to find his hat. The other, as big as he was, was squared off with him in that sullen, electrified circling stance of a fistfight.

Cas was obviously very drunk. He moved sluggishly with shuffling increments of motion, fixed, then moved again, his fists up close to his face. The sailor suddenly rushed him, arms flailing. Bonner took the full weight of the charge. It threw him back against the alley wall. Then the sailor was bodily lifted off the ground and hurled away. He went down flat onto his back, cursing. Bonner, slowly, wearily, lifted his fists again and took his stance.

Kiri yelled in French: "Watch out! The gendarmes!"

The second sailor came instantly to his feet. He glared up the alley, then turned, grabbed his companion by his collar, and dragged him into a smaller passage toward the bay. Bonner, fists still raised, turned slowly to face her as she walked toward him. His face was bloody. He swayed, trying to focus on her.

"*Bon soir, mon ami,*" she said, smiling.

He blinked. "Who the hell are you?"

"Kiri Valjean."

He thought about that for a moment, then slowly lowered his hands. He sighed and put his palm against the wall.

"You smell terrible," she said.

He laughed suddenly. "Damned if I don't."

She put her arm around his waist and they walked unsteadily up the alley. She drove him to her house, a structure made of teak logs on a hill overlooking Punaauia Bay, eight miles south of Papeete. As they pulled up before it, set in a thicket of *hao* trees and ginger fronds, it began to rain. She parked at the foot of the long stone stairway that led up to the house, and Cas followed her quietly. The steps were covered with moss and the rain dripping from the *hao* leaves released the heady aroma of ginger into the air.

He was just as mutely obedient when she administered to his wounds, though he watched her curiously. She then ran a bath for him, gave him a chunk of the native blue soap and a towel, and went off to her bedroom. It opened onto a small flagstone terrace that curved around to the right. This was one of her favorite spots, for in the late afternoon the sun came down on it through *pikaki* vines. Now the rain dropped off the eaves, sounding like elves whispering in the brush.

She undressed and got into her bed, a large, square frame set on the floor with a thick mattress and pale blue silk sheets. She lay and listened to the rain and Bonner in the tub and asked herself, "Why are you doing this?"

After first meeting him with Bourgerie she had made inquiries about him. When she found out he was a marine biologist working with the French government in a field station near the platform, she had made up her mind to nurture his friendship. He knew a lot of people and was undoubtedly a valuable source of information.

Yet now her anticipatory relish at the thought of seducing Bonner was confusing to her. Sex had always been a transient pleasure for Kiri, a physical thing with little more significance than the pleasing expulsion of sweat from a hard run, or a good night's sleep. As a result, she had always chosen her lovers for reasons totally apart from her emotions. They afforded information, a respite from boredom, or simply the assuaging of coital hunger. The possibility of love was ruthlessly proscribed. She had no intention of making herself that vulnerable to any man.

But now, suddenly, she had the uncomfortable feeling that with Cas Bonner it might be different. Watching him in the alley, being masculine and absurd, she had felt such a rush of blood that it had actually made her tremble. Now as she shifted her body slightly, felt the silk whisper softly across her already erect nipples, she realized that she couldn't wait to see where it would lead.

He finally came out of the bathroom, naked, and eased gently down onto the bed. He studied her a moment, then reached out and ran his finger over her lips. He smelled of soap and that faint scent of beer like freshly baked bread. Then he yanked her toward him and kissed her.

At first he was clumsy, running his big hands up and down her flanks, suckling her nipples roughly. Then, suddenly, the strength in his arms seemed to draw her in with almost desperate power. He entered her in full, throbbing erection. Engulfed by sensations, she clung to him, licked his face, shoulders. He groaned softly against her neck. When he reached orgasm, his burst triggered her own—again and again and still again, until she lay wasted beneath him as he pumped on, grunting, dripping sweat . . .

When she returned from the restaurant kitchen, her face was stormy. She plunked herself down beside Cas and snapped her finger at the barman. He instantly brought her a shot of vodka, which she tossed off neat. "Damn that Oriental son of a bitch," she growled. "I swear, I'm going to shoot that old bastard someday."

Cas watched her puckishly. She was talking about Leong, her *cuisinier*, a wizened old Chinaman who was the best chef in Papeete. But he was also as cantankerous as a wounded buffalo, and he and Kiri were always arguing, in screeching Cantonese.

"No, you'd never do that," he teased.

"You think not? You wait."

He leaned closer. "You know what I really think? You're just pissed off because you want to screw ole Leong and he won't have anything to do with you."

She whirled on him, eyes flashing. "You're a gross asshole,

Bonner." Then she saw him grin and realized he was ribbing her. She snorted disgustedly. "You and your goddamned sick American humor."

Out in the harbor, a high whistle sounded. A moment later, a patrol frigate from the naval arsenal docks moved slowly past, headed for the outer channel. Her bow wave curled a spreading V across the water, and on her afterdeck sailors with little red tufted hats were working deck gear.

Kiri slapped his arm. "Come on, comedian, make yourself useful. You can help me do the shopping."

With Bonner carrying a large coconut leaf basket, they dodged through the heavy traffic on Pomare Boulevard and headed toward the rue Ecole de Greres. The Pomare promenade was filled with sightseeing tourists, mostly clots of Japanese dutifully following guides carrying tiny Nippon flags. They took pictures of everything that moved, particularly the strolling prostitutes sheathed in expensive Dior dresses, with painted faces shaded under colorful *parapluies*, or umbrellas.

The Ecole de Greres was a narrow street lined with dilapidated two-story houses with salt-encrusted walls and split by balconies aflame with window boxes of bougainvillea. Under the overhangs, sullen young Tahitians and half-breeds squatted in the shade, drinking beer and playing *la fille* with polished stones. Nearby, Sony boom-boxes blared heavy metal music from a station in New Zealand. The air smelled of sewage and gardenias and the thick, dirty-sock stench drifting from the copra oil factory two blocks away.

Their destination was the main produce market on rue Leboucher, a vast, tin-roofed building filled with open stalls. The market was packed and raucous. Individual stalls were piled with all sorts of game and produce: fruits and vegetables trucked in from small native gardens around the island; barrels of live octopus and shrimp; counters filled with raw meat and gutted fish over which small boys morosely fanned away flies. There were stacks of straw shipping crates of cheap Algerian wine, and slaughtered pigs and goats tethered to cages containing tiny blue parrots and myna birds.

Cas dutifully followed Kiri around as she wove her way between stalls, pausing here and there to study a breadfruit or taste a sprig of lettuce. He nodded in admiration as she tested a tray of dressed barracuda, using a silver coin. If the coin had become tarnished, he knew it would have meant the flesh had been invaded by *ciguatera*, a highly poisonous marine fungus prevalent in these waters. She chattered with the vendors, yet there was no haggling over prices, since these were set by the French government.

Gradually the basket got heavier and Cas had to keep switching it from arm to arm. And the heat pouring down from the high tin roof was giving him a beer headache. Still, he made no comment, just plodded along behind, watching her go about her business. The fact was, he liked to look at her. She was so lovely, full and ripe. He studied her face as it changed from an animated smile to open delight to frowning concentration. Her eyes were a deep shade of green, like mossy jungle pools made deep and luminous in the faint touch of sunlight through trees. Like those pools, they were mysterious, cool, and elusive. Yes, she was a woman who had many secrets.

That much was clear by the way those eyes could paradoxically flash fire. In bed especially they would sometimes go flat and hard, and then she'd bite him or thrust against his body with such ferocity—power meeting power—that he was jolted. Afterward, with her hair mussed, her body drenched in sweat, she would silently study him with a vague look of puzzlement and deeper, way down, perhaps a tinge of fear.

On their way back to the restaurant, he told her about the dead pilot's body and what Bourgerie had found in its tissues. She immediately became very interested and plied him with questions. When he mentioned the confrontation with Plasque, she laughed. "Ah yes, that one. I know that pompous ass."

He went on to recount the incident with the albatross and what he had found in the lab, particularly his suspicions that the experimental platform was responsible. She watched his face harden and she fell silent, listening thoughtfully. They reached Pomare Boulevard and crossed into the shade beneath the willow trees in the Garden's foyer. There she paused and tilted her head to look at him. "You're going out to that platform, aren't you?"

"Yes."

"You fool. That's a restricted zone."

He shrugged. "So I'll get arrested. But before I do, I'll get a look at the waters around that damned thing and see just how much damage it's done. Then I'll write a report that'll stir up some attention."

She shook her head, but her eyes were bright with warmth. "How will you get there?"

"That's turned out to be a problem. I tried to charter a boat this morning, but the navy just closed the harbor. No commercial traffic in or out." He held up the shopping basket. "Look, what say we talk about this inside? This thing's making my arm numb."

They passed through the door and into the cool semi-darkness of the lounge. Suddenly she turned. "I can get you a boat."

"Where?"

"One of my customers, a doctor. He has a sailboat moored up at Point Venus."

"Yeah? Will he loan it to me?"

"No, but he'd let me use it."

He looked askance at her. "You want to go along?"

"Sure."

"Why?"

"Because I want to be with you, dumbbell. Besides, I like albatross, too."

Cas considered that a moment, then shrugged. "What the hell, why not?"

He telephoned SEO headquarters and told them he had something to follow up that would take him a couple of days. Skip wouldn't have to hurry home. The people at SEO were all excited over the downing of the Russian plane and wanted to know what the word was in Papeete. He replied wryly that rumor had it the Russians were going to invade any minute. That shook everybody up.

Kiri and Leong got into another Cantonese battle when she told him she'd be gone for two days. Afterward, she disappeared into her stockroom for a few minutes, then changed into a bikini and thongs, and they left.

They made two stops on the way. The first was so Cas could rent some diving gear, the second to pick up beer, cheese, bread, and packets of *kalua* jerky. Then they swung Kiri's little Peugeot out of town and turned north toward Point Venus.

During those few minutes Kiri had been in her stockroom, she had been thinking feverishly. Cas had just offered her an opportunity to test the platform's security net, see how much it had been altered, how jumpy the French were now.

She knew it could be risky—especially with Cas getting hard-nosed with everybody out there as she knew he would—but she was certain her cover would hold up. Hell, she knew every officer on the AlPaci staff personally, from Admiral L'Orange all the way down. She could claim that she had not known what Cas was going to do when he asked her to go with him.

The info on the pilot's body puzzled her. Cas's description of the man's flight gear made it plain that he had been ejected from a high-altitude surveillance aircraft, yet none of her dispatches from the agent in Auckland had ever contained high-resolution photos of the platform from aircraft other than the low shots taken by the Bears out of Cam Ranh.

She quickly raised Auckland. As usual, the agent didn't acknowledge reception clearance, but merely held down his mike button to let her know he was there. In a code-like patois, she told him about the pilot's body and asked if he knew anything concerning it.

"Negative."

Did he have any information on the downed fighter?

"Negative."

She told him she intended to probe security around mission object.

"Negative." His light went off.

"Screw you," Kiri said quietly.

Her second call was to Katevayo. Again using patois, she informed him that she was leaving with Cas to visit the "plantation." He asked, Why? She didn't waste time explaining, simply said it was to see whether the overseer had put on the extra guards as she had ordered.

"Bullshit," he sneered. "You want some more Yankee prong."

That dig drove her right out of the chair. Katevayo liked ribbing her about Bonner, and as soon as he had found out that it infuriated her, he poured it on. "You will be prepared to move when I say move, you obscene, grotesque bastard. Until then, fuck you!"

It took her a whole minute to regain her hostess face and return to Cas.

*   *   *

The MAQ platform looked like a great metal scab on the face of the ocean. The corrosive effects of the salt air had streaked her foundation pilings with dark rust. Fuel stains splotched her main deck. And the topside houses were smeared with orange rivulets, condensation runoff from the ventilation pumps and generator coolers.

Two miles off, three frigates were aligned in echelon, replacements for the *D'Estienne D'Vries*, since Lieutenant Cogne had been ordered back to Papeete for a full report on the attack. Throughout most of the early afternoon, the frigates, aided by platform divers in Zodiac boats, had searched the crash area, collecting whatever debris they could find. Now as evening approached, the divers were returning to the landing dock below the main deck.

Above them, in the main control room, Cotuse and his technicians were just starting the fourth test run of the main collider ring since Frenier's departure. Using a low-action neon plasma, they were checking for structural impurities in the weld joints and degauss effects in the main magnetic coil housings.

The appearance of the Russian aircraft had interrupted the second test run. When word came down, Cotuse immediately aborted it and everybody rushed to windows to watch. By the time Cotuse reached his office, the Russian plane had already been struck and was plunging crazily, spewing fiery debris. The sight horrified him. He had never before actually witnessed violent death. It shattered his concentration, already disrupted by Frenier's threats.

When he finally did return to the control room, he found that Savon had already set up for the completion of the test run. He felt a spurt of anger. Over the past few months, Savon's interference had become increasingly intrusive. He was now flagrantly usurping areas of command that were rightfully Cotuse's. Still, he said nothing but merely moved to his control pedestal and ordered the third run to begin.

Now, as start-up sequences were called off for run four, he settled himself into his chair and tried to force the sight of the fiery plane out of his mind and focus on his screens feeding in sensor-box data. Down along the underwater collider rings, dozens of these sensors had been placed to test structural and operational elements. The collider tubes themselves, two meters wide, were composed of inner toroidal magnetic shafts blanketed in lithium and surrounded by field magnetic coils. These were then encased in magnetic circuit lines and biological and reaction shields. The whole was then sealed in an antiradiation, carbon-based plastic piping.

The main control room was an amphitheater filled with electronic gear. The top bank contained velocity-monitoring screens and digitalized readout panels, magnetic-dispersal monitors that gave position fixes of the rotating protons, test generators, and oscilloscopes showing the acute alignment of proton target. Below these was a curved bank of more computers and control panels watched over by a team of fifteen technicians, each with voice-activated radio mikes. These ran circuit-board check grids; gamma and neutron radiation trunks that, when illuminated by proton-energy impulses, showed instant color graphics of phase levels; and dimension consoles with hundreds of number sequences arrayed.

Cotuse sat on the far right, in the center of an elevated platform with all the backup main control and monitoring screens completely surrounding him. Savon was directly below him in front of a similar but smaller version of his control board.

The test run began very rapidly as bursts of energy were sent through the neon plasma. Yet it would take several minutes for full monitor analysis to start feeding in. Gradually the screens to Cotuse's left began running printouts.

Everything looked clean. He was about to order another burst when a red light flashed. A magnet cluster in the C-14B sector was showing power dissipation. He punched a warning buzzer and instantly focus data came up on a screen. He squinted at it, quickly running down the mass of numbers and respond sequences.

"Run a power recheck on C-14B," he snapped.

Savon immediately executed the order.

A moment later, power-grid impulse stats flashed onto the screen. The power drop in the magnet cluster was eleven percent.

"Abort," Cotuse commanded.

Savon turned and looked at him. "But, Michel, it's only eleven percent. That's well within function parameter."

"Abort," he repeated.

Savon's face hardened. He was a muscular man of fifty-two who worked out every day with free weights on the main deck.

Although an outstanding quantum physicist, he lacked patience and was always riding the team members harshly. "I think it's wasteful to shut down now," he said. "That circuit sector can be repaired easily."

Cotuse's eyes lifted slowly. He stared at his deputy, saying nothing, until Savon looked away and hissed softly with disgust. They aborted. Cotuse waited until all his screens were clean. Then he rose and strode out of the room. He walked up to his wildflower garden. The sun was low on the horizon now, and its slanted light made the ocean look deep and impenetrable. He plucked a shriveled buttercup blossom and turned it slowly over in his hand.

"Cotuse," Savon said behind him. "I want to talk with you."

Cotuse stood slowly, still looking at the buttercup. "I think you'd best watch yourself, Savon."

"No, monsieur, you watch yourself. Dammit, look at me."

Cotuse whirled. "How dare you speak to me like that?"

The younger man stood with his hands defiantly on his hips. "You are deliberately delaying this project."

"That's a lie."

"No, it isn't. You constantly stall with unnecessary testing. You abort without adequate reason. We are ready for the Q run now and you know it."

"I will say when we're ready."

A strange look came into Savon's eyes. "But maybe not for long." Cotuse paled as his deputy went on: "Minister Frenier spoke privately with me before leaving. He ordered me to see that this project is completed at once if you are unwilling—or unable—to do it."

"You traitor!" Cotuse shouted.

"No, you are the traitor. Of your own project." Savon paused. "Either we execute full Q run within the next twenty-four hours or I notify Paris. They are prepared to appoint me project head."

Cotuse's eyes filled with such rage that Savon actually took a step backward. Then, recovering, he said, "Twenty-four hours." He turned and walked away.

Defense Minister Louis Frenier found President Vasillon in conference with his deputy secretary, Andre Guillume, and General Marshal of Armed Forces Henri Feramin when he returned to the Quai d'Orsay after a Concord flight from Sydney. Missing from the inner circle was Prime Minister Alain Chamboudet, who was in Canada for high-level meetings with the Canadian P.M. While abroad, Frenier had been informed of the shooting incident in Polynesia.

Vasillon, who had been holding constant meetings with his high-echelon staff people and key ministers, greeted Frenier grimly. "Thank God you're here, Louis. We need your thoughts on this damnable affair."

He quickly filled in details of the incident, then gave an update on the diplomatic situation. "Markisov is demanding an apology. He says we fired on an unarmed aircraft over international waters."

Frenier was taken aback. "That's idiotic."

"But it's not totally incorrect. That plane was unarmed."

"But how could we know that for certain?"

General Feramin leaned forward. "The aircraft was from a carrier south of the Polynesians. For it to have traveled all the way to the platform, it would have been necessary to exchange armaments for wing tanks. Besides, the on-site frigates found no missile debris."

Frenier frowned.

"As to the matter of international waters," Vasillon continued, "the Soviets are claiming the right of free passage along water corridors between the islands."

Frenier shook his head vehemently. "It's a political ploy."

"Agreed. But to what purpose? Did they deliberately send that aircraft in to create an incident? If so, why?"

"They were after the MAQ," Frenier answered flatly. "I know it, I feel it. That was the target."

The president studied him a moment before speaking. "General Feramin agrees with you. He believes they were trying to electronically disable the platform."

Frenier swung around to Feramin as the general said, "Just before our frigate launched its missiles, it experienced wild malfunctions of its firing system. The captain is certain he was under attack by some electronic weapon."

"That's it," Frenier cried. "And this—this absurd garbage about international waters means the swine are going to try again."

"That is a strong possibility," Vasillon murmured. "Then what must we do?"

"Stop them. Don't you see what this means? The Russians are conducting parallel Q-velocity experiments. Somehow they breached our security and knew Cotuse was close to the final run."

That statement struck home. Every man in the room knew what Michel Cotuse's work would give to their nation: a complete new physics, a technology so advanced that in the military sphere alone, it would hurtle France to the forefront of world power.

Frenier again turned to the general marshal. "What forces can we put into the Polynesians?"

"Only that carrier group in the Indian Ocean. But it would take several days to get on site."

Frenier turned on Vasillon. "We must reinforce AlPaci. The MAQ has to be protected at all costs."

Vasillon looked agonized. "Such a move would be highly provocative. This thing could escalate out of control down there."

"It doesn't matter, Monsieur President. We can't lose the platform. It's our future."

For the first time, Deputy Guillume spoke. "Sir, you are forgetting about the Americans. They dominate the South Pacific and would never allow an escalation, no matter what we do. As General Feramin pointed out earlier, they're already moving a strong carrier group into the area. Together we might intimidate the Russians enough to abandon any further attempts to strike at the MAQ."

The three men watched Vasillon. He sighed. "All right, order the carrier in."

Two minutes later, as if slightly off cue, there was a knock on the door. A new communiqué had just arrived from AlPaci Command. It stated that the Russian carrier force south of the Polynesians had begun to move. It seemed to be headed straight for the Societies.

The doctor's boat was an old forty-foot copra cutter with a Marconi crosscut mainsail and a Miter working jib. Her decks and cabin were made of teak, her hull of lap-straked ironwood stringers. She carried a small Volvo Penta diesel engine and a good marine transceiver. A tiny dinghy was mounted on the stern davits.

Cas parked the Peugeot at the head of the crumbling copra

dock where she was tied and they carried their supplies aboard. While Kiri cracked sail bags, he checked out the engine for fuel, oil, and coolant levels, started the generator, and stowed their gear.

Evening had fallen as they cast off the lines and drifted out into the channel with the offshore breeze. To the west, the peaks of Moeréa shone like an etching in the deepening sky. Cas fixed his course for NNE, which would bring them close in to Tetiaroa, Tahiti's sister island. Beyond the reef, he set the cutter on a long beat to windward as they cleared away from Tahiti, and the deck heeled to port until the lee railings were nearly submerged.

Kiri came aft, sat on the taff seat, and put her arms around Cas's chest as he hunched over the helm. Directly in front of him, the fluorescent numbers and lubber's line of the compass made a tiny glow through the spokes of the wheel. "*A'fe*, I've missed you," she whispered.

He chuckled. "*A'fe*? You're turning native."

"I want to. God knows, I love this place. It's like no place I've ever been."

The sudden swirl of a cat's-paw gust swept across the bow and made the mainsail luff slightly, popping. Cas eased the helm over, falling off until he could feel the wind shift again. When it did, he brought her up tight once more.

"Where *have* you been?" he asked casually.

When she didn't answer, he turned and looked at her. She shrugged. "Nowhere very interesting."

"Tell me anyway."

"No."

"Oh, oh! I forgot you're the lady with dark secrets."

She gave him a disgusted look, rose, and went below.

On they fled as night continued falling. Stars appeared, so sharp and bright that they looked like they would shatter if struck. The horizon, an uninterrupted line of blue-white ocean seen through the gauze of moon haze, seemed to mark a falling-off place to which they rushed.

After a while she returned to the deck, carrying a bottle of champagne she'd found in a galley closet. It was warm and blew a column of bubbles when Cas cracked it. They toasted Venus, sitting off the shoulder of the moon, and he threw his arm around her shoulders. Her hair perfumed the night as he nuzzled her neck, felt the warm flesh, the long, smooth line of her throat as, trembling, she lifted her face.

He locked the wheel and they made love in the well deck, both completely naked. Cas gripped the coaming rail against the boat's heel as he thrust, and Kiri, arms and legs enfolding him, met him with an energy that seemed to come straight up from the keel.

As he approached his climax, he felt her stiffen and draw slightly back. Opening his eyes, he saw that her eyes were wide open, too, staring wildly. He paused, lifting his body weight slightly on his elbows. He felt her hand come up, play across his lips, his eyes.

"I love you," she whispered, hushed with urgent wonder.

Then her face contorted. She threw her head back and twisted away from him. Their bodies disengaged, leaving Cas feeling suddenly pendulous and absurd. Before he could react, though, Kiri put her left hand on his chest and shoved, grunting, and then her right palm slammed him across the face.

The abrupt shock jolted him. For a brief second his eyes watered and he saw the moonlit deck as a shimmering, glassy blur. He felt her slip from beneath him, the long line of heated thigh drawing across his wetness. He reached out, grabbed a handful of hair, and pulled her face close up to his own.

"Damn you, Bonner," she hissed at him. "God damn you."

Astounded, he let her go and she bolted, disappearing into the cabin.

6

Del January had been sleeping in snatches all the way from San Diego, where the A-6 had stopped for refueling. Sitting in the radar intercept officer's seat, next to the pilot, a young black reserve lieutenant named Chuck Random, Del kept trying to concentrate on what he knew of the Russian aircraft, but then he'd doze off again, head down, body pushed against the seat harness.

When he came out of a final snatch of sleep, he realized that two F-14s had appeared off their right wing and were flying beside them. Their exhaust pipes formed huge candle flames in the darkness, and the pilots' helmets were shiny from their panel lights. Down below, the *Coral Sea* and her accompanying escort vessels were scattered across the sea for several miles.

Lieutenant Random began descending and the Tomcats stayed tight, escorting him in. As the carrier's approach control began vectoring, Del noticed droplets of perspiration on Random's neck below his helmet. A carrier landing was always a delicate affair, and for a reserve officer, short on fleet time, it could be hellish.

Ten miles out, Random linked his autopilot to the automatic carrier landing system and eased his hands off the controls. They began a radar-controlled descent, homing to the glide slope. Periodically, the voice of the landing control officer crackled on the radio, giving position and status reports.

Ahead, the *Coral Sea* began to come at them, growing steadily in size. Above the string of red drop lights off the fantail, the landing deck centerline lights trailed off. To the left was the column of the visual landing system: green lights with its meatball yellow in the center.

Unconsciously, Del braced his feet as they approached the carrier. Then the drop lights flashed underneath and they hurtled onto the ramp. The wheels slammed down hard. Random poured on full military power, making the two Pratt & Whitney J52-P-88 turbojets scream, and then the tail hook caught and the aircraft lurched as Random cut power. The engine sound died as if sliced. They rolled to a jolting stop, then rebounded as the catch wires drew up.

A fresh-faced ensign met Del as he climbed down the plane ladder. He thanked Random, slapped him on the shoulder, then followed the ensign across the busy flight deck, swept with chilly sea air and the smell of jet fuel and rubber. He was led through a seemingly endless complex of narrow corridors overhung with electrical conduits and fire gear, down a spiraling stairway to the O-3 level. Eventually they reached an officers' wardroom filled with air crews having breakfast.

Before two senior officers sitting alone near the door, the ensign braced and made the formal introductions. Commander James Gretton, the *Coral Sea*'s tall, rawboned executive officer, smiled warmly as he shook Del's hand. He introduced the other officer, Captain Richard Waltham, the carrier's air wing commander (CAG). "Sit down," Gretton said in a lazy, rich Texas drawl. "Breakfast?"

"Yes, please. I haven't eaten since Washington."

"Hell, we can't have that." He signaled a mess man, who hurried over to pour January a cup of coffee and took his order of eggs and pancakes. When Del turned back, he found both officers watching him closely. Waltham was a powerfully built man with a large, wide-open face and a prominent nose. His hair was graying, yet he had the look of a man who easily controlled his immediate environment and anything in it.

"Well," Gretton said, easing his elbows onto the table, "you come with some pretty high clearances, January. Precisely why are you here?"

"I want to locate a downed Russian spy plane."

Instantly, Waltham sat forward. "Downed where?"

"Somewhere in French Polynesia." He went on to explain while both officers listened attentively. Now and then his narrative was punctuated by the sudden, rumbling slam of an aircraft landing high above them. When he finished, Waltham and Gretton exchanged glances.

"So that's why Ivan's been running such heavy radar probes," Waltham said. He turned to Del. "Just how accurate are these altitude computations of yours?"

"My source is a helluva weatherman. He's always extremely accurate."

"You realize we're looking at an aircraft with capability far beyond what we have."

January nodded. "Very far beyond."

Frowning, Gretton interjected, "Something doesn't fit here. Granted this aircraft—if there is one—is something special. But would Ivan risk a war with France just to keep a few high-tech components secret?"

"I agree," Waltham put in. "And something else. Why make a run on that experimental platform?"

"It's possible we're looking at two different operations," Del said. "Or the Russian Forger could have merely been searching in the vicinity of the platform and the French skipper got panicky. CNO seems to hold that view.

"As far as the components are concerned—and this is just my hunch—I think the Russians have an advanced weapons system aboard. Something that could be decades ahead of us. The fact that they've been making such determined efforts to find it before somebody else does seems to point that way."

At that moment the wardroom loudspeaker blared, calling for Waltham and Gretton to immediately report to flag operations. Both men stood. "What specifically will you need?" the XO asked January.

"One of your Sea King helicopters."

Gretton winced. "The admiral won't like that."

"Will I be able to speak with him?"

"I'll see." He and Waltham left.

January waited for over an hour before another ensign came to retrieve him. They went along more corridors to a tiny elevator that took them up to the flag operations room adjacent to the carrier's bridge. Admiral Albert Passmore was seated in a large, raised leather chair, talking with another officer Del assumed was the carrier's skipper. All around him, seamen and officers worked numerous navy tactical-data system consoles.

When his ensign guide departed, Del stood around with nobody paying any attention to him. Finally the second officer looked his way and nodded him over. Passmore was almost totally bald, with only a line of wispy gray hair growing above his ears, and had a face set in a perpetual scowl. He swiveled around and looked Del over hard. "What's all this bullshit about you wanting one of my choppers?" he barked finally.

"Admiral, I realize this is an intrusion. I apologize. But I feel that—"

"I don't give a rat's ass for what you feel."

Passmore's abruptness jolted him, but he pushed on: "Have you been apprised of the situation here, sir?"

Passmore didn't answer, just continued staring. Then he snapped, "What the hell kind of a weapon is on this aircraft?"

"I don't know, sir. That's what I want to find out."

The admiral glanced at the other officer and then back. "What you're more likely to find is a French missile up your ass."

"Couldn't we notify AlPaci headquarters of what we're doing?"

"Right now the French don't want *anybody* poking around. Least of all a goddamned civilian aboard a U.S. Navy bird."

January flushed. He could feel his stomach tightening up. "Sir, would you at least contact OpNAV before you decide?"

"What in hell for? They've already discounted your spy plane theory."

"What?" Del barked in surprise.

Passmore nodded.

Goddammit, Del thought, those stupid assholes! Then he noticed a tiny smile playing on Passmore's lips.

"We just received something you might like to see," the admiral said, and thrust a yellow communiqué sheet at him. January glanced at it. It said:

TOP SECRET
01310Z*****46115

CIA/NIA CV-9: CORAL SEA; SIGINT BULL (RELAY STAT)
NZO—CALL YELLOW S1

MESSAGE FOLLOWS

ALPACI CC PAPEETE . . . RECOVERY OF PILOT BODY AT 1000Z YESTER-
    DAY . . . INDICATIONS RUSSIAN . . . HEAVY SECURITY . . .
    RECOVERY BY TWO (2) AMERICAN CITIZENS ASSIGNED TO SCRIPPS IN-
    STITUTE OF OCEANOGRAPHY (LA JOLLA, CA) RESEARCH OPERATION . . .
    ID: CAS BONNER (SS: 575-32-1969)/DAVID COWELL (SS: 578-45-1876). . .

XX

END SIGINT BULL

CIA/NIA: CV-9 (CS)

His head snapped up. "They've recovered the pilot!"
"Maybe."
"I want to speak with the men who found the body. Is that possible?"
"That's already being taken care of." Passmore studied him a moment longer. "All right, January, you get your helo. But you goddamned well better pray we don't have to come get you."

About three in the morning, Cas picked up offshore turbulence from Tetiaroa as the wind, circling, began to blow from the east again. He swung the cutter into it, riding tight. The air was turning chilly and he could now smell the crisp, cold tang of an approaching storm in it.
Kiri returned to the deck. She had found an old pea jacket smelling of mothballs. She sat beside him silently, facing the wind. Finally she turned and studied him, her chin on her palm. "Sometimes I can be very stupid," she called over the rush of the wind. "I'm sorry."
He grinned back at her. "No problem."
"That's all you have to say?"
He thought a moment. "No, there's one other thing."
"What?"
"You sure pack a wallop."
She ran her hand against his cheek, then playfully pushed it away. "Fool."

Ten minutes later, there was a soft, insistent buzz from the cabin. Bonner leaned over and peered down the companionway. "You leave the radio on?"

"Yes."

"Somebody's trying to raise us. Who the hell can that be?"

Eyes darting, Kiri jumped up. "I'll get it." A few moments later, she returned. "It's Skip Cowell."

What? he thought. He signaled for her to take the helm and slipped into the cabin. For a second he studied the call letters stenciled to the radio housing, then keyed: "MMN-D-188, go ahead, Skip."

"Where the hell are you?"

"About a hundred miles west of Arutua."

"What're you doing there?"

"I decided to take a run up and have a look at the Frenchie platform. What's the problem?"

"SEO just got a trace on us. From the USS *Coral Sea*."

"What the hell for?"

"They've sent out a chopper to search for an aircraft. Wanted one of us to show them where we found that body. I had a helluva time finding you. I finally got that old chink of Kiri's to tell me where you two were. Goddamn, that old bastard's a Chinese firecracker."

"Where are you?"

"Still on Raifavae. The LT-2's down. I think one of those damned albatross damaged the tail rotor."

Cas glanced around as Kiri came down into the cabin, watching him closely. He keyed: "Then I guess it's me."

"I guess so. Look, that chopper was supposed to be refueled by tanker, but they've requested a place in the islands where they can come in without ruffling too many French feathers. I'll raise 'em and vector to Arutua. You can meet the bastards there, and Nickie can give 'em all the fuel they'll need," he said, referring to Nicholas Fitzgerald, the manager of a large copra operation on Arutua. "How long before you reach it?"

"Maybe four hours."

"All right. Sorry I couldn't get too much poop on this thing, Cas. The carrier radioman was giving me all that navy shit. Sounded important, though."

"How long is this going to take?"

"Beats me. Until they find that damned plane, I guess."

"How long before you get the copter flying?"

"Tomorrow, maybe the next day."

"Okay, I'll see you back at Papeete. Whenever."

"Right."

"MMN-D-188, out."

In the minute before Cas hollered from the helm to help him bring the cutter around and begin tacking toward Arutua Island, Kiri remained behind in the cabin just long enough to flick on the radio and swing the dial for Katevayo's frequency. When he gruffly acknowledged, she said three words: "Arutua, be there."

Nine hundred miles to the south, Toomas Koik began a long, slow sweep as he held his Forger near stall and powered down the cruise engine. A mile ahead, the stern of the *Minsk* beckoned him, and his radio periodically blew orders from the carrier's LO officer giving him approach status. As he drew closer, he saw the deck's blast-resistant tiles looking luminous and the eight large white touch-down circles lined down the centerline. To the right, two Forgers were parked on the after platform above the storage bay, their wing panels folded back and intake slats open.

Gradually, Koik began the transition from cruise to vertical mode. The nose of the Forger came up, bobbled slightly as he powered the twin Kolesmov lift engines and slanted the Lyul'ka for a down thrust. As he hovered a hundred yards off the carrier's stern, her wake made a grayish churn that seemed to come from under the extended blast panel just above her trim line. In he came, inching. As the stern passed below him, he could feel cross winds cutting over his surfaces.

The upper curve of the number one TDC disappeared under his wings. Holding steadily, he lowered until he felt the wheels touch, then drew off power as he sensed the weight of the aircraft settling. At last he cut the engines. Deck crewmen came running and a brown-colored tow dolly scooted from behind the parked Forgers.

Several minutes later, he held a short debriefing in the pilots' ready room to ten airmen—six off Forger As, four from the two-seated Bs. There was none of the usual after-flight wisecracking. Everybody looked exhausted and grim. Since midnight, when Admiral Turesky had authorized renewed search operations, they had been running continuous "shotgun" flights: single aircraft in silent, on-the-deck runs. This time they had chosen to head north across the sparsely populated atolls of the western Tuamotus rather than risk the Marquesas Channel again with its air patrols out of Hoa and the heavy radar screen from the French Nuclear Test Center on Mururoa. But it was hellish flying, the kind that pinched a pilot's spine and made it tingle with tension. They had been going on total radio and electronic silence at tree level with only the moonlight to guide them, constantly avoiding lighted villages and mission stations, and always expecting a radio tower or hillock not marked on maps to loom up and turn their aircrafts into boiling balls of flame.

A lieutenant appeared and informed Koik that Turesky wanted an immediate report. Accompanied by his wing executive, Captain Second Class Vladimir Namovich, he returned to the flight deck and crossed to the carrier's island. The wind was brisk now and bore the feel of a storm from the Roaring Forties.

The admiral was discussing the group's storm deployment with Akhromayev and the flag executive, Captain Second Class Pilsar Omransk. The *Minsk's zampolit*, or political officer, Dmitri Vairov, was also present. Koik and Namovich stood at attention near the door until the admiral finished and signaled them in.

"So, Toomas, what did you find?"

"Nothing, sir."

Turesky grunted but made no comment, which was a sign of fatigue, Koik knew. Turesky's usual harshness always became more contemplative when he was tired. The admiral was an old-line officer with the best credentials: graduation from the prestigious M. V. Frunze High Naval School, the Soviet counterpart of Annapolis, and successful command of three fleet divisions and two flag flotillas. He had a sign on his desk: "*Without a sense of duty to Motherland, technology is worthless.*"

"We've received word that a large French carrier force is being diverted from the Indian Ocean to the Strait of Malacca," he said to Koik. "Reaction?"

"How long before they get here, sir?"

"About three days."

Koik shrugged. "It will create a bit of a problem, but nothing my pilots can't handle."

Turesky smiled, amused. "Good, Toomas. I always find comfort in your eternal optimism. One other thing, the American carrier group is also headed our way and reconnaissance indicates very active launch activity. It won't be long before Washington decides to overfly French waters to . . . warn us off. What do you say to that?"

"We can deal with it, sir," Koik answered. As he did, he noticed that the political officer was squirming, obviously anxious to say something. Turesky saw it, too.

"Comrade Vairov," he snapped. "You wish to say something?"

The *zampolit* flashed a pleasant smile. He was a corpulent man with a constant air of cheerfulness, unusual for a *zampolit*. "I merely wanted to remind the admiral that there is little need for pessimism. The French are frightened of us and the Americans are always hesitant. We are in complete control, as Moscow obviously assumes."

Turesky studied Vairov silently for a moment. "Fear and hesitancy. That's an advantageous combination."

"Indeed, sir." Vairov held his open palms upward as if indicating the obvious. "Superior Soviet beliefs and strength will always master the situation."

As the other officers exchanged mocking glances, the admiral snorted and turned back to Koik. "Continue the search runs. Intensify them. We had better find this fucking aircraft. I have little doubt that the secretary general will steam us right into these islands if we don't."

"Yes, sir."

His eyes lingered on Toomas's face. "I would advise you get some rest. If our 'hesitant' Americans decide to commit themselves, you'll need it."

"Yes, sir," Koik said. He and Namovich saluted, departed. As they walked along the outer corridor, the XO kept shaking his head, smiling ruefully. Toomas glanced at him. "You find something humorous in this, Vladimir?"

"Not humorous, definitely not humorous. Rather absurdly inevitable."

"Mm?"

"Some of us are going to die here, aren't we?"

Koik inhaled deeply, let it out slowly. "Perhaps, comrade."

Near dawn Captain Waltham was in early conference with two of his maintenance chiefs when his yeoman knocked lightly on the door. "Excuse me, sir. The admiral wants you in flag op right away."

"All right, Jess." He made a few final points to the chiefs, dismissed them, and stepped to his small basin to wash his face. It looked tired in the mirror. The around-the-clock operations they'd been running since sunset were brutal, kept everyone on the jump button.

A few minutes later, when he entered flag operations, Passmore was huddled with Commander Gretton and Captain Vince Stockdale, skipper of the *Coral Sea*, over charts and tactical printouts. Waltham braced. "Good morning, Admiral."

Passmore glanced up. "Hello, Dick. It seems we just got a little hind tit."

He explained. A red-op order had come in from COMMPAC. The Russian carrier south of Tahiti was still launching single-sections of Forgers and tanker helos. Logged time had been 1230 hours. Pearl notified Washington and the JCS had come right back. Apparently Washington was now going on the assumption that it was the platform the Russians were interested in. Since there was a lack of anything else substantial to explain the Soviet incursions, JCS had gone with what seemed obvious and turned it into policy fact.

The *Coral Sea* was to respond by sending relays of surveillance/strike flights *into* the Capricorn. But they were to assiduously remain east of the platform. If an actual Russian attack was observed, the final decision to engage would have to await direct orders from Washington.

"How deep will our penetration be, sir?" Waltham asked.

"As far south as the leeward islands of the Marquesas."

"Do we work the Channel?"

"No, I don't want to run the risk of our people running into either French or Russian fighters. I just want to be damned sure Ivan knows we're stretched out on his ass end if he opts to bounce the platform. Then if Washington decides we engage, I want to take those Forgers exiting the islands with their fuel reserves sucking bottom."

"What's our max range?"

"Seven hundred forty miles. So let's have some recommendations."

Waltham frowned thoughtfully. "What's the probability ratio for engagement?"

"JCS is still bouncing that ball in the air. I frankly don't think the silly bastards are even considering the possibility of an engagement. This is still a show-and-tell operation, so normal rules of engagement are in effect."

Again Waltham remained silent for a moment before saying, "I'd go with two split four-sections. One south, one southwest. We can run both Hornets and Cats. If we do bounce Ivan, the 14s can initiate intercepts and the Hornets can handle backup."

"How about armament?"

"With drop tanks aboard, we'll have to focus strictly on AAM units. I'd suggest Phoenix and Sidewinders for the Cats, and Sidewinders and Sparrows on the Hornets. But we'll have to refit for outboard tanks on the 18s."

Passmore nodded. "What's your launch estimate?"

"Thirty minutes, sir. And I'd like to take the first relay."

"All right. Better get on with it."

Waltham hesitated. "Sir, there's one other thing. What's the status with this January? The Sea King took off about two hours ago. With him wandering around out there, complications could develop."

The admiral leaned away from the table, sucking thoughtfully at his teeth. "I've considered recalling him. But, you know, I'm curious about this spy plane theory. Washington's discarded it, but sometimes those people can't find their pricks with both hands. I'd like to know for sure."

"Maybe we could vector him out of any potentially hot area, sir," Gretton put in. "Keep him west of the platform."

"Yes, I agree. If something blows, he can go to ground." Passmore turned back to Waltham. "All right, Dick, have a good flight."

Twenty minutes later, Waltham stood in heavy flight gear in the flight deck control room, watching through the window as the refitted aircraft were being spotted for launch. Amid the tumult of watch teams shouting status reports on flight deck activity, the CAG was frowning. He didn't like the smell of this operation. It was a political move that hinged on pure bluff. The fact was, sending aircraft nearly eight hundred miles from the carrier into a potential fire zone with only half weapon loads was just plain stupid, maybe even suicidal.

"Strike men up," the FDC officer called loudly. The pilots began filing through the door, handing in their weight chits. Outside, the flight deck was a seemingly confused mass of men in various colored jumpers scurrying among hordes of deck equipment. Engines whined, lights flashed, hose lines and pressure conduits were snaked everywhere.

Waltham walked to his F-14 and climbed aboard. His plane captain helped him buckle in, and he had chosen a young lieutenant named Billy "Sack" Bishop as his RIO on this flight. They ran through preflight checks, monitoring the Combat Information Center (CIC) on strike frequency. Three minutes later, the deck loudspeaker blared: "Launch strike. Launch strike."

The PC gave him the twirling finger for engine start. Waltham felt the power roar as his twin Pratt & Whitney TF30-P-412A turbofans came alive. Off to the left, the guard helo lifted, banked sharply, and whirled away as the *Coral Sea* came up into the wind.

Lieutenant Bishop called out checks as Waltham eased the aircraft up into alignment to Catapult Three. He inched forward until he felt the cat bar halt him and the shuttle take up tension. His eyes glued to the instrument panel, he pressed his head against the backrest and rammed on full military throttle. The F-14 trembled and he heard the whomping rush of his exhaust being deflected off the blast plates astern. He lifted his gaze and fixed it on a green light on top of the catapult officer's glass bubble.

The moment it went out, a powerful G force shoved him into the seat as the catapult shuttle hurled the Tomcat forward along the slot. A second later, the bow of the carrier flashed under him and he was airborne.

At twenty thousand feet, he grouped his people. His wingman lay off his sunup side. Farther back, in echelon, the two Hornets eased in tightly. He keyed: "Red Javelin Two-Zero-Four is at twenty and neat."

CIC came back: "Red Javelin Two-Zero-Four, your vector is two-two-three. One airborne blip one-seven-eight degrees your position at thirty. ID Boeing seven-two-seven commercial. Give us UDs at two-minute intervals until outer perimeter, over."

"Wilco."

With his course set up, Waltham settled back into his seat. Far below, the *Coral Sea* looked like a bar of soap floating in a tub. He eyed it affectionately. He'd been on seven cruises with her, as air wing exec and then CAG. Built in 1946, she was scheduled for decommission in 1993.

He was going to miss her.

The Jaune Palmier copra plantation covered six hundred acres of neatly arrayed coconut trees on the island of Arutua in the northern Tuamotus. Originally Dutch-owned, it had been sold in 1933 to the Australian company that still operated it. Its head-quarters, a flat-roofed, rambling house made entirely of porcupine wood, was surrounded by warehouses stacked with drums of coconut sugar called *jaggery* and huge coils of salt-water *coir* rope made from palm fiber, small cattle pens, and huge vats with the odorous, fly-covered coco-cake used for feed. Along the beach were drying courts, with small mountains of copra awaiting trans-port to the refinery in Papeete.

Nickie Fitzgerald was waiting on the rock pier when Cas brought the cutter up channel, swung her into the wind and, luffing sails, touched the pier head. He secured the bow line and came aft as Cas jumped to the pier and tied in the tailer. Nickie, dressed in khaki stubbie shorts and dirty tennis shoes, was a small, wiry man as dark as a *kukui* nut.

"Aye, Bonner," he roared, grinning broadly through his sun-bleached beard. "You goddamned Yankee bastard, ya." They shook hands warmly.

"How you hangin', Nickie?"

"Like a bleedin' bull with a goiter." Just then he caught sight of Kiri and his eyes flashed appreciatively. "Ah, been tart runnin', have ya?" When Kiri jumped to the dock and Bonner introduced her, Nickie beamed, showing yellow-stained teeth. "Glad to crack on ya, luv." He winked at Cas. "This one's a keepie, boy."

As he led them up the pier and through the drying courts, Cas noticed several plantation workers who had stopped to watch the cutter dock. They were all Tahitians, dressed in *pareus* tucked up to form loincloths, machetes strapped to their waists, dirty T-shirts, and straw hats.

"Have you heard from the navy chopper yet?" Bonner asked.

"Nah, but Skipperoo told me they were comin'. The dinks are probably lost."

"You got enough gas to service them?"

"Aye."

Cas clapped him on the shoulder and chuckled. "What happens if AlPaci finds out you're refueling a foreign aircraft?"

Nickie snorted. "Those dingos? They come whinin', I'll tell 'em to *allez vous faire foutre*." Pausing as he snapped out his middle finger, he glanced at Kiri. "Beggin' the luv's pardon if she speaks Frenchie."

The main house was cool and smelled of *lauhala* and leather and gun oil. The furniture was made of delicately curved, highly polished sisal boughs, and there was a large, square *punee* couch covered with a red-and-white quilt with Tahitian patterns.

A young native woman who wore a shark's tooth on a gold chain on her forehead served them ice-cold bottles of Foster's beer and *pu-pu*, strips of dried beef soaked in soy sauce—typical breakfast fare at Fitzgerald's. The small, lovely woman's name was Tafala, but Nickie called her Tifi.

Cas playfully pulled at her *pareu*. "Tifi honey, when're you gonna dump this old fart and come live with me?" She giggled and hurried away.

They were on their fourth Fosters, and Nickie was in the middle of a story of shark hunting in the Hebrides, when they heard the sound of an approaching helicopter. They hurried outside just in time to see it skim over the coconut trees and settle out near the drying courts, the wash of its blades kicking up turbulence on the shore water.

When they reached the pier, the copter's crewmen were squatting in the open hatchway, trying to make conversation with the workers who had gathered. A man in a blue flight suit jumped to the ground and came up to meet them. He looked pale in the early morning sunlight and wore glasses that had an opaque silver sheen.

"Which one of you is Bonner?" he asked.

"I am."

The man extended his hand. "I'm Del January. Look, I really appreciate your cooperation." As they shook, Cas noted that the man's grip was soft. Del turned to Nickie. "You're Fitzgerald, then?"

"Aye."

"You have fuel for us?"

Nickie cocked his head and looked Del slowly up and down.
"What say you show some courtesy first, mate?"

"Of course, I'm sorry. This is an emergency, Mr. Fitzgerald.
Time is very precious."

Nickie gulped down the last of the bottle he'd brought with him
and tossed it aside. "You'll have to chamois the lot."

"What?"

"Strain the bleedin' gasoline through a chamois. It's full of tank
debris. If ya don't, that bleedin' whirlybird of yours'll fart out first
thing."

"Oh, no!" January said, and hurried back to the helo.

It took three hours to refill the helicopter's tanks. She was a
Sikorsky SH-3 Sea King with a boat hull and extra tanks fitted to
her fuselage. Nickie's workers formed a long line from the maintenance shack, handing down ten-gallon cans of gasoline. The
radar man, a chief petty officer named Ray Capisotti, did the
chamoising on one tank while the copilot, Lieutenant Don
Woodcroft, worked on the other.

After a while, Del touched Cas on the arm and they moved off
under the coconut trees. All along, Cas had noticed that the man
was hyped with tension. And now he kept pacing while he talked,
his hands stuck into his rear pockets. "Here's the situation, Bonner. Somewhere out there is a Russian spy plane. It contains
something the Soviets want very badly." He brought his hands
out and punched a fist into his palm. "But, dammit, we have to
find it first."

"What's aboard?"

"We don't know. I think it's an advanced weapon system."

Cas tilted his head. "Was that son of a bitch really capable of
flying above fifty miles?"

Del's eyes widened. "How did you know that?"

"I talked to the AlPaci medical officer. He said the pilot's body
showed tissue burn that could only have come from those altitudes."

"Shit!" Del cried. "That means he bailed out at cruise altitude.
There won't be much of that fucking aircraft left." Grimacing, he
turned and jogged back to the helicopter.

Seeing that Kiri and Fitzgerald had returned to the house and
were standing on the veranda, Cas decided to join them. As he
came up, he heard Kiri laughing at something Nickie had just
said. She seemed a little tight from the Fosters. Nickie shifted

from foot to foot, eyes mischievous. "Bonner, ya great Yankee nong, ya," he called raucously. "Y've got yourself a choice one here, you 'ave."

A few minutes later, they heard the copter engines starting up. Turning, they saw January standing in the open bay, frantically waving them down. When they reached the beach, Kiri climbed aboard immediately. Del glanced at Cas. "Why is it necessary for her to go?"

He shrugged. "She goes or I don't."

January made a face, but silently followed her up the ladder.

The Sea King lifted off, heeled hard, and swung out over the channel. Cas and Kiri, sitting in the bay with their legs out, waved at Nickie. He saluted them with a beer bottle. Leveling, the copter skimmed close above the surface. Coral heads in green water flashed past, then the water turned to a sapphire color and finally to blue-black as they headed out over open ocean.

So intent was Cas on puzzling over the spy plane January had mentioned that it never occurred to him to wonder why Kiri was so eager to come.

7

Latif Gankin waited in the stairwell of his Moscow hostelry, nervously watching a young soldier and a girl necking against the wall just below the top landing. Sweating with nervous frustration, Gankin glanced at his watch. It was nearly midnight.

All day he had remained in his room, repeatedly going over his plan. Shortly after noon, it had started to rain and he opened the window and let the moist chill sweep over him. It brought back childhood memories of rainy days on the barren grassy slopes of Jaklitsk when he and Alexander had sat beside the fire and made straw dogs.

Twice he broke down crying, more from fear than sorrow. His very insides trembled. Once he even went out on the landing, determined to return to Riga and give up his insane plan. But the guilt of his being alive and his brother dead wouldn't let him leave. He returned to his room and sat before the rain-streaked window . . .

Finally the lovers parted. Gankin pressed back against the wall, holding his suitcase with both arms. The soldier passed him and gave him a friendly smile. He waited until the man had disappeared down the stairs before he charged up the steps to the roof.

Once outside, he noticed that it was covered with pools of rainwater. But the sky was clear now, and the pools held the reflections of stars.

He walked to the parapet and looked out at the lights of Moscow stretching out before him. Used to the bleak nights of Riga, the city looked intensely alive, almost quivering with human energy. He drew himself away and walked slowly along the parapet, searching for an ideal spot to set up the mortar. He chose a flat, tar-papered position near the building's electrical transformer, beside clotheslines clipped with women's undergarments strung between the transformer and the parapet.

He laid his suitcase on the ground and opened it. As he pulled the base plate out, it tanged gently against the transformer housing. Wincing, he looked around, and then quickly assembled the mortar. Once this was done, he took a pair of small binoculars and scanned along the Kremlin wall to Red Square. He could only see the side of it beyond the ramparts of St. Basil's, where men were working under lights.

He knelt beside the mortar and adjusted the range davits along the half-moon-shaped elevation span. The metal felt cold, and already a thin sheen of condensation had formed on it. When he was finished, he wandered around the roof, looking for something to cover the weapon. He found a large sheet of canvas that someone had used to shield a rooftop picnic from the sun.

With the mortar covered, he sat down beside it, his back against the transformer housing. He slid the empty suitcase under his legs, closed his eyes, and began his long vigil.

Just before four in the morning, Yuri Markisov bolted upright out of a dream. His body was drenched in sweat and his heart pounded with a terrible foreboding of catastrophe. Calming slightly, he glanced at his wife's body under the blanket. Her satin hair cap seemed faintly luminous. He looked at the bedside clock, then rose quietly from the bed and put on his robe and slippers.

In the outer hall, two guards were sitting against the opposite wall, nodding in a doze. They sprang to their feet at the sound of his door closing. He waved them back: "Stay, stay." But they followed him at a discreet distance as he walked up the hall and went downstairs to the kitchen. It was a huge, spotlessly white room that smelled faintly of cleaning solvent. He made himself a cup of tea and sat at the table, looking out the window.

The Markisovs lived in a small mansion three miles from the Kremlin. Set in a five-acre enclave of linden trees and unimaginative gardens, the house had once belonged to a court physician during the reign of Czar Nicholas II. The kitchen window looked out onto the neat lawns and scattered stands of trees in the Tbepckoh, the park that completely rings the Kremlin.

Markisov first mulled over the dire news that Titov had told him the evening before: of the New Zealand airliner incident, of the French recovery of one of the Saber's pilots. Now they knew the Saber was on automatic fire.

Then he returned to his dream, recalling that at first there had been lights, distant, pulsing, drawing closer. He was standing on a sand dune at night and there was wind blowing all round him. The lights, close now, seemed to warm him as they rushed past. He could actually feel their passage, yet there was no sound. They looked like the lighted windows of a silent train. As he watched them recede, they suddenly arced upward, as rapidly as the flaming tails of missiles. On and on they went until they burst and became stars that throbbed with points of hot light which washed down upon him . . .

He glanced down and found his hand trembling slightly on the teacup. From outside, he could hear birds rustling in the trees. He examined the dream, trying to find a meaning. Heat, light, explosions; fire and destruction. Yet they had climbed to the heavens. What did that signify? Triumph? Glory?

He sighed, suddenly feeling foolish for believing in dream portents. Holding the warm cup in his palm, he returned to his bedroom. On the chair beside his wife's dresser he sat and sipped quietly.

Atynal Markisov sleepily lifted her head. "Yuri? What's the matter?"

"Nothing, go back to sleep."

"What time is it?"

"Four o'clock."

"Are you rising now?"

"Yes."

"Will I see you after the parade?"

"Yes."

She snuggled back into her pillow. "Be careful."

"Yes," he said.

Shortly before that moment, Latif Gankin had also awakened to a feathery, chilling drizzle. His coat was soaked and sparkling with water droplets. He remained frozen for a long moment, watching through slitted eyes, for he heard people talking, machinery clanking. He finally realized that the sounds were far away and only seemed close in the stillness of the night.

He stood slowly and flexed his stiff muscles. Walking over to the parapet of the hostelry, he discovered Red Square still brilliantly lit with floodlights and swarming with people. To the right, all along Oktober 25th Boulevard, there was a river of lights and soldiers milling, tanks and missile carriers, their barrels and weapons shiny with the rain.

He leaned out and stared down at Kujbyseva Avenue. Moscow citizens were already assembling so they would have good seats for the parade, sitting under blankets and umbrellas on the sidewalks and cobblestones of the square. Policemen, mounted on horses with brass-studded reins, moved slowly among them, keeping them behind rope barriers strung along the parade route.

Seeing the crowds, then the police, Latif was struck with a wave of fear so intense that his legs began to tremble violently and he had to sit down. As he stared dumbly at the wet bricks of the parapet, the sour, sharp taste of bile came into his throat. He bent forward and vomited between his legs. After he finished retching, he crawled back to the draped mortar and huddled there.

What seemed like an endless stretch of time passed. The sky slowly lightened. There had been several intervals of heavy rain, but now it seemed to be moving off completely. Gankin's breath made little wisps in the air. He felt unbearably cold and could not stop shivering.

Slowly the sun rose through broken clouds. As it shone on the roof, the tar paper began to smoke slightly. Overhead, large stretches of pastel blue began to show and small *zdenti* hawks, the color of autumn leaves, drifted lazily over the buildings.

Suddenly Gankin whirled about in fright. The concierge's wife had appeared, carrying a laundry basket. She was a thick woman with a round Slavic face under a faded babushka, and she wore a dirty farmer's coat that made her look like a peasant. When she saw Gankin, she stopped, startled. "What are you doing up here?" she demanded.

He could only stare at her.

She noted his wet clothes with displeasure and snapped, "Ah, another parade watcher." She turned away and began to finger the line of undergarments hung on the wire. Finding them all too wet to gather, she turned to him again and nodded at the canvas cover. "What's that?"

Panic took hold of him. "It's—it's nothing."

"Let me see."

As she bent to lift the corner of the canvas, he lunged up and quickly held it down. "Please! It's just my camera tripod. I've set it so it's aligned on the square."

She straightened and snorted with disgust. "Parades are idiotic, boy. All show and no food." She shifted her basket. "The only thing more idiotic is a fool who sits all night in the rain to see one." She stamped off.

The encounter shattered Gankin's delicate control and he began to shake again. He felt the pit of his stomach draw up a new wave of nausea. He tried to will it away, whimpering softly with the effort.

Kujbyseva Avenue was now alive with engine rumble and the low, discordant murmur of voices. Latif closed his eyes. Desperately he tried to picture the face of his brother, that last, eternal look he'd had of him with blood spurting from his head where the Russian soldier had struck him with the edge of a shovel, how his hair cleaved into the wound it had made. But it kept fading, overwhelmed by his fear.

He sought something else to drive away the panic and recalled an ancient epic of his fatherland. He focused on each word, absorbed it, passed to the next:

THEY CAME.
UP OVER THE DISTANT GRASSY HILLS.
THEIR LANCES SHINING IN THE SUNLIGHT.
THE SOUND OF THEIR TRUMPETS, THE THUNDER OF THEIR HORSES'
*   HOOVES LIKE RUSHING WATERS.*

SKJHOLD FELT HIS HEART TIGHTEN.
HIS HORSE STAMPED, SNORTED, SMELLING THE WIND.
FROM BEHIND HIM CAME THE CLANK OF STEEL, BLADES ON SHIELDS.
SKJHOLD'S EYE SAW A FLOWER IN THE GRASS, ITS BLUE PETALS AS
DELICATE AS TEARDROPS THAT HELD THE SKY.

HE BELLOWED AND CHARGED . . .

Markisov entered his Kremlin office at five-thirty and found Marshal Petrov waiting for him. "Good morning, Comrade Secretary," he said. "I hope you slept well?"

"Good morning, comrade." Markisov motioned him to a chair and took his own. "I did not sleep well at all. From your appearance, neither did you."

Petrov shrugged. "A touch of indigestion, sir."

"Well, what's the latest with Admiral Turesky?"

"He has moved northwest and is actively continuing the search. No sighting yet."

"Have there been any further contacts with the French?"

"No, sir. The *Minsk* pilots have been very fortunate so far."

"Any word from Paris?"

"No, sir. But they did order their carrier force out of the Indian Ocean toward the Strait of Malacca."

Markisov grunted, ran a fingernail along his chin. "Perhaps I've underestimated them. I thought they'd be making anxious overtures by now."

"They're notoriously tardy when arriving at policy decisions."

The general secretary chuckled mirthlessly. "Tardy and emotional, makes a dangerous mixture. And what about our old friend, Bardeshevsky?"

Petrov's face clouded. "The man's been too quiet. I haven't picked up anything over the last twelve hours. I don't like it."

Markisov snorted with a tinge of repugnance. "Yes, beware of dogs when they stop barking. Incidentally, what's the general mood of your TVD commanders over this thing?"

"Predominantly they are ready and expectant."

Markisov's eyebrows lifted. "Predominantly?"

"Yes, sir. Some of the Old Guard officers are demanding we move immediately and sternly punish the French."

"That was to be expected."

Petrov's brow crinkled uncomfortably. "I'm afraid it's more serious than that, sir."

"Ah?"

"The fissure which exists between some command units is showing itself to be much deeper than I had anticipated. The French incident seems to be polarizing it."

Markisov leaned forward. "How badly polarized?"

"In some sectors, there's serious discord in the command structure. I'm particularly concerned over the rift between the KGB and GRU officers. As you know, Bardeshevsky's people are all through the GRU."

"Damn that son of a bitch," Markisov cried hotly. Noticing that Petrov seemed hesitant to continue, Markisov barked, "What else?"

The marshal sighed. "I've received reports that certain commanders have spoken of creating . . . fundamental changes."

Markisov slammed his fist on the desk. "Certain commanders? What certain commanders?"

"It's all rumor at this point, sir. I have no names."

Markisov leveled a finger at Petrov. "I won't have this, Sergie. Do you understand? You will stop this divisive talk at once."

Petrov nodded. "I've already implemented moves to do exactly that, sir."

"What moves?"

"I've placed suspected TVD commanders and deputy commanders under KGB surveillance. As well as certain ministers. This was initiated six hours ago."

Markisov was silent a moment. Then: "Is Bardeshevsky one of them?"

"Yes, sir."

Markisov swore vehemently. "We're returning to the old ways, aren't we? Petrov, we're *regressing*."

"The situation forces our hand, sir."

"*Damn* these fools!" Markisov rose and wandered distractedly to the window. "Well, the scum won't win. I'll destroy these dead souls before they destroy this country."

Petrov merely studied his hands.

Markisov exhaled, slowly calming himself. "Is there anything further, Sergie?"

The marshal looked up. "How do you intend to handle an ultimate refusal to apologize by Paris? Any hesitancy by you to force apology will only strengthen Bardeshevsky's position."

"I know. But we still have time. I'm counting on American pressure on Paris, along with world opinion. Vasillon is a damned neurotic about world opinion if it has any chance of affecting his constituency."

Petrov stood and came to attention.

"Thank you, Sergie."

"Sir?"

"What is it?"

"Do not attend the parade today."

"Why not?"

"A precaution, sir."

Markisov waved that away. "You don't seriously think they would attempt to kill me in front of all Moscow?"

"I just don't know, sir. I don't like this silence."

"No, no. I will attend. Not to do so would create too many complications. We don't need any more."

"As you will, sir."

After Petrov was gone, Markisov went into Titov's room. The old man was curled on a cot, asleep. Someone had thrown a blanket over him. He nudged Titov's shoulder. "Professor?"

Titov's eyes shot open. "What? What? Oh, Comrade Secretary." He sat up, rubbing his eyes. "Forgive me, I dozed."

Markisov moved to the professor's desk. The clutter of books and computer printouts and stacks of communiqués had grown. He punched the intercom and ordered breakfast be brought in for Titov, then returned to the old man. "Update me."

"There's been nothing concerning the Saber. None of the reports over the night indicate any activity."

Markisov nodded toward the door that separated the two offices. "There's a bathroom in my office you may use."

"Thank you, Comrade Secretary. I'll only be a moment." Titov hurried out.

A moment later, a soft knock sounded on the door and Markisov opened it. A young housemaid in a gray-and-white uniform brought in a tray of food. There was a stack of buckwheat pancakes called *bliny* and two *vatrushki* cheese tarts with a cup of heated honey and a carafe of tea.

When Titov returned and started eating, Markisov paced the room, arms folded. At last he paused before the desk. "Are you aware that two foreign flotillas are now approaching the Polynesians?"

Titov stopped chewing. "What?"

Markisov nodded. "French and American carrier groups."

"I didn't know. There's so much data—" He shoved out of his chair. "Comrade Secretary, you must stop them! They can't be allowed near the Saber."

"It may not be possible to prevent that."

"You can't! You mustn't! These flotillas will be carrying nuclear weapons!"

Markisov studied him narrowly. "What's the Saber's weapon range from ground level?"

"I don't know," Titov cried distractedly. "It could be two hundred miles or two thousand."

"What the hell do you mean, you don't know?"

"There's no way of telling, Comrade Secretary. The plane can utilize environmental elements to extend its range. Given a transiting satellite, a passing airliner, even a flock of birds, it could use it to deflect its charge beyond the line of the horizon."

"How precise would it be if the beam were deflected?"

The professor looked confused. "I can't know that either. It would depend on how the deflecting object was shaped and what it was made of. Metal would give a high percentage of accuracy. Glass or organic tissue—"

"Goddammit!" Markisov shouted heatedly. "I don't want suppositional parameters. I want ranges, precise ranges."

"Comrade, you still don't understand. I can't give you specifics. This is not just a machine we're dealing with here. The Kamov AI unit is capable of conceptual reasoning. If an enemy force comes within its range—whatever that range may be—it will figure out a way to attack it."

A half hour later, Markisov's Zil limousine, accompanied by its procession of security vehicles, exited the gate beside the Lenin Mausoleum, traveled the five hundred yards to the main reviewing stand in Red Square, and parked behind it. The stand was a permanent concrete structure that presented a slightly concave face to the square. There were two levels, and the second was invisible from the front. Neither level had seats or benches; the dignitaries would have to remain standing throughout the four-hour parade.

Thousands of people not only filled the huge expanse of Red Square, but overflowed into the radiating avenues and down onto the grassy slopes adjoining Karl Marx Prospekt. Directly across from the reviewing stand was a gigantic three-story building, a shopping complex called the GUM, which had a glass roof and wide glass wall partitions. Inside, lofty footbridges packed with people arched above a central courtyard of fountains and trees.

The general secretary solemnly took his place at the center of the stand. On either side of him were the Soviet President; Vasily Kilikov; Chief of the KGB, Anatole Yefiseva; Deputy Chairman of the Ministry of Defense, Yavi Kurtkakin; and the Council of Ministers Chief, V. A. Andalief. At the left end of the stand's center stood Bardeshevsky. As the parade began, Marshal Petrov quietly took his position directly behind Markisov.

The band leading off the march played a stirring rendition of the opening movement of Kilreskie's *Blood of the Motherland*, full of rolling drums and trumpets. Behind them came the elements of the 103rd tank regiment, great, lumbering T-72s and T-80s, their treads sounding like the steps of giants. Each vehicle had a stiffly braced crewman in the open hatch who saluted as he passed the stand.

Next came a motorized infantry regiment in armored personnel carriers. Then a parachute regiment, followed by mobilized artillery pieces: gigantic 203-mm. M-197s with long barrels that looked like battleship guns, and the smaller 2S3s and 2S5s. Behind them, stretched all along Oktober 25th Boulevard and beyond the overpass of Novaja Plazer, came more men and mechanized arms: naval infantry stepping sharply in their blue uniforms; a Spetsnaz regiment in green uniforms with red *khenkas* caps; and farther back, the heavy missile transports with Scaleboard, Frog 7, and Scud-B missiles canted upward on their launch ramps.

The minutes dragged by as slowly as the moving men and equipment. Markisov could already feel his legs getting tired. Shifting his weight, he felt a trickle of perspiration slip from his armpit. The spring sunlight was baking him through his heavy overcoat.

Then something odd happened. People started slipping under the rope barriers and merging with the marching columns. At first they came in ones and twos, then in small groups. Police tried to contain them, but they came on. Bright balloons were launched up into the sky, and out came banners and placards with brightly painted slogans: "PERESTROIKA, DA" "GLASNOST AND FREEDOM" "HUMAN DIGNITY."

As the number of civilians increased, the soldiers began breaking step. Pretty girls with red and green headbands tucked flowers in their tunics and kissed them on the mouth. People began singing work songs from the Kazakh steppes, sailor ditties, harvest songs of the Khabarnsk, and these were quickly picked up by others still behind the barriers.

The other dignitaries on the stand leaned forward in shock. As for Markisov, he watched what was happening and felt a warmth flooding his insides. As he glanced down the stand, he saw Bardeshevsky's rigid form. His face was as stark and deadly as a drawn saber.

At a sudden, thunderous roar from the sky, everyone looked up. Six Flogger G interceptors in phalanx formation appeared over the GUM. Behind them came four Mig-29 Fulcrum fighters. They hurtled past like silvered darts, their residual rumble echoing and rolling against the Kremlin walls.

As the last ripple faded into the blaring band music, another sound erupted: sharp and clean above the trumpets and the clangs of armored vehicles, it was a whistling sibilance like the violent ripping of canvas. People in the square again looked skyward in happy expectation. But here and there soldiers in the columns had instantly fallen flat onto the ground, causing several armored vehicle drivers to swerve aside to keep from running over them.

Markisov heard Petrov shout something, but couldn't make out what it was. He felt a chill cross his back. He turned his head and witnessed a slow-motion movie unfolding. Into the frame came agonized stop-action shots: Petrov's face and arms lunging forward; Deputy Kurtkakin's hands spread in confusion; a KGB officer's mouth open as if to scream. And at the end of the tunnel of his vision was Bardeshevsky's stark face, turning slowly, slowly, in utter shock. Then the old general bolted toward Markisov, his arms coming up, mouth opened.

Two seconds later there was a powerful but muffled explosion. From the left corner of the stand, human bodies were suddenly catapulted into the air, flung like discarded puppets as their limbs twirled crazily against the sun. Down in the square, a small armored vehicle with twin racks of 75-mm. artillery rounds was struck with white-hot shrapnel. It exploded, sending chunks of metal whistling through the air and bursting into fragments against the front of the reviewing stand.

Far across the square, the huge plate-glass facade of the GUM was shattered by the concussion. It just seemed to come apart, rushing down in a sparkling, glistening shower. Inside the building, people were hurled off the arching footbridges and plummeted disjointedly to the courtyard below.

As the sounds died away, the square was filled with a stunned, trembling silence, like a pause in the revolution of the earth.

A second . . .

Another . . .

And then a single scream rose up and set off chaos.

The moment the mortar round left the barrel, Gankin had collapsed inside. The sound had been so soft, just this metallic slap and then a hollow, throaty *whomp*. He'd expected a loud crack, had prepared his mind, tensed his body for it. The unexpected gentleness was like a misstep that made him cringe.

Crab-walking, he scurried to the parapet and peeked down at Kujbyseva Avenue. The parade was still advancing, but with a jerkiness caused by the ripple effect of drivers hitting brakes. With surprise he saw girls mingling with the troops and throwing flowers at them.

Then he realized that some of the soldiers riding in the armored carriers were standing and shouting at each other. Their heads were swiveling back and forth. Some were pointing up at the building. Without volition, he felt himself start peeing. It warmly drenched his underwear, slipped down his legs. With a groan he came to his feet, whirled, and ran.

Just as he passed the mortar, he heard the round hit, a dull explosion that made the roof of the hostelry shake. As he headed for the stairwell door, he felt a second explosion, much more violent and powerful. It seemed to contain smaller detonations within it. He could hear the distant sounds of things hurtling through the air and the concussions jolting along the avenues, making the air tremble above the buildings.

He wrenched the door open and bounded down the stairs, four at a time. At the first landing he collided with a man in coveralls, holding a large pipe wrench covered with grease. The collision knocked the man backward and he toppled down the stairs below, hollering all the way to the bottom. As Latif raced past him, he came up on one knee and swung the wrench at him. It missed, slammed into the wall.

Gankin made it to the small lobby. Several students were gathered around a piano, singing. They'd obviously been up all night and were still drunk. They stopped singing and watched him dash past. One yelled out drunkenly: "Hey, *tavarish*, what's the big hurry?" Another made a crude remark about somebody's boyfriend showing up unexpectedly. The others laughed and started singing again.

The sun was hot on Latif's back as he sprinted wildly along Ipatjevski Avenue. People lunged out of his way. Near the corner, a sailor with an obese girl in a blue dress saw him coming and tried to block his way, grinning roguishly at him, arms stretched out as if to make a tackle. Gankin ran head-on into him and knocked him into the gutter.

He ducked into an alley running beside a laundry. From conduits trailing down the side of the wall, bursts of steam issued from the bottom nozzles and drifted across the alley. From the main street someone shouted, "You, stop!" and there was the quick crack of boots on the pavement. Gankin threw a terrified glance back and saw a policeman and two soldiers giving chase.

The alley curved around and came out on Razina Boulevard. As he burst onto the street, he paused a moment in confusion, his heart pounding crazily. To his right, four blocks away, was the Basilius Kathedrale, and directly across the boulevard rose the Skrjabin Museum, a huge old building with a colonnaded entrance and a vast glass dome over a wing on the right.

He dodged across the street and headed down a sloping stretch of lawn with scattered fountains and statuary. So frightened was he now that he didn't notice how agitated the people around him were. They were pointing back toward Red Square, where a great pall of dark smoke was rising above the buildings. Latif reached the museum, flew up the steps, and dashed inside.

The inner court had a high ceiling and leaded glass archways. To the right was a large horseshoe arch that led out into an enclosed garden beneath the glass dome. Gankin stopped, nearly out of breath. One of the museum guards started toward him, a burly man in a green uniform with a large punch clock and a holstered weapon on his belt. Gankin turned and ran down into the garden.

Inside the conservatory, the air was warm and moist, and the sunlight slanted through the huge overhead dome and made smoky beams in the garden trees. Several doves frightened by his rush flurried off the walk and into the trees. Just below them, a man was kneeling on a concrete bench, focusing a camera on a small tripod.

Latif fled past him and into a small stand of Telerian pines on one side of an oval fish pond. As he stopped at the edge of the water, the *koi* fish within burst away from him, shattering the stillness of the surface. He went to his hands and knees and crawled under a thick growth of fireberry hawthorn. It had dark red berries and the leaves smelled of fumigant. The earth below it was covered with wood shavings. He crouched, his body shaking so violently it made the thin branches tremble.

The dome soon was filled with the hollow echoes of men shouting. Latif began to weep, inched back deeper into the hawthorn. Noting a short spade stuck into the ground near the trunk, he pulled it free and held it across his chest.

The voices quieted as his pursuers spread out. Now and then one would call out and another would answer from a different position in the garden. When Gankin peered out, he saw five policemen in knee-high black boots fanned out, advancing over the small meadow of grass toward the fish pond. Each carried a machine pistol raised, the misty sunlight touching the barrels and making them gleam.

Starting in fear at the sight of the weapons, Gankin felt his blood roar inside his head. *They came over the grassy hills, their lances shining in the sun.* As he detected other noises—the flutter of wings, the dim rustles of branches—they sounded like the rasps of swords unsheathing. *Skjhold felt his heart tighten . . .*

Gankin rose slowly, lifting up through the branches, holding the spade like a broadsword. He inhaled the scent of flowers, the musky odor of his own fear. Adrenaline exploded in him.

Skjhold bellowed and charged . . .

Latif Gankin bellowed and charged.

A policeman yelled. Another whirled and went to one knee. A second policeman shouted. On Gankin came. Three policemen fired at the same instant, and Gankin was struck squarely in the chest with fourteen rounds. The impact was so violent, it lifted him four feet in the air and hurled him back. He felt a lightning explosion of horrible pain, actually felt his back blow open. And then he was into the pond. As his eyes glazed and the water around him began to thicken with blood, the *koi* fish fled wildly away.

Three miles to the north, in Operating Room 2-B of the Anronikov Central Hospital, Dr. Dmitri Bonitskaya, the general secretary's personal physician, had just completed an incision into the chest of a forty-three-year-old lawyer on whom he was performing a coronary artery bypass graft.

He snapped an order to his first assistant, who immediately administered a mild electric shock to the patient's heart. This would stop its beating, preparatory to the implantation of the graft tissue taken from the lawyer's right leg.

Suddenly the door was thrown open and four men rushed in. Three were wearing dark suits, but the fourth had the uniform of a KGB officer. Bonitskaya glanced up, then bellowed, "Dammit, what's the meaning of this? Get out of here."

Ignoring him, they quickly surrounded the operating table, shoving assistants aside. The KGB officer roughly grabbed the surgeon's arm. "You will come with us immediately, Doctor," he growled.

Bonitskaya jerked back. "Get out of here at once, you imbeciles. You're contaminating the operating field."

The officer said nothing more, but instead bodily lifted the doctor away from the table and carried him out the door with Dmitri screaming in protest. As they went down a long hall, nurses darted out of the way. No one dared interfere.

Markisov's limo was waiting. The driver leaned over the backseat and opened the rear door. Instantly recognizing the automobile, Bonitskaya murmured something and climbed in readily. The

KGB officer and one of the other men got in beside him, carrying a medical bag. With a screech of tires they roared out of the basement.

"Where is he?" Dmitri asked the officer. "How badly hurt?"

The man didn't answer as the Zil rocketed onto Nezdanovaj Avenue, heading west.

"Damn you, man. What has happened to the general secretary?"

"He's wounded."

"How badly?"

"We don't know. There were explosions. He's been unconscious ever since."

8

Cas was lying on his belly, feeling utterly bored as he chamoised gasoline into the Sea King's port auxiliary tank. As far as he was concerned, it had been a wasted day. They had wandered aimlessly around the general area where he and Skip had found the body, swinging back and forth in low-level search loops blowing radar and magnetic probes. They returned once to Arutua for refueling and then went out again. At least, Cas thought, the helo had first-rate detection gear: an AQS dipping sonar, APN doppler radar, and an AQS-81 magnetic anomaly detector. In order to save weight, the craft's racks of sonobuoys had been off-loaded before she left the *Coral Sea* and twin auxiliary tanks installed.

All the same, Cas knew it wouldn't make any difference. There was just too much ocean out there. Unless they came up with a more specific area to focus on, the operation was doomed to failure.

Apparently, he wasn't the only one who felt that way. The command pilot, Lieutenant Abrams, had made it obvious he wanted elsewhere. And Lieutenant Woodcroft—a Texas burrhead, Cas had noticed amusedly—had spent most of the afternoon trying to put the moves on Kiri. Cas didn't know what the chief, Capasotti, thought, for the only time he opened his mouth was to spit tobacco juice.

In contrast, January just couldn't sit still. Early on, he'd worked out a contingency plan that he discussed with Bonner. If the radar or MAD scans picked up a likely target, they'd locate it and he and Bonner would go down in scuba gear to check it out. Cas's first question was: "You ever dive before?"

"No."

Cas shook his head. "Well, I'll tell you, there's obviously something else you've never done before: run an ocean search. You've got good gear here, but it's designed to pick up noise, not debris. What you really need out here is about a thousand more pairs of eyes. Even then, I don't think you'll ever find that ship."

"We have to try," January said simply and left it there.

Around four in the afternoon, Capasotti had picked up a strong but intermittent radar blip on his consoles. It was moving like a bat out of hell, down near the deck ninety miles to the southwest, and its velocity was creating a bad wash off the surface, causing the interrupted signal. The pilots discussed it and decided it was either a Russian Forger or a French Entendard fighter. Either way, they had to duck. They headed west until the signal faded. But that had lost them nearly thirty minutes of search time. They held for another hour and then Abrams, much to January's consternation, turned back for Arutua.

By the time they reached Nickie's plantation, the storm Cas had smelled in the night was blowing in full. Dark rain squalls were sweeping in from the south, and the wind gusted with the thick, wet coldness across the channel and into the coconut grove. They immediately set up the refueling line again. Kiri had helped for a while, but she said the gasoline fumes were making her sick, so Cas suggested she go wait with Nickie. Now and then he glanced up at the plantation house, wondering about her.

Out on the search run, he had discovered an entirely new side to Kiri: she was quite an electronics buff. Except for the times Woodcroft had been flirting, she had stayed pretty close to January and the chief at the consoles. As Cas watched her, he began to realize, from the way her eyes moved from specific input keys to screens to data prints even before either Capasotti or January did, that she knew exactly what she was seeing.

The discovery intrigued him. How did a restaurant owner know such things? The question provoked others. Where had she been? And with whom? he asked himself, thinking back on the way she'd slapped him on the cutter. She had said she loved him; she'd never done that before, no matter how aroused. Still, from the reaction, she obviously didn't like the idea.

When it came right down to it, he couldn't decide whether or not he did either. Love was something Cas eased around like a wary dog in a strange yard. Out of all the women he'd known, he'd only fallen in love twice, that hard, biting kind of love that takes hold way down there where it hurts. The first one he had married, a youthful mistake. The daughter of a Honolulu publisher, she'd wanted to fly too high and too fast and used drugs and other men to get there. He tried, as long as he could, then said "Screw it." But it still hurt. The second woman, Napah Gilchrist, had been a marine geologist. Their affair was still soaring when she was killed on an oil exploration in the Aleutians two years before. That one had left a great big hole in him.

A sudden whoop from Woodcroft in the cabin brought Cas up from his thoughts. The ensign had been monitoring frequencies for the last fifteen minutes. He whooped again and poked his head through the open panel. "Bonner," he shouted excitedly. "Get Lieutenant Abrams down here, fast."

Cas told the man handing up the gas cans to pass the word to Abrams. Two minutes later, the lieutenant and January came jogging down and climbed into the aircraft.

Curious, Cas eased along the tank until he was over the open canopy. He just managed to catch part of an incoming transmission. ". . . entire coordinate area east Marquesas. You are advised to monitor strike frequency one-four-four-three. Do you copy?"

Abrams, by now in his seat, keyed his helmet mike: "CH-Two-Four, roger."

"Maintain total radio silence and remain present position until further notice. Repeat, go to TRS and hold position, over."

"I understand. CIC, what is your present mount status?"

The answer was garbled with static. Slowly the words came back: ". . . strike alert in effect, full up. Watch your asses. Strike DDF One-Three clearing."

Abrams cleared, then slammed the mike down. He turned and glared at January, who was kneeling between the seats. "Well, that's it for this chicken shit operation, scientist."

"We can't stop now," January cried.

Abrams grabbed the front of his flight suit. "Listen, you son of a bitch, if it wasn't for you, I'd be back with my ship right now." He pushed him aside and stood up. "This chopper stays right here until I'm cleared. And then we're going home." He headed for the bay door.

Feeling someone touch him lightly on the shoulder, Cas whirled around and discovered Kiri beside him. "What's happened?" she asked. "I saw Abrams and January running."

Cas shrugged with his palms. He turned back and leaned into the open panel. "Hey, Woodcroft, what the hell's going on?"

The ensign glanced up. "Oh, man, some heavy shit. Somebody just blew away the Russian premier."

"What? He got assassinated?"

Woodcroft nodded rapidly, almost joyously. "Yeah, he's deader than a motherfucker."

When Cas turned toward Kiri to see her reaction, he was startled. Her face was blanched with utter, wounded shock.

Dressed in his night robe and slippers, the President had been in the White House library, browsing through the books, when he paused on a special favorite: Agatha Christie's *Ten Little Indians*. He'd read it several times and, despite the knowledge of its astounding climax, he still enjoyed reading it purely for its crisply structured plot.

He was lifting the book out when he heard someone running in the outer corridor. Frowning, he turned his head to listen. Someone knocked anxiously on the door. "Mr. President," a man's voice called. "Mr. President, are you in there?"

He hurried to the door and pulled it open. It was Secretary Lauderdale, looking stricken. "Secretary Markisov's just been assassinated," he blurted.

The President recoiled. "My God! When?"

"Twelve minutes ago. There was a terrible explosion in Red Square."

"Do you have confirmation that he's dead?"

"Nothing absolute yet. The reports are very fragmentary, but there was a great deal of damage in the square and many are dead and injured."

The President hurried past him into the red-carpeted hall. Over his shoulder he shouted, "Get Richfield, I want solid confirmation. And roust any Security Council member you can find. Here, ten minutes."

"Yes, sir." Lauderdale sprinted away.

The meeting was held in a small conference room in the west wing of the White House, under the dark, studied gaze of a Lincoln portrait. Four members of the NSC were present: Lauderdale, Admiral Hubbel, CIA Director Mark Richfield, and the President's chief adviser, Tim McQuisten. The remaining two members, Vice-President Gerald Sipes and Secretary of State Frank Aldridge were presently out of the country.

"All right, gentlemen," the President said grimly, taking his seat. "Let's get on with it. Richfield, do you have confirmation?"

"Not yet, sir. There's horrible confusion in Moscow, but the indications are very strong that Markisov *is* dead. One of the explosions occurred very close to the reviewing platform where he was standing."

"*One* of the explosions?"

"Yes, sir, there were at least two."

"Jesus!" The President's gaze glided over the shaken faces. "For the sake of options, let's assume for the moment he *is* dead. The obvious question is: Who did it? Let's have some thoughts. Richfield?"

The CIA director, who had been attending a dinner three blocks from the White House when told of the assassination, was still wearing a tuxedo. "The most likely source would be the Old Guard. Everything at this point puts the finger on them. We all know how much they hate Markisov, and recent reports show they've developed strong sympathies within the Russian military command. With this French situation, they could conceivably have figured it was a ripe time to take him out."

"All right, if not them, who?"

"There's the possibility of internal terrorists. *Perestroika* policies have released powerful nationalistic feelings in the Soviet Union, and some of the recent demonstrations have been put down. Yes, nationalistic fanatics could have done it."

"So where the hell does that leave us? First, if the Old Guard did it, and, second, if some nut did it?"

"In either case," Richfield said, "the situation within the Soviet Union is going to be very fluid and unpredictable. If it was the

Old Guard, we'll know soon enough. They'll move to take control of the government immediately and we can expect a complete one-eighty in policy. If it was a nut, there'll be a power struggle with no way of knowing who comes out on top until it's a fait accompli."

"Who has the inside track?"

"Constitutionally, Soviet President Kilikov would be in line to assume power," Richfield noted. Then he shook his head. "But he was on the reviewing stand with Markisov. No word on him yet. The hardliners are led by senior Politburo minister Bardeshevsky. One super hardass. If he takes over, we've got problems."

"How bad problems?"

"Bardeshevsky's the one who saved Leningrad, isn't he?" Hubbel interrupted.

"That's him," Richfield answered.

"Christ!" Hubbel said. "That son of a bitch's been raving for years about taking over all of Europe."

The President's head snapped back to Richfield. "True?"

"True. It wouldn't surprise me that if he does gain power, he'd immediately try to humble the French."

"Lovely," the President said disgustedly. "Absolutely fucking lovely."

"But what about the military situation in the USSR?" Lauderdale asked. "As you said, there's a lot of friction between commanders. Would this Bardeshevsky and his people be able to move freely?"

"That's a good point," Richfield put in. "The rifts are very deep between pro-Markisov and pro-Old Guard factions. Depending on how deep they are, the internal situation could become so chaotic even the Old Guard couldn't control it."

"You mean open revolt?" the President asked.

"Yes, possibly."

The President leaned back in his chair, fingering his upper lip, his eyes crinkling with thought. Finally he sat forward again. "Well, it seems no matter how the ball falls, we're on notice."

"Precisely," Richfield said.

For the first time McQuisten spoke up. "Sir, wouldn't the best reaction at this point be no reaction? As Richfield says, the situation is going to be extremely fluid now. Let's wait and see how things develop."

Hubbel turned and shot McQuisten a hard look. "That's downright stupid. With what's happening, you want us to sit with our thumbs up our asses until Ivan starts pulling triggers?"

"No, I'm not saying that. All I'm saying is to wait until definite trends develop. If we overreact to this, we could be exacerbating the situation in Russia."

The President was shaking his head even before McQuisten finished. "No, Tim," he said. "We can't sit on our hands now." He turned to Hubbel. "What are your recommendations?"

"First off, notify NATO commanders to be ready for anything."

"Agreed."

"Second, I'd start shoving more force down into the Polynesians. We can't provide whoever takes over further provocation than he already has. If that situation down there escalates, we're at war."

"I agree. Alert everything in the area and start mustering force."

"What about Passmore, sir? He's already got aircraft patrolling the eastern approaches to the Capricorn. Do we move him into French waters?"

"What do you think?"

Hubbel frowned. "Well, sir, as much as I'd like to penetrate in force, tactically it could be dangerous for Passmore. I'd suggest we simply order him to increase overflights, but stay out of bounds for now."

The President nodded. "Good, we'll go with that. Meanwhile, gentlemen, I want every source tapped until we find out precisely who the hell will be running the Soviet nation."

Alone, Kiri walked through the dark grove. High above her, the wind lashed through the coconut branches, bringing a hard rain that pelted her bare back. The ground was littered with downed coconuts and pieces of gauzy material from the tree heads, which whirled along the ground like dried newspapers.

Only by a deft concentration of will had she forced down the shock in front of Cas, and she wasn't sure she'd managed to completely pull it off. He had looked curiously at her for a long moment before asking, "How about that?"

"Brutal," she answered, then forced a casual shrug. "But leaders get killed."

"Yeah," he said, still watching with his head tilted slightly. "Right."

Now she walked with her head down, deep in thought. She had little doubt as to who had killed Markisov. Obviously, it had been the Old Guard factions. She knew how much they hated him. Still, the fact that they had actually assassinated him jolted her. He was their leader . . . Then she shook her head, disgusted at her momentary sentimentality. He was dead and that was it. What was important now was what would follow. Of course, there would be power struggles. In the end, it wouldn't really matter who came out on top. What did matter was that until the struggles were resolved, command structures would be dismembered. That would leave her and Katevayo on their own.

Ordinarily she would have relished the absence of the stolid procedure of checking and rechecking commands all the way back to Moscow. But now that link would be essential because things had suddenly, drastically changed. The MAQ platform was no longer the most important mission for her. No, now she had to do something else far more dangerous.

For the past day and a half, she had been probing for links between seemingly unconnected incidents: Bonner's dead pilot, the Russian incursions into Polynesian territory, Faaa Airport's radar malfunction and the nearly fatal airliner incident, the downing of a Forger, and now January on a hunt for a downed aircraft. These, overlayed with snippets of data gleaned over the last two years through KGB channels plus vague rumors during her sub-atomic research time at the Dzenshank facility, had gradually come together and jelled. The picture finally formed. Somewhere out in the ocean, an ICF-1 experimental aircraft was down. And *alive!*

She had hardly heard a faint rustle of sand before she felt a slight pressure on her back and then a knife blade against her throat. As she froze, a man whispered into her ear, "Very careless, Burmese."

The blade was withdrawn and Katevayo stepped around her. He was dressed in a wet suit, and the neoprene glistened softly from the distant lights of the plantation compound. Bending down, he slipped the knife into his small calf scabbard. On the inside of his other leg was a second holster, for the 9-mm. PC-6 pistol he was never without.

She made herself relax, but her heart was still pounding. "How long have you been here?"

"Since sunset."

"Where's the canoe?"

"Up the beach." He was silent a moment, leering his insane grin. Then: "Where's your Yank?"

She ignored the question. Instead she said, "Secretary Markisov has just been assassinated."

His expression didn't change. Through the leer he said, "What did you say?"

"Markisov is dead."

Slowly the grin faded, and Katevayo lowered his head. "Who did it?"

"The Old Guard, of course."

"Bullshit!" he barked viciously.

Her eyes narrowed. "It had to be them. Who else?"

"French swine."

"That's stupid."

Katevayo walked a few feet to the right and stared through the swaying trees at the plantation. When he returned, the grin was back. "I think we pay the pricks back. Now."

"What are you talking about?"

He jerked his head in the direction of the Sea King. "That Yank helicopter, it's got auxiliary tanks. With them and my gelegnite satchels, we could blow that platform"—he made a fist in front of her face—"to fucking hell!"

"No, Katevayo, listen to me. The platform has to wait, there's something more important we must do. One of our experimental aircraft is down out there somewhere and it's still functioning. We have to find it before either the French or Americans do."

He glared silently at her.

"Goddammit, will you listen to me? You don't realize how important this aircraft is. Worse, you don't know what it can do."

He snorted, "Fuck your aircraft." He started around her.

She grabbed his arm. "You can't do this. That helicopter is the only means we have of finding it."

He jerked her hand away roughly. "Burmese, you can come or you can stay. But right now, I'm going to kill me some Americans and grab that chopper." He turned and started off toward the beach, moving at an angle to the compound.

Frantically, Kiri searched the ground for a weapon. She spotted a huge coconut, scooped it up, and headed after him. As she lifted it to smash the back of his head, he whirled suddenly, blocked her strike, and shoved her back so violently she fell to the ground. He towered over her, snickering contemptuously. Then he bent and slipped his knife from its leg scabbard. He tossed it onto the ground beside her. "You said you'd kill me, cunt. Do it now."

Kiri, her eyes not leaving him for an instant, felt for the knife. He had carved a wooden handle for it and it felt heavy in her hand. Slowly she got to her feet and crouched. For a cold, sobering moment the fear of him overpowered her and then, suddenly, it was replaced by a wild rage. She steadied herself, the knife out and low in the classic fighting stance.

Katevayo also braced, lowering slightly. "Come on," he taunted. "Come in."

"You come, bastard."

He came in, almost casually, arms out and low, inviting the thrust of the knife. But she didn't thrust. Instead she rushed directly into his arms. As they bumped, she let her body give way to his forward momentum and he stumbled. Instantly she kneed him in the groin, then twisted off, guiding his body past her to the ground.

Bellowing, Katevayo tried to turn over, gripping his testicles. As he shoved one elbow into the sand, hauling his legs up under him, Kiri thrust the knife blade in just above his right pelvic bone. She had been trying for the kidney, but even though she missed slightly, she shoved it in all the way to the hilt, withdrew it, and slammed it in again.

He groaned softly and slumped as she reflexively leaped away from him. Slowly he rolled over onto his back and grunted something. Had there been obscene laughter in it?

"You fool," she hissed at him. "You stupid fucking fool. I needed you." She quickly knelt and unbuckled the 9-mm. holster. He twisted suddenly and tried to grab her, but she jumped out of reach. For a moment she considered finishing him off, but knew the shot would be heard in the compound. Without another word she turned and ran back through the grove, feeling the rain strike her face like bullets of ice.

*   *   *

Minister Bardeshevsky was not in any particular pain; he was merely dazed. He was sitting in the back of an old military ambulance, a Voskienski model as square as a baker's wagon, and he vaguely remembered that such vehicles had carted bodies off World War II battlefields. The minister's right hand was covered with drying blood, and he tensely held it between his knees as if it would fly away if let free.

In the terrible moments just before the explosion, Bardeshevsky had recognized the sound of the incoming mortar. It had frozen him for a fleeting second, then his instinct kicked in, and he started to run along the reviewing stand toward the back steps. The concussion of the explosion hurled him forward. His extended leg gave out and he went down flat, behind the parapet.

He lay there for what seemed an endless, chaotic passage of time as a second explosion went off and the shattering echoes roared and rebounded off the Kremlin walls. At last he lifted his head. Blood and grotesque chunks of human matter were splattered all over the place. Soldiers came pounding up onto the stand, their eyes dazzling hot, weapons ready. Hands touched him, moved away.

Lifting himself off the cement floor, he noted with quizzical surprise that his hand was bloody. "It was a mortar," he mumbled. "I heard it. A mortar." He walked down the back side of the reviewing stand and wandered away, impervious to the madness out in the square. Two hundred yards away, someone took him gently by the sleeve and helped him up into the ambulance and then ran off.

Now he gently eased himself back against an oxygen rack. The ambulance held the sharp stink of chloroform; it seemed impregnated in the metal frame. From somewhere near the vehicle, a woman was crying softly. Now and then her voice would lift, reaching for an hysterical note it never quite reached, and then it would drop, returning to its murmuring whimper. A medical officer carrying a small black bag stepped up into the vehicle. He wore a green uniform with blood caked on his gold braiding. He knelt in front of Bardeshevsky and stared fixedly into his eyes. "Comrade, do you know where you are?"

"It was a mortar."

"Yes," the officer said sharply. "Do you know where you are?"

Bardeshevsky lifted his head and gave him a scorching look. "Of course I know where I am, you idiot."

"Good. Are you wounded anywhere besides your arm?"

"No. Where is Secretary Markisov?"

The officer did not reply, but began gingerly trying to lift Bardeshevsky's tunic sleeve.

"Dammit, is Markisov dead?"

"I don't know." The doctor snapped open his bag and withdrew a pair of scissors. He cut the sleeve and undershirt all the way to the shoulder, exposing a long, shallow wound that ran across the minister's forearm.

Bardeshevsky turned and looked back at the reviewing stand. From his vantage point he could see most of the right front. There were shrapnel holes and large burn stains all across it, and gouges of broken cement along the top. Near the center, the driveline from a vehicle stuck straight out, driven like a lance deeply into the face. In the square itself were hundreds of soldiers and mounted police and rescue vehicles.

A moment later, he caught sight of a GRU officer and Deputy Minister Kandalov darting through the throng. Seeing him, they headed over. Kandalov's face was ashen, coated with perspiration as he lumbered heavily up into the ambulance. "Comrade," he blurted breathlessly, "you're alive. Are you injured badly?"

"Where is Markisov? Is he dead?"

"We don't know. His security people took him away immediately after the explosion."

"He was either dead or unconscious," the KGB officer said. The doctor cleaning Bardeshevsksy's wound paused and turned to stare at the officer for a moment.

"What about the others?"

Kandalov wiped the back of his hand across his mouth before answering. "President Kilikov and Kurtkakin are dead. Marshal Petrov is gravely wounded. They've already taken him to a hospital."

Bardeshevsky snapped around and barked at the doctor working on his arm, "Hurry with that thing, damn you." To the GRU officer, he said, "Where did they take Markisov? Did anyone see?"

"I don't know, sir."

The doctor was nearly finished bandaging the arm. Bardeshevsky roughly pushed his hands away. "That's enough. Get out."

"You'll need a shot."

"Get out!"

Wordlessly the medical officer closed his bag, climbed out of the ambulance, and walked away. Bardeshevsky bent closer to Kandalov. "Find Markisov," he hissed. "We must know if he's dead."

"Of course, comrade."

To the GRU officer: "You, do it now. When you find him, I want to know immediately. I'll be in the secretary's office."

"Yes, sir." The officer ran off.

Bardeshevsky's eyes were charged with feverish glee as he grabbed Kandalov's jacket lapel and growled into his face: "This is our chance. Now we can act."

Kandalov frowned. "Comrade, what do you intend to do?"

"Declare myself interim general secretary."

Kandalov jerked back. "But you can't constitutionally do that."

"Kilikov is dead. As far as we know, so is Markisov. As presiding chief minister, I have a duty to declare a state of emergency and act to preserve national order."

"But what if Markisov isn't dead?"

The intensity of Bardeshevsky's emotions was so powerful, it made his cheeks quiver. "Then we'll kill him."

Kandalov gave a guttural cry of shock. He studied Bardeshevsky's mad face for a moment, then turned away. "Do we dare do this?"

"You fool! This opportunity has been thrust on us. If we fail to exploit it instantly, such a chance will not come again."

Nervously, Kandalov again wiped sweat from his face.

"Well? Well?"

The deputy minister finally nodded. "Yes," he whispered. "Yes, you're right, our time *has* come."

The crab's feet made touches on the Saber's fuselage as faint as the raindrops. As the animal scurried along the base of the starboard wing and paused beside a finely milled fuel inlet, the cockpit monitors, feeding back through its flight environment sensors, picked up the tiny vibrations through the skin of the aircraft. It tracked the darting progress and sent data into the main computer. Analysis parameters were fixed:

WEIGHT: 914.285 GRAMS
COMPOSITION DENSITY: (SKELETAL) 0.285 SP
TEMPERATURE (MASS): 21C—RC (NON-HUMAN): 30.99
   PERCENTILE
GROUND VELOCITY: 0.0113 KNOTS

The Kamov scanned through memory ident banks. It came back:

NONFUNCTIONAL: REPEAT ANALYSIS

More sensor infeed ran through reels. Little electronic blips made pinpoints of sound in the cockpit:

ANALYSIS: SIMILAR

The Kamov asked the AI unit for a danger assessment. Its read said:

OBJECT: UNIDENTIFIABLE
STATUS: INSIDE NO-PASS PERIMETER
CMR: DESTROY

The weapon bay activated. The barrel aligned to the calculated intercept point along the leading edge of the starboard wing. The crab, though, did not move according to calculations, but hurried off at an angle. Once more the barrel realigned to the CIP. Again the crab moved elsewhere. Six times the barrel realigned. At last the crab did move through the CIP and instantly disappeared in a wisp of smoke. Beyond it, the beam cut a path into the water that sent a plume of steam into the night wind.

The Kamov shut down the fusion box and sat bristling, all sensors scanning for further intrusions. It swept the sky from one horizon fix to another. Like an angry old man sitting in a yard swing on a starry night, it watched the heavens.

A blip came up between grid lines, intermittent feed due to rapid cloud-mass interference. The Kamov homed. Ident banks formed P/C parameter working off earlier data tapes:

AMERICAN SATELLITE: NAVSAT (SEE TAPE NUMBERS:145-
  178-261)
CONCOIDAL RANGE: 20,000 KILOMETERS
TRAJECTORY ANGLE: 030 DEGREES, TRANSIT TIME 0.14
  MINUTES
COMMUNICATIONS ET: 145 IR CAMERAS, DTG CAPABILITY
  WITH TT RESOLUTION
LAUNCH DATE: 1-6-67

The AI countermeasure response was:

NON-LETHAL COMMUNICATIONS UNIT

The Kamov followed its orbit track across the sky. Six seconds
later, a second blip appeared. Once more the P/C procedure ran
through units, drawing up earlier ingested tape data again that
had indicated shadow debris. The Kamov decided to analyze this
time. Analysis:

SOVIET SATELLITE: COSMOS 346
STATUS: INERT/SYNCHRONATE ORBIT
CONCOIDAL RANGE: 2,000 KILOMETERS
CAPABILITY INVENTORY: LASER (FYTT), ACTIVATE
  CAPACITY: 0.0001 UNI-SECONDS

The Kamov registered: Friendly. It swung its secondary fix
sensors away and homed them on star constellations. Navigational memory banks fed pertinent data on the first:

CAPRICORNUS: (LT: GOAT HORNED)
ZODIACAL POSITION: MID AQUARIUS/SAGITTARIUS: 21 HOURS
  RIGHT ASCENSION, 20 DEGREES S DECLINATION
PASSAGE TIME: THREE HOURS, FOURTEEN MINUTES

Sensors shifted to the rising moon, registering interrupted
illumination due to rapid moving cloud masses. Navigational
data came up. The Kamov fixed on the Great Sea of Tran-
quillity:

US LANDING: 1-4-74 (?)
TOUCHDOWN SITE: SOFT, MINOR DUST DEPTH

DECLINATION AT TD: 10.14 DEGREES, AZIMUTH POSITION:
  56.00 DEGREES
SAMPLE RECOVERY: SPECIFIC GRAVITY: 0.198 LABS (PA 1100.01 DE-
  FLECTION INTERJECT)

Data bored, the Kamov clicked itself into hold. Suddenly a faint riffle of a ship's cavitation touched gently into the sensors. Instantly the computer came alive, adjusting direction. Identification parameters, however, were minimal, merely indicating submarine shaft cavitation. Working back from shaft and blade class standards to specific vessel peculiarities, the Kamov managed to outline a general ID:

ENERGY SOURCE: METALLIC, SINGLE SCREW (BRASS 74%;
  COPPER 24%; ZINC .012%; OXYGEN 0.80%)
VESSEL OUTLINE: ELONGATED HULL: TITANIUM IMPREG-
  NATED STEEL
DIMENSIONS: LENGTH: 81:4 METERS; BEAM: 9.5 METERS
PROPULSION SOURCE: STEAM TURBINE (45,000 SHP)

Within seconds, memory tape had focused on a solid identification:

ATTACK SUBMARINE: AMERICAN, STURGEON-CLASS
HEADING: 183 DEGREES
DEPTH: (FADE-READ): 31.25 METERS
RANGE: 422 KILOMETERS (TRA)

The Kamov held for a moment before going to AI assessment. Slowly, like the fading, whispered strains of a song, the American sub's blade noise disappeared as it moved out of sensor range.

9

At last Kiri was alone . . .

After the fight with Katevayo, she'd headed straight back to the cutter. She intended to raise her Auckland agent, inform him of the ICF-1, then, somehow, force January and the American pilots to resume the search. She deliberately didn't think about Bonner's place in it all. That was a confrontation she didn't want to deal with, not now.

As she reached the beach, though, she saw a pair of headlights coming along near the water. It was Fitzgerald and his Tahitian foreman in an old beat-up jeep. She held the 9-mm. down along her leg as they drove up.

"What the bloody hell, missy?" Nickie boomed in his perpetually half-drunken, joyous voice. "You look like a bleedin' drowned bitser. Come on, get your lovely arse up in here."

Holding the weapon below the edge of the frame, she climbed in beside him as the lanky foreman crawled onto the rear seat. They drove back to the plantation house with rain squalls sweeping across the compound, misting the lights. Water poured off the eaves of the porch, and down under the rafters small doves were huddled in tiny balls of wet feathers. Kiri furtively tossed the pistol into the darkness near the steps.

Cas, January, and Woodcroft were in the front room, the latter curled up on the large *punee* couch, sound asleep. Bonner turned as they came through the door, but he said nothing. Nickie immediately sent Kiri off with Tifi for a shower and change of clothes.

She returned a half hour later with her hair pulled back in a stiff bun, dressed in a pair of Tifi's Levis and a blue turtleneck sweater. She walked over and sat down beside Cas, winked at him, and took his hand. As she ran a fingernail intimately across his palm, Nickie noticed it and chortled lasciviously, "Well, shoot the crows, how bloody lovely." He shoved a freshly opened bottle of Fosters in front of her and then launched into a new story of his croc-hunting days in New Guinea.

To Kiri, time seemed to crawl past as Fitzgerald unfolded his tale. Eventually, Abrams came up. January instantly tried to talk to him, but the lieutenant waved him off. He went over and woke up Woodcroft and sent him down to monitor the helo's radio. It was well past midnight now.

Seizing the opportunity, Kiri stood up and stretched. "Nickie, luv, I'm sorry but I'm going to get some sleep."

"What?" Fitzgerald cried. "The night's still bloody young."

"No, I'm out of it."

"Ah, well, you can use my sack."

"Thanks, Nickie, but I'd rather go down to the boat."

"Nonsense! I won't have it." Kiri gave Cas a coy look, and the Aussie guffawed. "Ah, it's privacy you're wantin'." He got up and went off into another room, returned a moment later with a large denim jacket. "Here, missy, at least take a parka wi' ya."

Cas watched her leave without comment. At the foot of the porch steps, she retrieved Katevayo's gun and quickly strapped it to her right calf, pulling the leg of the Levis down to conceal it. On the way down the slope, she passed Capasotti coming up, his head tucked against the rain.

Quickly she slipped down the companion ladder into the cabin. The boat was jerking restlessly against the mooring lines, and she could hear the standing rigging thrumming softly in the wind. She found the hold hatch and descended. In another moment she had the auxiliary generator going, made sure the vent was clear, then returned to the cabin.

It took her eight minutes to raise the Auckland agent. At last her red light blinked as he keyed acknowledgment. Her first question was: "What is status at main plantation?"

Silence.

She keyed again. "What is status at main plantation? Over."

The speaker crackled. "Signal weak. Say again."

Dammit! she cursed silently. Then she keyed. "Is Father really dead?"

The answer came right back: "No confirmation yet. Confusion."

She paused, thinking over the words she'd use for the next transmission. Then: "Brother has crashed his aircraft in ocean. I am going to attempt locate. Over."

Once more the agent came back, "Signal weak. Say again."

"You asshole," she said aloud. She jammed the mike key down hard. "Brother has crashed his ICF-1 aircraft, repeat ICF-1 aircraft. Believed afloat and functioning. Intend to locate and pass coordinates to recovery crew. Americans also searching. Do you copy?"

A splurge of static rifled through the speaker, then a single word: "Understand."

"I must have link with recovery crew. Is this possible? Over."

There was a long pause before the agent came back. "*Poule.* South of Papeete."

Kiri frowned. He'd used the French word for "hen." What in hell did he mean by that? Wait, she thought, a mother hen, a carrier. Of course, there was a *skadra* force south of Papeete. That must have been where the Forger had come from. She keyed: "Understand reference. Can link be formed through you?"

"Affirmative."

"Will call when brother found. Over."

The only answer was a single-key interruption of the signal, and then the transmission light went out. Kiri exhaled, relaxing in the radio seat. For a moment she listened to a new flurry of raindrops on the deck. Then she turned around.

Cas was standing in the companionway, watching her with cold, narrow eyes.

Rene Joffre, dive master for the French MAQ project, skimmed close above the Forger's wing tank. Submerged in fifty feet of water, it had dark blotches where fire had burned the plastic outer coating, exposing bare metal disfigured from the heat. The tank was jammed between a network of electrical conduits on the MAQ's number 23 junction box, located near the southeastern curve of the outer collider ring.

Inside his mask Joffre cursed. Here was yet another unforeseen delay, this one potentially very serious. Ever since midafternoon, Director Cotuse had been running test checks hellbent, not even releasing his technicians for meals. Word had it he was resorting to shortcuts in test procedures, something he had *never* done before. Even when word of the Russian premier's assassination was radioed from one of the frigates, it had caused a mere ripple of shock but no interruption in the tests. Final Q-run was scheduled for dawn. That is, Joffre realized, unless the wing tank screwed up that deadline.

Gingerly he slipped below the tank and came up the other side. It was a miracle the damned thing hadn't exploded when the Russian aircraft plunged into the sea. Partially filled with fuel, it had floated just below the surface, hidden from sight. But he could see tiny bubble streams lifting off three seam points: fume leak. Apparently, the tank had been taking on water, slowly enough to dampen its buoyancy and drop it lower into the ocean. At fifty feet the storm current had rammed it with sufficient force between the conduits and junction-box housing. It had torn out several conduit locks. This, in turn, had depressurized the box, allowing seawater to seep in and short out the entire quadrant.

Several yards from box number 23 was one of the Weber antenna housings. There were four placed at points around the outer ring. Quadripole magnets, these antennae monitored magnetic buildup within the rings during the proton run. Huge and extremely sensitive, they were irreplaceable if damaged.

A second diver came up. His light was like a flare in the darkness. Joffre angrily waved him off, away from the fume bubbles. The continuing intake of water into the tank was forcing the lighter fuel upward, forming a compression state that vaporized the upper surface of the fuel. As a result, each bubble was a tiny explosive charge, and the tank itself was a bomb just waiting for a spark to ignite it.

Joffre circled the junction box several times, studying it from different angles. Finally he signaled the other diver to remain as he headed for the surface. Up above, a heavy swell was moving northeast, and storm combers loomed out of the night, their tops feathering off in the wind. He held his light straight up, and in a few minutes one of the Zodiac boats came to him, rising and plunging as it approached. As it slowed to pass him, he grabbed one of the gunwale loops and pulled himself aboard. The engine man swung into the swell and synchronized his speed so they would remain stationary.

Joffre thumbed the on-switch of the Zodiac's walkie-talkie: "CT-1, this is J-1. Over."

Cotuse came back: "Go ahead, J-1."

"We've got a ticklish problem here. A fuel tank from that Russian aircraft has wedged itself into the conduit lines of number 23. We've lost all pressure in the box and it's shorted out."

"What's your assessment?"

"We could string new conduit lines, but that tank's ready to explode. The fuel's vaporizing inside and leaking out. If we activate any electrical lines near it, it could create a magnetic fuse."

"Can we bypass 23 and rig a temporary box outboard the ring?"

"Yes, but it would take at least five, six hours. And I don't like the way that tank's moving in the current. Against those metal conduits, it could set up static ignition. An explosion could breach the ring and damage the Weber."

"Is there any way you can pull it free?"

"Yes, I think so. But we'll need more power out here. Send out two more Zodiacs with number 4 plastic-wrapped cable and some heavy-gauge hemp."

"Will comply. Over and out."

It took the other boats twenty minutes to reach the site. By that time Joffre was down near the junction box again. Around and around it he went, shaking his head. It was going to be a bitch getting a solid purchase on the tank. The mounting brackets had been smashed down; he couldn't risk metal contact trying to get them up high enough to hook onto. As he moved, he stayed completely away from the tank and its thin streams of bubbles, for the air mixture moving through his regulator baffles and breathing lines created tiny static electrical impulses. If just one of the bubbles lit, it could set off a chain reaction leading right back into the tank itself.

Two fresh divers came down with the hemp lines and U-jointed cables. One of the divers had a radiophone mask, and he and Joffre exchanged gear. Then the two of them began the slow, delicate process of "bunker" rigging the hemp lines around the tank: triple loops cut back with overhand locks and then out into a single lead. Working in unison, they held their breath as they darted in to form the loops, then gently backpedaled against the current. Inside their masks, they were both sweating profusely.

When the bunker was set, Joffre and his diver set up focus lights on the ring tube to illuminate the tank while the other divers quickly linked the single lead out to the U-joints on the twin pulling cables. Forty yards off the tank, their lights floated and dipped like silvery ghosts out in the watery void.

At last everything was set. Eyeing the cable lines lying in a deep, slacked curve, Joffre waved everybody back to the surface. He alone would remain near the tank as the Zodiacs began to pull. He floated over the box for one more inspection. Schools of small striped fish darted through the glare of the focus beams, skimmed along the hemp lines, nibbling at the fibers.

Joffre touched the voice activating springs at his throat. "Are you set up?" He saw the cables trembling, heard the periodic surge and fade of the boat engines overhead.

The earphones in his helmet crackled hollowly: "We've got the boats in position, chief."

"All right, start taking up slack. But slowly, slowly."

The dip of the cables began to tighten as the pitch of the engines rose. Seeing one of the cables go taut before the other, Joffre shouted, "Goddammit, ease up on the starboard boat. Keep abreast. Yeah, that's it. You got her."

When both lines were evenly tensed, Joffre called, "Go ahead."

A metallic screech came clearly through the water, and feeling vibrations on his hands, Joffre felt the hair on his neck stand up. He kicked his flippers, skimmed in close to the tank, and hovered over it, looking down. The cables jerked sharply, became taut again. The tank moved a little, twisting. Two unbroken conduit lines snapped.

Joffre went down a few feet, peered under the tank, and then backed away. He activated his throat springs: "She's coming. Just keep the pull as—"

He never finished the sentence. There was a sudden, rolling lurch of the tank and the left cable went slack. Joffre froze. One of the focus lights was torn away and went spiraling crazily down into the darkness.

A fraction of an instant later, there was a violent, rending explosion. Joffre was hit by the concussion, the power of it multiplied by the water. His mask was torn off and he went tumbling backward over and over, his ears sending sharp pain into his head as his eardrums ruptured. Upside down, he caught a fleeting glimpse of a four-foot piece of the tank whirling through the smoky explosion of bubbles.

It sliced him in two.

Kiri's hand automatically dropped to her right ankle, and she hooked her finger into the bottom of the Levi pantleg, waiting to see what Cas would do. He didn't move, just continued staring at her with those chocolate brown eyes hard as tundra. Her fingers recoiled. No, she thought, I can't do it. Not him. Her hand came back up and she let it rest lightly on the radio table. Then she swung her chair around completely to face him. "So, you heard?"

He said nothing.

She flashed him a disarming smile. "Casimir, my love, you should make more noise when you creep up on a girl."

"Cut the bullshit."

She sighed. "All right, okay. What do you want me to say?"

"You're a Russian agent, aren't you?"

Kiri's thoughts were awhirl. Why didn't I shoot him? she thought frantically. He's the enemy. He'll turn you in. Yet she made not the slightest move to regain the pistol, but sat rigidly, grasping for a way out. Play it by ear, she told herself, ride it out. "Yes, I am," she said evenly.

"Dammit!" Cas hissed through his teeth. "God dammit!"

"So? What do you intend to do about it?"

"I'd like to beat the crap out of you."

"Then what?"

He stared for a moment longer, then snorted in irritation. Stepping down fully into the cabin, he ignored her as he jerked open the galley refrigerator and took out a can of beer. Cracking it with a sharp wrench of his wrist, he sat down on the companionway ladder. He took a long drink, then fixed her with a glare. "You want to tell me about it?"

"All right. I'm KGB. My mission here has been and still is penetration of the French experimental platform. I also happen to be a physicist. That platform is a super-collider. The French are about to achieve a light-velocity proton collision. It's my job to find out if that's true and to hamper the attempt in any way I can."

She watched him carefully, but he merely grunted. A plan was forming in her mind even as she spoke, and she went on boldly: "Unfortunately, something of much more importance has developed," she said. "That aircraft we've been trying to find? January's right, it really is out there. And I have a good idea what it is. It's a secret Russian surveillance and interdiction plane called the ICF-1." She paused, measuring his reaction. "And I believe it's alive."

"Alive? What the hell does that mean?"

"Somehow—I don't know how—its weapons system is operating on automatic." Cas started to say something, but she held up her hand. "No, Cas, listen to me. This aircraft contains extraordinary capabilities. Technology far surpassing you Americans. The danger lies in its weapons bay. There's a miniature fusion chamber in it that can create a powerful beam of pure energy. You yourself saw what it can do. I'm certain that was what struck your albatross."

Cas lowered his beer.

"I'm also certain it took out the Faaa Airport radar system the other night. And it was probably responsible for the near crash of that New Zealand airliner, too. Conceivably it could even have caused the battle between our Forger and the French frigate by distorting the ship's fire-control system. The beam attacks all electronic weapon components within its range."

"Jesus Christ!" Cas said softly. Then his eyes narrowed again. "How do I know all this is true? Or not just more bullshit?"

"You don't. Nor do I, for sure. But everything points that way."

"Then I'll tell January. He'll be able to get a full search out here. When they find this ICF, the *Coral Sea* can hit it with a fighter strike."

"That's not possible. The aircraft's computer system is programmed to attack any enemy plane or ship that comes near it. Only Russian forces can approach it."

Cas arched back, smiling grimly. "I see. You're saying only you and your people can handle it?"

"Yes."

"I don't buy that."

Kiri's plan had reached its center point. This time she'd have to lie to him, make him believe that she was the only one there capable of disarming the aircraft. His reaction would be crucial since she needed his help. But even if he believed her, would he give it? Would it matter to him that she was an enemy agent? Oddly, she didn't think so.

Cas was a maverick, a man who thought on his feet, who looked at reality for what it was and adjusted to it. After all, that was one of the things about him she found so compelling.

Besides, the only other option would be to kill him. That, she knew, she was totally incapable of doing. Looking him straight in the eye, she went for it: "I'm the only one here who can defuse the ICF-1, Cas. I have to find it and I need your help."

Bonner's gaze held her for a long, hard, steady moment. Outside the wind surged, making the boat rock. He saw the intensity in her green eyes, that hard look which he'd so often observed across bed covers. Was she lying? Probably. Yet he also saw something else there, a desperation that seemed real.

He considered. All of this could be a scam. But where did the lies end and the truth begin? Was there really a plane out there? And if so, was it as deadly as she had said? It was certainly weird enough to be true. Well, he thought, what the hell? The only way to find out was to ride it through.

He smiled, dipped his head. "Then I guess we'd better go find the son of a bitch."

Kiri eased out of her chair and advanced toward him. She touched his shoulder tentatively, felt the cold wetness of his T-shirt and the powerful curve of deltoid muscle beneath. "Do you understand what you're doing?"

"Yeah, I understand. I'm helping a Russian agent fix a Russian mistake."

"Cas, I'm sorry for all this."

"So am I," he said. He tilted his beer, crushed the empty can, and eased out from under her hand.

They left the cutter and headed up the dock. The rain had stopped now, and the wind gusts were merely peppered with droplets. To the left, the open bay of the Sea King formed a large square of reddish light.

Cas stopped suddenly and put his hand on her arm. "Wait a minute. Do you know when the Faaa radar system went down? Precisely when?"

"No."

Wordlessly he turned and sprinted back to the sailboat. Puzzled, she followed. They leaped onto the cutter's deck and slid down into the cabin. "Find the radio-frequency catalogue," he ordered as he dropped into the radio seat and flicked on the unit. She probed through closets, finally came up with a thin booklet stamped: "SOUTH PACIFIC RADIO DATA."

He flipped through it until he found the commercial air frequencies, then swung the radio's selector knob. A moment later, Faaa Air Traffic Control came on. A voice as mellow as cream but as depersonalized as a bus conductor calling stops, was vectoring an aircraft designated Apache One-Four-Zero.

Bonner keyed: "Mayday. Mayday."

There was a long, drawn-out slur of static. Then the controller came back: "This is Faaa Air Traffic Control. We have received Mayday call. What is your designation and position?"

"Faaa, cancel the Mayday. I want information."

"Your signal is very weak. We are ranging for radio fix. Please key your transmitter at ten-second intervals. Do you copy?"

"Faaa, never mind finding me. All I want is information. When did your radar system go down?"

"Do not understand your request."

"Goddammit. When did your radar system go into malfunction yesterday?" he asked, emphasizing every word.

"Identify."

He had forgotten the boat's call letters. He squinted at the numbers taped on the housing. "This is MMN-D-188. It is urgent I know the precise time you recently lost radar capability. Over."

"MMN-D-188, you have declared Mayday. Please advise of your status."

"Faaa, cancel the damned Mayday. All I want is the precise time of radar malfunction. Please, for chrissakes."

There was a long pause, then: "Our network experienced malfunction at zero-zero-one-five hours, on—" The transmission faded.

"Goddammit!" Cas shouted. Keyed again: "Say again."

"—six-five-eight-nine."

Six-five-eight-nine. Twelve-fifteen, two nights ago. That was it! he thought.

"Faaa, thank you. MMN-D-188, out." Slapping the off switch, he began pulling maritime charts from the radio console. He spread them on the desk and flipped through until he found the one covering the northern Tuamotus.

"What are you doing?" Kiri asked, leaning over his back.

He didn't answer. Moving his finger across the map, he found Faaa Airport, traced an invisible line to the Scripps field station on Mataiva, and then continued on out into open ocean.

"That's it!" he cried triumphantly. "That's where that son of a bitch is."

"What? I don't understand."

"Don't you see? The straight line of the beam. It struck the albatross over Mataiva at the exact moment it hit the Faaa radar beacon. That gives us two coordinate points." He ran his finger through the points again, then out to sea. "That aircraft was somewhere along that line when it fired its beam." He turned and looked up at her. "Even with the drift factor, it's gotta be in the vicinity of that line."

As Cas and Kiri came hurrying up the slope to the plantation house, Nickie and two of his workers were on the roof of one of the storage warehouses. The wind had loosened some of the corrugated iron sheets and they were slapping noisily against the roof beams. Spotting them, Fitzgerald walked over to the edge of the roof, swaying unsteadily in the wind.

"Bonner, you sex-hungry nong," he called down gleefully. "I was wonderin' where you made off to."

They passed without comment. Cas, for one, looked grim. His girlfriend had turned out to be an enemy agent, and somewhere out there was a deadly weapon firing at will. He glanced over at Kiri as they started up the porch steps. "What's your real name?"

"Ilya Vashkin."

"Why didn't you use your goddamned pistol back there?"

She stopped, her head snapping around. "Why the hell do you think?"

He shook his head. "You better hope it wasn't a foolish choice."

Pausing at the screen door, he said, "Stay out here." Then he pulled it open and went in.

Lieutenant Abrams was asleep on the *punee*, snoring loudly. Chief Capisotti was sitting at the table, wolfing down rice and strips of pork. January was sitting off by himself, looking out at the dripping eaves. The chief grinned at Cas, lips glistening with grease. "Hey, Bonner, how you doin'?"

"Where's Woodcroft?"

"Still down at the helo."

Cas glanced at January, then asked the chief, "What's your first name, partner?"

"Ray."

"Just stay where you are, Ray."

"Hell, I ain't goin' nowhere."

"Good." He turned back to Del. "You, can you step outside a minute?"

Del glanced over his shoulder. "What do you want?"

"Outside."

When he returned to the veranda, Kiri was sitting in one of the wide-backed *tutu* chairs, hugging herself in the chilly, moist wind. Del came out, scowling. "What is it?"

"Let's step around here, out of the wind." Cas advanced to the corner of the veranda and January followed. Finding a sheltered spot, Cas sat down on the railing and crossed his arms. "What do you know about cold fusion?"

"What are you talking about?"

"You're a weapons expert, right?"

"Yes."

"Then tell me what you know about a cold-fusion weapon."

"There's no such thing. It's still in the theory stage."

"You sure about that?"

Del fixed him with a glare. "Yeah, I'm sure about that."

"Suppose there was such a weapon. How would it work?"

"What the hell is all this?"

"Would it focus its energy into a very small beam?"

Del shrugged. "Yes, that would be the most efficient way to deliver high-energy components. But why are you asking about this?"

"Would there be a high thermal content in the beam?"

"Extremely."

"Radioactivity?"

"Some, but very little. Fusion isn't fission."

Cas nodded. "Well, I've got a little surprise for you, buddy. You're wrong about there not being such a weapon."

Del stiffened. "What are you talking about?"

Cas nodded his head toward the north. "There's one out on that Russian aircraft of yours. And it's functioning."

Del's face instantly became hard. "What do you know about this? Dammit, what do you *know* about this?"

Cas laid out for him everything Kiri had said, finishing off with the twin coordinate points that went right out into the ocean. He watched Del's face as he talked, especially his eyes. They changed rapidly from wariness to confusion and finally clear shock. Cas paused, waiting for January to say something, to put some sort of capper on it.

But Del merely spluttered, "How in God's name do you know these things?"

"That's not important. But what is is my next question. Can a fusion beam detonate nuclear warheads?"

Del stared in astonishment.

"Can it?"

"Yes," January croaked finally, helplessly. "If it were powerful enough, it could disintegrate firing-system circuits. Possibly even cause a core-element collapse through magnetic-field heat."

Jesus Christ! Cas thought.

Del eyed him hard again. "Who the hell are you, Bonner? How could you possibly—" He stopped abruptly, held up his hands, palms out. "No, wait. I don't need to know any of that. But God, man, do you know what you're saying?"

"I know enough to realize that you'd better get some help out there. Damned fast."

"From where?"

"The *Coral Sea.*"

Del scoffed. "They'd never believe me. I don't have enough proof."

"Then I guess we'd better find this aircraft ourselves and get 'em proof."

"That fool Abrams refuses to fly."

"Then tell him."

They went back into the house together. Capisotti was pouring himself a shot of whiskey from a cut-glass decanter, and he downed it hurriedly when he saw them heading for the lieutenant. Abrams came out of sleep with sour grouch all over his face. He sucked at his tongue a moment, and then glanced up at them.

"What the hell do you want?" He cranked around and saw the chief. "What you doing up here?"

"Lieutenant Woodcroft told me to come get chow, sir," Capisotti said quickly.

Abrams rubbed his face vigorously before looking up again. "So?"

January was so keyed up, he couldn't relate the story coherently. Instead he gave it to the lieutenant in disordered chunks of emotional fact. Even to Cas it sounded like hysterical BS.

Abrams didn't let him finish. "What is this, January?"

"I tell you all of it's true, Abrams. Ask Bonner."

"Bonner? What the fuck does he know?"

Del flared, "Goddammit, you've got to listen to us, you fool. We've got to find that aircraft. Before it kills us all."

"No!" Abrams shouted. "Son of a bitch, I already told you that bird sits where it's at until I get orders."

"But, Lieutenant, can't you understand—"

Cas whistled for him to stop. Shaking his head, he nodded toward the veranda. Without waiting, he pushed through the screen door. Kiri glanced at him questioningly. A moment later, January came out, looking as if he'd just been told he had cancer.

"We've got to make that idiot realize what's at stake here," Del said desperately.

"Not him," Cas snapped. "We'll work Woodcroft."

"He'd never cross Abrams."

Cas ignored the observation. "Can you operate the radar system on that bird?"

"Of course."

"Can you fly the damned thing?"

"No."

Cas turned and looked at Kiri. She shook her head slowly. Just then Nickie came up the steps, grinning drunkenly. His beard was filled with raindrops that glistened like diamonds. "What the bloody hell's goin' on, mates?" he cracked.

Cas stepped down to him and put his arm around the Aussie's shoulders. "We got a little problem here, Nickie. Any chance you know how to fly a helicopter? That one down there in particular?"

Fitzgerald gave him a look as if he'd just smelled new shit. "I wouldn't set foot in one of them bleedin' killers."

Cas released his arm. "Too bad. I guess I'll have to do it."

Nickie peered up at him, swaying slightly. "You bloody crazy Yank. You thinkin' of nickin' off with that bastard?"

"Right."

Nickie threw his head back and roared with laughter. "Oh, you're a rippin' wild mug, Bonner."

Del poked his anxious face forward. "Can you really fly?"

"Hell no."

"My God! That's insanity!"

"Maybe not. I figure all I have to do is get the damned thing into the air. I've watched a buddy of mine fly a chopper enough times to be able to do that much. We're gonna take Woodcroft with us. And unless the lieutenant has steel balls, he'll take over from there."

Mumbling, Del walked away, then immediately returned. Kiri stood up and came over, shaking her head. "*Mon cher*, you're crazy."

"You got a better idea?"

"No."

At that moment Capisotti came to the screen door and looked out, cupping his hands on the screen. "What's goin' on out there?"

"Go have another drink, Ray," Cas said.

The chief shrugged. "You got it."

Cas turned to Nickie. "The minute we start cranking that bitch, Abrams'll come flying out here. You think you can stall him?"

"Aye, mate. I'll hit 'im so hard, he'll think his balls 'ave exploded."

"Thanks."

Nickie's grin snapped off and he gave Cas a stone-sober look. "Watch yourself on that killer, Bonner. Don't go clappin' out on me now."

"I won't."

As Cas, Kiri, and Del headed down to the helicopter, Cas touched Kiri's arm. "Give me your pistol." She hesitated for a second, then stopped, bent down, and came up with the 9-mm. She handed it over, and he studied it a moment. It was very light. He popped the clip, jacked the round from the chamber, returned the clip, and lowered the hammer. It was now empty. He slipped it into the waistband of his trunks.

Woodcroft was curled up asleep on the hammock seats, with

his back facing the bay door. Cas climbed up into the craft, Kiri right behind him. Remaining on the ground, Del walked around the chopper, eyeing it anxiously. He returned to the door. "There's got to be another way," he whispered harshly.

"No other way."

"For chrissakes, man, you're liable to kill us all."

Cas grinned down at him. "What the hell, January? You only die once."

"Jesus, that's a damned asinine thing to say to me right now."

Hearing their voices, Woodcroft lifted his head and looked over his shoulder. Cas walked over and squatted beside the seat.

"What's going on?" the ensign said, uncurling himself and sitting up.

"We want you to fly us out," Cas said.

"What? Where the hell's Abrams?"

"Never mind him. Listen, Woody, you got two choices. Either you fly us out or I will."

"You can't fly this bird. Can you?"

"No."

"Then, shit! What is this, a joke?"

"No joke." Cas slipped the PC-6 from his waistband and set its cold barrel against Woodcroft's cheek.

"What the fuck?" The ensign jumped, eyes shooting open as if someone had just shoved a heated prod up his butt.

"So, which is it gonna be?" Cas said.

"Goddammit, I'm not flying."

"Okay." Cas swung around and yelled to January, "Start pulling the rotor locks." Del's head disappeared.

"I'm getting the hell out of here," Woodcroft yelped, starting to come off the web seat.

"Hold it," Bonner cautioned. "You better strap in. You're coming with us."

"Goddammit, this is kidnapping. You know that? This is flat-out fucking kidnapping."

"That's what it is, all right."

"Oh, man! You guys are gonna be in deep shit you do this."

Cas handed the pistol to Kiri. "Shoot the bastard if he tries to move."

She took the weapon and pointed the muzzle at Woodcroft's temple. He swiveled his head slowly, looked desperately down the barrel as Del scrambled up into the bay. "The locks are out," he croaked.

Cas moved up to the flight-control deck and sat down in Abrams's seat. The space smelling of that familiar odor of electrical wires and instrument packing, reminded him of a submersible's control area. He searched around, squinting at dials and switches. He found a light knob, turned it up. In the glare he located the main power toggle. He switched it on. Instantly the control panel came alive, dials flipping hard over. There was a slight whine as gyros began rolling up.

He blew on his hands. They were steady but cold, and his heart was making solid surges against his rib cage. He furtively touched the control stick. It felt rough under his fingers, as if someone had sandpapered the finger molds. He leaned forward, ran his hands over instrument faces, trying to synch with what he had seen Cowell do a thousand times.

He finally located the engine console—to the left, a whole bank of dials and switches. There were red warning strips like Christmas tree ornaments above the instruments: throttle, heat indicators, pressure gauges, fuel-flow indicators . . . He scanned around the bank. There! The starter button.

Sweat was pouring off him now. His hand hesitated a moment, then he switched on ignition circuits, watched as dials started shimmying. Okay, okay, he thought. Where the hell's the throttles? There. Pumping them in and out, he primed up the engines. Woodcroft hollered, "You're fucking crazy!" Cas ignored him.

He punched the starter buttons. From outside, he heard the instant, compacted whine of the starter blowers come to life, a high-pitched sound and then the deeper, throatier coughing rush as the General Electric T-58-GE-10 turbojets came up. Through the Plexiglas, he saw the huge blades moving, cutting the cockpit light into segments that fused off into the darkness.

His seat was trembling. He could hear the tremble all the way through the Sea King, mixed in with Woodcroft's yelling for him to stop. Cas thought: "Here we go! Here we go!" And realized he was shouting it. He rammed full power in. With the crazy, groin-weightlessness of a fast elevator, they lifted off . . .

10

One hundred miles southwest of the Saber, the *Troikiska*'s loudspeaker crackled: "Control, Sonar, we have a contact. Bearing zero-one-four. Approximate range three-seven kilometers. Depth nine-zero meters."

The submarine had been holding a thousand-foot depth cruise down under a thick thermocline, boiling along at thirty-three knots on an adjusted patrol station. Captain Garesemov peered at the speaker from under his thick eyebrows, then cracked an order: "All stop."

"All stop," the echo came. The *Troikiska*'s deck pitched slightly forward, inertia pulling on her hull as her power went off.

"Rig for silence."

A moment later, confirmation came through the XO's power phone. "Boat secured for silence, Comrade Captain," Lieutenant Korotich said. As the submarine drifted into motionlessness, the only sounds were the tiny electronic pips off her panels and the soft whoosh of her reactor-coolant pumps.

Garesemov turned to his exec, eyes sinister. Earlier, the *Troikiska* had been informed of the disaster in Moscow during her regular satellite-linked position report. "So, what have we here, Stefan?" he said quietly.

The XO spoke into his power phone, listened a moment, then said, "Cavitation signature indicates an American Sturgeon-class attack boat, sir. Bearing holding steady on 268 degrees with approximate speed of 21 knots."

Garesemov sucked spittle against his teeth. Since word of the assassination, he had been working himself up into a withering rage. Still frustrated and shamed by the incident between the French frigate and Forger, his mind-set had inexorably solidified until the itch for an encounter had become an almost physical thing.

Now he eyed his XO with slitted eyes. "So, a Yankee Blueballer. Strolling through the fucking ocean like he owned it. All right, let's give the son of a bitch a surprise. Track him past."

"Yes, sir," Korotich said, and tilted his head to his mike.

Nine minutes later, the sonar watch aboard the U.S. attack submarine, *Scorpionfish*, picked up a diffused contact coming from deep water, faint and distorted. The watch officer ran it through the enhancement filters to clear out ambient interference and then through the BC-10 computer for analysis. He came up with indefinite read due to lots of scatter mixed in with the whistling echoes of a large school of porpoise moving somewhere to the south. Still, his magnetic-anomaly indicators were showing *something* moving below the thermocline. He relayed the news to the attack center.

Lieutenant Evelle "Blue" Winfield, a towering black ex-UCLA All-American, was momentarily standing command-duty officer while the *Scorpionfish*'s captain, Commander Ron Kassau, was in the head. Winfield immediately ordered the power to be cut and asked for an ident. The quartermaster dialed in the power command and a moment later came back with confirmation. The *Scorpionfish* eased to a stop.

Thirty seconds later, Commander Kassau came up, wiping his hands on a towel. Three hours before, his boat had experienced a stop signal on his ELF transmission system. The ELF network originated out of his command base at Bangor, Washington, and used an extremely low-frequency signal transmitted along the ocean floor. Any interruption indicated that he was to come to periscope depth to receive an emergency message from a TACAMO aircraft holding a fixed position off the tip of South America. The subsequent message had informed him of the assassination of Premier Markisov and had ordered him to change his patrol sector to reconnoiter the area adjacent to the French platform before moving down the Marquesas Channel to track the Russian carrier force to the south.

He took the conn. "Sonar, do you have a solid bearing?"

"Conn, Sonar, everything's coming in diffused. We estimate a span fix from two-five-zero through two-seven-nine degrees."

"What's the anomaly reading?"

"Needle divergence at thirty percent."

Kassau glanced at Winfield. "Well, we got *something* out there." He thought a moment. "Let's see if we can get the prick to show himself. Bring her to ten knots and start throwing some ping. Stand by to extend the towed sensor array and ready up for chaff blow on command." Winfield relayed the orders and the sub trembled slightly as she came back into motion. "Give me five degrees down planes."

"Helm, five degrees down planes, aye."

"Final trim at eight hundred feet."

The order echoed and the *Scorpionfish* dug her bow into heavier water with her BQQ-5 dome throwing pulses.

For the last fifteen minutes, the Saber's sensors had been tracking cavitation from both submarines with pulses shooting all over the consoles. The Kamov had focused on the cleaner read first and came up with a solid ident, running off parameters from previous tape fix:

```
ATTACK SUBMARINE: AMERICAN, STURGEON-CLASS, DD
   SCORPIONFISH
HEADING: 268 DEGREES
RANGE: 178 KILOMETERS
   ARMAMENT/ELECTRONICS:
   HARPOON/TOMAHAWK
   MK 63/ MK 48 TORPEDOES
   ASW: (NOM)
   SUBROC
```

The AI assessment came back heavy:

```
DANGER: EXTREME IF IN ATTACK MODE
```

The second cavitation read was diffused, coming up through water-temperature variances. But the Kamov managed enough data to form up an ident:

ATTACK SUBMARINE: SOVIET, ALFA-CLASS, DD TROIKISKA
HEADING: 097 DEGREES
RANGE: 191 KILOMETERS
TAPE PARAMETER: FRIENDLY

Suddenly the cavitation noises stopped, first from one target, then from the other. The Kamov reverted to calculating suppositional positions using drift data. Then a strong cavitation pulse registered, coming from the *Scorpionfish*-designated target. The wash patterns were strong, indicating a descending configuration. The computer focused, brought up an adjusted speed regime and position plot.

Captain Garesemov grinned icily when notified that the Yank was moving again and blowing probes. The fucker plays games, he thought, testing me. He tries to force me to expose myself by getting panicky and moving. All right, asshole, let's play games. "Bring us to ten knots and hold present course."

Korotich relayed. A moment later, the *Troikiska* moved sluggishly out of her drift and came up into movement, homing its sensors to the heat wash of its quarry. Now no longer on silent rig, the captain bellowed his orders, "Sonar, what do we have?"

"Control, target is pinging on quarter-second probes. But he's losing directional integrity because of thermocline degradation." There was a slight pause, then: "We are now getting flutter off a towed array, sir."

Garesemov swore contemptuously and cupped his hands against his temples like horns. "He lets out his big ears, eh, Stefan." Then his eyes went to that dark, dead look of a drunk who has just felt himself insulted. "Lash him," he growled.

An instant later, the *Troikiska*'s DUV-149 sonar dome hurled a fan of powerful electronic pulses through the water.

The *Scorpionfish* had just achieved trim level at eight hundred feet when the pulses struck her. They were so powerful that the AC watch could actually hear the soft pings like glass bubbles gently striking the hull.

Blue Winfield's dark brows came down. "Well, shit, mister! What's this motherfucker trying to prove?"

Kassau yelled, "Sonar, did you make definite fix?"

"Conn, we've got him. He's an Alfa-class boat, bearing off the bow is three-five-nine degrees, approximate range eighteen miles. Approximate depth running one thousand feet."

"Blow chaff. Stand by to give me ten degrees to the right on command."

"Conn, Helm, on command hold for ten degrees to the right, aye."

A few seconds later, a powerful cloud of electronic pulses blasted out of the BQQ-5 dome, literally filling the ocean with sound. Behind its protective shield, the *Scorpionfish* executed a rapid veer from course, a maneuver nicknamed the Barracuda after the propensity of that fish to hover and then disappear as if by magic.

Constant in-feeds of data had been coming into the Kamov. First it detected a new resonance from the designated Friendly target: a clean bearing and position fix and then a sudden, violent splurge of electronic probes from it. It analyzed, perceived Friendly in attack mode. Like a bystander in a street fight, it went into watch hold.

But this was followed by a blast of return pulses from the designated Unfriendly. They came through the sensors like an explosion's outthrow, so powerful it overwhelmed the sensor array with rebounds and forced it into momentary still state. Crazy lines and luminescent cascades appeared on the cockpit monitor screens.

As the splurge went fleeing off into the absorbent medium of the ocean, it gradually faded and the sensors came back onto line, once more throwing in-feed to the Kamov. Cavitation filter showed acceleration mode. Then, suddenly, the prop pulses ceased.

The Kamov ran all over its tape banks, trying to find purpose parameter. An unspecific response came back. As if frustrated, the computer went to the AI for assessment. The subunit considered for a millisecond, then came back:

STATUS: TIME-VARYING ACOUSTIC ENERGY BURST
FREQUENCY DOMAIN RATIO: 600-800 MHZ

```
AMPLITUDE BOOST: 3 GRID BASELINE (10 LOG:GG/GG-0)
DEFLECTION SPHERE: WA INTERFACE/B INTERFACE:
   SCATTER PROJECTION
ABSORPTION LOSS: (EST) 45%
ASSESSMENT: ATTACK MODE///EXTREME///EXTREME
CMR: CATEGORY FOUR RESPONSE
```

The Kamov homed its sensors to high-sensitivity location of the Sturgeon-class target . . .

Garesemov howled more obscenities when the American's chaff blast hit his hull. The fucking Yankee pricks were trying to hide, he thought disgustedly, like little girls covering their hairless cunts. At that precise moment an unfortunate petty officer crossed beside the captain. Frustrated into movement, Garesemov grabbed him by the shirt front and hurled him away. The man skulked off as the skipper, glowering, prowled.

"Sonar," he bellowed. "Where is he? Where *is* he?"

"Control, we are still ranging for locate."

"Find him, dammit."

A moment later, the loudspeaker came on: "Control, we have solid contact. Bearing three-four-three degrees. Approximate depth two-four-two meters."

Garesemov bared his teeth. "What's my depth?"

"Control, we are passing through two-eight-two meters."

So, the Yankee bastard was almost directly ahead of him and just slightly above. He tilted his head back and gazed through lidded eyes. He could feel the thud of his pulse in his head, could see whirling curlicues of light in the darkness. And beyond them, out there, he saw the cylindrical shape of the Sturgeon, mocking him, daring him into an achieve-and-track engagement. He felt his whole body tighten, as if his tissues and muscles were already braced for impact.

He whirled. "Come to new course of zero-one-three," he bellowed. Mock me? Let's see how you react to this! "Go to maximum speed when we attain trim at two-four-meters."

The control room was filled with echoed orders and confirmation relays. Garesemov waited, his jaw working steadily as if he were chewing leather. Then: "Torpedo room, blow tubes two and four."

Korotich's head snapped around in alarm.

Garesemov grinned frigidly at him. "You don't like that, Stefan? Well, let's see what the asshole does when he thinks he's under actual attack."

"But, Captain, we will commit—"

"Do it!"

The XO relayed the order, whispering. Watch seamen jumped to comply. Garesemov hung his thick arms over a conduit line. A moment later there was a rumble through the boat as the empty tubes were flushed with high-pressure air.

Garesemov listened to the wavy, rippling sounds of the blow go away from him and gave a throaty cackle of satisfaction. But then his rage was momentarily banked as a sobering thought struck him. What if the Yankee didn't back off and flee? He felt a moment of uncertainty. What if the chaos in Moscow had triggered American aggression? And that Yank out there was looking to kill?

An icy shiver swept down his back. His single moment of fury had just put him into a potentially for-real combat situation *with him playing a bluff on empty tubes!* Then his lips hardened into a frown. He was fully committed now: the sound of his challenge was already echoing through the ocean. To turn and run would show cowardice.

No, he'd have to play out his bluff, but be prepared if it didn't carry. His voice literally blew out of his mouth: "Seal tubes two and four, and arm three and five. Rig for wire guidance. Fire control, go for lock-on solution."

His command roared through circuit lines, and the seconds moved sluggishly past before acknowledgment came back. "Control, FC, torpedoes three and five in sheath and rigged. We are pinging for lock-on coordinates."

Garesemov stared at his shoes, mind working furiously. Run. Yank, you fucking bastard, run!

Inside the *Scorpionfish*'s sonar room, the four sitting monitor men and the sonar officer all jumped at the sound of the flooding tubes. It came in as cleanly and precisely as jets of steam shooting out in the ocean. Eighteen seconds later, another shock: the Soviet was pinging with one sixteenth-second pulses. Attack mode!

Kassau heard the news and froze in disbelief. His eyes sought

Winfield's and found the same look of dismay there. "Jesus Christ!" Blue uttered.

Kassau came out of his momentary shock. "Blow chaff," he hollered. "Activate torpedo-firing system and set up tubes one and three for wire guidance. Fire control, come up to solution."

As the orders crackled through the sub, Winfield headed for the plot room. As firing coordinator, he would now work with Sonar to calculate target coordinates and range for a firing solution. The junior officer of the deck, a young ensign named Ross Shelly, would now act as conn relay in his absence.

"Sonar, where is he?" Kassau yelled.

"Conn, target holding steady down-bearing line three-four-zero degrees off the bow. Distance approximate fourteen hundred yards, depth one thousand feet."

Dammit! Kassau put his head down, trying desperately to concentrate on what the Russian was doing and what tactical options he had. In a head-on situation, the *Scorpionfish*'s sonar probes would be inadequate for obtaining a proper firing solution. He would have to bring the sub to an angle off the bearing to get range and coordinate data to form a baseline for a fix.

Then it hit him: Ivan would have the same problem. How could he possibly have gained firing solution coming in on a head-on approach? That meant the motherfucker could be bluffing. But was he? Kassau had never run into this before. In the crazy underwater world of achieve-and-track, both sides had always maintained a certain distance, like World War I pilots attaining kill position and then waving off. But this fucker had crossed that unspoken line and actually armed.

He lifted his head. "Rig for fifteen degrees up planes and go to flank speed."

Ensign Shelly's high-pitched voice relayed the command. Helm came back: "Conn, rigged for fifteen up planes and going for flank speed, aye." The quartermaster rang down to the maneuvering room for the new power regime. Confirmation came back. The *Scorpionfish* picked up speed, lifted slightly.

"Stand by to retrieve array line."

"Standing by for BQ retrieval, aye."

"Retrieve."

A soft whine echoed through the ship as the thousand-foot cable of electronic sensors began to be reeled in. "Give me five degrees to starboard," Kassau ordered.

"Five degrees to starboard, aye."

Kassau closed his eyes again and brought up the mental picture of the entire scenario, seeing the Soviet sub, like his own, moving through the vast three-dimensional blackness of the ocean. Yet the paramount question kept flaring through his thoughts like an explosion: Why was the Russian showing such aggression? Bluff or not, Ivan was committing himself to battle. Kassau felt his testicles constrict at a new thought. Had it all started up there? Had the death of the Soviet leader triggered all-out war?

The realization presented him with a terrible dilemma. What the hell was he to do without concrete orders of engagement? Concentrating, he fixed on two necessary actions. The first was to obtain new rules of engagement. But that meant a run for the surface and a momentary hold at radio depth, where he would be vulnerable. That necessitated the second action: remaining in maneuvering control for full engagement.

He came up with a plan. He'd make for the surface, run quick radio relay, then cut into a hard, descending port turn that would bring him onto Ivan's stern. If the Russian held his present course and speed, he'd have a firing-solution angle on him as well as an upside position for a quick turn and broadside shot.

"Belay on array retrieval," he shouted. "How much is already in?"

"Conn, we have two thirds."

That meant over three hundred feet of array was still trailing, he knew. All right, that would give him adequate read, yet not foul up his turning radius. "Depth?"

"Conn, we are passing through six hundred feet and holding ascent angle of fifteen degrees."

"Give me up planes twenty degrees," he shouted. "Rig for red. Stand by for radio-buoy deployment on command."

The annunciator repeaters relayed and came back with speed confirmation. The AC lights dimmed to red as the *Scorpionfish* streaked for the surface.

Kassau ran through Alfa characteristics. He knew the Russian was incapable of torpedo line beyond eighteen degrees of his bow. But he also knew that the Alfa was a very fast boat, capable of over forty knots with a turning radius of less than eighty percent of his own. That meant he'd have to fine-tune his maneuvers in order to stay out of Ivan's bow flare as best he could. His partial array would help him there.

"Fire Control, get up here with FS, dammit."

"Conn, still ranging for parameters."

"Radio, lay up that buoy deployment for fast read. You've got forty-five seconds. I want engagement rules down here."

"Conn, radio, on stand-by and deployment watch."

Kassau turned slightly to check his depth indicator off the AD panel. As he did so, he noted with surprise that a calmness was taking hold of him. He'd be ready for Ivan, come what may.

The Kamov had watched as the American-designated target initiated a rapid ascent maneuver. It calculated a time-to-surface fix utilizing the target's present ascent angle and speed. Working off this data, it then formed up a range and trajectory command and shunted it to the weapons bay. Internal gears whirred softly as the firing barrel came up into hold position, awaiting activation and firing command.

Garesemov's eyes were narrow slits. The Yankee cunt was blowing electronic cover again. Was he running? Bent over the backs of his sonar panel men, he studied the brilliant wash of white patterns cascading all over the screens. "Find him," he roared.

Seconds passed.

"All stop." The submarine instantly tilted forward slightly as she slowed. "Sonar, dammit, do you have him?"

"Control, affirmative. Target climbing on heading off bow of six-zero-six degrees, range two-zero-point-eight kilometers."

Garesemov frowned. Why was the Yank climbing? He should have held depth position, gutted it out, and passed down their port side to go for a baseline coordinate. Wait. Yes, of course, the Yank was heading for radio-buoy depth to consult his superiors. That meant his engagement rules were normal and would remain so.

For the first time in the past few minutes, Garesemov relaxed. He even grinned. There was no war up there, he now knew. His overzealous bluff was going to carry after all. He was certain the Yank would be told to vacate the area in the face of an unprovoked aggressive action by a Russian submarine. That's what they always did.

He hissed contemptuously, once more cocky. "What's my depth?" he called out.

"Control, we are holding on two-four-two meters."

Garesemov considered a moment. "Give me fifteen knots and ten degrees up planes. Sonar, fix and track him until his position is directly amidships."

Korotich managed a timid glimpse at him. The captain leered back at him. "You don't like that move either, eh, Stefan? We give him upside advantage?" He slapped the XO on the shoulder. "It won't matter. When he comes down and around, he'll end up looking at our tubes. We'll give him a parting pucker to his asshole."

"Depth?" Kassau snapped.

"Conn, we're passing through 165 feet, holding fixed planes at 15 degrees."

"Stand by for buoy deployment." He waited for confirmation, then: "Deploy."

The echo of the command was followed by another sibilant rush of sound as the buoy's cable was reeled out. "Conn, we have buoy deployment and preparing for transmission."

Kassau moved aft to the sonar room, the conn instantly taken by Ensign Shelly. As the commander poked his head around the SR hatchway, he asked, "What's he doing?"

"He went dead for a few seconds, skipper. But now he's moving again, coming up on an approximate ten-degree port turn."

The captain frowned. The son of a bitch's tumbled to the radio run, he thought. All right, what's he setting up for? Again he closed his eyes, drew up a battle scenario. With the *Scorpionfish* on the upside, he had a slight advantage. In these high waters, his sonar reads would come clean while Ivan's would get heavy surface-bounce interference. Okay, then once Ivan passed amidships point, he could start into his descending turn. With his partial array out, he'd be able to get a solid coordinate baseline and lock-on before the jerkoff even knew where he was.

Yeah!

He moved on to the radio room and told the watch officer, "Code her out fast. Notify TACAMO we've got a Soviet Alfa boat showing heavy aggressive moves. Including flooding of tubes. Tell them I want some engagement rules down here fast."

"Right, skipper."

Kassau went racing back to the AC.

*   *   *

Several seconds before, the Saber's sensors had picked up the faint, wobbly resonance of the communications buoy and its cable. Instantly the Kamov ran through ident reels:

STATUS: ASCENDING, SMALL METALLIC OBJECT/UMBILICAL LINE
ASSESSMENT: COMMUNICATIONS BUOY//FIRING SYSTEM RELAY

The computer calculated a time-to-surface for the buoy and formed a new firing solution. It sent command to the weapons bay and then went onto hold watch.

Target time-to-surface: fifty-four seconds . . .

Commander Kassau paced around his pedestal seat, head down, absorbing everything that came to him. The AC was tense, no superfluous conversation. Into this compacted atmosphere the speaker blared: "Conn, sonar, target has achieved amidships position and has leveled out. Depth is holding at four hundred and fifty feet."

Goddammit, Kassau thought, the bastard was slowing again. Why? He had figured the Russian might understand his vulnerable position and quickly try to move away. He ran back over his own proposed maneuvers, trying to find a glitch.

"Conn, Radio. Buoy on stable platform depth thirty feet. Receiving TT code pulse, transmission ready."

"Start bringing her out. Trim to a hundred feet."

"Trimming for one hundred, helm."

"Run on count of sixty seconds—now. Radio, transmit."

"Conn, initiating transmission."

"Helm coming to one hundred and steadying . . . we have it. Fifty-three seconds and counting."

"Sonar, where the hell is he?"

"Target clearing down port side, coming to bearing one-nine-eight degrees. Depth holding steady at four hundred and fifty feet, speed on—Hold."

Kassau's head snapped up.

"Conn, we're getting heavy acceleration resonance." A pause, then: "He's really pouring coals."

What? Kassau thought frantically. Was the bastard finally realizing his vulnerability and trying to run?

* * *

The Kamov had encountered a slight trajectory problem. Its infed firing solution for target time-to-surface was no longer relevant. Sensor read indicated the communications buoy had stabilized *below* the surface and was now giving off transmission pulses.

The computer quickly refigured a new trajectory angle for an under-surface shot and hurried it to the weapons bay. The barrel gimbels began readjusting as chamber activation command came in. The chamber began to glow red as absorption heat filtered up through metal components. It throbbed and pulsed, awaiting final firing command . . .

Kassau, his eyes glued to the ship's chronometer, counted the seconds under his breath. 22—23—24— In his mind, he was already executing the lightning-quick maneuvers he would soon be initiating. It was to be a twenty-degree down-angle plunge coordinated into a complete one-eighty turn, a slewing, hard bank, with his sonar probing for coordinate base. If done smoothly, the *Scorpionfish* would level out at four hundred feet, facing the opposite way, and with a solid lock-on of Ivan.

"Conn, Sonar," the speaker blared. "Target executing high-speed turn to port and coming up. Passing through bearing one-eight-five degrees."

Kassau stiffened. The Russian wasn't running. Instead, the S.O.B. had suckered him and was now setting up for an ascending firing fix. Everything he'd planned just went out the window. If he tried a turning dive now, he'd present full broadside.

Countermove options slammed through his brain. He focused on the only one that made any tactical sense. He'd streak for depth now, before the Russian got fully around, and maintain the same radius of turn so he could stay out of the bastard's bow angle. "Rig for emergency dive," he bellowed. "Down planes twenty degrees and left rudder for coordinated one-eighty on one minute."

Orders snapped through the AC. A Klaxon blared loudly and crewmen gripped stanchions and uprights as the *Scorpionfish* drove her bow into the water, heeling sharply to port. Kassau touched his face distractedly, realized his fingers were freezing cold. The bastard was coming in for the kill! "Fire Control, go for solid lock-on. Blow tubes one and three."

"Conn, ranging for lock-on." A slight pause. "We have lock-on."

There was a rush of air as the tubes were blown. "Conn, tubes blown and outer hatch switches on in/up position."

"Open hatches and—"

Suddenly, through the hull and into the attack control space, a jolting wash of vibrations sizzled. Heads snapped up. What the fuck was that? For one tiny second Kassau felt fear rocket through his body. Had they been struck? There was a loud explosion within the ship, followed by a man screaming from the radio room.

In the AC everyone froze as a flash of pure energy seemed to come off the bulkheads and hurtle through the space like invisible lightning. Men's hair stood on end; their bodies felt as if they were glowing. Then monitor screens began exploding, throwing glass shards everywhere. Electrical panels sparked viciously, disgorging smoke. Men struck by the glass dropped to the deck. Kassau found himself staring at the teenage smoothness of Ensign Shelly's face, his eyes wild, his blond hair sticking straight up like the wires on a brush.

The *Scorpionfish*, now fully into her dive momentum, continued driving into deeper water as the faint glow of sunlight that had played across her hull during the radio run quickly faded and she plunged into darkness.

In the AC, the fire Klaxon was booming amid new explosions. Men yelled, more monitor screens blew out. Smoke and automatic extinguisher mist dimmed the red lights until the room seemed to be drenched in the last, fading glimmer of a tropical sunset.

Kassau came roaring out of his fright. "Damage Control, we have explosive malfunction and fire in the AC. Rig for fire. Status reports in here. Now."

As Shelly and his wire hair darted away, the captain felt his body pulsing with energy. His eyes caught sight of a main stanchion. A blue aurora pulsed off the metal, making peculiar little violet rainbows in the smoke.

"Conn, Helm, we're getting runaway. Losing total steerage integrity."

There was a powerful blowout of a panel bank. Its impact hurled a crewman into Kassau's back and both men went down hard on the deck. In trying to get up, the captain felt horrible pain shoot up through his hands as he pressed against the deck. It was scorching hot. He jerked back from it and came to his knees. The heat penetrated his clothing. The air in the attack center was hot as well and burned going into his lungs. He glanced up and gasped. Overhead conduits were melting, dripping red-hot down the bulkheads.

Now full panic ripped through him as he realized the sub's reactor plant was out of control. A terrifying vision hurled across his mind: the ship and everything in it melting down to a boiling, radioactive mass. The vision cut through his panic, drove him into action.

"Rig for emergency surface!" His voice came out just above a whisper. He tried again. "Emergency surface. Blow full ballast on emergency power. Engine, SCRAM your reactor." All around him men were wildly heading out through hatchways, up the stairs to the OPR space in the main sail.

Yet some men were still functioning. Kassau saw the huge body of Lieutenant Winfield charge through the smoke, his hands throwing men out of his way as he headed for the helm. The captain dove after him, his feet beginning to numb with heat pain.

Both helmsmen were gone. The dive officer, a skinny, bald lieutenant covered with blood, was trying to bring back both wheel pedestals. Winfield took hold of the starboard wheel just as Kassau entered the helm space. He ordered the DO to go aft and check the ballast panels, then dropped into the port helmsman's chair and began pulling back the pedestal. Neither he nor Winfield spoke, their faces pouring sweat in the dim red light.

Kassau heard the sudden rumble as high-pressure air began gorging the ballast tanks. The pedestal wheel trembled violently, followed an instant later by a sharp jolt from overhead. The submarine began to roll to the right.

"Goddammit!" Winfield screamed, straining against the wheel. "Bring her out of it!"

But they couldn't hold her. The roll continued, then abruptly steepened. Kassau, stunned, stared at a single dial forward the helm. Completely untouched, still polished and clean, it indicated that the starboard fairwater plane on the sail structure had jammed into full vertical position. He continued staring at it, overcome by terror as he and it and the rest of the *Scorpionfish* turned completely upside down.

There was a thunderous rumble as the ballast tanks, now completely open to the sea, began to vent their air. The boat shook and went on shaking. The lights went out. In the darkness, Kassau still clung to the control wheel while arcs and spirals of electrical shorts continued to crackle and explode around him.

It would take the *Scorpionfish* thirty-two minutes to plunge all the way to the ocean floor eight thousand feet below. By that time her reactor would go into contamination, and the steam explosions would blow out the after bulkheads. A few quick-thinking men would try to seal off compartments manually, but their efforts would be futile. The air system within the sub was soon contaminated with battery fumes. Every hand would be dead before she smashed into the ocean floor.

Ten seconds before the fairwater plane froze in full vertical, the fire-control system had gone into malfunction, shorting throughout its entire network. As it did so, tube hatches were flung open and torpedoes one and three were fired out into the ocean.

Side by side, they bore straight through the water for two hundred yards off the wire link. Then their onboard guidance systems, running in a low-speed search mode, homed to the large metal hull of the *Troikiska*, which was only two thousand yards away. Both torpedoes executed a one-hundred-and-four degree turn to the left, went into kill mode speed, and hurtled toward the Russian submarine.

One minute and sixteen seconds before, Captain Garesemov had been watching incoming data screens as the *Troikiska* went hammering through a hard turn to port, going for her setup. When the Yank did what Garesemov knew he'd do—execute a sharp, descending one-eighty—the prick would be broadside, like a fucking duck landing on a pond.

The captain chuckled maliciously. Of course, the bastard would then go into a deep dive, trying to get out of bow angle. Idly, Garesemov considered whether he would follow him down, constantly giving him bow to make his balls shake some more. Sooner or later, of course, he'd have to break out of the pattern and that would present a momentary vulnerability. But it wouldn't matter. He was absolutely certain now that the American only wanted away. Undoubtedly, at this very moment, he was shitting his pants.

He started another icy chuckle. He never got it out. There was the clear sound of an explosion. Unknown to him, it was the Saber's beam blowing through the surface water and imploding the American's communications buoy. Everybody in the command center jerked in surprise at the clean, powerful sound filled with hissing resonances and convoluted acoustic waves that impacted against the *Troikiska*'s hull.

A few seconds later, the loudspeaker blared, wrapped in a static wash: "Control, there has been an explosion in target's communications vehicle."

The captain's head jerked around. What the hell? There was no ordnance aboard a comm buoy or anything else that could cause that much blowout. Had the damned thing struck something? A mine? Then a new thought hit him: Was it a new American weapon?

"All stop," he hollered.

The command was obeyed instantly, and again the *Troikiska* pitched slightly forward as her power came off and she began gliding.

"Stabilize trim."

"Stabilizing on planes . . . we have trim."

"Depth?"

"Steady on one-two-one meters."

"Control, Sonar, target is executing steep dive and angled turn to port."

More sounds came through the water. They pinged gently against the hull, yet with enough force so that those in the command center heard soft, crackling pops.

Sensing something radically out of sequence here, Garesemov searched wildly for reasons. The Yank was going into a rapid dive before expected. But what else was he doing? And why?

"Bearing?"

"Control, target passing through three-five-four degrees."

"What is projected turn rate?"

"Thirty degrees per minute." A few seconds slid past. "On present descent rate, full head-on position will be achieved in five-point-four minutes."

Garesemov was jolted by the thought that he might have miscalculated the entire scenario. Perhaps he did intend to attack.

"Go to three knots and track," he roared.

Before acknowledgment could be echoed, the loudspeaker blared, "Control, we're getting heavy ballast venting. Rebound indicates an increase of target mass."

Increase of target mass? Garesemov wondered. What the—son of a bitch! he realized. The American was *rolling* in the water, showing his beam profile. And then he himself actually heard the faint, distant rumble of the ballast venting.

"Control, target is in inverted position."

Garesemov hissed through his teeth and a glint of amusement flashed through his eyes. The poor fucker was in malfunction. A fatal one, from the looks of it.

"Control, we're picking up torpedo-launch blow resonance and high-speed screws. Bearing three-five-zero degrees off the bow."

Every head in the room jerked upright. For one crazy moment Garesemov was stunned into speechlessness, unable to believe what he'd just heard. Then he came out of it, hurling commands: "Full emergency up planes. Blow EDB chaff and come to flank speed."

As if jabbed with electric shocks, men all over the command center jumped to obey. Status confirmations came cutting through the air as the *Troikiska* lifted her bow sharply and headed for the surface.

Five seconds passed. Then Garesemov and everybody else in the CC heard, very faintly, the sound of the incoming torpedoes: a soft *shushing*, humming sound as they drilled two-foot holes in the ocean at fifty-five knots.

"Control, torpedo distance nine-zero-one meters. Two screws. Cavitation on homing mode."

The captain shivered. Nine hundred meters away was much too close for evasion maneuvering. Now it was a race. Would they reach the surface before strike? The torpedoes would kill by exploding beneath his sub, creating a fatal pressure bubble. If he could reach the surface and vent hatches, some of the crew might live.

Then something cold and hard entered his intestines: the certain knowledge that he was going to die. As he balefully scanned his command room, he saw terrified eyes everywhere staring back at him. "Rig for missile impact," he said quietly.

The command was obeyed with frenzied quickness. Throughout the sub compartment doors were slammed shut and dogged. All unnecessary electrical circuits were shut off. In the engine spaces, SCRAM switches were thrown to the reactor plant, and power was instantly shunted to the emergency battery backup. Status confirmations came echoing back like ricocheting bullets as men braced their bodies, tried desperately to maintain control over themselves.

When the *Troikiska* was less than seventy-five feet from the surface, the two torpedoes exploded directly below and slightly aft of her hull. A gigantic vacuum bubble formed. Caught within the sudden pressure drop, the Russian submarine literally blew apart. Seams in her outer hull were ripped open, hurling gyrating chunks of plating through the water. Inboard, compartment bulkheads were sundered and their rivets flung like bullets. All electrical systems exploded in blue arcs. Crewmen were thrown toward the overheads by the concussion and then they dropped back in crumpled heaps. Blood and internal tissue blew through body apertures, sprayed across smoking panels.

The forward section of the *Troikiska* continued hurtling upward and rammed through the surface like a breaching whale. When its momentum was spent, it plunged back down and lay on the surface for a few moments, disgorging huge bubbles of air and steam and bits of debris. Finally, almost gently, it dropped below the surface and started its long, fragmented plunge to the bottom.

11

Apparently, the metal content of Lieutenant Woodcroft's testicles was quite high. It took him nearly three and a half minutes to lunge wild-eyed into the Sea King's cockpit and wrest the controls from Bonner. He did so none too soon.

Cas had managed to get the helicopter airborne, straight up like a mortar shot, but as soon as it cleared the dampening effect on the wind created by the nearby groves, the aircraft jolted sharply and heeled hard to starboard, the blades cracking through the air. Cas held on, trying to stabilize by putting as little pressure on control units as he could manage. Somehow he got the thing moving forward, but only skimming just over the tops of the palm trees, the leaves scraping loudly on the underbelly.

Everybody gave a general gasp of horror and clung frantically to stanchions and web belts. Kiri missed a web and fell down right onto her buttocks. Beyond her, Del was coiled around a stanchion, his face pressed against the slender metal tubing.

Up front, Cas said, "Oh, shit!"

Woodcroft let out a bellow. "Jesussweetmother, we're all going to die!"

Cas was desperately trying to find the altimeter gauge. In his frenzy he thought that if he found it, it would magically tell him that they were very high. Meanwhile, his feet were jabbing with excruciating timidity at pedals, his hands barely touching the stick. As the aircraft rolled and pitched, the engine roaring and fading, he muttered, "Oh, Christ, why did I do this?"

Suddenly something crashed against the helo's struts, followed by a snapping of coconut fronds lashing across the cockpit windows. Letting out an involuntary yell, he reflexively twisted away from the impacting palm branches. In so doing, he somehow manipulated the controls and felt the sudden lifting sensation in his groin as the helo boosted straight up again.

It kept going up. He became aware of the changing pitch of the sound off the blades, clearer, more solid, as if they were in wide-open space. He settled into the seat, thinking, All right, all right. Here we are. The stick trembled in his hand like a newly boated marlin and jostled all over hell. One red light blinked on the panel, then another. A loud warning buzzer cried out at him. Over it he heard Woodcroft scream: "Hold power and trim her up! Trim her up, you stupid fuck!"

Cas ran his trembling fingers over the throttles. The engines wound up and one red light went out. Trim? Trim? he wondered. Where in Christ is the trim button? He furiously squinted at dials and switches, but couldn't make out the worn, unintelligible words.

The Sea King yawed violently to the left and started to roll. Again he punched hesitantly at controls. Sweat was coming off his face like water out of a squeezed sponge. He lifted his head. "Woodcroft! Get your fucking ass up here!"

The lieutenant's face suddenly appeared over his shoulder, grotesque with rage and terror. "You son of a bitch!" he roared into Cas's face. "I'm gonna have your ass. I'm gonna have your goddamn motherfucking son of a bitching ass!"

He hurled himself into the copilot seat. Hands flying, he took over. The helo instantly leveled up, the engines evening out. Now they hurled forward, skimming through darkness.

Cas rested his chin on his chest. Sweat covered his entire body, and a large droplet slipped into his eye and stung it. He drew in a deep breath, filled up every square inch of his lungs before letting it out. His heart started quieting.

Glancing aft, he saw Kiri and Del both sitting on the deck,

looking into space. As he watched, Del pulled himself up onto the radar console man's seat and fell into it. When Kiri looked at Cas, he winked.

Woodcroft was glaring at him. "You stink," he snarled.

Cas grinned back at him and poked a finger into his ribs. "Gotcha."

"Fuck you," Woodcroft said.

Commander Ron Sorrel, CO of the small U.S. Navy satellite-tracking station on Phoenix Island, fifteen hundred miles southeast of the Hawaiians, was awakened by his Yeoman First Class, Stan Evans. "Sorry to roust you, sir, but Chief Hedges says he's got something you ought to see."

Sleepily, the handsome, brown-haired young officer got out of bed. Wearing only his skivvies and a baseball cap, he and Evans walked across the compound to the main communications Quonset. The night was warm, with the faintest touch of rain in the air, and high, lacy clouds from a storm far to the south skimmed across the face of the waning moon. In its light the neatly painted white stones marking the walkways looked like balls of ivory.

Electronics Chief Don "Big D" Hedges was hunched over a code machine when they came in. The comm shelter was twice the normal length, filled with radio consoles, computer banks, and tracking displays. Hedges twisted around. "Sorry about getting you up, sir. But we got something hot here. Came in on P-SS USAF channel."

"You got decode yet?" Sorrel asked, bumming a cigarette from one of the other panel men.

"That's one of the problems. My update book doesn't jibe. But there's something weird about the transmission. It was broken and very short. Came in out of normal sequence schedule."

"What do you think?"

"I got a feeling there's a sub in trouble out there somewhere."

"What's your code sched?"

"Zero-five hundred, sir."

"No wonder. Pearl changed up two days ago." He turned to the yeoman and tossed him a set of keys he wore with his dog tags around his neck. "Go get my CS log from the safe. And don't stop to look through my pussy magazines."

After Evans hurried out, Sorrel wandered around, checking

update tracking reels. Besides Chief Hedges, there were two men lounging casually on watch. Seeing a can of Budweiser was on one of the men's consoles, Sorrel picked it up and took a long pull.

Evans returned with the codebook. Sorrel read off input numbers and Hedges fed them into his decode machine. Then they reran the transmission. The sound of it was a wavering bass, like that from a record player that had been slowed to a near stop. The printed decode came out on a yellow strip of paper.

When the machine clicked off, Sorrel tore the strip off and read it. Frowning, he handed it to Hedges. The message, prephrased with automatic ident and transmission data, said:

```
PA TRANS OPEN/CODE INTER (23LL2//2345)
PEARL COMM: USAF—691 SCORPIONFISH: ET/OOS 691
TIME: 1123Z

MESSAGE FOLLOWS:

HAVE MADE CONTACT (ATQ) RUSSIAN SUBMARINE . . . ID: ALFA
CLASS . . . BEARING: ZERO-NINE-FOUR DEGREES . . . TARGET
CONTINUALLY EXECUTING RAPID DEPTH-CHANGES—TUBES CLEARED—
PERCEIVE AGGRESSIVE INTENT . . . AM COMING TO FIRING POSITION
ON . . . ON . . . ON . . .

STOP

STOP
```

Hedges looked up. "Jesus, Commander, this looks like he got nailed."

"Get on the horn to Pearl," Sorrel snapped. "Relay this in."

As Hedges leaped out of his chair, Sorrel bummed another cigarette and stood there with it unlit, scowling.

The Old Lion of Leningrad was trembling with exhilaration as he ensconced himself in Secretary Markisov's private office. It had all been much easier than he had anticipated. Paralyzed by the power vacuum, men eagerly responded to someone, anyone, issuing orders.

And he *was* giving orders, with lightning swiftness: commands for brutal suppression of ethnic unrest with thirty-four Red Army units; widespread arrests of Markisov supporters; instructions to TVD commanders to come up into war-contingency alert. To implement this last set of orders, he activated STAVKA, the wartime state of the Supreme Military Headquarters.

Four hours earlier, GRU officers loyal to him had taken over the entire Council of Ministers building, barging in swiftly, boots cracking, machine pistols bared. Markisov's huge staff went into immediate shock, and the few gutsy enough to pose a challenge were instantly hauled off to the holding cells in the Kremlin Arsenal. Markisov's personal aide, Trofimov, stood firm, only to be clubbed to the floor and carted after the others. The rest of the staff, seeing the fate of their colleagues, cooperated with surprising alacrity.

The real coup came when Bardeshevsky obtained Markisov's personal transmission codes. With these he had the power of the general secretary's office to control every division and command headquarters. And people snapped to, just as they had in his World War II days.

Bardeshevsky prowled around the office, smelling a total victory in the air. With him were ministers Kandalov and Herzen and General Poporonov, senior staff officer of the Supreme Military Command under Marshal Petrov. He was now openly issuing orders in the marshal's name, for Petrov, barely conscious from his wounds, had refused to cooperate with the usurping regime. GRU officers simply sealed off his hospital wing, isolating him and thus giving Poporonov command base control.

The general secretary's office, which was being deluged with updating status reports from around the world, now received an urgent incoming request from Red Fleet headquarters in Vladivostok asking for parameters for Pacific deployments. Within the overall scenario was a high-priority interject for definite orders to Admiral Turesky's Skadra HC-3, presently in the Polynesians.

Bardeshevsky called for maps. He studied them intently, then glared at Poporonov. "Run his ships right through the fucking French islands. Challenge the goddamned swine to come out and fight."

The order was sent, but minutes later, Vladivostok came back with questions. Turesky's order would initiate provocation. Should the Red Fleet move into bastion positions east of Sakhalin Island

and south to the Sea of Japan? Further, should Cam Ranh sortie carrier support for Turesky's *skadra*?

Bardeshevsky's answer was one word: "Affirmative."

For Professor Titov, terror had reached a new plateau.

He had witnessed the carnage in Red Square from his window, after the first explosion had drawn him from his work. The second and third had shattered windows throughout the building. Immediate confusion had erupted in the outer corridors. Titov, shaken, rushed out. People were dashing out of offices, faces white. Someone yelled that the general secretary had been killed. The words pierced Titov to the heart. Dumbly, he withdrew to the sanctum of his room.

Ever since Markisov's departure earlier that morning, the professor had been assiduously monitoring incoming feed, still filtering out anything from Polynesia. So far, nothing had indicated Saber activity. Moreover, he noted that a storm had crossed into the Capricorn, and Turesky was holding in storm deployment just south of French waters.

Within a few minutes after the explosions, however, his machines were flooded with incoming local transmissions rapping into the teletype and computer modules. The secretary's command to link him with high-priority intercepts still held, but the rush of data was so heavy, the machines were shunting off information into reel-storage components.

By eight-thirty, Titov could see the repercussions of the bloodbath in Red Square. Reports came in of demonstrations and even rioting in numerous cities throughout satellite and border republics and at least two revolts in Red Army garrisons. Confusion reigned everywhere.

By ten o'clock in the morning, he heard renewed activity in the outer corridors. He chanced a peek. GRU soldiers and officers filled the halls and men were clustered throughout the general secretary's suite of offices. Others scurried in and out of Markisov's personal office next door. Closing and locking his own door, he went to the inner wall to listen, but heard only a soft murmur of voices.

Within minutes, his machines began showing a divergence in the incoming transmissions. Outgoing commands were being issued directly through the secretary's staff equipment, some carrying his personal code. For an exhilarating moment Titov interpreted that to mean the rumor he'd heard of Markisov's death had been wrong. His hope was short-lived.

A pattern quickly developed in the outgoing orders. It clearly showed the commands could not have come from Markisov. They were too aggressive, brutal. Police contingents in Latvia, Georgia, and Azerbaijan, fortified by elements of the Red Army, were being ordered to put down demonstrators at all costs. Moscow itself was being put under martial law, and dissidents were being rounded up. As Titov studied the orders, he saw that key members of the Politburo known to be supporters of Markisov were being targeted. Clearly, a purge was developing.

By noon Titov's anxiety reached fever pitch. It was then he noted an even more ominous development coming across his machines. Whoever was in command was now initiating orders beyond the USSR. The first move was a diplomatic note to the French, in effect, an ultimatum! Immediately afterward, orders were sent to all commanders along the Warsaw Pact frontier to come to Orange Alert and begin power exercises.

But the worst was yet to come. At one o'clock Titov's computers intercepted a command communiqué to the Red Fleet headquarters at Vladivostok. A carrier force was to sortie from Cam Ranh Bay and rendezvous in the northern Solomons with Admiral Turesky's group. The second part of the order brought Titov right out of his chair. Turesky was commanded to pass directly through the Societies as a deliberate show of power and defiance to the French. That would bring Turesky's nuclear-laden vessels within range of the Saber!

Someone suddenly pounded on the door, and Titov whirled, startled. Another flurry came and a man's voice shouted, "Open up in there." The doorknob was jiggled. Then the man swore and went away. A moment later, he was back. "Kick it in," he snapped.

Something heavy struck the door. Again. Then it flew open, hurling wood splinters from the frame. A tall GRU colonel barged in, followed by two soldiers with Kalashnikov assault rifles.

When the officer saw Titov, he barked, "Who the hell are you?"

Stricken, the professor could only stare back at him.

The colonel came forward, wading through the drifts of computer printouts strewn over the floor. "What is this crap?"

Titov found his voice. "Colonel, I'm Professor Andrik Titov of

Moscow University. I am here on a personal assignment for the general secretary."

"What kind of assignment?"

"It is very complicated."

The officer turned his head slightly and ordered, "Arrest this man." Instantly one of the soldiers stepped around him and roughly grabbed Titov by the arm.

"Please, Colonel," Titov cried out. "I must speak with whoever is in charge here."

"Out," the officer snapped. "Put him in the Arsenal and guard this room until I can send someone up to tell me what all this shit is."

"Please!"

The soldier dragged him through the doorway and pushed him ahead down the corridor to a small elevator. It went down very slowly. On the main floor, Titov was taken through a door beside the main entrance. The soldier prodded him across an expanse of lawn and scattered apple trees to the twin-storied Arsenal. The largest structure in the Kremlin, it had arched windows under which were placed cannons that had been captured during Napoleon's invasion of Russia. Inside the building, they crossed a high, domed hall and went into a large room bisected by a heavy screen. The soldier spoke with an officer, and then a brutish-looking sergeant with a bald head took the professor down some stairs.

They entered a narrow corridor with a string of bare, dirty lightbulbs down the middle. The walls were made of stone, and there were small cells on both sides. This had once been the famous dungeon of Peter the Great, where hundreds had been tortured to death.

Titov could hardly move. His insides were mush and his legs trembled. As he passed the cells, he saw clean-shaven men, all in civilian suits. He thought he glimpsed a well-known Politburo member. Near the end a KGB officer was standing close to the bars, dressed in full parade uniform. He watched them insolently as they passed.

The cell Titov was shoved into was no larger than an oversized closet. The walls were stained with moisture. It had a bucket and a rusty pipe with a spigot. Below it a trough ran under the door to flush the water into a larger trough in the corridor. A single red blanket was rolled up on the floor. When the sergeant slammed the door, the sound echoed back up the corridor.

Titov stood a moment, feeling stark terror and despair. Inhaling, he took in the acidic stench of excrement and disinfectant, of ancient metal. The walls seemed to reek of dark violence, the faint memory of agony imbedded in the stone. In another moment Titov had blacked out and crumpled to the floor.

Admiral Turesky received the command to move north with ambivalence. On the one hand, he was relieved that Moscow seemed to be reestablishing command. Ever since word had reached the ship of Markisov's assassination, he had been churning with anxious confusion. Under Russian military command structure, a field commander could never act on his own. Everything had to be cleared through channels, all the way back to Moscow.

Still, the actual command deeply disturbed him. To move directly through the Society Islands instead of transiting the Polynesians south of Cook Island and Samoa was tactically idiotic. His *skadra* was potentially exposed to attack from either or both French and American strikes, and he was deprived of any open-sea maneuvering room. No, he decided, the man who ordered this knew nothing of naval warfare.

But at least it was an order. And with any luck, it would get him out of this damnable situation. Turesky turned and scanned the dark ocean and the running lights of his vessels scattered beyond him. It was a decent battle group, he knew, comprised of the twin Slavas-class cruisers, the *Asov* and *Izentzi*, six Krivak- and Riga-class frigates, two auxiliary fuelers, and the gigantic replishment vessel *Berezina*. But they were a long way from home and about to enter enemy waters in an American-dominated sea.

He signaled the *Minsk*'s skipper to his seat. "Vitaly, redeploy the units. Bring the *Asov*, two frigates, and the replishments into tight formation. And put the *Izentzi* on point with a flank of frigates on the east. We're going to slice through the islands in column and at full speed. I want to break westward as soon as we clear the Leewards."

"Yes, Admiral."

"Get Koik up here."

A moment later, the carrier's wing commander appeared and snapped to attention. As Turesky explained what they would be doing and why, Koik's face was devoid of response.

"Toomas, I want constant air cover and two-minute alert status."

"Yes, sir. Will we continue the search runs?"

Turesky thought a moment, then nodded. "Yes. We've been lucky so far, so let's keep at it. But I want nobody without ordnance now. If you have to, sacrifice range. I also want a two-flight far out on our starboard quarter. If the Americans vector their fighters in this direction, I want to know about it instantly." The admiral eyed his wing officer steadily. "Be prepared for anything. This could be prelude to open war. You understand?"

"Yes, sir."

The Sea King made its way steadily northwest, slowly making big zigzags at two hundred feet. Sunrise found them slightly east of Bonner's station on Mataiva. As he looked out, he saw that the storm had moved on, pulling long swell chains from the south in its tail. The tops of the swells were dished, and the sunlight bounced off them, giving the ocean a deep opaqueness.

Woodcroft had resigned himself to being a hostage. But every now and then he'd glance back with a sly smirk. Sooner or later the helicopter was going to need fuel, and then he'd have to turn back to Arutua. He couldn't wait to see what would happen then.

Meanwhile, Del was hunched over the APN 130 radar console, sweeping the ocean with probes with a dark, brooding intensity. His console was a constant checkerboard of blips as *motus*, tiny islets, and an occasional native fishing canoe came up. Running rapid ident read calibrated to metallic parameters, he was constantly discarding targets. Only once had he gotten excited, when the radar had picked up a fair-sized metallic object in a *motu* field. But it turned out to be the rusting remains of a steel-hulled copra schooner that had obviously gone aground years before.

Bonner and Kiri hung out the bay door, web straps around their waists, scanning through binoculars. It was hard on eyes as the sun threw pinpoints of harsh light back through the lenses, leaving pulsing throbs on their retinas. Finally, disgusted, Cas offered Del a suggestion. Since they were looking for a surface object, why not go down on the deck for a while? Maybe they could pick up a silhouette fix.

Del agreed. He set up his radar probes for pure horizontal and informed Woodcroft to descend. The Sea King dropped heavily and leveled out at forty feet. The improvement was immediate to Cas. Now they were able to scan the horizon and everything back of it with images coming in clean and sharply etched.

Two minutes later, Woodcroft hollered something. Del leaned over, listened a moment, then signaled Cas to come forward. Cas hauled himself back and crawled up.

"There's something screwed up on the under side of the fuse-lage," Woodcroft shouted over the engines. "I just felt something give and I'm getting drag." He shot him a glare. "You probably damaged our after section, you prick."

"You want me to check it out?"

Woodcroft nodded. "Web yourself and climb out on the spon-son. From there you'll be able to see the entire stern."

"Right."

"Check the rotor and tail-wheel assemblies. If you don't see anything, come back and go down into the after bay. The hatch is behind the stern bulkhead."

Cas eyed him wryly. "Make sure you keep this bitch level. I don't want to go falling through those blades."

For the first time Woodcroft grinned. "You got it."

Cas proceeded to double-line two web belts, one around his waist, the other to hold onto. Then, with Kiri giving slack, he went out the bay door, inching around the after portion of the starboard auxiliary fuel tank. The down rush of the main blades whipped savagely at him, and their sound was a constant, chopping thunder.

Though there were few handholds on the smooth tank, by bracing his body between it and the main fuselage, he managed to get a view of the stern rotor. It seemed all right. But the curved, pregnant duck bulge of the hull prevented him from seeing the bottom side of the fuselage. For that he'd have to go all the way down to the sponson strut.

He tried several times, hands clawing at tiny rivet heads in the tank. It was no use, it was too slippery. He signaled to Kiri to brace up. Then, pivoting on the hand line at his waist, he swung himself upside down. It was a grotesque position, what with the mirage-like whirl of the giant main blades above his feet and the horizon rocking back and forth like a blue ceiling. Still, he got a quick view of the undercarriage. The after bay door was open.

He swung upright again and, going hand over hand, returned to the ship. "Your after door's open," he told Woodcroft.

"Shit! All right, go aft through the upside hatch and see if there's any interior damage. You won't be able to pull the bottom door shut, so don't fall out."

The inside hatch was on the after side of the main cabin bulkhead. Cas slipped through a small oval opening in the wall. The space was dark and smelled of frame packing and cable grease. He could hear the rush of the airstream coming up through the bottom door.

The hatch was flat on the deck with a swing lock in a shallow recess. It was frozen. Using the back side of his fist, Bonner finally got it moving. He twirled it, lifted the hatch, and leaned into the lower bay.

Into his face was thrust the muzzle of a Skorpion MP-3 machine pistol. Behind it were the feverish gray eyes of Valentin Katevayo.

12

Like Viktor Turesky, Admiral Passmore aboard the *Coral Sea* had already crossed that invisible line that fighting men somehow sense as a situation heads inexorably toward confrontation. Already he was psyching up for it, like a boxer warming up for a match. And when satellite and recon reports showed that the *Minsk* force had broken out of its holding pattern and was now headed straight for the Societies in speed, his mental gears clicked up another notch.

Judging from the stream of communiqués he was receiving from COMMPAC, it was evident Washington was also getting antsy. Information on Markisov's assassination was still hazy, but field intelligence sources were beginning to relay evidence of sudden hard-line policy shifts toward internal dissidents, plus evidence of arrests of Markisov supporters. That could only mean the Old Guard had gotten the upper hand.

Meanwhile, in the Pacific, things were coming to a head. A strong carrier force had been sent out of Cam Ranh into the South China Sea, undoubtedly to support the *Minsk* against flank attack from the French flotilla coming through the Strait of Malacca. Further, a broken message had been picked up from an

American attack sub that said it was being aggressively run on by a Russian sub. Had it been sunk? No one knew for sure, but it looked ominous as hell.

At this point, Passmore's foremost concern was the French reaction when the Russkies steamed through the Societies. Would AlPaci Command dare challenge Turesky's ships? If they did, the *Coral Sea* would undoubtedly be ordered in. That possibility made Passmore wince. Twin carrier flotillas and a Mickey Mouse strike force from Papeete all mashed together in archipelago waters without seaway to deploy? That would be a massacre all around.

At 0400 hours, he received a Joint Chiefs' red-op instructive via Pearl COMMPAC that ordered him to head slowly west and launch daylight interceptor runs toward the Leeward Islands of the Societies. He was also informed that CVN-68, with the *U.S.S. Nimitz* as flag, was already making a sortie to take up support positions off Radak and the Marshall Islands.

For the *Coral Sea*, Passmore knew, the assignment was more saber rattling. Except this time Washington wanted more aggressive tactics. Since the Russians apparently hadn't already gotten the message, JCS wanted to make sure the bastards knew that the United States would not sit still and allow a sea war to erupt in the South Pacific. And they wanted it done before the mess escalated out of hand.

With dawn only forty-five minutes away, he gathered his staff in flag op: *Coral* skipper Stockdale, Commander Gretton, and CAG Waltham. He laid out the overall mission, then turned to Waltham. "JCS wants some teeth bared this time, Dick. If you make contact, maintain normal rules of engagement, but show Ivan some bounce moves. Let the pricks know what you can do if you have to."

Waltham nodded. "What if they jump the bait and engage, Admiral?"

"My impression of JCS is they don't expect that." Passmore shrugged. "But if it comes to it, kick ass. And do it fast. Make a point."

The three officers eyed one another and nodded.

Passmore went on: "All right, gentlemen, we'll go for strike launch at first light. I know that limits time, Waltham. But get your men up here as soon as possible."

*   *   *

Lieutenant Danny "Ditto" Wolfe, strapped into his F-14 Tomcat fighter, was set up on the five-alert section of the *Coral Sea*'s
flight deck. All his systems had been checked and preflighted.
Now he and his radio intercept officer, Lieutenant Phil "Bubba"
Penskie, were waiting for the launch order.

Wolfe was brimming with nervous energy. The short prestrike
briefing had been heady, for Captain Waltham hadn't minced
words. They'd be making close-in dry-fire runs on Forgers, tick-
ing the Russkie suckers on the ass. Wolfe was delighted to ride
wing for the CAG in a four-flight with the other two Tomcats
laying far out for cover. Afterward, he and Waltham had huddled
a few moments to go over procedure. They would go in on the
deck until contact was made, then throw some fancy shit at the
Forger pilots. Shake 'em up good.

His earphones suddenly crackled: "Red Javelin, Two-Zero-
One, Vanguard Strike, go secure."

Wolfe keyed: "Roger." He flipped his radio scrambler and waited
for the synchronization tone. When he got it, he keyed again:
"Vanguard Strike, Two-Zero-One is secure."

The four-flight was updated by the carrier's combat decision
center. Then the flight-deck loudspeaker blared: "Launch strike!
Launch strike!" Four minutes later, Captain Waltham was hurled
from catapult one and Wolfe came right after him.

As the bow flashed by beneath him, Wolfe hauled in the landing gear and trimmed up, nose slightly high. He scanned his
instruments and saw no warning lights. Accelerating, he brought
the flaps in and followed Waltham, their noses pointed to the sky.

At fifteen thousand feet, the four Tomcats formed up in echelon. Ditto checked right, left. The sky was a faded blue, washed
with new sunlight. Against it the other aircraft looked perfectly
motionless, suspended. Forming data links with the Hummer,
the E-2C electronics surveillance aircraft flying the out line, they
were vectored to course one-niner-two. Ten minutes later, Waltham split the flight, and he and Wolfe dove for the sea.

The early morning sun low off their port wings threw the
shadows of the two F-14s onto the ocean twenty-five feet below.
With the light coming in at such a shallow angle, to Waltham
the sea chop had a three-dimensional solidity, making it look like
inky granite flashing past.

The covering Cats, with lieutenants "Sally" Lane and Dayton Dietrich, were on flank position sixty miles to the northwest.

Waltham's mission scenario was simple. While Lane and Dietrich stood off at eight thousand feet, he and Wolfe would hug the deck until a bogey contact was made. As definite ID was secured, they would execute hard verticals and cross close by the incoming fighters. Once past, they'd go into high-low split, with "Banger" —Waltham's nickname from his days at the navy's Fighter Weapons School—holding the vertical as Wolfe broke into a hardass horizontal turn.

The maneuver, if timed perfectly, might jolt the Soviet pilots into thinking they were under attack. That would be a reasonable assumption with two American fighters suddenly shooting up at them from the radar clutter and visual haze off the sea. At the very least it would carry one helluva strong message. And if the Russkies panicked and started crabbing for lock-on, Waltham and Wolfe would go for the kill as the other two F-14s barrelled in for cover.

Waltham keyed his radio. "How you doin', Ditto?"

"Hanging clean, Banger."

"Sally?"

"Holding separation neat. Have you on scope, but we're getting a lot of sea clutter."

"Hell, it's pretty down here."

In Waltham's rear pit, his RIO, Lieutenant Commander "Jobber" Joberlesky, was scanning with his AWG-9 Doppler radar. This close to the sea, the readouts were heavily diffused. Unlike the more advanced digital radar gear aboard the Hornet F-18s, the A-WOG was a touchy bitch that needed constant handling. But Jobber was the best RIO in the outfit, with a sixth sense for interpreting read.

Waltham flipped his channelizer and listened in on the link Joberlesky had with the outlying Hummer E-2C. ". . . frigates holding close transit CC. Relative bearing one-seven-three, distance from you two-three-zero miles. Hold vector two-niner-one and watch for passover of reach limit. Counting two-zero seconds . . . now."

"Roger, two-zero seconds," Jobber acknowledged.

Once beyond the radar range of the Hummer, they would be radar dark, since Waltham had chosen to go in without probes, using only passive read and visual. He wanted as much surprise as he could get when he and Wolfe came up off the ocean.

The most delicate part of the mission was fuel. Wherever they struck the bogeys, their turn-and-burn time on site would be hard-pressed. Instead of extra tanks, they were carrying full complements of AIM-7 Sparrows and AIM-9 Sidewinders. To cover their asses on return, a K-A3 "Whale" tanker would be waiting for refueling. But on-site engagement could be critical.

A burst of static blew through his earphones. "Two-Zero-Zero, you are passing through RL. Maintain vector two-niner-one. Switch to strike frequency now, over." Jobber wilcoed and flipped the channel selector.

Waltham keyed. "Vanguard Strike, Red Javelin Two-Zero-Zero for switchover. Holding vector two-niner-one on the deck."

"Red Javelin Two-Zero-Zero, we have you on radio pilot. Be advised one double-up, one holding on alert five. Whale airborne at angels ten and will reach rendezvous position at zero-five-two-two."

"Roger."

Waltham settled back into his seat, scanning the sky above him, made gauzy by the ocean haze. Directly in front of the nose of the Tomcat, the sea was gathering needle points of sunlight that sparkled and shimmered as he flashed over them, holding the F-14 at a steady four hundred and fifty knots.

Three hundred miles from the carrier, Jobber informed Vanguard Strike they were going into R-and-R silence and shut down the A-WOG's active probe unit. Over the intercom, Banger said, "Keep an eye out, Jobber. We should be near Ivan's patrol area pretty quick."

Four minutes later, Jobber came back: "I've got twin bogeys. Heading three-four-zero at angels five. The SMC looks like Forgers."

Waltham glanced off to his right. There! He thought he saw two tiny dots appear and disappear in the soft silver-blue of the sky. He twisted about and glanced at Wolfe, flying thirty yards off his right wing. He made a V with his fingers, then spread all five, and pointed toward the northeast. Wolfe nodded, made the OK sign with his thumb and forefinger.

"They're coming on us, Banger," Jobber called out. "Separation is one-eight miles."

Waltham squinted where he thought he'd seen the dots. Finally picked them up again.

"Separation is one-four miles."

Waltham was listening intently for his ECM buzzer, which would indicate they'd been made by the Forgers' radar. It remained silent.

"Separation one-one miles."

He settled back into his seat, trying futilely to relax. His fingers tapped nervously against the stick, and in his head, he counted: one . . . two . . . *three.* "Here we go!"

He reefed back hard on the stick, slamming the F-14 into a sixty-degree, four-G vertical climb, afterburner smoking in V zone. Back and away, Wolfe followed right with him. In his heads-up display, Waltham watched dials and needles whirl. Four seconds later, his firing picture came on as Jobber switched on active radar. It formed a dark circle with spikes and a T. The twin blips of the incoming Forgers were far to the right.

He held to the blips, tightening slightly in their direction. For a brief period his airspeed indicator eased through Mach 1, then back again into subsonic range as the Cat began losing climb energy.

The blips blossomed into the green pencil lines of two tiny aircraft. They wobbled and jinked around the firing circle. And then, off his starboard wing root, he saw them: thick green fuselages dark against the sky.

"Break right," he yelled. "Break right."

Ditto's voice crackled back: "Breaking! Breaking!"

Waltham kept climbing vertically, but his speed was dropping rapidly as climb energy continued dissipating. He glanced over his right shoulder and caught a glimpse of Wolfe executing a hard right turn. When his speed neared three hundred knots, he felt the controls getting mushy. He snap-rolled, pulling hard over, and made the apogee inverted, the Gs going to momentary zero state. Then he started down into a zoom, picking up energy again and rocketing toward Mach 1.

Dead ahead, two miles out and down, one of the Forgers was coming straight at him.

For the last six minutes, the Saber, one hundred miles to the south, had been tracking the atmospheric wash of approaching jets: one set from the northwest, the other from the northeast. As the blips drew into danger range, the Kamov began running an identity scan.

It immediately made the Soviet fighters, for the signature wash pattern created by the distinctive vector baffles on the engine exhaust ports was clean. It assessed Friendly, moved to the second target. The wash ripples crossing through the air were sharp and precise. Direction of source was zero-four-three degrees, altitude six thousand meters. It also registered a third, fainter disturbance fuming up off the ocean beyond the curve of the earth. The Kamov shunted that one into stand-by priority and focused on the higher contact.

Parameters began feeding in:

```
RANGE: 150 KILOMETERS
BEARING: ZERO-FOUR-THREE DEGREES
SPEED: 450 KNOTS
ALTITUDE: 6000 METERS, HOLDING
```

The Kamov scanned through its memory and focused on qualitative, volumetric, and gravimetric evaluations of the wash read. ID came quickly:

```
INTERCEPTOR: AMERICAN: GRUMMAN (DES) F-14: NCB
CREW: 2
ENGINES: (2) PRATT-WHITNEY TF-30F-412A
SPEED CAPABLE: MACH 2.5
DIMENSIONS: 19.3 METERS/ GROSS WT: 30 MASS (TONS)
ELECTRONICS: AWG-9 RADAR
ARMAMENT: (VM) PHOENIX; SPARROW; SIDEWINDER MISSILES WITH
    NUCLEAR CAPABILITY
```

A second passed. The Kamov scanned the AI read:

```
DANGER ASSESSMENT: POTENTIALLY EXTREME
TARGET ARM STATE: UNACTIVATED
```

The computer ordered the firing chamber into active and tracking fixes. In the cockpit, lights flashed in sequence lines of orange dots as the Kamov set up convergence points. It homed the firing barrel to coordinated time merge.

That's when the sensors began cleanly picking up the diffused read beyond the horizon. Two separate targets were climbing rapidly right off the ocean in an almost pure vertical thrust. A whistle sounded sharply in the compacted silence of the cockpit.

The Kamov instantly redeployed its sensor focus to the previously side-shunted read. Range and numbers flicked onto cockpit displays. ID followed almost instantly: American F-14s.

The weapon received a new convergence fix hold, but the chamber gimbals were too slow to implement the Kamov's rapidly changing number sequences as the targets ascended through lightning-fast altitude and position maneuvers.

The computer went to the AI for solution. It pondered a fraction of a second, then came back. Bypass convergence run . . . Utilize angular splay (CT-TTF-12 mm.) . . . CMR update: Danger Extreme.

The Kamov hurled new instructions to the fusion chamber's firing unit.

Two seconds before the American fighters flashed by his starboard wing tip, Captain Koik had sensed their presence by pure instinct. He'd heard no radio transmissions and his short-range ECM radar probe had given him nothing. Yet he *knew* they were coming.

As the ghostly gray F-14s rocketed by, he was already reacting. He bellowed to his wingman, Lieutenant Vasily Nitlitzin, to make a scatter turn, then threw the nose of his own Forger up, shooting full throttle and afterburners to his Lykal and Kolesov engines.

He and Nitlitzin had been flying the outermost patrol sector northeast of the *Minsk*, in-and-out loops for maximum scanning. The procedure had pleased Toomas. The search runs had been too static for him; now he was flying solid tactical missions.

As he climbed, his thrust engine vectored all the way back, he picked up the black dot of an American far ahead. It flashed so quickly in the immense expanse of pastel blue sky that when he blinked, he lost it momentarily. Quickly he relocated it.

He knew he could never catch an F-14 in straight vertical, but he also knew the propensity of the American fighter to lose climb energy rapidly. Soon the pilot would have to turn back into a dive to regain momentum. And this would bring him into a head-on closure.

Koik's bloodstream made little ticks against his temples. This was no ordinary achieve-and-track maneuver. The way the Americans had come silently off the deck indicated they had other intentions. A faint smile touched his mouth under the mask. *I'm here, Yank.*

For a split second he took his eyes from the F-14 to scan his rear quarter. And cursed, as he always did, at the fact that his intake hump blocked his view. Still, he did manage to catch a fleeting glimpse of Nitlitzin in a triple-twisting barrel roll.

As he swung forward again, he saw the Tomcat before him arcing in apogee. For one still moment it hung in the sky above him. Then it came down the far side of the arc and started zooming right at him. He adjusted his trajectory line slightly and went for the fighter, closing at six hundred meters a second.

Ditto Wolfe felt the adrenaline spewing into his blood like jets of pure energy as he made his break to the right. He went screaming out in a flat horizontal run with his RIO's voice whooping through the earphones: "Fuckass, baby! We got 'em shook. Hold 'em! Hold 'em!"

He keyed the ICS: "Where are they, Bubba? Where are they?"

"One in vertical, the other cranking into a horizontal to the right. Bring her to—"

The transmission was suddenly filled with heavy static, and Wolfe cursed. The cocksuckers were throwing radio jam. He threw the F-14 into a fangs-out, six-G bat turn, afterburners flaming, wings configured forward to full speed for high-lift component. As his body seemed to merge into his seat, he watched the sky revolve in silence. And then they were around. He leveled, cutting burners, and hurtled forward, his head swiveling back and forth as he tried to locate the horizontal Forger.

Suddenly it crossed above him in an angled pass, then *wham!* shot right across his view. "Shit!" he bellowed, and slammed the aircraft into a pure vertical, snapping a three-sixty roll at the same time. He picked up a flashing glimpse of the Forger doing the tightest turn he'd ever seen a jet do. Dammit, the motherfucker was using his vector nozzles to slow him down. The maneuver would bring him onto Wolfe's tail.

He held every ounce of power he could and reached for the sky to break out of the sixes zone, the area where he was squarely in

Ivan's sights. "I've lost him!" he shouted. "Can you see him? Can you see him?"

Static peppered Penskie's words: ". . . on . . . around . . . Jesus! . . . six . . ."

Feeling the Tomcat was mushing up, Ditto threw it into a one-eighty roll. Saw the Forger coming out of a zoom, headed for his stern quarter. He pitched the Cat down hard, trying to get more momentum. Two seconds later, the Russian hurtled past. Ditto went into another vertical, saw the Forger turn, yawing crazily, and then it disappeared off his port wing tip. Oh shit, oh fuck! Wolfe cursed. The prick was solidly on his tail. He started another roll to the right.

Out of nowhere, a thousand yards ahead, he saw a strange, fan-shaped distortion appear in the air. At least a hundred yards wide, it looked like a smoking spray of electrified mercury. Wolfe had barely time to blink in surprise before he hurtled right into it.

He felt his body jolted with a burst of energy so powerful that in one blinding moment he felt his every tiny cell vibrate violently.

The aircraft's instrument panel blew open. Glass, metal, then canopy, and frame struts, everything disintegrated. Even as the atoms within his throat aligned themselves into a curdling scream, he and the Tomcat were enveloped in the explosion of his fuel tanks and missiles.

As the Forger came in for head-on closure, Waltham angled slightly to the left so the Russian's gun azimuth would be off. He held to the position, his aircraft rapidly accelerating. The airspeed passed through Mach 1 . . . 1.5 . . . 2.0 . . . He heeled the Cat over in a balls-to-the-wall pullout. Ocean and sky rolled past his canopy. Through it the Russian crossed in a blur.

"Goddamn!"

His radio crackled fragments from Jobber: ". . . ger . . . they got . . . Holy, holy shit—"

Waltham twisted about and glanced over his right shoulder. Five miles away, he saw a cloud of fiery debris sailing leisurely in the sky. Curling spirals of smoke floated away from it.

Jesus, they got Ditto! Waltham thought in jolting agony.

At that moment tracer rounds zipped past him, leaving streaks of light on his retinas. He hurled the Cat into another vertical climb. The open-furnace oval of the sun made a hot flash through his canopy. Up he went, through Mach numbers, reaching for sky.

One second flew past . . .

Another . . .

He lifted his head. Less than a hundred yards away, the Russian Forger was climbing with him, canopy to canopy. With a curse he hit full afterburners and jacked away from Ivan as if he were standing still.

In the momentary pause his mind raced through maneuver options. This was no ordinary Soviet pilot he was dealing with. This son of a bitch was putting his Forger into performance parameters it wasn't supposed to possess. Worse, he was gradually boxing the heavier, less maneuverable F-14 into his fight.

Waltham erupted in rage and screamed into his mask: "You think so, motherfucker? Well, come on. Let's see you do it."

At the precise moment his climb energy faded, he hammerheaded, revolving right around on the plane's fore-and-aft axis, throttles back full. As he came around, he caught sight of the ocean twenty thousand feet below. The Forger came up hard, its cannon pod blowing flashes.

Waltham jammed forward into a spiraling zoom. The Forger pivoted in the sky and came after him. They went down in a series of interchanging positions—a rolling scissors—each trying to gain stern angles on the other.

Neither could.

Waltham's airspeed was dropping steadily as the tight turns dissipated his energy. He broke out of the scissors to build momentum and plunged for the sea. The water came steadily at him. He jacked the aircraft into a tight pullout, coming so close to the waves that his tail pipes threw spray. Once more he rammed into a pure vertical climb.

Almost instantly the Forger was tight on him, canopy to canopy. He could see the pilot's black helmet, the dulled reflection off the dark green fuselage. Up they went, skewering ever higher. Six thousand . . . nine . . . eleven . . .

By now the Kamov had repositioned for a second angular splay shot homed to the other F-14. Trajectory data was hurtling through position fixes, tabulated and fed to the firing mechanism. The target picture showed the American and Russian aircraft in a sharp, steady climb.

Suddenly a secondary radar pickup punched into the system as a new target came up into clean read. It was to the southwest—close, slowly skimming low over the ocean. The Kamov posted high-priority to the F-14 target and sub-ran ident on the new one. Ident and assessment was instantaneous:

```
RANGE: 6.9 KILOMETERS
BEARING: ZERO-NINE-EIGHT DEGREES (RELATIVE)
SPEED: 140 KNOTS
OBJECT: SIKORSKY SH-3 SEA KING HELICOPTER (EE US NAVY)
CREW: 2 PILOTS, 2 SYSTEMS OPERATORS
ENGINES: 2 GENERAL ELECTRIC T58-10 TURBOSHAFTS
ARMAMENT: 2 MK 46 TORPEDOES
ELECTRONICS: AQS-13B SONAR; APN-130 DOPPLER RADAR; MAD AND
    ECM SYSTEMS
```

The threat assessment and AI countermeasure followed:

```
THREAT POTENTIAL: FIRING GUIDANCE SYSTEM
CMR: DESTROY
```

One millisecond later, the Kamov fired its angulated charge at the primary F-14 target, registered non-contact. Instantly it swung its focus to the incoming helicopter and began bringing up a new firing convergence fix . . .

Waltham saw a gigantic V of smoking air burst into the sky directly above him. The edges of it were as precise as a Kabuki fan. Energy ripples made convoluted patterns within it, like those formed when white-hot steel is plunged into oil.

Using pure reflex, Waltham hauled back on the stick, slammed throttles full back, and threw on his air brakes, idle and boards. The Cat almost instantly dropped three hundred knots of airspeed.

But still he rushed toward the fan of smoking air.

He whirled the F-14 into a sharp, inverted roll and caught a glimpse of the Forger also making an emergency vertical reverse. A burst of smoke blew out of the Russian's tail pipes as the pilot came around in vector-baffle deceleration. Both aircraft seemed to float through their apogees, then descended at full speed.

This time Waltham was in the rear.

The Soviet immediately slanted into hard-rolling three-sixties, again and again, absorbing momentum, all baffles straight back. Waltham went after him, blowing burners.

As they streaked toward the ocean, a target fix was forming up in Waltham's heads-up display. The line drawing of the Forger bobbed and swung across the firing circle. Waltham began throwing switches, coming to master-arm state. His eyes watched as the T centered up. The circle changed color, went to red. "Yeah!" Waltham yelled. Centering of dot, the optimum missile-launch position, had been achieved. A buzzer went off as the Cat's fire-control system locked onto the Russian.

"Fox two on six."

Waltham pressed the firing button on the back side of the control stick. An instant later, he felt a Sidewinder leave his wings, jolting the aircraft as if someone had slammed a baseball bat against the fuselage. Then a trail of smoke spiraled away from him.

Straight below, the ocean hurtling at him.

Again the T centered within the circle. Lock-on buzzer.

"Fox two on six, repeat."

The second Sidewinder was fired.

The first missile missed, curving slightly to the left of the Forger as it spun into another series of three-sixties. As it passed the Russian, he leveled, beginning a pullout.

Two seconds . . . three . . .

The second Sidewinder struck the Forger directly in the exhaust pipes. A burst of orange and black smoke erupted. The forward section of the aircraft continued flying, but its stern came apart. Then the forward section exploded. Debris whirled outward, gyrating slowly, slowly against the blue-black sea.

Waltham jammed the stick into his crotch, feeling the Gs draw his face down hard as he wheeled out. Bits of debris flew past his canopy. Up he went. At eight thousand feet, he rolled and headed down again. Through his earphones Jobber's voice, free of static, yelled excitedly: "You flamed him, baby! Goddamn beautiful. Fucking goddamn beautiful."

"Where's the other one?"

"He's gone. The chicken shit bastard's gone."

As they skimmed over the ocean, Waltham saw a single plume of smoke drifting up. His hand started to swing radio channels.

At that instant, he saw something flash on the southwestern horizon: a hair-thin line of light as brilliant as a sunburst. He blinked, looked again. It was gone.

He found channel and keyed: "Vanguard Strike, do you read?"

"Red Javelin Two-Zero-Zero, we've got you. Fan-fucking-tastic! We are vectoring cover section to you."

"Negative. Vector all aircraft out of this area. We visualed a strange energy this sector. Do you copy?"

"Red Javelin, do not understand reference."

"I don't give a fuck if you understand or not. Vector all aircraft out of this sector."

"Wilco, Red Javelin. What is your fuel status?"

He turned Vanguard transmission over to Jobber, not wanting to talk anymore. His heart was still thundering, making jerky muscle tension in his body. For a moment he closed his eyes and brought up the vision of Wolfe's aircraft fragmenting into smoky bits and pieces. Saw again the strange energy fan dead ahead of the nose of his plane. Shimmering and discoloring the sky.

Christ, he thought. What the hell's happening here?

13

At 5:31 P.M. Moscow time, fifty-three minutes before the dogfight in Polynesia, Yuri Markisov came out of his coma. He found himself lying on a dilapidated couch in a small, dimly lit room, wearing an oxygen mask. He vaguely eyed stacks of files and book shelves against two moisture-stained walls. The room smelled of dust and old book bindings.

Suddenly he realized his head was pounding and his left arm felt numb. He glanced down at it. He had no shirt on and the arm was bandaged from the shoulder to the elbow. He heard a man say something and an instant later, Dr. Bonitskaya appeared in his view.

"Yuri, thank God," the doctor whispered. He ran his hand lightly across Markisov's throat, then lifted an eyelid to peer deep into it. He unclipped the mask and pulled it away. "How do you feel?"

"Where am I?"

"In a storage room of the Arsenal library. No, lie still."

Turning his head slightly, Markisov saw the tops of two oxygen tanks and a portable EEG machine. Several other men stood farther away. All looked grim, and all had their machine pistols at the ready. One was his security chief, Rotuf Parunin. Seeing him triggered a rush of memories: Red Square, explosion, darkness.

"What happened?" he asked Parunin, aware that his voice sounded slightly high and lazy.

Parunin came close and knelt beside him. "They tried to assassinate you, sir. A mortar blast in the square."

"They?"

"We're not sure yet, but—"

"Dead?"

"Yes, many. President Kilikov and Kurtkakin."

Markisov closed his eyes for a moment. Then they snapped open. "My wife!"

"She's safe, sir."

The general secretary sighed wearily. "Where is Marshal Petrov? And Yefiseva?"

"The Marshal was taken to the emergency unit at Sklifosovsky Hospital. KGB Chief Yefiseva has been here and will return soon."

"How long have I been unconscious?"

"Nearly ten hours, sir."

"Dammit!" The vehemence of his cry made his head throb with pain. He waited a moment, then tried to sit up. Bonitskaya sprang forward and put his palm against his chest. "Please, Yuri, just lie there."

"No! Parunin, come, help me."

The security chief eased him upright. For a blinding moment he felt a terrible dizziness that made his stomach heave. He sat motionless and gradually the sensations faded. He looked at Parunin. "What happened while I was out?"

Parunin hesitated a moment, glancing at the doctor. Then he said, "Minister Bardeshevsky has apparently taken control. He's using your code systems and has put the city under martial law. GRU officers are arresting people left and right."

Markisov's eyes quivered with speechless rage.

There was a soft knock on the door. Parunin whirled, his weapon coming up. One of the other men edged to the door. "Who?"

"Director Yefiseva."

Parunin turned to Markisov, who waved his hand. "Come in."

As Yefiseva entered swiftly, Markisov saw out in the hall at least a dozen more armed men. The KGB chief, a very tall man with heavy, bony features, had a bandage on his ear, another on his right hand. "Comrade," he blurted, hurrying to the secretary. "I was just told you regained consciousness. Are you all right?"

"Yes. You?"

"I was very fortunate. Nothing."

"Parunin has told me about Bardeshevsky. Where is he now?"

"In your office. He intends to convene an emergency session of the Central Committee tomorrow and declare himself interim general secretary."

Markisov hissed. "Goddammit, is anyone challenging him?"

"Yes, but there's a great deal of confusion throughout the nation. People are anxious for someone to tell them what to do. Bardeshevsky's taking advantage of the paralysis."

As Markisov cursed, another surge of pain skewered across his forehead. Not waiting for it to fade, he cried, "What about Petrov? Is he cooperating, too?"

"No. He defied Bardeshevsky's lapdogs, but he's gravely wounded. His left arm was amputated and he has internal injuries. The GRU has sealed off his entire ward at Sklifosovsky."

"Who else defied them?"

"All my KGB units. Actual gunfire has erupted between them and GRU. There's also much confusion in TVD districts. Most commanders are obeying simply because the orders bear your security codes. But there have been mutinies."

"Ah?"

"At least two that I have reports on. One at the Nyorodo Naval Base on the Caspian, and another at the Krmikillian Military Barracks. But it looks bad for them since they're openly defying STAVKA."

"STAVKA! You mean the jackal's activated STAVKA?"

"Yes."

Markisov's brow knitted so fiercely that Doctor Bonitskaya once more stepped forward and tried to calm him. Markisov roughly brushed him aside and pointed a finger at Yefiseva. "This madness stops now!"

"Yes, comrade. But unfortunately it can't be done without you. You must show yourself to the ministers, the people. Prove you're alive and still in command."

"That's exactly what I intend to do," Markisov snapped.

The others remained silent for nearly a minute while their leader stared into space, formulating plans. When he spoke again, there was no hesitation.

"Gather as many members of the Central Committee as you can find in Moscow," he ordered crisply. "Pick our people. Those that have been arrested, free them with whatever force is necessary. See that I have a complete quorum. If you can't make one, appoint proxies, anyone you're sure of."

Yefiseva nodded, a thin smile beginning to play on his lips.

"Also, I want as many foreign journalists present as possible. And they will be given immediate access to overseas communications facilities. What time is it?"

"A little before six in the afternoon."

"All right, you have until seven-thirty. At that time I'll convene the emergency meeting in the Presidium."

"Yes, comrade, good."

"What tank regiments are still in the city?"

"Elements of the 1136th and the 1178th."

"Use the 1136th. Colonel Chkalov is a personal friend. I want his units *in* the Kremlin compound. And fortify him with two detachments of your Spatnez."

"Yes, sir."

Around the room, everyone was starting to stir with anticipation. The KGB men, smelling a fight, glanced at one another, their fingers scratching at their weapons. Markisov turned to his security chief. "Parunin, your job is to grab Bardeshevsky and bring him to the Presidium. Kill anyone who attempts to stop you."

Parunin nodded.

"Don't move too soon or too late. I want him in the Presidium hall at precisely one minute before seven-thirty."

"Yes, Comrade Secretary."

Markisov paused, then glanced at Yefiseva. "What has he done to Professor Titov?"

The KGB chief frowned, puzzled. "Titov? Who's that?"

"Parunin?"

"I don't know what's happened to him, sir."

"Find him. Turn this damned city upside down if you have to, but find that man. Take him back to his workroom beside my office."

"Yes, sir."

"All right, everybody out. Except Dmitri."

When the room was empty, Markisov turned to his physician. "Is there a possibility that I could relapse into unconsciousness again?"

"I can't be absolutely certain, Yuri. You have a concussion, possibly a subdural hematoma. Unfortunately, your people would not allow me to move you to adequate equipment so I could be sure."

Markisov nodded toward the portable EEG machine. "What did that show?"

"No abnormalities and your vital signs appear good. I would prefer, however, you lie down again."

"You know that's not possible."

"Yes. How is your head?"

"Hurts like hell."

"I can give you something."

"Will it affect my alertness?"

"No."

"All right."

Bonitskaya dug into his medical bag and came out with a hypodermic needle and a small vial. As he drew up the shot, he paused, anxiously studying his patient. "When you show yourself, Yuri, they might try to kill you again."

"Yes."

"Ah, I fear for you, comrade. Are you still powerful enough to challenge them?"

Markisov didn't answer. He stared into the air directly in front of his face as inwardly he weighed probabilities. Were the unleashed forces too far committed for him to stop now? How much damage had Bardeshevsky's betrayal created? How were the Americans reacting? And behind these, like an approaching whirlwind, always the vision of the Saber . . .

He came up from his thoughts. "I don't know, Dmitri," he said softly. "But we'll find out soon enough, won't we?"

At that precise moment—while Captain Waltham and Lieutenant Wolfe were still hurling their F-14s just off the ocean and the dogfight lay minutes in their future—Kiri turned from the open bay and watched Cas climb back through the narrow after hatch, instantly noting the set look of his face.

Is there serious damage to the helicopter? she was about to ask him. Then she saw Katevayo's face in the hatch and her heart jarred. Without thinking, she twisted and went for the pistol still strapped to her leg. But before she could reach it, Valentin had his Skorpion on her.

She fell stark still with the sudden knowledge that she was about to die. But Katevayo didn't pull the trigger. Instead, with his wild gray eyes dancing, he laughed contemptuously at her. In Russian he snapped, "You don't kill so good, eh, Burmese?"

Then he roughly prodded Cas with the muzzle and stepped fully through the hatch. He was wearing only the bottom half of his wet suit, and his upper body was naked save for a makeshift bandage he'd wound around his knife wounds. He nodded at Kiri's pistol. "Take it out slowly," he ordered, "and slide it over here."

Holding his stare, she obeyed. The weapon thudded dully against the bulkhead at his feet. He picked it up and tucked it into his waistband, then reached back through the hatch, and brought out two gray satchels of gelignite explosives.

Bonner was still facing forward with Del watching open-mouthed directly in front of him. Cas's eyes darted back and forth as he tried to gauge the precise position of the Russian behind him. But then the Skorpion's muzzle jabbed him once more in the small of the back, and Katevayo ordered him to sit down on the deck.

Kiri quickly said, "Do it, Cas."

He studied her a moment, then slowly, deliberately, squatted with his back to the starboard bulkhead aft the bay door. His eyes fixed gelidly on Valentin as he came around him.

For a moment Katevayo stopped and looked at the sophisticated electronic gear of the consoles. January stared up at him, terrified. Katevayo shoved his face down until his nose almost touched Del's. "Put your fucking hands up here where I can see them," he hissed.

Instantly, Del obeyed. His fingers looked white against the metal desk. Valentin grinned at him, quickly stepped past and up onto the control platform hatch frame. Covering the others with the machine pistol, he took out Kiri's P-6 and shoved the barrel against the back of Woodcroft's head.

The ensign, unaware of what had been taking place in the main bay, jerked around. His eyes shot up. "Jesus Christ, another one! Where the fuck did you come from?"

"Head this aircraft toward the French platform," the Russian shouted over the engine noise.

"What?"

"The French platform, you fuckass. Do it! Move!"

"Do what he says," Del cried, still looking down at his panels. "He'll kill us all."

"I don't know where that damned platform is," Woodcroft said.

Katevayo gave him its coordinates. Shaking his head disgustedly, Woodcroft put them into a sharp bank and they swung toward the east.

Valentin eased himself down against the hatchway frame so he could keep everyone in sight. He put the P-6 back into his waistband and laid the Skorpion across his knees. With his right foot he pulled up the satchels he'd dropped beside Del's chair. Then he settled back and grinned his crazy grin at them all.

Across the bay, Cas watched him closely. He'd noticed how the man had winced several times in pain. He was also deathly pale under the veneer of his sunburn and his wounds were bleeding, the blood slipping down into the rubber folds of his suit.

Katevayo caught him staring and stared right back. For a long moment neither man flinched. Then a wave of anger seethed up through the Russian. "Come on, Yank," he taunted Cas. "Try it."

Kiri, seated in one of the web seats with her legs drawn up, had been frantically searching the copter's bay for a weapon, but all she could find was a three-foot iron bar used to brace the door and now lying in a deck trough. As she looked up, she realized what was passing between Cas and Katevayo and yelled, "No!"

At her cry, Cas tilted his head slightly and Katevayo's lips came up into a dark sneer. Gently he lifted the Skorpion, pointed it at Cas's head, and went, "Bing!" Then he chortled lasciviously and relaxed back against the frame.

Kiri let the air out of her lungs, felt her stomach trembling. That was damned close, she thought, too close. She turned back and glared at Cas. Sooner or later, she knew, the damned fool would try something and get blown away in the process. Wait, you asshole, she screamed silently at Cas, trying to convey it through her eyes. Can't you see how weak he is?

But Cas ignored her, gazing unwaveringly on Valentin's face. Then he reached up and took his lighter out of his pocket. He flicked it once. "Hey, asshole," he called to Katevayo. "You got a cigarette?"

Oh, shit, Kiri thought.

Katevayo lifted his eyes slowly, his chin down. He again locked into Cas's stare.

"And don't give me one of them native smokes," Cas went on evenly. "They taste like rolled dog shit."

Kiri hissed at him. "Stop it, you fool. Don't push this man."

Katevayo's gaze slid to her, watching her anxiety from under his eyebrows with a dark merriment. "What's the matter, Burmese?" he asked tauntingly. "You think I'm going to kill your Yankee cunt-licker?" He shook his head, snickering. "No, not unless he's very stupid. I'm going to make *you* kill him."

"No cigarettes?" Cas said, his own eyes flashing. "Jesus, you fucking Russians don't come prepared, do you?"

On that one, Katevayo went rigid. Instantly, Kiri leaned forward, forcing him to whirl toward her. "All right, Valentin," she shouted in Russian. "You win, we'll do it your way. You want to blow the platform? We'll blow it. Just tell me what you want me to do."

She hurled a quick glance over her shoulder at Cas, and was jolted at what she saw in his face. He was going for it! She could see him shifting his weight almost imperceptibly, changing position so as to coil for a full spring. She jerked back to Katevayo. "Come on, you son of a bitch," she cried. "Tell me how we'll do it."

But Katevayo was no longer listening to her. His own body was coiled now, the insane gray eyes blazing. The barrel of the Skorpion lifted off his lap . . .

The radar console let out a sudden, raucous buzzing that sent punching jabs of sound into the tense air. Everyone jumped, startled. Del's eyes shot up and he stared at the screens. Two bright dots of light were moving rapidly like darting, glowing insects on the glass. From the cockpit, Woodcroft hollered. "We've got interceptors out here. January, run me an ident."

Two more blips appeared on the screen, coming from the upper left quadrant. Del's fingers now scurried over the switches, energizing the Doppler to analyze the encoded impulses and waveforms through the signal processor for range and direction. The returning read came up, numbers flashing: Primary: 275 degrees (relative); 400 + knots; 5000 feet; 90.03 miles//Secondary: 273 degrees (relative); 430 + knots: 500 feet (adj.); 90.01 miles.

Katevayo cursed, then shouted at Del, "Who the fuck are they?"

Before Del could form an ID, Woodcroft gave a whoop. "They're Cats! I've got 'em on frequency. They've bounced a couple of Forgers." There was a pause, then: "Holy shit! They're engaging!"

Glancing back at Cas, Kiri saw that he was up on the balls of his feet, body wired. Her gaze swung back to Katevayo and, seeing him distracted, she slid her legs off the web seat and bent down for the metal bar on the deck.

Six seconds later, the radar screen went wild, blowing shimmering white streaks that cascaded downward like molten liquid. And beneath the streaks, a pulsing, blinding ray of light emanated from the ocean. Del gasped, "That's it! There it is!"

Katevayo's eyes were darting from the screens to Cas, to Kiri and back. "What is it?" he yelled.

As quickly as it had erupted, the violent interference on the screen disappeared, leaving the jet blips clean again. But now there were only three and, close in, a flickering dispersion of tiny lights. Explosive debris!

Suddenly the helicopter dipped sharply to the left. Everyone was thrown, Cas slamming to the deck, Kiri grabbing for webbing, and Katevayo tilting heavily, stiffly, like a metronome. In another moment, though, he recovered, snapping up the machine pistol, scanning everywhere wildly.

"Give me a heading," Woodcroft was yelling. "Goddammit, January, give me a heading. They've splashed a Cat. I'm going after it."

At that instant the screen went crazy again, more white rain that held rainbow colors. And below, the unbelievably powerful beam of light splayed like a molten fan of fire.

Del came to and began furiously throwing more switches, thumbing dials in an effort to encode pulses and make the range and direction of the strange energy source. Numbers began to appear. They shimmered and glowed, fusing into wash smear. Then it was gone, and the screen again showed three blips gyrating furiously. Seconds hurtled past. Suddenly there were only two blips and another sprinkle of flashing dots.

"Oh, shit!" Del moaned. "I've lost the fix."

Katevayo lifted himself. Blood, pooled in the creases of the wet suit, spilled onto the deck. Training his weapon on Bonner, he turned his head slightly and shouted to Woodcroft, "Pilot, turn this ship back to the platform."

Woodcroft screamed back, "Fuck you!"

"I said, turn it back!"

Del shifted in his console seat. "Listen, you fool," he yelled at Valentin. "That's *your* spy plane out there. We've found it!"

Enraged, Katevayo swung the muzzle of the Skorpion on him and fired. The bullets tore into Del's body with such violence that they lifted him out of the chair and slammed him against the radar console. His body went limp. The back of his flight suit was ripped apart and blood cascaded across the panel.

In the fraction of a second that Katevayo's weapon turned away, Cas lunged across the deck and crashed into him with his shoulder, ramming him against the hatchway. Grunting, Katevayo tried to twist away from him as Cas smashed him just under the left ear, snapping Katevayo's head back. All the same, the lunge had carried Cas across the Russian and up against the console seat, and Katevayo rolled, his hands searching for the Skorpion. Unable to find it, he came up with the 9-mm.

Before he could fire, Kiri hit him with the iron bar, slashing it across his shoulder. The pistol went skittering across the deck. And Cas was on him again, pounding Katevayo's face against the edge of the hatchway.

Another furious buzzing crackled from the radar console.

There was a violent, wrenching burst from overhead, like the blowing crack of a nitro-fueled engine throwing a rod. With it came a rasp as if the rotor blades were tearing through something solid.

The Sea King faltered and began to shake violently. A high whine erupted, as sharp as a scream. For a wild moment Cas felt his entire body energizing. Every molecule of his skin seemed to take on a separate, charged, glowing state.

Directly behind him, the radar console exploded. As smoking glass shards hurled across his back, the explosion knocked him forward like a powerful rabbit punch. Thrown away from Katevayo, his knees hit deck and he rolled, coming up.

Katevayo held the muzzle of the Skorpion six inches from his forehead.

Mindless shock hurtled through him with the explosive force of power lines shorting. Twisting, he tumbled to his left. There were three quick shots that came so close together they seemed parts of a single blast. For one fleeting, tortuously confused instant, he thought it was the Skorpion, waited for the thunderous surge of pain. Then he saw Katevayo's face open with a look of outraged shock. His body arced over Cas and fell limply onto the deck. Kiri had put three 9-mm. rounds into the base of his neck.

Cas had no time to feel relief. As the helo rolled sharply to the right, he heard Woodcroft yelling as the violent movement hurled him off the deck. Cas grabbed wildly for webbing and watched as Katevayo's body sailed through the bay door and into the tilted blur of rotor blades. There was a rapid, mushy thumping, and bits of flesh and rubber clothing and blood blew back through the door.

Choking back his revulsion, Cas held on wildly as gravity pulled him in crazy directions. He threw a glance over his shoulder and saw Kiri clinging to a seat stanchion, body splayed out, legs thrashing near the bay door. He braced himself against the jolting bulkhead and catapulted his body toward her. As he plowed into her, he grabbed her waist, twisted, and pinned her body against the after-webbing shroud. There they hung, gazing out through the bay door at the shimmering blue-green ocean, thirty feet away, rushing at them.

The Sea King hit the water with the heavy crunching metal sound of colliding boxcars. The impact came up through the deck with such force that it made Cas's ankles and knee joints slam with pain. Water rushed in through the bay doorway, a solid column that blew in with the sudden, pounding weight of a flash flood. With all his strength he held onto Kiri and the webbing.

Sounds came out of the water: the shattering of Plexiglas, the violent sizzle of the hot engines as they sank into the ocean. Up through the aircraft came sucking sounds and soft squeals and creaks; frame struts groaned under far more weight than they had been designed for as the heavy engines and transmission housings plunged the copter toward the sea floor.

Gradually the sounds began to subside. The water pouring in grew less and less until it was merely swirling inside the aircraft. Cas and Kiri were floating. And then they banged lightly into the inverted bay deck. The helo continued sinking. He could fuzzily make out the arch of the doorway. Beyond it, the ocean went off into a green haze, light shafts shimmering. He patted Kiri on the head and pointed out the door and up. Braced against the near bulkhead, he propelled her toward it, felt the gentle swirl of her leg kick as she skimmed out.

Turning, he made his way through the cockpit hatch and found Woodcroft slumped forward against his seat harness. Blood fumed off his face and swirled gently up through the smashed Plexiglas dome. Cas's chest was beginning to hurl oxygen-starvation pains through his muscles. Quickly he unbuckled the lieutenant's harness and hauled him through the cockpit frame into open water. One of the huge rotor blades had smashed down onto the starboard tank. Gasoline was streaming out, making clear patches of water. The edge of the rotor blade was trembling in the plunge surge as he dragged Woodcroft by the collar of his flight suit and headed for the surface.

The silvery counterpane flashing sunlight seemed a desperately long way off. His body was pounding, demanding oxygen; his chest burned, heart roared away inside as if suspended in space, isolated. Long seconds later, he blew through the surface.

The swells were distorted with crest foam and they lifted him and Woodcroft up, eased them down. He caught sight of islands off to his left about two hundred yards away. Reassured by this, he scanned quickly at each rise, looking for Kiri. At the next dip he turned his attention to the ensign. Blood was coming from a deep gash in his chest, stretching from nipple to nipple.

Kiri's voice sounded far away and then near. As they rose on another swell, he saw her up near the surf line of the closest strip of land. He waved her toward it and saw her return the wave. Then he slung his arm around Woodcroft's chest in a swimmer's carry and headed after her.

As he drew closer to the small island, he could see its contours: flat, sandy with a few stunted Samoan palms and sea grass. There was a wide channel at its southern end, but it was too far away. Woodcroft was losing too much blood. Cas knew he'd have to go straight through the surf line.

The combers were moderate-sized—ten, twelve feet high—but they came in steady series, curling up on the reef. For a fleeting instant he saw a dark body streak through a rising comber. Then another, off to the right. Sharks! Woodcroft's blood and the concussions of the crash were already drawing them.

As Cas reached the main break, he felt the pull as the swells rolled into neat curls and then smashed down, making a layer of foam as they raced toward shore. Without hesitating, he went into them, felt himself lifted. To his left the curl break came toward him and hollowed out. He gripped Woodcroft's body with both arms as it struck.

Over and over they went in crazy barrel rolls, the water thundering and hissing all around them. Woodcroft's dead weight tried to tear away from him, but he held on tightly and then they were gliding through foam. Cas laid his feet out, touched reef, skimmed, touched. In four minutes, he made the beach, with Woodcroft draped over his shoulder.

They tore strips of Kiri's shirt to bind the lieutenant's chest wound. As they tightened the bandage, he moaned softly. Cas was astounded the man hadn't drowned. They felt around his body. No bones were broken, but there was an ominous mushiness to his stomach. His face was pale, his lips blue; he was going into shock. They covered him with sea grass and his limbs trembled.

Suddenly a high-pitched whistle drifted in out of the surf. Cas caught sight of a sail, then a twin-hulled native *natarua* skimming just beyond the surf line. It cut suddenly and started toward the shore with the swiftness of the wind. Two men were in it, one standing, his legs braced on the cross struts that linked the two hulls, riding the surf surge like a skier. In they came, the steersman correcting sharply, and then they shot straight in, the sail popping as it shifted to the wind, and they hurtled over the foam, running as lightly as fall leaves in a sharp breeze.

Six of them, with Parunin as leader, assembled in the fading twilight at the north end of the Arsenal below St. Nicholas' Tower. Under their disguise of workmen's coats, coveralls, and hard hats, each man concealed a short-barreled AKR machine pistol, a boot-holstered P-6, a knife strapped upside down on the inside of his left biceps, and three antipersonnel grenades hooked to his belt.

The seventy acres within the Kremlin walls were strangely quiet. Many of the lights normally on the great golden onion domes of Cathedral Square were dark. In the Kremlin Garden, the fountain lights were also out, with the only illumination provided by the tiny pathway lights.

One by one the men crossed the two hundred yards to the rear of the Council of Ministers building, where they reassembled beside a small concrete tunnel. Parunin led them off in single file through a maze of basement corridors until they reached a narrow staircase with a red fire door. The bar latch chunked loudly as they slipped through and echoed hollowly through the basement.

On the second floor, they entered a large storage room filled with office furniture. A connecting door led into the building's mailroom, where two old watchmen were sitting on overturned boxes, eating their supper. They glanced up as the KGB men barreled in. Seeing the men's weapons, the watchmen silently raised their hands and got down on the floor. They were quickly bound and gagged.

Parunin pulled the outer door open a crack. It was at the end of a wide red-carpeted corridor. At the other end were the general secretary's suite of offices, and the last door along the corridor was the one to Markisov's personal office. GRU soldiers guarded each of the five doors and there were two guards and an officer before Markisov's. The office suite had halls that spoked off the corridor, where secretaries and junior GRU officers were shuffling continually between rooms.

Parunin mentally measured the distance to Markisov's office: two hundred feet. He eased the door shut. "Seven guards and an officer," he whispered tensely. "All armed. We'll go in echelon. Move quickly and shoot to kill."

The men nodded and braced their weapons, muzzles pointed straight ahead. Their bodies smoked with repressed energy and they shifted slightly from foot to foot, coming up on their toes.

When Parunin pulled the door fully open, they burst out like paratroopers exiting an aircraft, running with their weight high and fanning out in echelon across the corridor. They covered forty feet before one of the soldiers turned and saw them. His mouth opened in surprise for a split second, then he yelled something and started to swing his Kalashsnikov off his shoulder.

Parunin's opening burst spattered him across the chest, hitting with the sound of mallets striking a hung rug.

As the other guards snapped around, the GRU officer yelled, "Parunin!" and began clawing for his pistol. The guards behind him dropped to one knee, bringing their weapons up. Explosions roared up the corridor as Parunin's men opened fire, and three of the GRU men were struck almost simultaneously.

One soldier was hit in the head. His body caromed violently in the hall, blood blowing from his skull. Another twirled to the deck and the officer was slammed back and into Markisov's door before he slid to the floor, his legs stretched out. The other guards instantly froze.

Parunin and the man directly behind him covered the remaining distance in five seconds. Three others went pounding past and into the suite halls, dodging into offices commando style. The remaining two braced in the center of the corridor, their weapons poised to shoot.

As Parunin reached Markisov's door, it was flung open and a fat GRU general lunged toward him. Parunin dipped his shoulder and drove into him. They both hurtled into the room and to the floor. Instantly, Parunin was up, his AKR sweeping. He found Bardeshevsky standing near the window, then two other men: Kandalov and another Politburo member named Herzen. For one stultifying moment no one moved. Then Bardeshevsky drew himself erect and faced Parunin, eyes flashing.

Parunin barked, "Minister Bardeshevsky, you are under arrest by order of General Secretary Yuri Markisov."

Bardeshevsky scoffed insolently. "You fool! Markisov no longer orders anything."

"Come here," Parunin snapped.

The old general didn't move.

"I said, come here. Now!"

Bardeshevsky finally obeyed. Stiffly, arrogantly he came around the desk and planted himself squarely in front of Markisov's security chief. "You'll pay for this, Parunin," he growled.

"No, comrade," the other answered with an icy grin. "You will. Put your hands out."

Bardeshevsky drew himself up again and sneered.

Parunin jabbed the tip of the AKR's silencer into his chest. "I said, put your fucking hands out."

At the poke of the weapon Bardeshevsky went pale. With his eyes still blazing, he lifted his hands. Parunin quickly snapped on handcuffs. As he herded him and the others out into the hall, all of them heard a distant clank of tank treads drifting through windows. Bardeshevsky and Kandalov exchanged alarmed glances.

By now Parunin's men had emptied all the suite offices and disarmed the GRU men. There was a throng in the connecting halls. Parunin shouted to them, "Vacate the building at once. It's been dynamited. Everybody, out!"

At that, people surged en masse for the main staircase. Bardeshevsky whirled on Parunin. "You wouldn't dare kill us all," he cried.

The security chief jabbed his weapon into the old general's ribs and nodded down the hall. "Move. That way." They retraced their steps to the basement. Once outside, Bardeshevsky, Kandalov, Herzen, and the GRU general were formed up into a line. Everywhere soldiers were hurrying and T-64 battle tanks were coming up the Trinity and Borovitsky Gate roads, the rumble of their treads echoing between the tall spires and splendidly ornamented facades and colonnades of Cathedral Square. In lock step, Parunin started his little group across the short walk to the northeast side of the Presidium of the Supreme Soviet building.

All through the long, crazy day, Quentin Alsop, Moscow's bureau chief for the Associated Press, had been fighting a vicious hangover. Diarrhea had sapped him of energy, forming gas with the inevitability of fermenting grapes. It was still roiling now at seven-fifteen as he sat in a stuffy, stolidly furnished anteroom within the Presidium of the Supreme Soviet building. With him were thirty other international newspeople.

It had been a day of unbelievable excitement. He had been watching from the third story of the GUM building to observe the parade when the explosions took place. Bleeding from glass cuts, he had reached the bottom-floor entrance in time to see people fleeing hysterically, trampling fallen bodies.

He'd turned toward the Pravda building, a half mile away off Marx Prospeckt. Every other newsperson in Moscow had apparently had the same destination, for the outer lobby was packed with a mass of shouting people. Using Pravda as his base, he spent most of the afternoon scouring the city. Police squads led by GRU officers were roaming everywhere, brutally making arrests. Rumors were flying that Minister Bardeshevsky and the Old Guard factions were taking over. No one had any word of Markisov's whereabouts or condition. The whole city seemed gripped by panic.

He returned to the Pravda offices shortly before a cadre of KGB officers came in, hot-eyed like Cossacks among villagers. They grabbed newspeople at random and jostled them toward the entrance. A man with extremely foul breath hooked into Alsop's arm. "You Americansky?" he demanded in his face.

"Yes."

"Big paper?"

"Yes."

"You come with me."

Now, waiting impatiently in the anteroom, he felt his stomach roil a faint warning. He clamped down on his groin and the surge passed. A KGB officer came in, a burly, pugnacious-looking man wearing a dark suit that didn't fit his chest. "You will all come with me, please," he ordered. "This way. But go slowly and in a single group."

The newspeople trooped down a long corridor with the fading portraits of Russian revolutionaries on the walls. They were stopped at a large, ornate door. The KGB man said, "There will be no questions. You are merely observers here. But you may take pictures. As many as you wish."

Nigel Broadstreet of the British News Service dipped his head close to Alsop's ear. "Sounds like a bleeding schoolmarm, doesn't he?"

They were herded onto a high balcony in the rear of the main meeting chamber. Finding no chairs, the newsies jostled one another getting to the railing. Below them were at least three hundred people scattered throughout the sloping chamber, all men. Armed Red Army soldiers roved the aisles. The journalists began taking photos. The soft *ziiiip, click* of their cameras sounded loudly in the vast room, and some of the men directly below the balcony glanced up, scowling.

Alsop could feel the tension in the chamber, and he leaned out over the balcony rail to study the people below. He recognized some of the faces, members of the Central Committee of the Communist Party. But many others he'd never seen before. It finally dawned on him that the chamber was being packed with proxies, ringers. He glanced at Broadstreet and saw that he realized it, too.

A murmuring suddenly swept the hall, and people began standing, pointing. From a side door on the right of the main stage, four KGB officers emerged. Behind them came Bardeshevsky, Kandalov, Herzen, and General Poporonov with four more KGB officers following.

Broadstreet gasped, "Bloody hell, Quenie, will you look at that? And the muckers are cuffed."

Down in the hall, the men's appearance set off shouting, and two scuffles broke out, quickly stopped by the soldiers. But the shouting continued and the faces of some of the assembled men were reddened with rage. Alsop thought: Markisov's alive.

As if taking his cue, the General Secretary appeared, entering slowly from the right side of the stage. Though he walked erectly, he wore the same suit he had worn at the parade, which was covered with dust and dark stains, the jacket draped over a bandaged arm. Instantly everyone fell silent.

His face pale, Markisov took the rostrum. All through the chamber, seats clattered as the ministers sat down. From the balcony, cameras were zooming in, their flashes popping with tiny metallic clicks.

"Comrades," Markisov began. "I have convened this plenum for two reasons." Loudspeakers around the chamber gave his voice a powerful resonance. "First, to show you that I am still alive." He paused and his gaze swept the entire hall and the balcony. Then they fixed on Minister Bardeshevsky. "And second, to once and for all tear out the disease that eats at Mother Russia's heart."

The chamber stirred with coughs and rustles of men shifting in their red-leather seats.

He continued: "All of you here, comrades, have been witness to the stagnation of our country, that blind adulation of the past which has doomed this great Union to a lingering and inevitable death. *Worse* than the threat of any foreign enemy. Because here we *ourselves* are the enemy. We do not leap the tombs but fall back into them."

As he paused again, faces turned to look at other faces. Broadstreet said softly, "Oh, my."

Markisov finally went on: "You have all heard the insidious calls for a return to the grim, dark times of Stalinism. 'When Russia was great,' they say. 'When we Russians were kings,' they say. Kings? Hardly. Only those at the top lived with the power of kings. And only because they waded through the blood of their countrymen."

Emotion was beginning to seethe in the lower seats, and many of the younger ministers began nodding emphatically.

"And where do these calls come from?" Markisov demanded, his voice rising now. "Who has sought to beguile you? You already know. Today they saw their opportunity to turn back the clock, and they struck like vipers. You've already seen their poison. Some of your comrades have already suffered their betrayal." He dramatically lifted his hand and pointed at his heart. "*This* was their target now." His voice dropped to a low hiss. "How soon will it be yours?"

A tumult exploded from the chamber as ministers and proxies sprang to their feet, spearing the air with clenched fists, shouting Markisov's name. At that moment Bardeshevsky leaped up. Instantly some of the noise quieted.

"*You* are the poison," the old general bellowed, pointing his cuffed hands at Markisov. His face was contorted with rage, flecks of spittle at the corners of his mouth. "*You* destroy us." He stopped, his head swiveling, neck tendons bulging, like a lion at bay driven beyond reason. Then he turned to face the full assemblage. "Kill *him*! Grind this man's body into the dirt with the rest of the vermin!"

Markisov walked to the edge of the stage and balefully regarded Bardeshevsky for a long moment. Enraged, the old general lunged toward the stage. Two KGB officers hurled themselves at him, and all three went down hard onto the floor. Bardeshevsky screamed. Behind them Kandalov was openly weeping.

Markisov watched, his eyes narrow and frigid. At last he lifted his head. In the stunned hush, with only the sound of Bardeshevsky's muffled cries, he pointed at the old Lion of Leningrad and he said, "Comrades, *there* is your past!" He paused, the silence like thunder. "Make your choice now. His way—or mine."

The roar came slowly. First one man cried Markisov's name. It was answered by a few more and then a few more until the vast chamber was thundering with cries of "Markisov!" *"Perestroika!"* "The future!"

Quentin Alsop released his breath. "Son of a bitch," he whispered, awed. "Markisov, you brilliant bastard, you've pulled it off."

In his dungeon, Professor Titov had heard nothing save the tremble of his own heart and the occasional scurry of rats.

An eternity seemed to pass.

Then he heard the loud slam of a door and boots cracking down the stairs. As they headed down the corridor, men in the cells murmured with surprise. In front of Titov's cell, two KGB officers stopped. They were carrying small automatic pistols and their faces were stony. "Here," one shouted. The huge sergeant who had brought the professor in came up. He peered into the cell, then looked at the two men. "I have no orders to release this man."

One of the KGB men lifted his pistol and placed it against the sergeant's throat. "Here's your order. Get him out."

The sergeant eyed the weapon casually, shrugged, and opened the cell. The two men rushed in. They bodily picked up Titov, one on each arm, and hurried him out and up the corridor. As they passed the cell where the imprisoned KGB officer was standing, one of the men yelled to the other: "Yari, him, too."

Titov was paralyzed with fear. For one stark, vivid moment, he knew he was about to be executed. The thought was so overwhelming that his legs gave out, and he crumpled against the man carrying him. The man grunted at the dead weight in his arms and hissed sharply, "Don't panic, comrade. You're safe now."

He was hustled across the Kremlin compound to the Ministers Building. He could see tanks and milling soldiers as he was taken through a small door beside the main entrance.

In the hall in front of the general secretary's personal office, Titov gagged at the sight of the four dead soldiers lying on the floor. Blood was everywhere, looking dark and thick. It carried a slaughterhouse stench. He shied away like a skittish pony.

"What has happened here?" he cried.

The KGB man didn't answer, but merely threw open the door

to the office where the professor had been stationed before. "Comrade," he said quietly. "Secretary Markisov will be here soon."

Titov's mouth opened with shock. "Then he's alive?"

"He orders you to return to your machines. He wants a report on the aircraft as soon as he arrives."

"Yes," Titov blurted, his heart lifting with hope. "Yes, of course."

The KGB officer reached for the door. "Pay no attention to anything that happens out here. You understand?"

The professor hastened to his consoles. Nothing had been touched; the floor was still littered with messages and military communiqués and long strips of computer printouts. Hurriedly he began going through material that had come in since his departure. The printouts had overflowed the teletype cage, and because one of the computer's printers had jammed, the in-feeding sheets were tightly wedged under the printing head.

For the next two hours he worked methodically through the confused mass of military orders and activation responses, GRU-dominated: intelligence reports, riot-suppression reports, status reports of Moscow garrisons, overseas intelligence summaries.

And buried in the mélange of transmissions, he found two that formed ice crystals in his blood.

Markisov came into the room quietly. His face was drawn and there were dark circles beneath his eyes. When he moved forward, he walked gingerly, as if treading on unstable swamp ground. Overwhelmed, Titov rushed to him and threw his arms around his shoulders.

Markisov did not move. When the professor drew back, he asked simply, "What is the news?"

Titov, too choked up to speak, went to his desk and produced a sheaf of glossy transcription parchment. He handed them over silently. Markisov edged closer to the desk and began to page through them.

The first sheet was the high-priority RSR from the *Minsk* relayed through Cam Ranh and the Pacific Red Fleet headquarters at Vladivostok reporting the dogfight between their Forgers and F-14 Tomcats from the American carrier, *Coral Sea*. The rest of the report concerned follow-up status of positions and Turesky counter moves. Markisov went slowly through the pages, but when he reached the last two, he reread these. They were a summary of an interview with Lieutenant Nitlitzin, who had been Captain Koik's wingman during the engagement. He had survived a shrapnel strike to his aircraft, but had managed to limp back to the carrier intact. Nitlitzin claimed he had not shot down the American fighter, had not even fired his weapons. Nor had Captain Koik, engaged with the other F-14, until *after* the American had exploded. Something else had struck the U.S. aircraft, something strange that made the sky flame and smoke.

Markisov lifted his eyes and stared at the professor.

Titov nodded. "Yes, the Saber."

"You are certain?"

"Yes. What this young pilot described was a flare charge from the Saber's weapon."

Markisov put his head down and sighed.

"Comrade Secretary, the Saber is now in Category Four."

14

Father Claude Joxe was well over six feet tall, but weighed less than a hundred and forty pounds. He had a long, reddened nose, deep sun wrinkles, and wore a filthy straw hat and a dirty black cassock that smelled of rum. He was the pastor of a scattered collection of fishing villages in the outlying Tuamotu reef islands. His church, on a slight hill, was made of coral and cement with a rusty tin roof. A grove of anemic *mape* trees surrounded it, and the ground around the building was packed as hard as asphalt.

It took nearly forty minutes for the *natarua* to reach Joxe's parish on the island of Tuariva. The canoe was old and stank of dead fish. There were nets in the holds and wooden buckets of live octopus and eel. Its sail, made of *lauhala* fiber, hummed softly as they ran southward, flying across the wind.

The priest's shack, to which Cas and the two fishermen carried Woodcroft, was like a monk's cell. It contained little more than a coconut frond bed with a thin woolen blanket and fruit box shelves containing medicine bottles and books. The books were mostly novels: Proust and Genet and translations of Hemingway. The sand floor was mixed with coconut husks and filled with tiny black sand beetles. The only pieces of technical gear were a small short-wave radio and an ancient record player with a faded emblem of a fox terrier sitting before a Victrola.

Father Joxe hovered over the ensign stretched on his palm bed. Shaking his head, he turned to his shelf, searched for a moment, and came up with a syringe and vial of yellow-colored liquid: morphine. He injected it into the lieutenant's deltoid muscle, watching Woodcroft's face closely. Still shaking his head morosely, the priest rigged a glucose bottle, hung it on one of the spindly roof beams, and put the needle into the ensign's forearm.

Only then did he straighten. "*Mon Dieu*, this young man is very badly hurt." He made roiling motions with his slender fingers. "Inside, he is in tumult." He fixed his sorrowful eyes on Cas. "What happened?"

"A helicopter crash."

"Ah, how sad, how sad."

Cas nodded toward the radio. "Can you get help out here?"

"Yes, I can call the Hoa airbase. They have good medical equipment."

"Raise them. But instruct them to come in from the south and remain low, close to the sea. Be sure they understand that."

Joxe's brows lifted. "Ah? Why is that?"

"I can't explain, Father. Just do it. Please."

The priest looked at Kiri, then shrugged, and moved to his radio. Cas stepped outside for a moment to thank the two fishermen for their help. Big, husky men who wore dark glasses and straw hats, they grinned embarrassedly.

When Cas returned to the shack, Father Joxe was peering into Woodcroft's eyes. Cas squatted down and ran his fingers over the ensign's forehead. It was hot, clammy. "How is he?"

"Somewhat better. His color is more natural. But he needs some serious medical attention."

"Is Hao sending someone?"

Joxe nodded but gave him a strange look. Kiri filled in, "Hao thinks we might be terrorists." She smiled at him.

The priest stood up, eyes darting. "What do you intend to do with me and the fishermen?"

"Relax, Father," Cas said. "We're not terrorists." He nodded at the radio. "Will that thing raise a ship north of us?"

"No, I will not help you."

Cas nodded. "I understand your hesitancy, Father. But before you make up your mind, I have something to tell you. We're *not* terrorists. I'm an American marine biologist and she's a Russian scientist." He jerked his thumb toward the northwest. "Somewhere out there is a Soviet spyplane that crashed into the sea. I don't know how, but it remained intact. Inside it is a weapon, a fusion weapon. That's what caused us to crash and why I told you to instruct the French pilots to come low from the south. This thing is deadly." He paused. "It's actually capable of triggering nuclear warheads anywhere within its range."

"Mon Dieu!" the priest cried, quickly crossing himself.

"We intend to find its exact location so that it can be destroyed. There's an American carrier force about six or seven hundred miles to the northeast. If we find this aircraft, they must be told where it is."

"If what you say is true," Joxe cried, "you must tell *my* government."

"No, you've already heard their reaction. They'd never believe us."

"But this—this is monstrous. They will listen."

Cas shook his head. "We can't take that chance, Father. There isn't time. I'm hoping my countrymen *will* listen."

The priest turned away. He shuffled about for a moment, mumbling to himself. Then he reached behind the radio housing and brought out a bottle of rum. The liquor was as dark as tar. He took a drink, studied the sandy floor, took another, and distractedly handed the bottle to Cas. The rum was like fire in his throat. He handed it back.

"We couldn't reach a ship that far with this radio," Joxe said at last. "It isn't powerful enough."

"Could you link with someone else?"

Father Joxe took a third drink, then nodded. "Often I talk with a ham-radio operator who lives in New Zealand." He shook his head. "A very sad case. He's confined to a wheelchair from an auto accident. We talk of many things and sometimes I play my hymns for him."

"Would he be able to raise the carrier?"

"Yes. He's very smart with radios and has lots of power."

"Will you contact him?"

"Yes."

Cas stood up. "Thank you, Father. There are two other things."

"Ah?"

"Will those fishermen let us take their canoe?"

"If I ask them."

"We'll also need a radio."

"This is the only one for miles around."

"How do you power it?"

"Car batteries."

"After you speak with this man in New Zealand, we'll have to take it."

Father Joxe looked at the radio. He said something softly to himself. Cas understood how he felt. Stuck way the hell and gone out here, it was probably the only thing that had filled his long, lonely nights. It would be an irretrievable loss. At last he sighed. "Yes, of course."

"Do you have explosives?" Kiri asked.

The priest looked at her. "Explosives? No, of course not."

"Gasoline?"

"Yes. I keep a small drum for my parish people when their outboard engines run out. But it's contaminated and would have to be filtered."

"That won't matter," she said. "Where is it?"

"Up near the church."

"We'll also need empty bottles and soap. And some cloth and waterproof matches."

Puzzled, Joxe nodded. "I have these things."

Kiri darted out.

Cas said, "Father, raise your New Zealander."

The priest knelt before his radio and began adjusting the dial. He talked softly into the mike, repeating the call name "Wheelman," then paused, listening. Contact came back quickly, a powerful signal that reverberated through the radio's speakers: "Aye, Father, what a bloody pleasant surprise."

Joxe explained about raising the *Coral Sea*.

"The Yank carrier? Aye, I've been trackin' the ruddy thing on my charts. Big ado up there, eh, Father?"

"Can you raise it?"

"I'll damn well have a go at her. She's a bit outback, but sounds like a bingo exercise."

Cas tapped the priest's shoulder. "Let me speak to him." Joxe handed him the mike. "Wheelman, my name's Bonner. We've got an iffy situation here. Too long to explain. I appreciate your help."

"Lay me up, Bonner."

"We'll need a clear link to the *Coral Sea*. But we're moving the priest's radio, so our range will be very limited. Possible?"

"No problem. I've got big ears. Just scatter and I'll home to you in a tick."

"When you raise the *Coral Sea*, identify us by saying we were aboard the helicopter CH-42 with January, Abrams, and Woodcroft. Do you copy?"

"Abrams, Woodcroft, and what was the first?"

"January. Like the month."

"Got it, mate."

"Tell them the chopper was shot down by an energy beam. January dead and Woodcroft wounded. The beam is capable of detonating nuclear ordnance."

There was a second's pause and then Wheelman came hurling back. "Bloody hell, Bonner! Is this fair dinky-di?"

"Every goddamned word. And time's running out fast."

"Sounds like a bleedin' gack."

"It's that and more. Please."

"Good-oh, I'll stick."

"We'll be moving now."

"How long will you be clear?"

"I don't know, maybe several hours. What's your squawk frequency?"

"One-five-three-point-one."

Just then Kiri stepped back into the shack, the P-6 in her hand. "Hold it," she said. Cas and Joxe swung around. Kiri waved the muzzle of the pistol. "Stand away from the radio."

"Shit!" Cas said disgustedly.

"Just go quiet, Casimir," she said. "Please don't be an asshole." She looked at Joxe. "Father, step away from the radio."

Frightened, the priest obeyed.

"Did you copy that, Bonner?" Wheelman asked.

Kiri swung the frequency dial away from him. The loudspeaker buzzed softly for a moment as she homed up to her Auckland agent's call frequency. It took nearly three minutes to bring him back, all the time Kiri calling and watching Bonner and the priest closely.

At last Auckland clicked on.

"Raise the *poule*," she said. "I am very close to Brother's aircraft. It is somewhere north of Tuariva. Will have more precise heading within next four hours. Copy?"

"Yes."

"Ship in extremely dangerous state. If recovery impossible, I intend to destroy it. End transmission."

The speaker hummed again.

Father Joxe was staring wide-eyed at her. "You *are* a terrorist."

She ignored him. "All right, Cas, you and the priest start dismantling the radio."

Cas looked at her in sardonic amusement.

"Goddammit," Kiri snapped. "Please don't give me a hard time here."

"You don't need that."

"What?"

"I want to find that goddamned plane as bad as you do." He smiled broadly at her. "We can debate what we do with it after we find it."

"I don't trust you."

He shrugged. "Then shoot us." Father Joxe's eyes went wide.

"Damn you!" Kiri cried. Then she hissed, shook her head. With a quick dip she lifted her Levi pantleg and slid the pistol into its holster. She straightened. "Happy?"

"I've been happier."

On the MAQ platform, Michel Cotuse sat stiffly at his control board, feeling displaced pulses of energy in his body similar to those hurtling through his collider tubes. The final Q-velocity run had just started.

So far everything was coming up clean on the reading displays. Eyeing the sequence numbers rolling without red interject, Cotuse thought it a miracle that they were functioning at all. The explosion on the SE-144 quadrant had done extensive damage to the precise balance of circuit integrity. Fortunately, the all-important Weber antenna had not been damaged. As for the rest, the divers had needed nearly four hours to bypass the destroyed junction box, string new conduit connectors, and rig a "floater" panel suspended from buoys. Finally everything was linked up again and working.

The loss of Joffre had struck the platform's personnel like a violent, dark wind. All that had been left of him, the divers reported, had been a cloud of blood and scattered chunks of flesh. Paradoxically, though, the incident had also somehow reenergized the entire team, particularly Cotuse. It had taken the death of a colleague to burn out the last of his lingering doubts and infuse him with a resurgence of his old determination.

At precisely 8:08, he ordered hydrogen gas jetted into the injector chambers. The low-power magnet system was activated. Gauss readings came up swiftly as clusters of protons fumed off the hydrogen nuclei and were started from natural state into initial hurl. Within nanoseconds the clusters, narrowed into a beam, were allowed into the first accelerating ring. Section "four-pi" monitors came on line, feeding detection imput into the control consoles, where it was digitalized and processed.

Cotuse momentarily held the proton mass at a steady velocity of eighty thousand miles per second. As station calorimeters registered momentum energy levels, the read indicated the mass was in the million-electron-volt range.

Head swiveling back and forth, Cotuse scanned his monitor screens. To his left were the flux-return detectors, which measured and identified the angulation of the protons' trajectories. The data was taped before being displayed on the imaging tubes. So far the patterns were well within primary-model limits. Heat and gamma factor monitors, which registered the force created by the increasing mass of the accelerated protons, remained in the green zone.

Cotuse ordered the second proton mass activated in the linear injector. It was instantly driven to entry speed and given access to the first accelerating ring. Seconds passed. Once more all field checks showed a satisfactory run state.

At 8:16 he ordered beam access to the second accelerator ring. This chamber contained three times the number of magnets of the first ring. They were denser units utilizing high-temperature, superconducting wire coils that created greater deflection speeds. Both proton masses climbed in velocity, crossing into the billion-electron-volt (GeV) range. Monitored velocity was now clocked at one hundred and ten thousand miles per second.

Again Cotuse held steady state while his computers ingested data. The emergency reaction circuits were automatically activated. Instantly, high above the control room, secondary transformers kicked in, held stability level as the second-ring magnets began eating up megawatt power. Now the four Weber antennas started showing a first-sign deflection read of four nanometers as their GF-detector needles eased gently up into the outer range of green field.

He ordered increased power to the magnets and held it there. Proton mass velocity leaped to one hundred forty thousand miles per second. Energy range moved to eight trillion electron volts (TeV). Data chains were coming off the "hot-feed" analyzers directly onto span-imaging displays. The trajectory tracks indicated a slight divergence of momentum resolution.

When Cotuse yelled for flux-return check, the order created frantic arm movement among the down technicians. Switches clicked, hard sequences came up. Michel peered at them so intently that a pain began to form behind his eyes.

Below him, Savon was inducting data, muscular arms darting. Around the room technicians were calling fix rates. Flux return indicated a stabilization of the trajectory track with a steady velocity state holding.

Michel took it all in and sighed in relief. So far, so good. At 8:22 he ordered beam access to the third and final accelerator ring.

To the southwest, the Saber's computer began bringing up analyzed parameters of a new magnetic wash:

```
SOURCE: (TAPE X113):RANGE 150 KILOMETERS/BEARING 067 DEGREES
MAGNETIC FIELD BUBBLE: HARMONIC INDUCTION: 200 MEGAWATTS
MAGNETIC TORQUE DIVERGENCE: (BASE: 1.25664 X 10/-6): 10% GAUSS
   (MAXWELL)
TRACE ELEMENT: PROTON PLASMA FUME (MAGNETIC CONFINED)
PLASMA STATUS: NON-READ ELECTRON VOLT RANGE
```

The Kamov hurried through its memory banks for ident analysis. The answer was: Non-entry??? As it rescanned, the sensor reads suddenly jumped dramatically. The computer ingested:

```
HARMONIC INDUCTION: 250 MEGAWATTS
MAGNETIC TORQUE DIVERGENCE: (B): 30% GAUSS (WEBER)//FLUTTER
   INCREASE//LORENTZ FORCE: 10/10
```

PLASMA STATUS: SECONDARY FLOW (ID: PROTON)/ GAMMA COMPONENT/
MILLION ELECTRONVOLT (MEV) RANGE

Again the Kamov searched its memory banks. Once more the answer was: Nonentry??? It went to the AI:

STATUS: PROTON BEAM CHANNEL
SUPPOSITIONAL PURPOSE: PROTON COLLISION (?)
EMR: POTENTIAL EXTREME: MONITOR/MONITOR

The entry of the proton beams into the third and final accelerator ring went smoothly. The third ring would operate in three power stages, each increasing the velocity of the proton masses. The last stage would accelerate them to the speed of light: one hundred eighty-six thousand miles per second. One trillionth of a second before this was achieved, a series of quadrupole magnets would automatically deflect both beam masses slightly out of flux trajectory and into a head-on track. Collision would then occur at precisely the moment both masses reached Q-velocity.

As in-feed data rolled in with astronomical rapidity, boost power click-ons energized computer and analyzer circuits to their maximum limits. In the huge generators on the main deck, the output passed three hundred megawatts.

The tension in the control room was like a greasy steam, so congealed it seemed to stick to objects. All around the room, men were sweating freely now. They jumped, blinked, recoiled at the slightest flicker of their screens. The experiment was now entering an area of proton velocity no human had ever witnessed before. The first power stage brought the beam masses to twenty trillion electron volts. Mapped velocity: 155,000 miles per second.

Seeing that the flux returns were showing slight trajectory "flare," Cotuse ordered a check hold. Background field waves were forming on the outer perimeters of the accelerator channel. Analysis indicated lepton fumes were surging out of the swing orbits. But the muon detectors registered low-range, non-interference, parallel assimilation. Still, the Weber antennas were showing that deflection had increased to ten nanometers, and the read needles were easing into orange range.

Cotuse considered a moment, then ordered the second power stage. Proton energy jumped to thirty trillion electron volts. Mapped velocity: 168,000 miles per second. Infeed came spewing across console screens, throwing light panels into rapid sequential flows. The imaging equipment formed crazy-quilt patterns of trace lines as brightly green as glowing emeralds.

Cotuse felt his bowels constricting, then an overpowering urge to defecate. He tried to swallow. His mouth was as dry as mummy dust. He willed himself to control his body, focusing his concentration to a needlepoint of intensity. He would need all of his will power to make the final decision.

The Kamov was busy constructing overview graph displays of the increasing magnetic, harmonic, gamma-throw, and proton-velocity voltage ranges when another sharp jump came through the sensors. The computer rapidly collated and fed to analysis banks. A few seconds passed before parameters returned:

HARMONIC INDUCTION: 300 MEGAWATTS
MAGNETIC VECTOR DIVERGENCE: (B): 60% GAUSS (WEBER)//EDGE OF
   SENSOR CAPABILITY
PLASMA STATUS: (EST): APPROACHING LIGHT VELOCITY//FRICTION COM-
   PONENT INCREASING//20 + TRILLION ELECTRON VOLTS (TEV)

The Kamov went to the AI:

STATUS: PROTON PRECESSION IMMINENT//CONFUSED PARTICLE COLLI-
   SION WITH RADIOACTIVE THROW
EMR: EXTREME: CATEGORY FOUR: INFUSION, REDUCTION

The Kamov activated the fusion chamber and began feeding in azimuth, range, and discharge time data to the firing-barrel system. The home fix was the weather tower's occulating strobe light.

Cotuse ordered the third power stage.

Along the outer accelerator ring, tiny bubbles were forming in the metal seams as tremendous heat pulses created by the friction of the lepton fume chafed the channel walls. Air bubbles popped off the seams, made tiny fluorescent pockets, shaped like umbrellas that wobbled toward the surface. Energy state was now at fifty trillion electron volts. Mapped velocity: 184,000 miles per second.

Red lights began flashing on consoles all around the control room. Savon yelled something that was instantly joined by technicians' voices along the second bank. In his master seat, Cotuse was mesmerized by what he was seeing on his screens. Imaging displays were breaking into kaleidoscopic chaos. Trace tracks of every color in the spectrum, and colors unseen before were creating vividly glowing curlicues, arcs, pinwheels.

Cotuse blinked, trying to clear his retinas of the colors, but couldn't. He looked away, then back. A single dial face sprang out at him, the one with little sparkles of light on it, residue of the track screens. It was the Weber antenna read. The needles were beyond the red zone.

Unmeasurable gravitational force!

His mouth shot open. Out of it came a scream: "Abort! Abort!"

The Kamov ran rapid-firing sequence checks. The return numbers were hurled onto displays in the cockpit, internally evaluated, marked off. Two seconds later, it sent the firing command.

The beam struck the radio beacon light, transferred itself to the tower girders. With lightning speed it traveled down the tower to the platform. Harmonic tremors and powerful waves of energy swept through decking, infused conduits, struts, and lines. High above the main structure in the power station, the charge was hurled into the control panels. Instantly a massive shortage took place in the circuits that were carrying the gigantic amounts of electricity to the accelerator. All along the system there was a violent power surge. Everything—five hundred million watts of power—in the storage capacitors blew through the system at once.

The thousands of accelerator magnets around the outer ring instantly surged. The proton masses, now on the very edge of the speed of light, were given a tremendous magnetic boost and hurled into full Q-velocity. At the same moment, as the surge blew out all control units, the quadrupole magnets that guided the trajectory of the proton masses automatically altered them into convergence alignments.

The masses collided!

There was a blinding, white-hot flash of luminescent energy at the impact core. From it was hurled a glowing soup of quarks, leptons, and gamma particles. Arcing trajectories crisscrossed each other, creating new collisions.

0.000001 seconds . . .

The main collision momentum, still packed with kinetic energy, surged through the time/space fabric. Energy became matter. Out of nothingness appeared infinitesimal particles of matter, axions a hundred million times denser than a proton.

0.00001 seconds . . .

A gravitational field formed around the axion mass. It was one billion times more powerful than normal proton mass gravity vector. Instantaneously gravity waves were hurtled away from it. Traveling with the speed of light, they warped the surrounding gravitational field in an expanding sphere that would travel through outer space forever.

0.0001 seconds . . .

Every molecule of matter within a radius of sixty meters from the impact core was sucked inward toward the center of the axion gravity field . . .

Michel Cotuse had felt the massive infusion of energy as the Saber's beam hurtled throughout the MAQ platform. It fused right up through the decking, crackling like a lightning bolt. He, like everyone else in the control room, froze. All he could do was stare, his mind momentarily blank, yet his visual sense was so acute that he could see the entire room with the clarity of a hundred lenses. That single moment in time was frozen against the retinas of his eyes. His heart thudded. His eyelids started to blink . . .

He felt a horrendous force lift him and his chair up into the air and hurtle him toward the opposite wall with a velocity too violent for his mind or nerves to comprehend.

His body struck the wall, *became* it. And it became the upper bulkhead and the bulkhead the decking. Wood, metal, glass, flesh, blood, air, sea, rock, all of it was compressed into a single mass of matter.

0.001 seconds . . .

As the converging matter rushed toward the axion core, molecular space was being squeezed tighter and tighter. Now the compression began to close even the atomic space between electrons and nuclei. As the mass grew even more dense, its internal heat rocketed to galactic levels.

At the same time, the axion particles were nearing the end of their life span, going into decay, and their gravitational vector force was beginning to lessen. At this point, hydrogen ions, running out the final vestiges of impact momentum, formed curving arcs and, pulled by the axion gravity force, hurtled back toward the center. There heat had now reached three thousand million degrees Celsius. Critical temperature!

The hydrogen ions instantly fused into helium, then carbon, and finally iron. Since the fusion of iron creates an exoergic reaction—the giving off of heat—a thermal backlash was created inside the axion core. Heat waves traveled through the incoming matter as the axion gravity force dissipated still further. Now the axions began decaying totally and crossed back through the time/space continuum to become energy once more. But the fusion heat, now spreading through the momentarily motionless incoming matter with tremendous speed and aided by the core heat, exploded outward.

The stupendous forces reversed their flow. Only now there was no envelope to contain the energy. An area three hundred yards around the impact site was instantly consumed by the massive thermal blowout. Whatever was left of the platform and the top layers of rock simply evaporated.

0.03 seconds . . .

There was a pause. A tiny speck of time. And then the ocean poured into the vacuum. Violent steam explosions followed. The thermal energy surging outward was instantly absorbed by the massive volume of the ocean. But then, like a runaway train, the temperature gradient plunged past normal, headed downward.

It passed the temperature of the surrounding ocean: 22 degrees Celsius . . .

Passed 10 degrees . . .

Passed 0 Celsius, freezing temperature of water . . .

Crossed minus 15 degrees . . .

Now it began to dissipate, losing momentum. But by then an area of ocean a half mile wide around the site had turned to solid ice.

15

In the mess hall of the Phoenix Island tracking station, Commander Ron Sorrel took his eye momentarily off the television screen to sop a biscuit with egg yolk. He popped it into his mouth and glanced back. On the screen two women and a man were contorted in a ménage à trois. One of the enlisted men had recently received several X-rated videos from home, and someone from the night watch had left one of the cassettes in the VCR. Now the off-duty men were running it as they ate breakfast.

The overhead loudspeaker cut through the groans and female squeals: "Mr. Sorrel, Track Shack. Jesus, you better get over here, sir." The commander grimaced, wondering, What the hell now? He pushed his plate away and got up gingerly so as not to squeeze his hard-on.

Chief Hedges was still overseeing the track watch, and he whirled completely around when Sorrel came in. "We got a fucking nuclear detonation!" he blurted.

Sorrel's penis went *zip*, straight into miniature. "What did you say?"

"We just got a satellite thermal fix. In Polynesia."

"It's gotta be the Frenchie nuclear testing site." Then he thought: No, the French suspended testing over two years ago.

"It's not from there, sir," Hedges countered. "The fix is seven hundred miles north, off the Tuamotus." Consoles all around the room were clicking furiously, ingesting reads from the NAVSAT and in-linked scientific and British/New Zealand satellites. The readouts were showing tremendous gamma-ray pickup and a gigantic burst of radio-wave impulses.

Sorrel planted himself behind the chief, his heart pounding. "Run back your thermal tapes."

As Hedges did, the pictures came up with white chit marks along the edges. The rest was solid red, with streaks of blue and green. "Skipper, look at this!" one of the other men shouted. "I'm getting out-of-sight gravitational readings."

"Run up a gravitational track plot."

A second console man yelled, "A new thermal fix coming in, sir."

Hedges's thick fingers flew over his keyboard as he began bringing in the new fix.

The first panel man called out, "Here comes the GT plot." Sorrel was beside him in two bounds. The screen was filled with white grid lines that formed a matrix of gravitational-force lines around the curve of the southern part of the earth. Right away Sorrel saw something peculiar. In the entire Capricorn quadrant, the lines were turned inward in opposing positions.

Sorrel backed away a little, studying the picture. Something vaguely familiar about it struck him. Where in hell had he seen it before? College, . . . astronomy class. That was it: It was the classic pattern of the advance of the perihelion of Mercury. He sucked in his breath. That meant the earth's gravity in the Capricorn had experienced *gravitational-wave distortion!*

Holy shit! he thought.

He charged back to Hedges's screen, a new thermal picture had already been brought up. It shimmered with electronic quiver but was totally changed. Everything that had been red on the first fix was now blue. Malfunction, Sorrel thought. "Reprocess the tape," he bellowed.

Seconds passed. The reprocessed picture came on. It was the same. Both men leaned way in, nearly poking their faces against the glass. Hedges said, "I don't believe this. We're looking at fucking *ice*."

Sorrel whirled and started toward the radio room. Then he stopped dead. Something was missing. There was no radiation pickup, he realized. If it had been a nuclear blast, then where the hell was the goddamned radiation read?

One second after the core collision in the MAQ's collider ring, all ships of the *Coral Sea* task group lost their communications.

The carrier and her escort vessels had been holding three-sixties four hundred fifty miles ENE of the platform, following new, explicit orders from COMMPAC. Reacting to the aerial battle, Washington had decided to pour more force into the Capricorn and areas west. Passmore was to hold station until the CVN-68's elements could achieve their positions southeast of the Marshall Islands. Surveillance indicated that the *Minsk* group was still sheltering among the Societies, undoubtedly also waiting for its own reinforcement from Cam Ranh. All in all, it was beginning to look like a major naval engagement.

Amid all the stepped-up action, though, Admiral Passmore found himself bothered by something else entirely. His debriefing with Waltham and Joberlesky had been a strange one. The CAG was visibly depressed, jumpy, not at all like himself. And when he recounted the sequence of the combat, he stressed repeatedly that Wolfe had been shot down by a mysterious energy force and not by the Russian Forger. Jobber backed him up on it. Neither knew what that energy source had been, but it was sure as hell there.

JCS, working off their own assessments, wrote off the report of this energy force as due to combat stress. To Passmore, that was bullshit. These were vets, good flyers. Further, their report corroborated what that January fellow had said about a weapon out there. In any case, he decided not to press the issue with Washington, particularly since his orders specifically forbade him sending further aircraft into the general area for now.

When all of his communications went totally haywire, Passmore received the news with something akin to dread. Even as he ordered everyone momentarily to resort to the old blinkers and signal flags, he called for a complete report from all sectors. Sure enough, it turned out to be weirder than a communications malfunction. Reports were coming in of all sorts of other equipment going crazy: generators, capacitors, magnetic storage cells. Even the main engine compartments reported a millisecond of power dropoff before automatic backups kicked in. Throughout the entire task force, buzzers and Klaxons started blaring, and some of the crewmen swore they had heard their hulls *humming*.

Of the aircraft flying defense positions, only the two Hawkeye Hummers experienced serious problems. Although all aircraft had lost communications, the Hummers' Allison T56-A-422 reciprocating engines had simply died. Boom, same instant. One of the Hummers didn't get its engine restarted until it was almost into the sea.

The *Minsk* wasn't that lucky . . .

The report of the aerial dogfight and loss of his air wing commander had shaken Admiral Turesky. Here he was, alone in a southern ocean caught between American and incoming French naval forces, and support elements from Cam Ranh might be too late to deploy adequately to protect his flank. Added to that was the confusion in Moscow. His instructions from Cam Ranh were showing a decided turn to aggressiveness. But what did he have to be aggressive with? The admiral was no coward, but he was also no fool.

When Lieutenant Nitlitzin returned from his mission, he, too, had a strange story of an energy beam that had in fact shot down the American F-14 and triggered the engagement between Koik and the other Tomcat. Turesky grilled the young pilot himself, but the lieutenant stuck to his story, leaving the admiral thoroughly puzzled. He dutifully sent off an extensive report of Nitlitzin's debriefing to Vladivostok and Moscow, hoping they could figure out what the hell was happening.

By now the *skadra* had reached the northern fringes of the Leeward Islands of the Societies. Turesky ordered a slight course adjustment to the west and regrouped the formation between the last two islands of the chain, Bellingshausen and Mopelia, before breaking into open ocean. It was at that moment when the effect of the French collider's Q-velocity explosion reached the *skadra*.

Computers and communications consoles throughout the bridge went silent after a crackling surge. Crewmen and officers jumped, startled at the sudden silence. Like a crossing sunbeam, a minute energy wave seemed to pass through the air. To the right, a small compass encased in anti-magnetic glass suddenly shattered.

Turesky felt a cold shiver touch him, penetrating deep into his tissues. Looking up, he saw in the faces around him that the others had also felt it. He looked toward the bridge window. Aft, above the skyline of antennae and radar dishes, he saw a Forger that had just been settling onto the number three in-board TD circle. He watched as in agonizing slow motion the aircraft began to drop out of its slanted position. Exhaust blast blew off the deck, scattering crewmen. The Forger nosed down, twisting violently.

The port wing tip collided with the deck and folded inward like paper. The impact instantly whirled the fighter over, exhaust ports showing white-hot, the nose coming down hard on the deck, crumbling. The aircraft swiveled crazily, like a wounded bird flapping helplessly out of control, then there was a violent, blinding explosion as the jet's tanks went up.

Every person on the bridge cowered in reflex as debris splattered across the outside of the port bulkheads. Shrapnel, trailing smoke, went hurtling past the bridge window. On the deck, a roiling blossom of burning fuel erupted upward, laced with black smoke and fire. The accompanying concussion threw the admiral from his pedestal seat.

Turesky found his face pressed against someone's shoe. On his hands and knees, he tried to get up. At last hands grabbed him and brought him to his feet. He swayed a moment. The *Minsk*'s skipper was near the bridge barking orders; Klaxons were blaring furiously. Outside, the crash site burned fiercely, hurling steady, boiling clouds of smoke.

On Mururoa Atoll, site of the French Centre d'Experimentation du Pacifique, the first sign of trouble was an explosion in a lime quarry near the nuclear storage bunkers, located on the north end of the twenty-five-mile-long atoll. A blasting crew had been shooting lime with shallow wall charges of Telex dynamite running off electrical fuses. Three men were still on the blasting face when a mysterious splurge of electrical energy flashed through the lines. The fuses ignited and all three men were killed.

Seconds later, red warning lights throughout the huge monitoring complex of control bunkers, warehouses, and communications buildings began flashing. Only a skeleton crew of engineers and maintenance technicians was still on the island, for the previous day, AlPaci Command, uncertain of the Russian *skadra*'s intentions, had ordered evacuation of most of the four thousand workers at the base. The remaining Foreign Legionnaire patrols, bolstered by a company from Hoa, drove through the huge, cement-domed nuclear-mass caches lined along the northern beach. Within these bunkers, only sixty feet underground, was raw fissionable material with a blast potential of five million megatons.

In the main control building, watch crews bristled with anxiety as their monitors reported gamma radiation calibrated at galactic levels. Thermal readings as well left a sharp upthrust on tracing displays. But the most astounding reads were the gravitational fluctuations. Tapes came up showing complex patterns of altered gravity grids.

The initial analysis was thermonuclear detonation. Position fix: coordinates: 146:30/10:10, six hundred miles NNE. The MAQ platform! Frantic technicians raced to their radios to raise AlPaci. But it took them several minutes to establish contact. All internal and overseas communications had malfunctioned due to sudden overloads in transformer units. And when they finally did raise Papeete, the receiver consoles warbled distortedly as if the incoming signals were being filtered through water.

Cas had just fitted the last of the five car batteries up under the canoe hull's starboard coaming. Like the others, it was wrapped in *lauhala* matting to keep it dry. Father Joxe and one of the fishermen struggled out with the radio, carrying it between them, and deposited it into the port hull.

Straightening, the profusely sweating priest pressed his palms into his back. He gazed for a long moment toward the north, then looked at Cas. "I do not understand these things, Monsieur Bonner. All I know is that they make me very frightened."

"I wish I could reassure you, Father. I can't."

"Are my people in danger of dying?"

"Yes."

"Ah, sweet Virgin Mother." He shook his weathered head sadly. "I will pray for you and"—he nodded toward Kiri—"the *feminist voleur armé.*"

"Thank you." As Cas shook the priest's hand, he noticed it was horny, like the hand of a coal miner.

Joxe said, "What must I tell the men from Hoa?"

"I leave that to you."

"I cannot lie." Joxe thought a moment, then brightened. "To get through the reef, you'll first have to point toward the south, will you not? I will therefore not be guilty of a lie if I say you—"

The onset of a bizarre force in the sky cut off the rest of his sentence. Cas felt it wash over him—like wind riffling in the air, but these penetrated his body, down so deep they seemed to make his inner organs vibrate. Pulses thrummed through tissue. He lifted his arm and stared at the hairs on his forearm. They were standing straight up.

He glanced at Kiri across the mast stays. The hair on her head was also standing out, lifting as if from a powerful blow dryer. Beside her, the linnet cord stays were humming. The big Tahitian who had helped Joxe with the radio suddenly farted loudly, and his eyes opened with surprise. "*Afe!* My *opu* feel funny, Father."

As the vibrations faded, Cas placed his hand on the solid koa gunwale of the canoe, testing it. Then he lightly touched the metal of the radio housing. In it he felt an energy force. Suddenly the windows of the church up the hill blew out, spreading glass shards onto the rock-hard ground. Cas's eyes shot up at the sound, stared. The church's tiny steeple held a faint halo of bluish light around it! And the withered *mape* were also glowing.

"*Sainte Vierge!*" Father Joxe croaked, crossing himself three times. The Tahitian fisherman swung around and lunged toward the beach, plowing through the thigh-high water.

"Kiri," Cas shouted. "What the hell is it? The plane?"

A shadow seemed to cross over them. But it was neither a shade nor darkness. It seemed a light-on-light variation. Everywhere. Cas looked up at the sun. It was shimmering and it, too, held a faint blue aurora. He heard Kiri whisper, "Oh my god!"

"What is it? What the hell is it?"

Her face was stark. "It's a plasma-wave turbulence," she said, in the hushed tones of a woman watching a tornado streaking toward her house. Distractedly she moved along the canoe, staring at the sky.

Bonner was suddenly aware of her scent. A fear odor, but more. It was as if his senses had been suddenly tuned to such a high level that he could actually smell all of her: hair, saliva, vaginal secretion, skin, armpits. "Get down," he snapped and reached for her.

Kiri shook her head. "It won't make any difference. Something's already happened out there, something unbelievably powerful."

Cas instantly placed both his palms onto the coaming, pivoted himself and went into the water. He grabbed the prow of the canoe. "Lay out on the center brace," he yelled to her. She obeyed without question, crawled out onto the mid-struts, and stretched out on her stomach.

Cas reeled in the stone anchor and tossed it onto the coaming. Then, bracing his feet in the sand, he shoved the canoe out into deeper water, held on, and let its momentum pull him aboard. As he scampered across the mid-brace, he released the sail booms.

They snapped down, opening the triangular sail. For a moment it fluttered, then caught the wind, swinging the twin hulls around sharply. Cas crawled over Kiri and lay out on the after mid-strut, the tiller locked under his arm. The canoe began picking up speed, sweeping over submerged coral heads.

As the twin prows hissed through the water and threw spray, Cas grinned at Kiri, a cold, narrow-eyed, enraged grin. He'd had enough of this bullshit. It was time they found this fucking monster.

Nanoseconds after the MAQ explosion, the Saber's cockpit panels and light boards had come up into full display. Warning signals were blinking furiously, buzzers humming. The incoming feed was so immense that the Kamov sensed a jolt throughout its systems, a millisecond of power interference. It came back on bristling, sensors alive and power probing. The read was chaotic. Data banks were automatically running through ingested parameters, trying desperately to locate a ground base so as to work from it.

The Kamov was flashing through material with lightning speed, yet its sectional banks were proving inadequate for analysis. The computer overrode input, went to the AI unit. It demanded isolation fix and analysis.

The artificial-intelligence unit was momentarily quiescent, as if confused. Inwardly, however, it was creating projected scenarios in an effort to box and identify the mass of in-feed into real-time parameters. On the cockpit displays these scenarios made high-velocity picture shifts: stick figures, trigonometric patterns, whirling helixes. At last it began to draw conclusions and hurled them back to the Kamov:

GAMMA FUNCTION: (COHERENT RANGE): 0.005–0.5 NANOMETER WITH
    ISOMETRIC RADIATIVE TRANSITION
THERMAL GRADIENT: 3.4000000 TMM/C
RADIATION: 0.01333 (ERP COMPONENT)
ATMOSPHERIC DISRUPTION: 88.55 %
SEISMIC PRINTOUT: 0.115 KILOSECONDS/ FACTOR 7.7

The AI formulated danger assessment:

DD-E FIX: MAXIMUM
ANALYSIS FIX: NUCLEAR EXPLOSION
CMR: GO TO CATEGORY FIVE

16

A nuclear detonation?

The report struck Washington like a Carolina hurricane. Admiral Hubbel was the first member of the National Security Council to hear about it, enroute between the Pentagon and the White House. A few minutes later, he burst into a luncheon meeting the President was holding with other NSC people in the conference room adjacent to the Oval Office. "Somebody just hit the nuclear button," he blurted.

The four men around the table—the President, McQuisten, Richfield, and Secretary of State Aldridge, just in from London—jerked up, forks and coffee cups poised.

"There's been a powerful nuclear explosion in Polynesia," Hubbel went on. "Track shows it was on the French platform."

For a moment the tableau at the table remained motionless. Then the President swore vehemently and slammed down his fork. "How bad?" he snapped.

"Data is sketchy, but it blew the platform away. That much is certain. There's also been some very strange phenomena."

"What phenomena?"

"Satellite photos are showing large sections of ice on the ocean."

"Ice?"

"Yes, sir. And warpage of gravitational fields in the area."

"Jesus Christ," Richfield said. "What the hell kind of nuclear blast is that? That's not normal, is it?"

The President glanced at McQuisten. "Tim, get NASA on the horn, and NORAD at Cheyenne Mountain. I want some questions answered."

McQuisten rushed out. One of the telephones beside the conference table buzzed. Hubbel, the closest to it, picked it up. He listened for a second, then replaced the receiver.

"That was Director Levi at NASA, sir. Nobody's picking up any radiation readings or powerful seismic reports from anywhere in the Capricorn. They doubt it was nuclear, but don't have any idea what the hell it was."

"Goddammit," the President cried. "What the hell are we looking at here?"

"Could it be a new Russian weapon?" Richfield put in.

"You tell me."

The CIA chief, trapped, put his palms up. "If it is, sir, the bastards have kept it tighter than anything I've come up against."

Aldridge leaned forward. He was a distinguished-looking man, the image of the aging Harvard lawyer with the aura of judicial aloofness. "Perhaps it was an accident. We don't really know what the French were doing on that platform. Maybe the whole project just got out of hand."

The President shot a glance back to Richfield. "Possible?"

"I doubt it, sir. My scientists tell me that they were running super-collider experiments out there. Nothing that could generate this kind of power."

"Well, shit."

"Sir," Richfield went on, "the more I think about it, the more I'm thinking secret weapon here."

"Then why didn't they use it sooner?"

"Maybe Markisov was holding back. Now, with the hard-liners apparently in control, they gave the green light."

The President glared at him. "We're going to talk about this later. I won't accept this kind of intelligence lapse."

"Yes, sir," Richfield said quietly.

He turned to Hubbel. "What's your assessment?"

"I think Richfield may be right. It fits."

"So what do we have? Nuclear blast or a secret weapon capable of this?"

"Let's assume nuclear parameters for the sake of reaction."

"All right, then give me operational options."

Hubbel found a seat and lowered himself into it. "Once nuclear threshold is crossed, our reaction strategy specifies three primary objectives: immediate military transition to defensive war condition; isolation of detonation zone to contain escalation; and rapid deployment of countermeasure forces to negate further strikes."

Although every man present had repeatedly heard these same phrases in strategic briefings, the words suddenly took on terrifying proportions. All about the table men readjusted neckties, folded hands, tapped fingers. The President was the first to speak: "How long for your people to get me an ST-1 report with recommendations?"

"One hour, sir," Hubbel snapped.

"Then get on it. And I want constant updates until it's here."

The admiral hesitated. "Mr. President, I'd recommend you do three things immediately."

"Which are?"

"First, order the *Coral Sea* into French waters."

"No! Not yet."

"Then will you at least allow Passmore to move into an offensive position so he can bottle up that Russian carrier force in the Societies? Before it tries to break out into open ocean. CVN-68 can sea deploy to intercept the Cam Ranh sortie. Sir, if those twin Soviet carrier groups link, we could have one helluva sea battle on our hands."

The President thought a moment, then nodded. "All right, go ahead with that. But keep the *Coral Sea* out of AlPaci territory. I don't want that situation getting any more mucked up than it already is. What else?"

"Order deployment of Coordinated Europe Forces into the Norwegian and Danish Seas. They could blockade the Russians from setting up sea-missile platforms for strikes against NATO."

Again the President nodded. "Agreed. But let's not go at this thing hog-wild. If the hardasses *are* in control over in Moscow, that would give the pricks just the provocation they'd need to call for a full-scale war."

Another phone buzzed. This time the President took it, listened, hung it up. "NORAD backs up NASA. The explosion was not nuclear."

"Well," Aldridge said, "at least we've got that much."

"Which may still be nothing," the President countered. "Go ahead, Admiral."

"My third recommendation is to lay out our attack subs to counter the Soviets from moving into bastion positions in the Barents Sea and the northern Pacific." Bastioning was an accepted concept under U.S. maritime strategy. It supposed the Russians would, in wartime, gather their missile subs into pockets adjacent to their territorial land areas with attack subs running outer guard. From these sanctuaries their missile boats could launch intercontinental-ballistic strikes against the United States.

The President eyed Hubbel for a long moment, then sighed. "Okay, start redeployment. Again, go slow. Don't hurtle our subs in like the fucking cavalry with sabers drawn."

"Yes, sir."

"All right, move, move."

Hubbel hurried away.

The President turned to Aldridge and Richfield. "Bill, start hitting diplomatic contacts. Start with the French. I want to know their reactions. If you run into tremors from Paris, I'll talk to Vasillon myself."

The secretary of state nodded.

"Richfield, I want everything your field people can get on world reaction. And, goddammit, tell me what the hell is going on in Moscow. You think you can handle that?"

"Yes, sir."

The door swung open, and McQuisten rushed in. "Mr. President, we've just got word that Premier Markisov is alive." The President swung fully around in his chair to look at him. McQuisten was nodding joyously. "News reports are flooding in. The general secretary just held a special session of the Supreme Soviet and faced down the Old Guard. Minister Bardeshevsky has been arrested."

"All right!" the President shouted. He leaped out of his chair and scurried around the room, distractedly rubbing his elbow. "We've got a reprieve." Then he stopped beside the window and turned to Aldridge. "Can he maintain control of the situation?"

"There's no way to be sure, sir. Old Guard momentum could be too strong."

"Richfield?"

"Bill's right. Markisov's power could be very tenuous. The thing might blow up in his face."

The President started prowling again, his brow furrowed. He crossed the window twice and finally paused. "Notify Hubbel of the situation. Tell him we're still go on the options we discussed. Tim, I want key congressional members up here by the time Hubbel returns with his report."

McQuisten nodded and dodged out.

The President turned to the other two. "I want minute-by-minute updates on what's happening in Moscow. And everything, *everything*, that foreign embassies are picking up." He studied them coldly. "And let's just pray to Christ, friend Yuri is strong enough to keep kicking ass."

French President Vasillon had spent the past few hours in a rising pitch of anxiety. Now faced with a Russian ultimatum for immediate apology over the downing of the Forger, he was caught in a whirlwind of indecisiveness.

Defense Minister Frenier had continued his exhortations to stand firm against the Soviets. "Moscow's in turmoil," Frenier kept pointing out. "The Bolshevik bastards will not fight."

Prime Minister Alain Chambaudet, who had just returned from Canada, was in opposition. He'd been shocked at the aggressive tone of the newspapers in Paris, who hailed Lieutenant Cogne's actions as heroic. When told of the ultimatum, he had immediately advised negotiations be conducted with Moscow to find a viable resolution to the situation.

Vasillon and Chambaudet were alone when Frenier rushed in with word of the explosion in Polynesia. The defense minister was so shaken, he could hardly get the words out. He thrust a communiqué onto the desk, which Chambaudet picked up and read in stony silence.

"What does it say?" Vasillon cried desperately.

"Apparently a nuclear device was detonated on the MAQ," Chambaudet answered softly.

"*Mon Dieu!*" Vasillon croaked. Then, recovering, he whirled on Frenier. "You imbecile! You said they would not fight."

"Monsieur President, I—" Frenier stammered. "I am over-whelmed."

"Now what do we do?" Vasillon demanded furiously. "Now what in the name of God do we do?" He seemed near fainting. "Sweet Mother, this means war!"

Chambaudet came out of his silence. "Vasillon," he said sharply. "You must immediately contact the Americans. If the Russians have done this—and we are not certain they have—Washington's reaction is our only salvation. The Pacific belongs to the United States. Any retaliation or diplomatic thrust must come from the American president."

Vasillon stared at him, and then a look of relief came over him. "Yes, of course, Alain. Yes, we must speak to the president."

Chambaudet turned to Frenier, who was still staring ashen-faced at the desk. "You, I want everything you can find out about this explosion. Dammit, Frenier, do you hear me?"

"What? Oh, yes."

"Now!"

The defense minister left, moving slowly, shaking his head. Chambaudet stepped to Vasillon's side and lightly touched his arm. "We must not panic, Pierre."

"Ah, Alain, this is horrible. Are we looking at the beginning of the end?"

"Perhaps."

"*Mon Dieu!*" It was a cry of pure pain.

"Steel yourself, Pierre," Chambaudet snapped. "I'm going now to establish your link with Washington."

"Yes," Vasillon said. "Yes, hurry."

When full communications were finally reestablished on the *Coral Sea,* the first message from COMMPAC put flag op into momentary paralysis. A nuclear blast in Polynesia had been recorded! The news went through the ship with the velocity of light. Barely a minute after receipt of the news, Waltham and Gretton barged through the bridge door, too overwhelmed to go through the formal ritual of entry.

By then Admiral Passmore had recovered his senses enough to explode in a flurry of curses. The CAG and XO exchanged glances: Passmore's behavior told them clearly that the scuttlebutt was true.

The radio officer who had first received the message timidly approached Passmore's seat and held out a verification of the original communiqué. The admiral whipped it out of his hand. "God damn the bastards!" he growled, as the radio officer scurried away.

Waltham and Gretton stepped forward, and Passmore fixed them with a steely glare. "What's available?" he roared at Waltham.

"Four planes down, sir, one F-18 and three 14s. If we make shortcuts, we can have nearly a full complement. Where was the hit?"

"The French platform."

"Jesus," Gretton groaned. "I didn't think they'd actually do it."

"Who the hell did?" Passmore snapped. "All right, CAG, load 'em up. I know fucking-A well what the joint chiefs will recommend to the president: full-out strike on the Russian carrier. And I goddamned agree. You will be ready when word comes down, do you hear?"

"Yes, sir."

"I want complete readiness reports in thirty minutes."

"Aye, aye," Waltham said, darting away.

"Gretton, contact group skippers. Notify them we are likely to be going after the Soviet carrier group. I want status reports from them here in fifteen minutes."

"Yes, sir," Gretton said, starting to turn away.

"One other thing. Instruct them to rig for radiation. There are strong winds aloft from the south. Christ knows what we'll be catching in about two hours."

"Aye, aye, sir." Gretton fled.

Passmore dropped into brooding silence for a moment, then sprang from his seat and headed for the door as the watch officer called, "Attention! Admiral leaving the bridge."

Before his stateroom door, his marine guard braced, Passmore brushed by him, slammed the door, and made straight for a safe beside his desk. He spun up combinations, inserted a key hung on a silver chain around his neck, and pulled the door open. It was small but heavy, made of finely milled carbon steel.

Inside were stacks of brown manila envelopes. He sorted through them and chose two. He relocked the safe and sat at his desk. The envelopes bore thick red diagonal lines across their fronts. Stenciled on the first was: ADVISORY: NAVAL WAR COLLEGE: TACTI-

CAL SCENARIO OF CARRIER-ON-CARRIER. The second said: MARITIME STRATEGY IMPLEMENTATION: SOUTHERN PACIFIC/DESIGNATE: CZE-1.

He picked the second envelope first. Before he opened it, though, he paused to study his hands. They were steady. Good! he thought. He had seen combat several times—first as a lieutenant in the Battle for Leyte Gulf in World War II, then as a strike pilot over North Korea—and he suspected that things were about to get very hairy, very fast. Not only would the Russians be ready for his thrusts, but there was a solid chance his own vessels would come under intensive air strikes. He scanned the MSI report first, then went back and picked out specific items. He went on to the next envelope. He was nearly through when his intercom hummed softly. He snapped his hand over the switch: "Go."

"Admiral, Bridge. We've just received a red-op code from COMMPAC. The President has given the go-ahead for location-and-track of the Soviet *skadra*. But no entry into French waters."

"Location and *track*? What about strike contingencies?"

"No solid update on rules of engagement yet, sir."

"Good Christ!" Passmore growled.

In Moscow, Yuri Markisov had moved with ruthless rapidity to consolidate his control. His physical presence had shaken many of the Politburo members who had been wavering. Like most politicians, they immediately saw which way the wind was blowing and fell into line. Those who refused followed Bardeshevsky into KGB holding cells.

But the military situation wasn't as easily resolved. Bardeshevsky's brief but bellicose tenure as de facto secretary had released long-pent-up frustration among many commanders. With blood up and blood flowing in many satellite cities, with massive movements already under way along Warsaw Pact frontiers and in northern maritime sectors, a new confusion met Markisov's early commands to stand down. Sporadic fighting broke out between KGB and GRU contingents. And STAVKA was swamped with calls from infuriated TVD field officers demanding to know just who the hell was in charge. As a result, the chain-of-command links ran into deliberate stalls as distant military headquarters were recycling orders for repeated validation.

One of the most affected chains was the Vladivostok-Cam Ranh-Minsk link. On returning to his office, Markisov's first order had been for Skadra HC-3 to immediately vacate the Polynesians. Turesky had not yet received that command.

Meanwhile, Titov labored on in his room. The professor was nearing complete exhaustion and the lights overhead were giving him an excruciating headache. Since his conversation with Markisov, he had been tracking not only the events in Polynesia, but also the plethora of military and KGB data on the situation within the USSR following Markisov's return.

Then it happened. Lancing through the mass of Russo-European communiqués came a frantic overseas transmission, an intercept from an Australian air command base in Brisbane. Its weather-satellite tracking office had registered what appeared to be a nuclear explosion fixed somewhere north of Tahiti.

Titov froze. The displays continued throwing info into the flickering darkness, but he didn't absorb it. One single word governed all of his thoughts: Saber!

Only after several minutes did Titov purge his mind of his initial shock. And as he did, he found that the news of the explosion had released his mind from the fixed perspective it had been locked into for days. New vistas appeared, fresh possibilities.

Soon he was back at his consoles, hurling questions, studying background feed, shooting more questions. The displays flashed and flickered like speeded-up movie reels as they ingested data bytes directly off the gigantic main frames at Moscow University to which he had gone for depth analysis.

Among the frenzy of data coming in were: meteorological tapes gleaned from intelligence intercepts of British satellite feed; position reports of French, Russian, and American naval units; tabulation and distinct categorization of previously ingested data on unusual phenomena delineated Capricorn Quadrant-Environs; analysis of correct mathematical/digital order alignment.

He formulated simple analog projections on two screens that gave potential parabolas of general coordinate sequences. Hands flying, Titov drew up new concepts and methods of approach based on what the displays were giving him. By nine-thirty he beheld a complete electronic landscape. And was awed.

"It's possible!" he shouted. The discovery propelled him from his seat. As he skirted his desk, he stopped, startled. Secretary Markisov was standing in the doorway, watching him. Titov rushed to him, gripped his shoulders, actually shook him. "Comrade, I've found it! I know where the Saber is and how to destroy it!"

Markisov responded quietly, "There has been a nuclear explosion in Polynesia."

"No," he cried. "It wasn't nuclear."

"What!"

"There has been no radiation nor significant seismic reactions recorded in the Capricorn. It could not have been nuclear."

"Then what was it?"

"I'm not sure. Something extremely powerful which created unbelievable atmospheric and gamma phenomenon."

Markisov came close. "Was the Saber involved?"

Titov's face quivered with an intensity so profound it seemed to give his gaunt features an inner glow, as if the blood coursing there were visible. "Yes. It probably triggered it."

Markisov's eyes widened in shock. "Then it's now in Category Five!"

"Yes."

The general secretary recoiled and thrust his fingertips against the desk to steady himself.

"But there's a chance we can destroy it," Titov blurted. He put his hand on Markisov's shoulder. "Come, comrade, let me show you what I've found." He led the secretary to an adjacent console and pointed to one of its screens. "See that? Those are trajectory analyses."

Markisov's eyes narrowed, studying the picture. "I don't understand."

"Every individual, particular incident that has happened in the Capricorn was like a signpost. But I was so concentrated on the Saber, I failed to see what should have been obvious. By fixing trajectory vectors and calculating power distances and general ocean currents in that area, I would have been able to isolate the Saber's track. Now I've done just that and I *know* where it is!"

Markisov's gaze lifted from the screen. He studied the professor darkly. "But is it too late?"

"I don't know."

"You said you could destroy it. How?"

Titov dropped into his seat and began punching in override commands. The second screen went black for a moment, then brought up a picture of arcing lines. "Those are satellite orbit tracks. There, that one's the American NAVSAT communications vehicle. That one far to the south is an Australian meteorological unit." He then pointed to another arc line running nearly parallel to the NAVSAT's flight path. "But that one is our satellite. The inert ASAT Cosmos 346."

Markisov shook his head, confused. "I still don't—"

"The Cosmos contains a laser unit as its primary weapon," Titov interjected. "If we can focus its beam directly on the Saber, the laser could cause a massive thermal explosion within the aircraft's metal subframe. It would blow apart."

"Is that possible?"

"Yes. If I have two things, I can destroy it. First, a precise firing fix on the single strip of exposed metal in the Saber's external frame. And, second, a power boost for the Cosmos from the American NAVSAT."

Markisov's face went slack. He hadn't completely grasped everything the professor said, but he understood enough to realize that such requirements—particularly the latter—were impossible to achieve. He shook his head, started to speak.

Titov cut in before he could. "Yes, comrade, these are difficult things to do. Very complex and perhaps beyond our abilities. But it is the only chance we have. We must attempt it."

His head down, Markisov rubbed his fingers gently across the curve of his eyelids. He felt the pressure seep a throbbing pain into his eyes. Then he snapped his head up. "Yes, of course. Tell me what to do."

"Contact the president of the United States and ask for his help."

As he saw Markisov's face harden, Titov hurried to explain:

"The Cosmos ASAT doesn't have sufficient power to send its laser beam all the way to the aircraft and still trigger a thermal explosion. We have to feed it more power. The only strong enough source in that sector of the sky is the American NAVSAT satellite."

Markisov started shaking his head, moved off into the flickering gloom. "This is too complicated," he said distractedly. "Even if the president agreed, it would take too much time."

Titov's feverish eyes studied him narrowly over the top of his consoles. "Yes, time, comrade. There is none left to think anymore. Only to act. I haven't told you all of it."

Markisov stopped dead and his eye was caught by the console lights, looking like embers in the semi-darkness.

"Within sixty-seven minutes, the NAVSAT will cross into angulation range of the Saber's lowest beam trajectory. By bouncing off the American satellite, the aircraft could detonate the entire store of fissionable material at the French nuclear testing site on Mururoa."

For one long, crystalline moment, Markisov stared at Titov in horror.

Then he bolted for the door.

Above the Saber, the sky lay like blue eternity.

Inside the cockpit, a complex series of adjustments was being made in the Kamov analyzer systems. Now that Category Five had been accepted in function, all low-level danger assessments were ordered into low-priority shunts, accessible only for emergency retrieval. Full monitoring sensor power was called up and directed through intricate check-off component relays that would trigger fusion-chamber alignment and focus.

Within the chamber, outer shield plates were electrified to maximum magnetic deflection. Louver linkages were finely calibrated to full aperture spacings. Reaction springs were coiled into position so as to give instantaneous release for total ray exposure.

Meanwhile, the Kamov was studying incoming data. As each system reached on-line status, red lights in the displays began flicking on, replacing orange ones. As the banks completed out, the computer went into prefiring stand by.

The sensors swept the heavens, the surrounding ocean. As it made momentary contacts, each was analyzed, tabulated into a priority rating, and fitted into the C5 scenario. A solitary seagull wheeled into the sensor pickup, trembling stationary in the sea wind, but the Kamov rejected it. Weak bursts of radio waves wandered in from the southwest. The Kamov discarded them and moved on.

Now the computer searched only for nuclear mass.

A solid blip came through the sensor infeed. Analysis: satellite. Its track was angulated, in slow horizon differential. Kamov pinpointed ID from its previous tape:

AMERICAN: NAVSAT (DESIG): COMMUNICATIONS UNIT
TRAJECTORY: GEO-STATIONARY: COORDINATES NON-FIX, ANGULATED/
    ADJUSTED
HEADING: 013 DEGREES

VELOCITY (OEP): 16,000 KILOMETERS PER HOUR
ALTITUDE: 700 KILOMETERS

One second later, sensors located a second target. Again the Kamov ran an analysis, triggering previous track tapes. The read was clean: Cosmos 346: Soviet: inert, nonthreatening.

The computer discarded the read. Returning to the American satellite, it asked for a deeper assessment from the AI unit. Parameters of NAVSAT on-board gear came right back:

HIGH FOCAL TELEVISION CAMERA/RELAY: MULTI-SCAN WITH DIGITAL
    COMPREHENSION
MULTI-SWEEP SENSOR AND PANEL-SPECTRUM CAPACITY
TELEMETRY COMMAND MODULE
SOLAR POWER ACTIVATION UNITS
REAL-TIME IMAGING CAPACITY

The Kamov interrupted the readout: Give nuclear mass component. The AI considered. Responded:

NUCLEAR MASS: 0
POTENTIAL USE AS NUCLEAR MISSILE-GUIDANCE UNIT: 100%

17

"Good evening, Mr. President."

The voice that traveled across five thousand miles sounded restrained but also burdened and exhausted.

The President said, "And to you, General Secretary."

The call had come while the NSC was going over Admiral Hubbel's report, and the President had asked to take the call in the Oval Office. The Washington-Moscow direct line came through a small computer-like box with a red phone. It contained no buttons or dials and looked like a simple intercom unit.

Markisov said, "There is very little time, Mr. President. I plead with you to listen to what I have to say and then think very seriously on your decision."

But the President had a question: "What caused the explosion?"

"I don't know."

"Were your people responsible?"

There was a pause. "Yes, indirectly."

"I don't understand."

"A secret aircraft of ours is down somewhere in the ocean near Tahiti. It was the trigger. But not the explosive. Whatever that was belonged to the French."

The President was bewildered by this response. Russian triggers and French explosives? "Forgive me, Mr. Secretary, but I don't know what you're talking about."

"Then listen to me," Markisov snapped. "It's difficult to understand and believe, but you must believe it. There isn't time for doubt. In less than an hour, incalculable destruction will be unleashed in the Pacific. Only you and I can prevent it."

You and I. Already stung by the Russian's retort, the phrase rang a warning bell in the President's mind. "How cleverly you phrase that. *You* send your planes against a helpless experimental station, but now it's you and *I* who can stop it."

"I've already said we were not directly responsible."

"I don't believe that."

"Then you're being a fool."

"And you're a liar."

In the silence that followed, the President closed his eyes, felt blood pounding in his temples. He would get nowhere trading insults. He forced himself to be calm. He opened his mouth to apologize.

Markisov beat him to it. "Mr. President, please forgive me. Anxiety creates idiotic outbursts. I again plead with you, listen to what I have to tell you."

The President inhaled softly, let it out as gently. "Yes, Mr. Secretary," he said steadily. "I, too, apologize for my remark."

"Then you will listen?"

"Yes."

Markisov spoke quickly, explaining what the Saber was, what it could do, what it had already done; Titov's projections and plan to destroy it; the disaster of the incoming fleets; the danger of the French nuclear arsenal at Mururoa.

As the President listened to the tale of disasters, then to the unimaginable horror only minutes away, he could not help wondering if he was being conned. It was so fantastic, so grotesque.

Markisov concluded: "There is one slim hope. But I can't do it alone. I need you."

"In what way?"

"At this moment, one of our inert ASAT satellites is very close to your NAVSAT. It has the capability, if extremely precise conditions are achieved, to destroy the spy plane. Two things are essential. The ASAT must receive a power boost from your satellite, and we must have a precise fix for the firing." Markisov paused a moment before launching his plea: *"Will you help me?"*

The last words had such intensity, such a tormented beseeching, that for a moment the President felt as if the contact had been physical, a link forever unimaginable by anyone but the two of them.

"Your requirements are impossible. Is there any other way?"

"The only alternative is to withdraw all nuclear mass from within the aircraft's weapon range."

"Isn't it too late for that?"

"I agree. But perhaps there's some way the French can seal their deposits on Mururoa. At the very least, all naval forces in the area must jettison their nuclear weaponry into the sea."

The President sat upright at that.

The general secretary bore on: "And all this must be initiated immediately. Can you convince President Vasillon to seal his storage bunkers? And will you order your vessels to dump their missiles?"

The President's eyebrows narrowed in disbelief. This man was asking him to disarm and then coerce the French into disarming, too. It was unthinkable! "What about your own carrier forces in the area, Mr. Secretary?" he shot back.

"My order to jettison all weapons aboard the carrier *Minsk* and the ships of Skadra HC-3 has already been sent." He waited for the President to comment. When there was silence, he said, "You do not believe me."

"I'm hesitant."

"That's understandable. But think about this, Mr. President. In less than fifty-eight minutes, the Saber will detonate the Mururoa bunkers."

"It's a goddamned trap," Admiral Hubbel cried when the President explained the reason for Markisov's call. "Jettison our missiles? Jesus Christ, the son of a bitch must think we're idiots."

Across the table, Richfield, McQuisten and Defense Secretary Lauderdale were staring open-mouthed. Finally, Richfield said, "It's too complicated, it can't be true. It's got to be some absurd ruse."

"This is ominous," Lauderdale added. "I don't like the look of this thing." Another thought struck him. "My God, the whole assassination plot could have been phony. Just part of some—some complicated scheme."

The President replied softly: "What if it's true?"

"It can't be true, sir," Hubbel shouted. "A downed spy plane? Where? We've had no indication of such a thing."

"Are you certain?"

"Yes."

McQuisten suddenly leaned forward. "I say believe him."

Everybody's head swung around at him. Seated to his right, Lauderdale drew sharply back as if a bird's droppings had just landed on McQuisten's sleeve. Hubbel's look was as scorchingly contemptuous as a laser.

McQuisten ignored them. "We have no choice, Mr. President," he said slowly. "If we don't cooperate with Markisov and he's telling the truth, there'll be unbelievable destruction. If I remember the figures, the French nuclear test site contains enough raw fissionable material to create worldwide nuclear winter."

He let that neat little statistic sink in before continuing: "On the other hand, if he's lying and this *is* some fantastic ploy, we'll soon be in a war anyway. But maybe one that could be kept conventional. If I have to choose, God help me, I'll go for the second one."

He sat back and scanned the faces around the table. They still looked sour in disbelief, but now doubts were flickering in their eyes. Even Hubbel was momentarily quiet.

The President clasped his hands and leaned back in the chair. He stared into space directly in front of him, thinking. Then he sat forward sharply. "Before I decide, I want some solid data on this. Hubbel, I want to know if there is a Russian spy plane out there. Run every one of your goddamned communiqués from anything in the area over the last three days. You and your people might just have missed something."

The admiral looked skeptical, but silently he moved to the bank of phones. Within seconds he was talking with his chief of staff.

"Tim," the President said to McQuisten. "Get Levi at NASA." McQuisten twisted out of his chair and picked up a second phone. The President's eyes slid to Richfield. "What agency handles the NAVSAT?"

"It's a navy satellite, sir. I believe control is with the Naval Communications and Weather Data Center at Santa Paula, California."

"Get 'em."

"Right," Richfield headed for a third phone.

The President swung to Lauderdale. "Get President Vasillon. Use my office."

"Yes, sir." Lauderdale rose and slipped out the door.

McQuisten said, "I've got the NASA chief, sir." He handed the receiver over.

The President paused. "Are the congressional people here yet?"

"Yes, all key members except Minority Whip Henderson. They're in the Blue Room."

"Tell them I'll be there in a few moments."

"Yes, Mr. President." McQuisten hurried away.

NASA Director Jess Levi had a sharp voice on the phone that sounded youthful. After identifying himself, he listened silently while the President laid out the situation the Russian premier had presented. Finally the President asked:

"What are we looking at here? Is this for real?"

Levi could only manage a gasp in reply.

"Come on, man," the President snapped, "tell me."

"Sir, I'm afraid this is beyond my field. May I have permission to bring one of my staff onto conference line? His name is John Prescott. He's Chief Coordinator for Atmospheric Phenomena and has a solid grasp of related military aspects."

"Make it quick."

Two seconds later, Prescott came on line. "I'm here, Mr. President."

"Fill him in, Levi."

The director hurriedly explained the situation. The President could hear Prescott grunting occasionally, as if the sound were the clicks of his mind absorbing data. When Levi finished, the President said, "All right, let's have some specific opinions. Could the Russians have a spy plane with this kind of capability?"

"Yes, sir," Prescott came right back. "It sounds like a fusion weapon. The Russians are far advanced in that technology."

"This idea of linking our satellites. Is it possible?"

"Very improbable, sir. It would be an extremely touchy maneuver."

"Why?"

"First off, a physical linkup in space would be necessary for a transference of power. The NAVSAT has stored electrical power

from her solar panels, adjustment units, and eclipse-time batteries
—a fairly potent charge, in fact. But the only way to pass this
power to the Soviet ASAT would be through direct contact of hull
surfaces. And if the touch were in any way violent, both satellites
could tumble out of control."

It was the President's turn to grunt. He ran his hand through
his thick brown hair. "But is it possible?"

"With extremely delicate command inputs, yes."

"How long would such an operation take?"

"Once initiated, a matter of a few minutes. But whoever is in
control will have to have command codes for both the NAVSAT
and Soviet ASAT. Is that possible, sir?"

"I don't know."

"There are other factors, Mr. President. Even if we assume the
Soviet satellite is capable of generating enough power to throw a
beam to this—this target, an extremely fine fix would be needed.
I'm assuming the ASAT contains a laser setup. This would mean
offset deflection of the beam as it passed through the atmosphere.
Unless the Russians have an absolutely precise fix on the target,
the beam could over- or undershoot. Or it could be drawn off by
any massive metallic object within the firing perimeter. And once
the ASAT fired, its total energy would be expended. There'd be
no second shot."

"Shit!" the President sighed. The whole thing was getting too
precise, too—impossible. Momentarily overwhelmed, he once more
raked his hand through his hair, gazing desperately into space.

"Sir?" Levi put in softly.

"What?"

"There's one other major problem with all this."

"What? What?"

"If we attempt a space link, the NAVSAT could tumble out of
control as Prescott pointed out. If that happens, it would elimi-
nate all military surveillance in the South Pacific."

"Sir?" Prescott said. "May I ask a question?"

"Of course."

"If the Russians do have a precise or even general fix on this
aircraft, would there be time for us to put someone aboard?"

"I don't know. Why is that important?"

"If we could get a homing device on the plane, we'd be able to
negate any atmospheric or metallic deflection. The device would
draw the laser beam to itself."

The President nodded in satisfaction. He liked this Prescott. He was steady, coolheaded, just the sort of man needed in a crisis. "I'll try to get answers on that and have them for you immediately."

"Thank you, sir."

"Meanwhile, I want you people moving. Get the Santa Paula center in direct link with you. I haven't made a final decision on this yet. But when I do, I want them and you ready to jump."

"We'll be ready, sir," Levi answered.

"You, Prescott, I want every aspect of this thing you can think of," he said, fully aware that he had just bypassed Levi. Too bad, there wasn't time for considering egos. "I'm putting you on a clear line to an aide. I want constant in-feed of your thoughts."

"Yes, Mr. President."

Beside the table, Hubbel was signaling to him. The President said, "Hold a moment." To the admiral: "What do you have?"

Hubbel looked embarrassed. "There's a strong possibility a Russian high-tech aircraft *is* down in the Capricorn."

"Goddammit, Hubbel!"

"We've tracked down a photo from NCC's astrophysics division that was taken over two days ago. It looks like an aircraft in rapid descent."

"Why in *hell* wasn't I told of this?"

Hubbel shrugged helplessly. "CNO apparently downgraded its importance."

The President snapped, "Fax that photo to NASA on the double." He glared at the admiral as Hubbel began barking orders into his phone. Then he returned to Levi and Prescott. "NCC's faxing a photo of what might be an aircraft to you people. I want your evaluation in five minutes or sooner."

"Yes, Mr. President," Levi said.

He slammed down the phone. Hubbel was still chewing ass on the other line. He glanced at his watch. Eight minutes had slipped past since his talk with Markisov.

A half minute later, Lauderdale poked his head through the door. "I've got President Vassilon." The two men hurried to the Oval Office.

The French president came on with a rush: "Ah, Monsieur President. At last, at last."

"I think we're in serious trouble, Pierre," the President said.

"God, yes, I know. The Russian swine have created—"

"No, no. Something more imminent than that."

As the President explained, Vasillon sighed and gasped with ever increasing vehemence. The President concluded with a pointed question: "Are your Mururoa facilities capable of being sealed?"

Agonized silence.

"Vassilon, for God's sake! There's no time to waste. Can your bunkers be sealed?"

"There's a—yes, a flood system, I think."

"Will you order them flooded?"

"But Monsieur President," Vasillon cried desperately, "can we believe this—this Bolshevik? He asks us to become naked."

"I believe him." And it was true, he realized as he said it. At that moment the President's decision was made. "He's telling the truth. And if we don't help him, we're looking at Armageddon. Will you order your bunkers flooded?"

After a long pause a thoroughly deflated voice replied: "Yes, Mr. President. I will do as you ask."

As he hung up the phone, Hubbel came through the door. "NASA just came back, sir. It *was* an aircraft."

"Get the *Coral Sea* the hell out of the Capricorn," the President shouted. "And dump every nuclear missile they've got into the sea."

Wordlessly the admiral disappeared.

His return call to Markisov lasted all of four seconds. The general secretary said: "What is your decision, Mr. President?"

"I accept your word."

Three and a half minutes later, twenty thousand feet over New Zealand, the Soviet ASAT Cosmos 346 received a click-on signal command running 5930 MHz from Sary Shagan Satellite Control.

Inert for nearly a year since its launch, the small satellite instantly began automatically setting up. Designed on a dual-spin configuration with a spin axis fixed to the perpendicular, its central rotor activated to create gyroscopic stability to the communications/command platform that contained position/orientation repeaters and antennas which instantly homed to command direction.

Secondary jets fired, positioning the vehicle out of its free-float orbit into a synchronous attitude and spin-up. Sensors—three oriented to the earth, two to the sun—linked with on-board computers to establish a relative position of inertial attitude and platform control baseline. A third sensor, tuned to metallic rebound, began sweeping a three-hundred-and-sixty-degree scan, searching for foreign satellite bodies nearby. It instantly homed to the American NAVSAT drifting two miles away in a slightly higher orbit.

Internal infrared detectors—these protected the heat-sensitive components of the command unit—came on. Sub-power systems clicked on. Nickel-cadmium batteries sent electrical surges to de-spin platform components that contained electronic-repeater, telemetry, and command grids.

Deep within the vehicle, the laser unit came alive. It was composed of a solid bar of pure ruby enclosed in a flash shield. When activated by its separate lithium/magnesium battery system, it would be saturated with high-frequency light bursts. The atoms within the ruby's oxide crystal lattice would then release photons to form a beam of high-intensity light capable of creating a thermal-expansion explosion within a target's metallic mass. The laser's directional barrel now went into immediate coordinated alignment with the command computer and locked onto the NAVSAT.

As each of the vehicle's elements came into green state, the Cosmos's main transponder, running at a 33.0 dBW frequency range, answered the Sary Shagan's telemetric status inquiry: unit fully activated and aligned: PO coordinates (solar) 113.0 transorbital with divergence factor of 0.000074.

In that position it went on hold to await final firing command.

Bonner, still stretched across the *naturua*'s after mid-strut, listened to the wind. It came in surges, stretching the crab-claw sail and making the stays and koa mast tremble with strain. He had been holding a steady northerly heading. Now and then coconut trees and bits of beach appeared beyond the swell crests to the east.

Kiri had moved from the forward brace and was now curled in the port hull near his feet. With loose strands of hair plastered over her face, she looked like a forlorn waif. Under her seat, Father Joxe's empty rum bottles and a single five-gallon wine jug tinged softly together beside the radio. The bottles were filled with gasoline and flakes of soap—which combined, formed a compound similar to napalm.

"Where are we?" she yelled.

"I figure about two miles from where the chopper went in."

After a few minutes, they began to catch glimpses of palm heads on a long atoll to the west. Several seagulls were feeding nearby. They dipped down in long swoops that took them out of sight below the swells and then they'd come shooting up again, sometimes with fish, and catch the wind, hovering to feed.

"That's Iritua," he told her, pointing. "Best black pearls in the world come out of that lagoon." She gave him a wan smile.

Ever since leaving the priest's island, Cas had been turning over in his mind the best way to go about this. Finding anything as small as an aircraft would not be simple, even with a general fix. Still, he had something to go on: the exact sequence of events when the helicopter had been struck. The initial shock, the direction of the heel immediately after from left to right, meant the port engine had been hit first. Using that as a beam-direction fix, it cut the search in half.

His gut feeling, however, was telling him the Russian plane was northwest of the crash site. He knew that area contained reef and *motu* fields that drew the northern currents. Since the aircraft had to have been floating, it was more than likely it had grounded somewhere in the field. At least, it would be a good place to start.

He signaled for Kiri to take the tiller. As she crawled past him, she touched his arm lightly and smiled at him. Her eyes looked unbelievably large and clear. He winked at her.

Out on the forward cross brace he stood up, his back pressed against the port boom. Scanning ahead, he studied the ocean for signs. An experienced eye could decipher subtle indicators: a delicate change in color that indicated depth; passing flotsam that showed the direction of the current. Even the smell in the air—the dry smell of coconut fronds, the scent of heated sand, or the faint iodine tang of tide-exposed coral heads—helped give him a fair approximation of his exact position.

He turned his head and shouted to Kiri, "Bring her up about eight points to port." She eased the tiller over and the canoe responded instantly, sliding gently as the sail shifted. They went up the back side of a swell crabbed slightly, leaving a patch of perfectly smooth water off the lee side. Then the canoe, adjusted up, went scooting over the swell and down the front.

They ran for another five minutes. Gradually the water color began to lighten and the swells lengthened out, smoothing along the crests. Their forward faces steepened and the canoe went up and down in swift, gliding bounds. The sound of pounding surf drifted to them from the right, and they could see break mist lifting into the air.

As they came up onto another crest, Cas caught sight of the reef field. Stretching toward the northwest, the first *motus* and small islands began about a half mile away. The water was now a soft, shimmering blue and he could see the patterns of coral and white sand pools on the bottom, some fifty feet below.

He turned and pumped his arm toward the north. "Run across the swells," he hollered. Kiri gave the tiller a sharp pull to come about, and the canoe twisted, then darted forward as the sail refilled with wind.

Cas shifted his weight, letting his legs absorb the pitch of the craft like a skier. He glanced back at Kiri. She was hiking out, letting her body weight hold the tiller shaft as her stretched legs counterbalanced, showing the long, fine curve of thighs and calves and pointed toes. The swells were now almost sheer walls as they drew friction off the shallowing bottom and became combers. The canoe, absorbing some of the wave energy, picked up speed, bows knifing through the water.

Cas whooped, riding the flying main brace as the comber lifted them, and they crested with that momentary weightlessness of roller-coaster riders just topping a crest before the next plunge. Watching the wave move under them, his eye followed its passage toward the distant horizon. Just then he spotted the coral heads glistening with water runoff and the slivers of sand islands and . . .

There it was!

Its incongruous black color stood out starkly against the pastel greens and foamy whites and sun-shimmering blues. With its wings stretched, its cockpit glass like devil's eyes holding tiny flecks of reflected glare, it looked like a gigantic bat on the sea in malignant repose.

The Saber!

18

When Kiri saw Bonner come scrambling over the mid-struts like a monkey, she jerked upright. "What's the matter?" she yelled.

Cas reached the stern. "I just saw the son of a bitch," he bellowed. "We're headed straight for it."

"Oh, my God!"

As he dove for the tiller, he shoved her aside, and she had to grab for stays. He threw the tiller all the way over and they gunned around in a slewing one-eighty. The sail fluttered limply for a moment and then the booms swiveled around on their linnet bindings, cracking like the double reports of pistols.

"Bring the low boom around," Cas hollered, hauling in slack on the yard sheet. For a moment they floundered in a trough. Then the canoe broached another high swell and slid off the face, nearly capsizing as the sail caught a gust. *Whomp!* He put all his weight against the tiller, bringing the head of the canoe around, aiming for the reef line.

As they were lifted onto another steep crest, Cas squinted at the sun glare off the water, frantically searching for an open channel through the surf. The canoe shot past an exposed coral head to where the crests began breaking, and Cas glanced over his shoulder. Three huge swells were forming out of the deep water behind them and lifting into thirty-foot walls. He shot a look to the right, along the back side of the comber that had just thundered down ahead of them. About sixty yards out, its break tapered off, told him there was a channel there.

"Hang on!" he hollered as he yanked the tiller hard over. The first of the three incoming combers came on, starting to curl fifty yards away. Its feathering made rainbows in the sunlight. Quickly it drew into a massive escarpment, shiny as polished emerald, flecked with skittering foam. Its fore slope moved under the stern of the canoe, lifting it and ramming the twin prows deep into water. A deluge hurled back over them.

Cas put the tiller over as far as it would go and the canoe, responding, shot away from the curl and rocketed down a clean face. The comber broke astern, roiling, foamy turbulence following them. With tremendous velocity they sailed across the wave face. Cas heard Kiri yelling and the curl cracked down, forming a hollow tube that threw spray out of its tunnel like gravel.

Gradually, the energy of the wave began dissipating as they reached its outer edge. The canoe lowered, no longer skimming. It was instead plowing sluggishly, so filled with water that the gunwales were level to the sea. Back and to the left, the next comber had already crashed down, but they were out of the break zone and its turbulence merely threw a four-foot wall of foam into the canoe that drenched everything anew and then shoved them toward the edge of the channel and shallows.

A hundred yards to the east was a low strip of land. It had a spine of sand dunes, broad patches of sea grass, and a few stunted Samoan coconut palms near the edge of the high-water line. Cas slipped over the side into water over his chest. He winced as the bottom of reef coral sliced at his feet. Kiri dropped off the forward strut and together they sculled and hauled until they got the swamped *natarua* finally up onto the sand.

Immediately, Cas took off for the dunes. Calling after him, Kiri said, "Cas, wait. Don't show yourself."

Hearing the urgency in her voice, he dropped instantly to his hands and knees. He was crawling forward when she caught up to him. "Do you have any metal on you?"

"My zipper."

"Strip it off. The aircraft can home its beam to metal."

Wordlessly he rolled over onto his back and pulled off his shorts. Kiri was doing the same with her Levis. She wore nothing underneath, and the holster strapped to her calf looked like a grotesque growth.

"Dump the pistol," he snapped.

She shook her head. "It's okay, it's made of carbon plastic."

He shot her a disgusted look and started forward again. She grabbed his leg. "Cas, listen to me. Goddammit, listen to me! That thing out there's out of control."

"Then we'll blow it."

"No, you don't understand. We'll never be able to approach it. It's too far off." As she crawled up beside him, her wet hair glistened in the sunlight. Her face, though, was an ugly, distorted mask. "I lied to you. I don't know how to defuse it. But even if I did, it's too late. That thing we saw in the sky, the aircraft caused it. I don't know how, but it did. I'm sure of it."

He considered what she had said for a moment, then headed for the dune crest again. Once they reached it, they lay side by side in the sand. Feeling it scorching his penis and testicles, he wriggled his hips until he found cooler sand. They peered cautiously over the dune.

The Saber lay about two hundred yards away.

Cas slitted his eyes against the glare and studied it. From this angle he could see the full sweep of the left side of the wing, could clearly make out the huge, tunnel-like engine exhaust ports. Bracketing them were the twin vertical stabilizers, cutting the sky, curved like the dorsal fins of two gigantic killer whales.

He drew his eyes from the aircraft and scanned the distance dividing it from his islet. A coral plateau under about fifteen feet of water was pockmarked with sandy pools and connecting channels. He noticed one particularly large channel that wound and curved unbroken to the right of it and then fanned out into veins that fed tidal runoff into deeper water.

Kiri had slid back down the face of the dune and was lying on her back, staring at the sky. When he rolled down next to her, she said, "We need help out here, Cas. That monstrous thing has to be destroyed."

"I think I can reach it with a couple of gasoline charges."

"No! Even if you made it, those bottles wouldn't be powerful enough. We need stronger explosives and somebody to tell us how to approach it."

"Then we'll raise the *Coral Sea*. They'll lay a strike in here."

She shook her head, her wet hair whisking back and forth against the sand. "They'd never get near it. No, there's only one chance. I have to contact my people."

He snorted. "Jesus, don't you ever quit playing secret agent?"

With a single practiced move, she reached out and grabbed his hair. "Idiot! Don't you yet understand? There aren't any boundaries anymore. No Russian or American. That fucking airplane will kill us all if we don't take it out. And the only ones who know how to do that are the bastards who built it."

Cas softly lifted her hand away, but what she'd said struck bone. She was right: the Russkies were the only way out. He snorted and gave her a sly sidelong glance. "Put your pistol on me."

"What?"

"Point that gun at me." Then he flashed that wide, easy, mischievous smile that had always made Kiri go stupidly weak. "I don't like being a traitor without duress."

She shook her head. "Fool."

"Commie spy."

Returning to the boat, they found that the radio was soaking wet in its *lauhala* wrappings, and the batteries were submerged in three inches of water. The gasoline bottles floated inside the canoe hull, bumping dully against the cross beams. Cas braced himself and bodily lifted the radio out, got it up on one shoulder, and hauled it to the beach. Kiri brought up the batteries and set them in a semicircle around the unit. While she wiped everything off with handfuls of seagrass, he strung the coil of antenna wire to one of the small coconut palms.

Above them three petrels drifted in over the surf, hovered a moment with dark eyes curiously watching, then glided away. The beach sizzled with heat as Cas began connecting the batteries in series. His hands were bleeding from the terminals when he finished. He hooked up the lead-in wires to the radio and nodded. "Okay, give her a shot."

Kiri threw the master switch. Nothing.

"Shit!" Cas growled. He went back over the entire series,

checking terminals, tightening down wires as hard as he could. "Hit her again."

This time the tiny red power light flicked on. "We've got it," Kiri shouted. With the frequency dial still on her Auckland agent's carrier cycle, she keyed the mike and began calling, repeating his code name over and over. She continued for two whole minutes, then slammed the mike down into the sand. "It's no use. Our signal's too weak for him to pick up."

"Try the Wheelman. Maybe he can link us through. One-five-three-point-one."

Kiri's hand lifted toward the frequency dial. Before she reached it, the loudspeaker blew a wash of static and then the Wheelman's cheery, Aussie-accented voice came through: "Hello, luv. Havin' a bit of a fizzer, are you?"

Admiral Passmore felt physically sick as he watched his tactical-missile warheads going into the sea. Down on the main flight deck, a steady stream of aviation ordnance crewmen in their red jerseys were bringing up dollies filled with the nuclear units of Sparrow, Sidewinder, Maverick, and Phoenix missiles—slender canisters silvery in the sun as they came up on the outboard elevators from the magazines deep within the ship.

The *Coral Sea* was dead in the water as the warheads were dropped off the fantail. On the flight-operations deck, aircraft were parked everywhere; the entire wing was aboard with the only planes aloft being the two electronic Hummers. Ranging out in the ocean around the carrier, the other elements of the task group were also jettisoning their nuclear armaments.

Passmore found it difficult to look at anybody; he was certain that he would see contempt in their faces. He was stripping his ships of the most powerful ordnance they carried. Although strategic use of these tactical nuclear units was limited to an extreme contingency situation and only authorizable by a direct order from the president, Passmore recoiled at the thought of lessening *any* of his options. His task group would remain a conventionally potent force, but in view of the way things were going in the Pacific, a contingency situation might just possibly be right over the horizon.

Earlier, when the order to jettison had come through from COMMPAC, it had drawn gasps of disbelief and a volley of obscenities throughout the flag bridge. Passmore's reaction was: "What the fuck kind of order is this?"

His acidic demand for verify was hurtled back to Pearl. The answer came back dripping with threats. This was a goddamned presidential directive, COMMPAC said, and it would be goddamned complied with and goddamned instantly.

CAG Waltham, his face blazing with fury, soon stormed into the bridge. "Admiral, what in hell is this insanity?" he demanded. Under carrier-force steaming order, the wing commander had the final word on all dispersal of weaponry aboard. Not even the *Coral Sea*'s skipper could order it used or even moved without Waltham's explicit compliance. Only the flag admiral could override that.

Passmore said, "It's a presidential directive."

"Jesus H. Christ!" Waltham cried. "Why? That fucking Russian carrier sure as hell won't be dumping *its* nukes."

"It's a presidential order," Passmore repeated hotly. "And it will be implemented at once."

Waltham just stared, dumbfounded.

"Goddammit, Dick," the admiral said more quietly. "I know it doesn't make any sense. But we're just gonna have to live with it. Now see that it's done."

The CAG inhaled, still livid. "Yes, sir."

When he was gone, Passmore looked wearily through the bridge window. Far out, his ships were still in motion as the jettison order was now being transmitted. In his mind he was already envisioning the complicated sequence of maneuvers that the second half of the COMMPAC order had specified: a complete one-eighty turn to the northeast and out of the Capricorn Quadrant . . .

His radio officer approached. "Excuse me, sir."

Passmore turned and glared at him.

"I've just been informed, sir, that twenty minutes ago we picked up a peculiar transmission from a ham operator in New Zealand. The man claimed that he had word the helo we sent out with January was shot down."

The admiral's eyebrows shot up. "What's that?"

"This guy actually knew the names of officers Abrams and Woodcroft. He said one of them was wounded, and that another man named Bonner told him they were shot down by a spy plane."

"My God!" Passmore cried. "January was right! Where's this Bonner?"

"The ham said he was somewhere near the plane."

Passmore blinked, then grabbed the radio officer's arm. "Jam that message to COMMPAC. Code it up Red. Go, go."

At AlPaci headquarters in Papeete, President Vasillon's orders set off all sorts of fires. The first was that all military, commercial, and private air traffic in Polynesia be grounded. The second commanded that any operational nuclear warheads be immediately dismantled with their cores sealed in lead. The third instructed that the storage bunkers on Mururoa be flooded.

After a brief flurry of politician bashing, AlPaci obeyed. Unfortunately, on Mururoa compliance was not as simple. The test site did indeed contain emergency flooding systems designed to counter a radioactive accident, but they had been left unmaintained and the large induction vents that drew sea water into the bunker channels were now clogged with seaweed. Divers would have to be dispatched to clear the passageways before the huge intake pumps could be started. Estimation of time for full flooding was three hours.

Another facility, the Hobart, Tasmania, satellite-tracking station of the Australian Oceanic and Meteorological Society, was also in for a shocker direct from Australian Prime Minister, Ian Hook. Station scientists were told to destroy the tiny geological satellite VV-5, which was at the moment transiting through coordinates 149.11 E/40.23 S, above Chatham Island southeast of New Zealand.

NASA, now tracking everything moving through the Capricorn sky, had advised the President that the VV-5—running in a low-orbital surveillance of the New Zealand/South Victoria land area—could present a potential bounce platform for the Russian aircraft eighteen minutes before the NAVSAT approached.

The President spoke to Hook and the order was immediately sent out: Tumble the VV-5 from its orbit. Four minutes later, it made a fiery streak across the southern sky.

*   *   *

It took Titov less than three minutes to move from his room to the main communications section of STAVKA. He was driven across the Kremlin compound in Markisov's limo with the blood dark on the floor rug.

The Secretary did not accompany him. Again ensconced in his office in the Ministers building, with his full complement of secretaries and section supervisors, he continued the solidification of his power.

One of his first orders after the second conversation with the U.S. president was to Turesky: Skadra HC-3 was to immediately turn out of the Polynesians, jettison all nuclear weaponry, and go into total radio and electronic silence. Compliance response from Admiral Turesky took exactly ninety-one seconds.

At STAVKA, Titov was met by sullen senior operations officers of the supreme military center. No explanations from the general secretary's office had come with the order to give Titov full cooperation, so nobody really knew what the hell was going on. They responded to his commands sluggishly, like delinquent boys designated to do menial chores. However, they did obey.

Titov's first task was to interface the STAVKA computers to the main frame at the university. Within the KORMAC unit's gigantic memory bank was data on any and every scientific or technical project in the past twenty-five years. Plus damned near everything else that had occurred in the world that could conceivably affect the USSR. Before leaving his room, he had alerted the team from the university, and they were standing by when he formed the link-up.

His next assignment was to establish a direct radio line to the Sary Shagan Control Center. Its network included two field stations that shifted command control of Cosmos satellite 346 as it moved along the quadrants of its orbital path. The first station was at Pointe de Camau on the southern tip of Vietnam; the second sat on the perpetual ice of Rennick Bay, located on the edge of the Lillie Glacier in Antarctica, a secret installation that had been constructed by submarine crews.

As this hookup was being set, the university main frame was supplying geological and marine topographical data within the general area that Titov had pinpointed the Saber: present wind conditions, standard and deviant sea currents, atoll configurations. Using these, the KORMAC was projecting likely grounding positions for a free-floating object.

At last, Titov, constantly checking the time, came to the most unpredictable connection: direct access to NASA headquarters' command/control section, which had overseeing capability for the NAVSAT satellite. Although the U.S. president's pledge to Markisov presupposed the link would go smoothly, there was always room for a glitch.

It came in Europe, where STAVKA radio operators ran into ground transmission-line problems. Transmission traffic was horrendous due to the heavy load from NATO and Warsaw field units, and interjects and security verifies continually interrupted the probe. Then a junior officer, intrigued by what Titov was doing, suggested a northern link, via the Soviet KOSTIC satellite now transiting across southern Greenland.

A few moments later, NASA came on the line. Prescott did the talking: "You are Professor Andrick Titov?"

"Yes. You?"

"John Prescott, Chief for Atmospheric Studies. It seems we have a little problem here, don't we, Professor?"

"Yes." Titov spoke little English, and found he had understood only part of what Prescott had said. "Please, Mr. Prescott—you will wait a moment?"

Titov twisted and hissed at the nearest officer: "Get me someone who speaks fluent English." Then he cursed himself for forgetting the obvious hurdle.

Moments later, a major hurried forward, a large man in the spotless blue tunic of the Sevetminst Field Artillery. "Comrade, I speak English."

Titov handed him the mike. "Interpret."

The major, whose name was Igor Garolovsky, said into the mike, "Whom do I address, please?"

"Prescott. For chrissakes, man, let's get on with it."

"Yes."

With Titov formulating the questions, the three-way conversation went forward rapidly. No words were wasted. Garolovsky said, "Your command unit for the NAVSAT is Santa Paula, California. This is correct?"

"Yes."

"Can we take over total control of your satellite through our Sary Shagan Command?"

"No."

"Why not?"

"The link would be too complicated. Better *we* control both satellites."

Several of the senior STAVKA officers, beginning to sense the urgency of what was going on, had gathered around the radio unit to listen. At this statement, though, those who understood English started shaking their heads. Ignoring them, Titov snapped off a question and Garolovsky said into the mike: "Will this method expedite the maneuvering?"

"Yes."

"Then we shall do it that way."

"We'll need complete access and command codes for your vehicle as well as internal structure components. Are you people fax capable?"

Garolovsky looked indignant. "Of course."

"All right, start running it through. What is your projected time frame for position-firing angle vis-à-vis Mururoa?"

The major frowned. "Please say again. I do not understand—"

Titov slapped his hand on the man's shoulder and spoke quickly. Garolovsky said into the mike: "Twenty-three minutes."

"Jesus Christ!" Prescott was silent for a moment, then: "One other point. We have updated word that an American air crew is somewhere near your plane. Will this alter procedure?"

Titov literally grabbed the major in excitement. He'd understood *that* statement. He began rattling off a whole string of questions. Garolovsky shook his head. "Slower, please."

Titov calmed himself, and soon Prescott heard: "Is the crew capable of planting a homing device on the Saber?"

"Saber? Is that what you call it?"

"Affirmative."

"I don't know. Maybe."

"Are you in radio contact with them?"

"Not directly."

"Comrade Titov says he must speak to these crew. Can we link?"

"Again, I'm not sure of that. They were in contact through an amateur radio operator in New Zealand. His call name is Wheelman."

"Can we link through this Wheelman?"

"Hold a moment."

Titov leaped to his feet and paced agitatedly. "A map! Bring me a radio map of the South Pacific."

Ten feet away, a panel man instantly tapped in a command to the KORMAC. Eight seconds later, radio grids began splaying across his monitor. The professor studied them for a moment, then returned to the major with instructions.

"Prescott?" Garolovsky called. "Prescott?"

"Yes, go ahead."

"We believe we can establish a link line to Wheelman. Our satellite DID-7 is transiting the Bay of Bengal. We can boost to your naval radio station on Mindanao, then to the ham AA satellite over the Gilberts to Auckland. We must have Wheelman's frequency and clearance through your naval facility."

"Jesus, that's one hellish link chain," Prescott said. "Will you have clear traffic access?"

"Affirmative that."

"Okay, I'll clear to NRS, Mindanao, and wash the AA satellite for single run. I don't have Wheelman's frequency yet, but will notify Mindanao of it. Punch through in two minutes."

"Will comply." Garolovsky listened to something Titov added. "Do you possess more precise Saber fix?"

"Negative."

"Is there anything you wish to add?"

There was a pause, then Prescott said: "Just a prayer that the shit doesn't hit the fan."

The major cocked his head. "Shit hit the fan"? He didn't comprehend the phrase. Titov was tapping his shoulder, whispered into his ear. Garolovsky said, "We pray, indeed."

One minute later, STAVKA received word that Sary Shagan Command was refusing to turn over access/control codes for the Cosmos 346 to NASA without written order from the general secretary.

Cas quickly leaned over the radio and took the mike. "Wheelman, this is Bonner. We were about to raise you. We've found the aircraft and need your power. Over."

"Pig's arse, mate!"

Cas keyed: "What the hell's the problem?"

"You ginks are playin' silly bugger wi' me. I monitored your tart's transmission to her bleedin' cozy in Auckland. And then that flamin' Paddo raises a bloody Russkie warship! Who in devil hell are you bast'ds, anyway?"

"It's a complicated situation, Wheelman. But believe me, we're in some heavy shit out here. Christ, don't jack up on us now."

There was a long pause, then: "You a friggin' Russkie, Bonner?"

"Negative." He frowned, then keyed again: "But my tart's a KGB agent."

"Bloody hell!" The loudspeaker crackled with sharp slashes of sound, like exclamation points. Finally the Wheelman came back: "All right, I'm game for a listen. But don't gi' me any more shit hot."

Bonner explained the situation as rapidly as he could and keyed off. There was another long pause before the New Zealander spoke again. "I'm bein' a dickhead, but I'll stick. What do you want me to do?"

"Have you contacted the *Coral Sea?*"

"Aye."

Seeing that Kiri was signaling him for the mike, Cas handed it over and she keyed: "Wheelman, you'll have to link with the Soviet carrier. Can you do that?"

"What about your Auckland chummie?"

"He won't risk answering you now."

"We might have a problem with the Russkie ship. I've been running monitor trace on the bitch, but they cut off the air in a blink. I think they're running radio silence."

"Dammit," Kiri growled. She keyed again. "Will you try anyway?"

"Aye, but gi' me their standard operating frequencies and entry-code designates so I can home a solid fix."

"I don't have the codes." She thought a moment. "Look, use Russian when you call up. I can give you the phrases phonetically."

The Wheelman came back laughing. "That'll be a flamin' rip. But go ahead, lay 'em out."

She spoke the words slowly, distinctly, breaking them into syllables. They meant: "Attention, Soviet carrier . . . Have KGB message." She made him repeat them several times. They came back distorted in Aussie tongue rolls and a sudden racket of interference.

She keyed sharply: "Wheelman, we're losing you. Can you still read?"

Now his voice was chopped into bursts of word fragments. Then even these faded, leaving only a distant rustle of static.

The Wheelman was gone.

Earlier, like a spotlight picking out a single face in a crowd, the Saber's sensors had isolated from other ocean vibrations the slapping pounding and hissing of an incoming canoe's bow as Cas and Kiri came into range. Instantly the Kamov came out of its watch state and began tracking for identity, range, and speed.

Although in Category Five, with nonnuclear targets being shunted to monitor status, the system still maintained its close-in environmental safety perimeter, the AESP warning plot. Anything breaching that area automatically triggered a response from the Kamov.

As ID components began feeding back, the sensors suddenly lost the canoe's track as Bonner had wheeled it around and sent it into the overriding sound of the crashing surf. Still, the sensor grid continued scanning, trying to pick it up again.

Thirty seconds passed without regaining contact. The Kamov then isolated the read and put its tape into the quick-retrieval level. Then it turned its attention back to the approaching satellites.

19

"Vnemania, Sovietskaya aviamatka . . . Yest KGB soobshenia."
Over and over the Wheelman threw signals at the Skadra HC-3, fixing on each gradation of the frequency range Kiri had given him, but nothing was coming back. He paused a moment to wipe perspiration from his forehead, then scooted his electric wheelchair to the tiny air-conditioning unit in the window of his radio shack.

The shack stood on an isolated bluff overlooking the Bay of Islands near the town of Russell in North Island. His name was Nigel Samerson. He was forty-two years old and lived with his mother, Esther. Ever since he had lost the use of his legs in an auto accident at age twenty, he had lived the life of a recluse. Yet he was a man with an incisive wit and his radios were his deliverance. Returning to his main transmitter/receiver, he chortled softly, aware that he had never felt more alive.

"Vnemania, Sovietskaya aviamatka . . . Yest KGB soobshenia."
Again and still again.

Suddenly a clear, crisp transmission blew into his secondary receiver: "AOS code Wheelman, this is U.S. Naval Radio Station One-Three-Zero Mindanao rolling on frequency band one-three-five-point-two. Do you copy?"

293

He jerked around and stared at the speaker, astonished. What the bloody hell? he thought. Then he swiveled and keyed the second unit: "NRS, Mindanao, Wheelman on one-three-five-point-two, receiving clean and clear. What's the strike, mate? Over."

"We're carrying signal from Moscow via Bengal satellite, Wheelman. Understand you are linked with crew on-site designated downed aircraft in CQ quadrant. Verify."

"Aye, Mindanao. I've had them on strong read but have lost signal. Heavy interference here."

"Affirmative. We register strong, fluctuating gamma waves your sector. Urgent we raise crew. What is transmission frequency?"

He gave it.

"Wheelman, we will attempt to raise. With unstable air in vicinity, we request you monitor in case we cannot receive crew signal. Can you wilco that?"

"I'll be here, mates."

"Roger, Wheelman. Thanks. U.S. NRS Mindanao, One-Three-Zero, out."

For the last few minutes, Kiri had been frantically trying to regain the Wheelman. She had periodically picked up his call, fuzzy and indistinct, riding static surges. While she cursed, Cas paced around the radio like a caged animal. Then, more for something to do than anything else, he began hauling up the gasoline bottles and making Molotov cocktails, using strips of his T-shirt. Now he was wholly naked, the deep copper ligaments and muscles of his body clean in the sunlight.

There was a violent explosion of static, and then a powerful male voice boomed through the radio's speaker: "*Coral Sea* crew, this is U.S. Naval Radio Station, Mindanao. We have your frequency fix and will be transmitting via AA satellite unit. Can you copy?"

Kiri jumped. For a tiny moment she hesitated. In that space of time, Bonner whipped the mike out of her hand. "Mindanao, yes, we are receiving your signal very strong. Over?"

Silence.

Then: "*Coral Sea* crew, your signal too weak. Key answers. One for yes, two for no. NZ operator Wheelman has also lost your signal. Can you still read him? Over?"

He keyed twice.

"We have negative. Stand by. We're patching through transmission, origin Moscow. Scientist designated Andrik Titov will give you instructions on downed aircraft. Do you understand?"

Kiri jumped again at the mention of Titov. "My God, I know of this man!"

Bonner keyed once.

"We have affirmative. Stand by."

Cas looked at her. "Who's this Titov?"

"One of Russia's most outstanding aeronautical physicists. He probably built that ghastly thing out there."

"Son of a bitch," Cas said, grinning. "I don't know how, but we've got the one prick who can make a difference." They bent toward the receiver, waiting. Nothing was coming through but rolling, drifting static. Thirty seconds went past. Cas flicked the mike key several times impatiently. "Come on, Andrik baby, let's get it on."

Instead the Wheelman's sing-song voice came warbling through the speaker. ". . . am scanning on open. Come in, luv. Ohhh, luv?"

Cas went right back to him. "Wheelman, God damn. We've got you again."

"Ah, there you are, mate. We're havin' a mucked-up time here, aren't we? Never saw such atmosphere bounce. Must be friggin' sun spots. I see Mindanao made you."

"Yes, very strong for a while but now nothing."

"Looks like the Yanks are havin' a bit of stink, too. Hold a ding and I'll see if we can rig up for direct through me." He went off.

Kiri stood up and walked around, hugging herself as if she were cold. She paused, staring at Cas. "Can you feel that thing out there?"

He nodded, cradling the mike against his cheek. It was true, the aircraft had a lurking, waiting presence, like something alive. As he turned and looked toward where it lay hidden behind the rise, he saw the sky etched against the thin branches of the palm trees, looking ridiculously serene.

The Wheelman's cheery voice came back. "Stand by, mate. I've got bloody Moscow on the tap. Transmit so I can fix relay. Over."

Cas keyed and began repeating the single word: "Wheelman." He kept at it for ten seconds, then fell silent.

The New Zealander came back: "Mindanao not receiving my

boost. Damn, I was afraid of that. All right, let's go for tri-relay. Stand by."

For what seemed an agonizingly long time, they heard nothing but tiny pippets of static. Kiri sighed and stared at the sand. Cas said, "Shit! Come on, come on."

When the Wheelman came back, his voice was strangely clipped, his cheer all gone. "Home tight, Bonner, I'm running with a joker tagged Titov. He's got a bloody lot to say. First, is the aircraft damaged at all or totally intact?"

"No evidence of damage. Wheelman, inform him a Russian KGB scientist is present."

Silence as Wheelman went back to Titov. Then: "Have you attempted approach?"

"Negative. Is it possible?"

Long silence.

"It's possible, Bonner, but extremely dangerous. There's a baffle angle of a few degrees directly astern where the ship's weapon can't reach you. Mark that close, mate. This is one snarky machine you're messin' with."

"Understand."

"Do you have any ordnance?"

"Affirmative. Gasoline bottles made into Molotov cocktails."

More silence as Wheelman went back to Russia. Then: "Not sufficient. Hold."

Again silence.

This time Wheelman blew back hard: "Sweet Mother Mary! These dingos want you to place a homing device on the damned thing. The Russkie says you will have to break down your receiver and use the crystal unit as a homing device. Can you do it?"

Kiri's eyes snapped up to Cas's face. "Affirmative," he said.

"I don't like this, mate," the Wheelman shot back. "I don't like what this kinko's tellin' me. That bloody plane of his is even capable of readin' your body heat and pumper if you come up on it. You still willing to give it a go?"

"Affirmative," Cas snapped.

There was a long stretch of silence. Then Wheelman came back, his voice low and throaty. "I think you people better take a fair suck on the sauce bottle, Bonner. They've just upped the stakes. You've got seventeen minutes to place the device so a bleedin' satellite can fire a laser and—" He faded off.

"What?" Cas cried. "Goddammit, what was that? Wheelman, we're losing you. Come back."

"Read this! Read this! If the laser misses the air—" Again he was gone.

"Shit!" Cas bellowed. Desperately he keyed: "Did not receive last message. Say again."

". . . your bloody aircraft . . . detonate the . . ."

"Repeat!"

". . . can comp . . . detonate nuclear mass at Mururoa four secon . . . I am . . . Jesus . . ." Then he was gone completely.

Bonner jerked around to face Kiri. "Did he say what I thought he said?"

She nodded slowly, eyes wild. "The aircraft's homing to the Mururoa test site."

"Oh, Christ!"

Suddenly, Mindanao NRS blew in again, shattering the silence. ". . . can you receive? Wheelman indicates he has fadeout. Can you receive our signal? Over?"

Cas didn't comprehend what he was hearing, so large was the looming thought of Mururoa. Then he keyed once, absentmindedly.

Mindanao came back: "We have affirmative. Repeating Wheelman's last transmission. Homing device must be placed within sixteen minutes or detonation will occur in French nuclear test site. Can you accomplish?"

Cas's thumb came down hard on the mike key. Once. Affirmative!

Titov had come close to apoplexy at Sary Shagan's refusal to turn over access codes to NASA, running around the STAVKA communications center, howling helplessly. One of the senior officers immediately called Markisov. The general secretary's subsequent transmission to Sary Shagan Command came back through the STAVKA radios, and the sitting operator ran it into the overhead speakers. Everyone in the room froze, listening.

Markisov minced no words. He informed the on-site commander that if relay of the Cosmos satellite codes were not sent to the U.S. NASA headquarters immediately, he would order the KGB commandant to execute every Sary Shagan officer in sight.

Sary Shagan came back, voice oddly quavering, to say that the codes were being transmitted.

Commander Sorrel had one hellish headache. It crawled around his frontal lobes like a spider, spreading fire. Everything was coming at him at once. He felt as if he were seated in the center of the earth with magma booming all around him as it went driving toward the surface.

His entire command was now in the main tracking-control room, and those not on consoles were moving around gingerly, giving one another "Oh, man!" looks. Their primary link was still Santa Paula, which was throwing constant data sequences at them straight from NASA's Command Control with COMMPAC communications linked in. Included were interjects from the U.S. Air Force Space Center in Cheyenne Mountain, Colorado, which was using its main frame for the projection of maneuver and guidance data.

Sorrel paused in front of a console giving NAVSAT position sequences and saw the secondary satellite close by, which had suddenly shown life minutes before. What had previously been categorized as space debris had turned out to be a damned Russkie killer satellite. For a split second he had a vision of the ASAT destroying the NAVSAT with everybody right up to the President watching. His headache shifted around, seemed to be poking a hot knife into his left ear.

"Skipper," someone shouted, "we're getting Russian access commands now."

Sorrel gritted his teeth and started rerunning proper sequence procedures through his mind. It was going to be one double-hump son of a bitch, all right: reposition of the NAVSAT; lockdown of capacitor network; constant reaction adjustments to prevent tumble. And then, as he watched the fax prints coming up off the receiver, he suddenly realized the ASAT might have to be rolled. "What's convergence time?" he bellowed. "Goddammit, give me the time!"

"Angular convergence approximate is one-seven minutes, zero-four seconds."

Sorrel closed his eyes and thought: Here goes nothing. It's balls or bust!

*   *   *

A huge satellite, the NAVSAT was shaped like a reinforced cylinder thirty-two feet long and weighing eight tons. It was a dual-spin-designed unit with its spin axis perpendicular to the orbital plane.

On the apogee, or upper, side was a long array of photovoltaic solar cells. Through heat exchangers and a closed system of pressurized vapor, turbine, and condenser units, it constantly created electrical power, which was then stored in a bank of batteries located in the stern. These, in turn, supplied a steady power source for its telemetry and command electronics, all sealed in temperature-controlled packets. The operational unit would last for eight years, the life span of the crystalline and amorphous silicone materials that made up its solar panels.

In addition to this system, the satellite contained a secondary power grid of nickel-cadmium batteries that activated its redundant jets for position-orientation adjustments during orbital flight; its apogee motor was used for large repositioning maneuvers when an emergency orbital divergence was registered.

The main command platform, using fix positions through earth and sun sensors, retained stability through a gyro that kept the communications/command repeaters and antennas constantly aligned to receive incoming pulses from its primary command station on Phoenix Island.

Total reposition interjects were now coming in constantly from Phoenix, and the tiny computer units within the NAVSAT were clicking off reaction follow-throughs. The satellite hummed and riffled with electronic pips as the computers shunted appropriate commands to various subsystems. Antennas slowly shifted through microscopic divergence spans, adjusting up.

Command: Locate and fix to adjacent vehicle.

The antennas scanned slightly and found the Soviet ASAT. Computers quickly calculated distance, elevation, and mass weight. The NAVSAT sent compliance code.

Command: Lock platform gyroscope.

It was done, compliance sent.

Command: Fire starboard redundant jets. Burn time: 0.1 seconds. Swing through ninety-degree arc and hold.

In the silence of orbit, two tiny flecks of sound came as twin tongues of fire jetted, leaving riffles of heat. The huge satellite, responding like a stick on a string, pivoted slowly to the southwest. Forty degrees . . . sixty. A retroactive port jet fired. The NAVSAT settled, ninety degrees from original position.

Command: What is relative position of adjacent vehicle?

Astern.

Command: Go to pre-ignition of apogee motor. Projected burn time: 1.08 seconds.

Apogee motor on pre-ignition and holding.

Command: Apogee motor ignition.

Jets of compressed air blew into the motor along with fuel spray. A spark shot across terminals. A soft, hollow whoosh erupted from the forward end of the satellite and scooted it ahead, trailing wisps of condensation.

0.5 seconds . . .

1.08 seconds . . .

Ignition kill.

Now moving on momentum, the NAVSAT headed for the Soviet Cosmos.

Sixteen minutes.

Trying his damnedest not to think of blooming mushroom clouds or tsunamis as big as mountains, Cas dropped to his knees and began tearing at the back of the radio. Even though he cut hell out of his hands along the edge of the plate, his frantic efforts were useless. He couldn't move it. He leaped to his feet and raced to the canoe and started flinging out *lauhala* matting and grass and bits of dead fish. He felt up under the gunwales, along the under coaming, and came up with a rusty hunting knife that had been jammed into the mast seat. He raced back to the radio.

Kiri had taken over the mike again, and Mindanao was blaring through the speaker: "*Coral Sea* crew, transmit verbal. We want to test your signal strength. Over."

Kiri keyed: "Yes, still receiving your signal."

"We have you, faint but readable. We need to know your radio type and model. Transmit."

She began frantically searching all over the radio casing for markings. Just then Cas came back, slid to his knees, and started using the knife blade on the back plate screws. "They want the radio model," she yelled at him. "Where the hell is the model plate?"

"I don't know—on the front. Shit!" The knife blade had snapped.

She finally found it, a tiny stainless steel plate on the bottom right corner. It was so worn, she had to kneel way down to make out the letters. She keyed: "Radio model is Halicrafter X1B-dash-3. Three hundred watts. MIL Series DC-dash-40. Did you copy? Over."

"We have the numbers. Stand by."

Anxiously she glanced at Cas. He had worked out two plate screws, using the broken end of the blade. She grimaced as she noticed the knife's wooden handle was bloody from his cuts.

A different voice came through the speaker, this time Russian. "Crew, this is Andrik Titov. Listen very carefully. Time is desperately short." As he launched into a series of rapid-fire Russian phrases, Cas's eyes lifted and stared questioningly at Kiri. "What's he saying? Can you get it?"

"*Da! da! Andastaend!*" Kiri acknowledged to Titov, then listened again, head bowed. Her hand clutched the mike so tightly, the skin on her knuckles showed white and her ruby ring, sparkling with crimson sun shafts, looked like a tiny pool of shimmering blood on her finger.

Cas finally managed to pry one side of the back plate up by the time Titov stopped talking. As Cas glanced up again, he saw Kiri staring fixedly at the loudspeaker. Then she looked up at him and said "*Da*" once more and gently laid the mike down.

"What the hell did he say?"

The radio came on again, the same Russian voice but speaking English now: "Crew, words do not sufficient. May all gods help you and us." With a click the transmission ended.

Bonner eased back on his haunches, feeling an overwhelming sense of isolation descend over him. Ten-foot stone walls seemed to have lowered around the tiny islet while the rest of the world lay a million miles away.

Then the radio gave a tiny spur of static, and the Wheelman's voice came, faint as a whisper: "Good luck, mates." Then he, too, was gone.

Cas forced himself out of his daze: "How much time?" he growled. Kiri blinked at him, momentarily locked into her own visions.

"Goddammit, how much time?"

She shook herself. "I don't know. Ten, twelve minutes."

He bent down the back plate and peered inside. Smelling

electrical circuits and burnt wax, he pulled the main power lead off the batteries. "What component do we need?"

"The crystal."

"What does it look like?"

"A small Bakolite unit the size of a cigarette lighter."

"Where?"

"It's beside the tuning grid. There'll be four brass screws holding it on. Pull the entire unit. It has to be placed on a small metal strip along the exhaust vents of the plane's engines."

Peering into the radio again, he spotted the crystal and reached in. The hot tubes burned him as his fingers scurried over the unit. He couldn't feel the screws. He withdrew his arm, braced his knee, and with brute strength pulled the entire back plate off.

Within fifteen seconds he'd pried the crystal unit free and held it in his palm. It was nearly weightless, the plastic sealant discolored with heat burn. Clutching it like a diamond, he headed for the line of Molotov cocktails. Hooking a forefinger through the eye of the gallon gasoline bottle, he pulled the T-shirt material out and began dumping the fuel and soap mixture. It looked like thick, gray-yellow sludge in the sand.

Kiri followed him. "Cas, we also have to submerge all metal in the area. Any metal might draw the satellite's laser."

"Get the antenna wire. I'll get the radio."

She ran up the beach to the stunted palm and began reeling in the copper wire. Cas dropped the bottle and hurried over to the radio. He hefted it up and carried it out into the water until he found a deep hole in the reef and let it sink, bubbling, to the bottom.

Back on the beach, the last of the gasoline had flowed out of the gallon bottle. He retrieved it and squatted at the edge of the water. He washed it out twice and then recapped it with a piece of dry T-shirt material. With the crystal unit in one hand, the empty bottle in the other, he streaked for the dune line and once more went to ground just before he reached it.

This time he didn't feel the heated sand. His every thought was on measuring the channel that wound out toward the Saber. It was going to be one long underwater swim, at least two hundred yards before he reached a position astern of the plane. Hopefully the air in the bottle would give him one good breath on the way.

He studied the coral heads spread along the channel and picked out one halfway there, a kidney-shaped formation with a spur of coral protruding above water. He scanned farther, saw another coral head directly astern of the aircraft. This one had sharp, dark crevices on the beach side that tapered down into a huge sand pool.

When Kiri touched his shoulder, he twisted around, startled by the delicate feel of her fingers. She kissed him violently on the mouth, teeth banging teeth. He pulled back. Her eyes were wide, shining. He ran his fingers along her sweaty cheek and grinned at her.

Then he raised himself to his knees. Holding the crystal unit behind his back and the gallon jug tucked under one arm, he sprinted over the dune crest, bent over, the sand scorching his feet until he reached the water. Then he sprang in a swimmer's gun start into the surf. On impact the gallon jug's buoyancy wobbled against his arm, nearly pulling free. Ahead of him the frothy, misty green water spread away, and all around him shafts of sunlight pierced through to make the sandy bottom glow softly. Churning underwater, Cas headed up the channel toward the Saber.

Steady in-feed was coming off the NAVSAT to the Saber's sensors, reaction verifies and compliance returns from all sorts of command interjects that were coming from a strong radio source somewhere toward the north. The Kamov began dissecting the command inputs in an attempt to project its maneuvering purpose.

This process was interrupted by a sensor infeed indicating that the satellite's photo gear had just relayed a pickup of a new land mass coming into its scan periphery. Once more the computer ingested it and brought up comparative terrain maps for ident:

MORANE ATOLL: SOUTHERNMOST ISLAND OF TUAMOTU ARCHIPELAGO
COORDINATES: 148:01 W/16:01 S
GEOLOGIC STATUS: ATOLL; MAX ELEVATION: 18.3 METERS
NEAREST LAND MASS: FANGATOUFA ATOLL (106.8 KILOMETERS), MURUROA
    ATOLL (301.5 KILOMETERS)

The Kamov stopped the ident run as a high-priority warning came off the memory bank. It focused on the last entry:

MURUROA: SITE OF CENTRE D'EXPERIMENTATION DU PACIFIQUE: FRENCH
    NUCLEAR/TESTING COMPLEX
STATUS: (KGB REPORT 7TI (1/8/88): STORAGE (NC/SS): U235: 453.51 KIL-
    OGRAMS (1,000 POUNDS) THORIUM/URANIUM (CARBIDE FORM):
    4535.14 KILOGRAMS (10,000 POUNDS)
DEUTERIUM: 680.27 KILOGRAMS (1,500 POUNDS)
DEUTERIUM OXIDE (D2O): 2267.57 KILOGRAMS (5,000 POUNDS)

The computer went to the AI unit, infed MB parameters and
called for priority DAS. It came back with red lights flashing:

STATUS: DANGER: EXTREME/EXTREME/EXTREME
CMR: FULL ANGULATED DESTROY/ACTIVATION MODE

The Kamov instantly began running an angulated firing solution with the NAVSAT satellite as a bounce platform. Intricate
number sequences flashed as the computer tracked speed and
orbit pattern of the satellite, set up a maximum convergence
point, range, and trajectory of ricochet beam angles.
    It boxed the firing fix. Instantly the fusion chamber went into
pre-activation hold as the angle coordinates were fed into the
barrel system. A moment later, the Kamov injected automatic
firing sequence with its countdown time: 600.25 seconds . . .

The Phoenix tracking room had fallen into an impenetrable
hush, broken only by the clicks and soft pips of its electronic gear
and the whispered exchanges between Commander Sorrel and
his console operators. Verbal transmissions were no longer coming out of Pearl's COMMPAC. All incoming instructions were
now coming through the radio-computer analog sets that displayed number sequences. Cheyenne Mountain had now taken
over total overall operational command from NASA with Santa
Paula merely acting as transit base.
    The whole thing was coming up off an extraordinary linkup,
primarily on the command interjects for the Soviet ASAT. Sary
Shagan was sending command codes and maneuvering data
cleanly, but the system was oriented to a Russian language se-
mantic base. Everything had to be run through Cheyenne's se-
mantic content analysis system, which broke down the Russian-based
commands into English equivalents through digital "frame" ref-

erences. These were then reconstructed into numerical command sequences that were passed on to Phoenix Island.

Sweating, pumped up on adrenaline, Commander Sorrel watched the momentum glide of the NAVSAT carefully. He knew that after all the technical bullshit, the down-and-dirty of it came to manual touch. This was going to be one piece of hairy business.

A panel man to his right twisted toward him. "Commander, I'm picking up ultrahigh-frequency 'inquiry' impulses on the NAVSAT's infrared transmissions."

"What's the source?"

"No fix. Somewhere in Polynesia."

Goddammit, Sorrel thought. Something or someone was tracking the NAVSAT's off-feed. But why? And what was it? He had no time for speculations, though, and forced himself to focus on the bright numbers that came up on his command module, which was now projecting the NAVSAT's momentum and distance to touch point:

SPEED: 30.09 MILES PER HOUR
TRAJECTORY ANGLE: 018.00 DEGREES (SUN ORIENTED)
CONVERGENCE DISTANCE: 280 YARDS
                      260 YARDS
                      240 YARDS

"Do we have lock-on for auto-retrofiring?" he barked.

Someone came back: "Retrofiring data in and locked."

Sorrel waited, his mushy bowels sending more urgent signals than any he had ever felt in his life.

Meanwhile, Chief Hedges had been monitoring the incoming Soviet ASAT span sequences. Hedges was pissed and tense. The damned tiny Russkie bitch, compared to the NAVSAT, was simply a weapon sailing around in space. It should have been simple to handle. But in this scenario, it was becoming agonizingly complicated.

Running a third of the mass-weight of the NAVSAT, it contained a complex communications-power-firing system. Telemetry and command modules were sealed in high-tensile plastic cartridges, as were the small C-band radar-homing unit and laser-weapons systems. The firing fix depended on the primary radar unit, but this sub-powered system had a maximum range of only ten miles. There was a backup, however, formulated in the event of radar jam. It utilized four position mirrors, located fore and aft, top and bottom, of the vehicle. These found a target visually and positioned it in computerized cross hairs. The internal computers then read the mirror bearings and formed up a coordinate firing fix.

This was the system that would have to be used to fix on the Saber. By inputting artificial mirror bearings to the fire-control unit, a "false" target would be fixed and then fed to the laser cannon. That's where it got sticky. In order to force the on-board computer to accept the artificial bearings, all four mirrors would have to be focused downward. That meant the ASAT had to be turned ninety degrees from an orbital position. Since it was a free-spinning vehicle that normally completed a single revolution along its orbital axis every hour, the precision of touch and firing had to be worked out to within centimeters and timed perfectly to the incoming NAVSAT.

Positioning of the ASAT began. Sorrel called backup moves as the chief tapped them in. The tiny satellite began its revolution. Degrees clicked off. As it neared the ninety-degree position, Sorrel called for retrofiring, stopping the twist at eighty-eight degrees so that the natural spin of the vehicle would coincide with the NAVSAT touch.

This touch point was critical. The entire battery system of the ASAT was a short-lived energy-cell grid. It was good for only six hours after activation of click-on, since the satellite had been programmed for immediate destruction of adjacent enemy satellites. This factor raised a serious problem.

Fortunately, Titov, cranking out constant data from the STAVKA comm room, had already foreseen it and had the solution. The Cosmos 346 contained a single design component that could be used for energy transference. The vehicle had two antennas: a high- and low-gain circuit. The low-gain unit, protruding eighteen feet from the satellite's main mass, had a niobium-tin alloy lead-in wire. Since niobium has the astounding property of dropping its resistance to near zero in low temperatures, the convergence and final touch of the satellites was programmed to occur while the low-gain antenna was on the out-spin position, away from the sun. There the ambient temperature would be minus one hundred degrees Fahrenheit. The instant the NAVSAT made contact, automatic commands would trigger all operational power units aboard to activate at once, creating a massive short. The niobium low-gain antenna, with its near-zero resistance, would then suck in the electrical energy like a sponge.

There were two major questions: Would the transfer of power actually take place? And if so, could the small ASAT batteries take the sudden infusion without exploding?

MERGE DISTANCE: 90 YARDS . . .

Sorrel was staring at the screen so intently his eyes were watering. Ignoring the tears, he murmured, "Come on, motherfucker. Blow the retros."

The automatic command interject shot through the satellite's computers. The Phoenix displays adjusted up: Ignition of RJ units . . . Burn time: 0.031 seconds.

The commander, unable to contain his mounting anxiety, yelled, "Is she slowing? Goddammit, is she slowing?"

The console man monitoring the main NAVSAT screens called, "Momentum velocity holding one-five MPH."

A second firing.

"Momentum velocity down to four-point-one MPH."

Sorrel squinted at his display. Distance-to-target merge was thirty-five feet. He started cracking his knuckles, making sharp pops.

"Momentum velocity now zero-zero-four MPH."

The NAVSAT was sliding in like a butterfly back-winging for a fragile alightment.

"Is the ASAT antenna in touch position?" Sorrel bawled to Hedges.

"She's fixed hard on. Temperature grid registering minus nine-three degrees."

The commander took a deep breath. "Shut down the NAV's automatic system."

"OBAS off."

"Distance?"

"Target merge to one-five yards."

"Slow her up."

One second.

"She's accepted it."

"Give her a jack."

"Burn zero-zero-zero BT. Got it."

Sorrel closed his eyes. With utter clarity he watched in his mind as the satellites came together: their metallic surfaces polished by sun glare, the shadows on the dark side as blue-cold as the bottoms of ice floes. A million miles away and right in the room.

"Here we go," he whispered.

Touch.

All the NAVSAT's in-feed consoles instantly went black.

"What's happened?" Sorrel shouted, his voice echoing throughout the room. "Did the son of a bitch take power?"

Hedges was leaning down to his console screen as data began feeding in. "ASAT power grids showing clean intake and holding stable. Yeah! No fucking explosion."

Sorrel felt a howl of joy start out of his chest. Before it reached his mouth, though, Hedges said, "Shit! We're getting tumble."

"Goddammit!"

"Orbital deflection developing. I'm getting three degrees—no, five degrees."

"Hit the ASAT retros."

Hedges complied. One second passed. "They're ignited. Burn on parameter of quad-second."

Frozen, Sorrel just stared and stared.

"We got her, we got her," Hedges cried. "She's stabilizing." The silence following his cry seemed to fold down again like the onset of evening. Then he said: "Oh, no!"

"What now?"

"The NAV's locked into her wash. The combined weight's pulling them both out of orbit track."

"Hit her retros again."

Hedges glanced over his shoulder. "That could aggravate the tumble."

"Do it!"

The chief obeyed, shouting out ignition and burn parameter. Sorrel refused to look at the screens. Instead, he put his head down and closed his eyes. Two seconds passed—three. "Is she cleaning?"

"Wait ... yeah, I think so. She is!" Hedges turned around,

teeth showing through the sun-bleached beard. "She's stabilized with the NAV still riding wash."

The commander whirled, growled triumphantly, and then another wholly new problem hit him. The maneuvering had altered the ASAT's orbit slightly. All previous setup calculations had just gone out the window. He rushed back to Hedges.

"What's her orbital-angle loss?"

"One-four-point-three degrees."

"Shoot it back to Cheyenne. They'll have to work up a new firing solution for her mirrors." Hedges was already doing it before he finished. Sorrel turned to a second console man. "How much time before they reach the Mururoa bounce position?"

There was a slight pause, and then the man came back: "Nine minutes, thirty-four seconds, sir."

20

Deflection Angle Convergence: 9 minutes, 33 seconds

Cas was having an impossible time making headway. Not only did the bottle of air keep slipping from under his left arm, trying to float to the surface, but with his other hand holding the crystal unit, he was forced to paddle with a fist. He moved along like a wounded turtle, mostly using scissors kicks of his legs. But that was eating up his stored oxygen rapidly.

It was no use, he finally decided. He had to let the bottle go and risk skimming for breath, just his face out of the water for a quick fix. He gripped the crystal unit between his teeth. Now, with both hands free, he started really cutting water.

Through the haze he saw the kidney-shaped coral head coming up. It looked like a block of black cement washed in diffused sunlight. As he drew closer, a school of *Manini* fish erupted from a slanting crevice in a flurry of darting black and yellow stripes. He hardly noticed them, though, for his need for oxygen was becoming overwhelming. He wouldn't be able to hold off much longer. He rolled completely over, gliding on his back, and angled for the shimmering blue-silver surface above him. As his nose cut through the water like a stone in a stream, he snorted out, sucked in as deeply as he could, then arched, and plunged for the bottom again, until his toes just scraped the surface. A moment later, he veered slightly off the first coral head, rolled, and started toward the second.

His heart was pounding like a drum and he could actually feel the warmth of his blood as it surged through his veins. With this queer sensation came frightening thoughts. *It can bloody read your body heat and pumper,* the Wheelman had said. Feeling utterly naked, he tried to hug the bottom as tightly as he could, staring forward through the dancing green light to see the aircraft's shadow.

All the same, he was starting to flag. Such ominous thoughts were stimulating an instinctive desire for self-preservation. Squeezing his eyelids, he forced his mind to concentrate on the very things he wanted to hide: his body's heat, vibrations, the smooth, oil-like slide of water down the full length of him, the vaguely pleasant whip of his penis back and forth as he rolled, and the interchange of strain and relaxation in his muscles.

As he did, he seemed to merge into the ocean itself: to the chatter of a million reef creatures, to the soft rustle of water whooshing across exposed coral heads, to the echoing boom of surf in the distance.

The Kamov found him . . .

In the midst of adjusting its firing fix to compensate for an odd divergence of the satellites' orbit, it picked up his approach as he breached the safety perimeter. Instantly data went to the memory banks to form an ident:

```
TARGET: ELONGATED OBJECT
DIMENSIONS: 1.92 METERS (LENGTH)/0.6 METERS (MAX WIDTH)
MASS WEIGHT: 95.6 KILOGRAMS
TEMPERATURE: 99.1 DEGREES
MASS DENSITY COMPONENTS: FLUID (98.1 PERCENT)/FIBROUS CALCITE
     (24.2 PERCENT)
STATUS: HUMAN (ORGANIC)
```

A second sensor read came in with a flashing warning: *Interject/ Interject.* The Kamov went to it. A crystalline entity was registering. AI unit fixed parameters and assessed danger response:

TARGET UPDATE: CRYSTALLINE AURA PRESENT
DAS: CRYSTAL LATTICE COMPONENT POTENTIAL HOMING DEVICE FOR FIRE-
    CONTROL SCAN
EMR: DESTROY

The Kamov sent a temporary hold to the chamber's firing sequence. Range and elevation were worked out of the incoming crystalline target and fed to the barrel system. Immediately it was adjusted to the new incoming target.

As Cas neared to the huge shadow of the aircraft, he drew up for a moment, trying to pick out the shadows of its vertical tails. But it was impossible. The shape of the shadow was too indistinct.

From his left a burst of objects shot from between coral heads and went past him: faint yellow *papio* fish. Right behind them was a shark skimming close to the bottom, the snap of its tail kicking up sand. It passed directly below him and disappeared up the channel.

Cas estimated his distance to the plane: forty, forty-five yards. It was too far, for his lungs were nearly bursting. He paused, considering. Did he dare come up from this position? Would he be within the stern angle? Finally he decided he had no choice. He had to try it.

He broke the surface gently. Tilting his head, he expelled ever so softly and inhaled, sucking in air around the lump of the crystal unit. Then he saw that he was facing the plane. This close, the immensity of the aircraft jolted him. Then a fresh realization seared through him like fire. He was outside the stern angle!

No sooner had he seen this than he heard a minute click of gears, an almost inaudible whir of motors. Then a reddish glow suddenly fused up into a glass dome just aft of the cockpit's down curve.

"Jesus!" Cas thought. "It's homing to me!"

A wave of fear hit him full bore. Frantically he plunged, trying to somersault and head for the bottom. As he came around, the water whipped the crystal from between his teeth. Watching it flutter off in his own turbulence, he cursed. He checked his spin and leveled out, reaching for the unit. But like a wisp of paper caught in a breeze, it rode more turbulence out beyond him.

Just as he started for it, there was a violent sizzle and something came at an angle into the water. It looked like a pencil thin tube filled with plasma energy. Instantly the crystal unit exploded, as powerfully as a grenade. In reflex Cas's muscles had already begun drawing him back into a protective ball before the unit shattered. The concussion hit him, ramming through and past him. For a second the underwater world was transformed into a hell of roiling water and bubbles and sand sucked up by the explosion.

Simultaneously he felt himself propelled through the water. Backwards! Then he was free of the water and he felt a burst of intense warmth of the sunlight and the slight chill of rushing air. He flipped over once and went down into the water again.

He vaguely tried to move his arms. They felt numb. His legs ached, and the right one was burning. He lashed out at the water, like a man struggling in a nightmare. It was shattered into thousands of tiny, bursting sun needles. Through it he vaguely heard the sound of the explosion going off through sand channels like thunder dissipating in a canyon.

He reached the surface, but only managed a feeble breach. He sucked in air, went down, came up again, sucked in more. Then it seemed as if he was cartwheeling crazily in dimmed sunlight.

Lying flat on her belly on the lee side of the sand dune, Kiri had seen Cas surface before the explosion. Her heart lurched. He was outside the stern angle! Even as she screamed at him, she saw the red fusion of light in the after dome. It flickered and throbbed, as if a fire had started in the aircraft. But she knew what it was. The ship's weapon was energizing, homing to Cas.

Without thinking, she lunged to her feet and sprang over the dune crest and down the other side. There was a violent hissing sound, followed immediately by an explosion. Water erupted in a huge bubble that fractured open, throwing spray and steam into the air.

She reached the surf line and hurled herself into a level dive. Just for an instant, she caught sight of Cas hurling out of the water. He back-flipped completely over, blood droplets flew off him, glistening brightly in the sun. And then she herself was into the water, heart racing wildly as she broke the surface and began stroking with abandoned frenzy to where she had seen him.

*   *   *

After the destruction of the crystalline target, the Kamov instantly returned the firing barrel to NAVSAT/Cosmos fix and began scanning its immediate environment. The explosion momentarily flooded the sensors with heavy vibrations. Then slowly the grid began giving a clear read. New objects emerged out of the ocean like ghosts from mist. The target designated organic/human was intact, thrashing discordantly, but no crystal status remained. A second object, elongated and moving swiftly, had just entered into the no-pass zone. A moment later, three more identical objects hurtled in.

The computer drew up an overview analysis of the intruding targets:

> STATUS: ELONGATED OBJECT
> DIMENSIONS: 4.10 METERS (LENGTH)/0.8 METERS (WIDTH)
> MASS WEIGHT: 239.1 KILOGRAMS
> TEMPERATURE: 67.01 DEGREES
> ASSESSMENT: CARTILAGINOUS MARINE LIFE/DES. *CARCHARHINUS MILBERTII* (SANDBAR SHARK)

Suddenly red lights began flashing on the cockpit's target/track-sequence grid, indicating a fire-solution disruption. The Kamov sidetracked the shark read and focused on the disruption. Radar bounce was indicating the NAVSAT/Cosmos target was moving slightly slower than pre-merge velocity, and this had created a beam-trajectory problem.

The Kamov quickly analyzed and found a solution. With actual radar read of the target still low on the southeastern horizon, it projected a forward track point of the known angle, timed the target to that point, then calculated velocity. Within nanoseconds it had a new fire solution to bounce angle fix. Updated time to satellite CPF: six minutes, twenty-two seconds.

Returning to the sharks, it found an *Alert* sensor interject. Read was showing a metallic component within the shark bodies. The sensor system was so precise it was actually picking up the high concentration of iron salts within the animals' livers. The Kamov consulted the AI. Answer:

> STATUS: INTERNAL METALLIC CORE/POSSIBLE MISSILE CHARGE
> ASSESSMENT: DANGEROUS (PRIORITY 11)
> CMR: DESTROY

Once more it drew off the firing barrel fix and began running motion azimuths and range calculations to the nearest shark target.

The Cosmos ASAT refused Cheyenne's new firing fix. Its return display simply showed ?????. Sorrel didn't even curse this time. Instead he twisted and bellowed to his radioman: "Tell Cheyenne the little bitch refuses new fix."

Seconds went by sluggishly. Cheyenne came booming back: Why the hell didn't it accept? Had Phoenix inserted the correct sequences?

"Goddamned right we did," Sorrel shouted. His answer began its long link back to Colorado. But now heads in the control room were beginning to shake slowly, eyes knowingly meeting other eyes. This sucker just wasn't going to work.

"What the fuck is wrong?" Sorrel asked desperately.

Hedges shrugged with his palms. "Christ knows, skipper. Maybe the power link blew out small circuits."

"It can't be." The commander paced back and forth, head down. He ran the ASAT's fax printout through his head for the hundredth time. "It goes there," he mumbled, "and then there. And then . . . Whoa!" he shouted. "That's it!" Looking up, he snapped to the chief, "What's the orbital divergence angle?"

Hedges glanced at his panel. "Six-point-two degrees."

"That's it!" Sorrel yelled. "The mirrors are in maximum cant position, but with the divergence, it's not steep enough to provide an artificial picture for the new firing fix."

"Jesus, you got it, skipper," Hedges cried. "But what the hell can we do to bring her up?"

"Retro the starboard jet. Roll her a little."

"But we're liable to blow stability again."

"No, just give her a one one-thousandths burn. That should slide her around like a slippy dick."

Hedges's eyes shifted worriedly. "Skipper, you're putting your ass out. Maybe you better get clearance from Cheyenne first."

"Fuck Cheyenne," Sorrel growled. "Burn her."

The chief obeyed, tapping in the command. Almost instantly the slow-moving number sequences on his monitor began speeding up, flicking through changing patterns. "She's got burn," he called. "And still holding stable."

"See if she'll accept the new fix," Sorrel ordered.

Hedges did so.

Return: ?????

"Son of a bitch! Hit her again. Same burn."

They went through the procedure once more. Suddenly one of the radios boomed out: "PITC, PACCOMM TT-3, we're getting updated on—"

Sorrel whirled around: "Turn that prick down." The radio faded to a soft murmur.

Hedges said, "She's positioning and holding stable."

"Give her the fix command."

Two dozen pairs of eyes anxiously stared at the chief's screen. On it the number sequences began rapidly shortening, forming an inverted pyramid. At the bottom was a single time set, clicking off in half-second adjustments: 5 (m) 47 (s) . . . 5 (m) 46.5 (s) . . .

The Cosmos 346 had just accepted the firing fix and was counting down.

Floating in a confused haze, Cas saw Kiri's face come at him through the soft, fuzzy green water, her eyes magnified, her features grimacing with exertion. Until that moment he had been bobbing up and down, unsure of where he was or what had happened. His head rang and warbled with internal sound. Now and then he would feel something go by him and catch a glimpse of dark shapes. Vaguely, without any particular anxiety, he realized there was blood on his face, around him in the water.

Kiri grabbed his hair and started pulling him. The wrench on his scalp, more than anything else, brought him up sharply. He shook himself loose and stared at her, terribly irritated. She gasped something, seemed to be pleading with him.

And then it all came back in a violent rush. He whirled around in the water and saw the aircraft sixty yards away. It was as black as death, its coal-soot skin fuming heat rays off the broad expanse of its wings, the gigantic tail fins awesome. And right in the center, the dome with its scarlet light was pulsating again.

"Go under!" he shouted to her. He dove and saw the slivery envelope of her dive close by. Immediately thereafter he heard an explosion. Its sound came through the water in muffled surges, which were instantly followed by a burst of frantic clicks and squeaks as the reef animals scurried away from the blowout. Near panic, he and Kiri drove toward the beach.

Below them, the reef gradually gave way to sand pools, which lengthened out and became ripples, and then they were into the shallows. Lunging, crawling, they made the beach and ran for the small tidal bank at the foot of the palms and went hurtling over it into a wash trench thick with dry sea grass.

Gasping for breath, Kiri turned her head. "I thought you were dead. Where are you hit?"

Bonner wiped the blood off his face. Examining his fingers, he found it was watery, pinkish. His ears were still ringing, and his nose and forehead felt as if he'd taken a fist squarely between the eyes. The concussion had ruptured several veins in his nasal passages, and now the blood started flowing again heavily. He closed off his nostrils, and sucked up, tasting the salty tang of the blood in his throat.

They heard a hollow *zippp*, then a crackling sizzle like water poured onto a hot griddle, followed by another explosion. Cas lifted slightly to look out. Bits and chunks of a shark, enveloped in a spray of bloody drops, blew through the surface.

"Jesus!" he hissed, recoiling as the gory sight drove home the full impact of the aircraft's deadliness. Like a maniac gone berserk in blood lust, it was now slaughtering anything that came in range.

Staring at the spy plane, he felt the most intense hatred he had ever experienced in his entire life. He hungered for a weapon—a bazooka, a mortar, a grenade—any goddamned thing that would blow that malignant son of a bitch to hell. *Yet all the while he knew that his one weapon was already gone!*

Kiri had also been watching. Now she quietly slid down and turned over onto her back and began sweeping the sky intently. He finally eased down beside her. There was another explosion and a few seconds later one more. He didn't bother to look this time. He wiped more blood from his nose. It was gradually stopping. "It got the crystal," he said.

She nodded but said nothing. Seeing where she was gazing, he lifted his head and looked at the sky, too. It arched over them in pure blue majesty, unutterably vast and deep. And somewhere in it, beyond their own vision, floated a silver object that held their lives and those of countless people inside its electronic heart.

But now, he knew, it didn't matter. Without the homing crystals, the odds of strike were beyond probability.

On Phoenix Island, Commander Sorrel's victory was short-lived. Forty-seven seconds after the ASAT accepted new firing fix, they experienced a power fade. This time Sorrel did cut lose with a string of expletives. That little Russian bitch was garbage, he roared. A flying piece of Soviet shit not fit to be in the air.

Hedges cut him off: "Wait a minute, sir."

"What?"

"I think I know what it is." The chief punched in a command. Instantly the screen lit up again, but it was blank.

"What're you doing?"

"I figure the unit was simply running a pre-firing check on the power grid and ran into a blown circuit. I just punched in a check override to see if she'll re-initiate switch-on."

The screen flared brightly and the same countdown number that had been registered when power had failed came back on again: one minute, fifty-six seconds . . .

"We got her!" Hedges and Sorrel yowled together.

Someone said, "Hey, but won't the firing fix be off now?"

"Oh, fuck, that's right," Hedges moaned.

Sorrel stared at the seaman who'd spoken, as if he wanted to smash in the man's face.

"How long were we off?" Hedges shouted. "Goddammit, didn't anybody time it?"

No one spoke.

Hedges cursed. "That means we've gotta go back to Cheyenne for another fix."

"There isn't time," Sorrel snapped. "We'll estimate down lag." He swung to the nearest man and shouted right into his face. "Estimate! Estimate!"

"Jesus, I don't know. Eight, ten seconds?"

To the next man: "You?"

"Ten seconds, sir."

Sorrel wheeled back to Hedges. "Ten?"

"Yeah, that's about right. But, Christ, we're shooting in the dark."

"Adjust the countdown ten seconds."

The chief tapped in the command. The screen went on with

the working sequences for two seconds, then went blank and came back with a new countdown.

One minute, twenty-eight seconds . . .

Cas had never felt so frustrated and helpless. He was lying on his ass in sea grass while eternity ticked away. At the same time, like a triggering mechanism, his mind began that panic-laden acceleration into terror, his heart thumping ever louder in his chest. He felt Kiri's hand grip his arm, and her own terror trembled in her fingers like a hot energy. He put his hand over hers and turned to look southward. What would it be like when Mururoa went up? he wondered. Would they see the mushroom cloud? Or would the explosion be so horrendous that its concussion wave alone would send this pissant island and them straight out of sight like an elevator plummeting to hell?

He closed his eyes and for a delirious moment grappled with the realization of death. It was a strange encounter, full of specters. Like all men, Cas had always hoped that death would come swiftly, unexpectedly. Not with himself primed up like a man in front of a firing squad, waiting for it. What a shitty way to die, he thought.

He suddenly stiffened in rage. If he was going to die, at least he was going to take it standing up. He twisted over and released Kiri's hand. Putting his palms against the grass, he started to lift himself up. Frowning, she glanced at him in alarm. As she moved to pull him down beside her again, the sunlight sparkled off her ruby ring.

Cas paused, staring at it. And something in his mind went *wham*! Memories of chemistry classes at Scripps came flooding back. Ruby: corundum from the Hindi word *kurand*. Molecular sign Al_2O_3: aluminum oxide. Composed of hexagonal crystals capable of *piezoelectric resonator effect* . . .

With a half yell, half curse, he grabbed Kiri's hand and began frantically trying to pry the ring off her finger. She moaned with pain and curled over, eyes blazing at him. "Your ring," he yelled. "Get it off! It'll draw the laser beam!"

For a second, she was puzzled and then her eyes shot open. "Oh, my God!"

It was hung up on her knuckle. Cas plunged her finger into his mouth, slimed it with his saliva. Then, whirling it over and over, he worked it off her finger. It slipped out of his hand and fell into the sand.

"Shit!"

Clawing at the sand, he finally found it. He popped it into his mouth and clamped down. In one clean lunge he was on his feet and charging over the rise of sand and coral and then down onto the beach, sprinting toward the water.

He took a quick glance at the aircraft to position himself and then dove in. His final, wild dash back to the Saber had begun.

Chief Hedges's fingers curled almost gently over his computer keys, their tips just touching. He kept calling aloud as the ASAT's countdown flashed on his console: "Firing fix now on 31 seconds."

Sorrel was leaning against his shoulder. Behind him, every man in the command was standing around with a nervous, wild-eyed look. Sorrel growled at them, "Back off, dammit. Back the fuck off." The men shuffled slightly, but stayed right where they were.

"Twenty-five seconds and counting," Hedges said.

"Verify firing command."

Hedges's fingers went *tit . . . tit . . . tit.*

In a corner of the chief's screen, a light flashed: Verify accept///Verify accept.

"She's on. Coming to 19.5 seconds."

"Give her full automatic release."

Tit . . . tit . . . tit.

"She's on her own," the chief said.

That's it, Sorrel thought. His job was over. He felt deflated as his whole being went down, crumbling toward his groin. He whirled and headed for the toilet.

The Kamov was now completely disregarding any sensor pick-ups of moving bodies close to the aircraft, even those within the no-pass perimeter. Once something had actually touched the ship, which sent a bursting quiver through the sensor system. But the computer was now fixed on the high-priority processing. Like a human brain, it refused to deviate until completion of the primary firing. Quad-seconds flashed on cockpit monitors.

Time to NAVSAT CPF: 17.25 seconds . . .

*   *   *

A shark came at Cas. Straight out of the green haze, moving with that humped, erratic motion of feeding frenzy that had been triggered by the explosions and the blood. Through his blurred vision, Cas saw the dark, blunt snout and swung at it with his fist. He felt it strike and then rasp over skin as rough as slivers of glass. The animal veered sharply, throwing turbulence into his face.

He angled down and scooted into a narrow crevice between coral heads. As he passed through, an edge of the coral sliced across his shoulder, stinging. He plunged to the sandy bottom and pulled himself along. When he looked up, he saw the shadow of the aircraft's stern silhouetted against the faint blueness of the sky.

A red glow fused into that blueness, spread over the surface, and gave the dancing, sunlit dimples a pinkish tinge. Feeling all his senses come alive with gorged blood, he drew his legs into a crouch, planted his feet, and then uncoiled. He shot up, angling slightly forward, his arms gathering in massive amounts of water and shoving them back as he rocketed to the surface.

The Kamov was running constant update checks of the fusion-chamber ignition, barrel alignment, and firing-convergence time fix. Everything came back green, cockpit panels throwing tiny dots of glowing turquoise light. In the pilot's heads-up display, grid lines were converging to a point as the NAVSAT CPF clicked up into 6.50 seconds . . .

Seeing the dome of the aircraft glow, Kiri felt her heart clutch. The illumination fused crimson, yet it carried a horrible darkness, a lethal viper's strike that would in seconds strike Cas and sunder him into bloody bits.

Although the death of millions hovered all over the sky, at that moment her only thought was of him. Mindlessly she sprang out of the wash trench and ran down to the water's edge, screaming, waving her hands madly.

The Saber continued to glow. Cas was nowhere in sight. Cursing, she bent, yanked out the P-6 pistol, and started firing.

Cas blew through the surface like a dolphin. Directly in front of him, not three feet away, was the large mouth of the aircraft's left exhaust port. As his upward momentum dissipated, he flailed out for a handhold and managed to grab the upper edge of the port and swung himself in.

His body dangling, he clung there. He was looking right up the exhaust tunnel: baffle channels, milled surfaces showing metal discoloration from jet burn. It smelled of residual fuel and the sharp acetate stench of resin. The entire ship was vibrating gently, like the quiver of a frightened animal.

Kiri's rounds sundered the air and then *whanged* against the aircraft's fuselage. As two richocheted nearby, Cas glanced back at the beach. She was standing near the water's edge, feet planted, arms braced in a policeman's stance.

He was overcome with fury. "Get away!" he screamed. "Get down!" Suddenly the firing stopped. A sudden silence rolled over him, disturbed only by the soft hum of the fusion dome and the gentle quiver of the metal beneath his hand.

He turned back to the port. Studying the outer rim, he saw a tiny strip of highly polished metal around it. Less than an inch wide, it glistened in the sunlight like platinum. Grunting, feeling his limbs trembling with panic, he spat out Kiri's ring into his right palm. It rolled across and onto his fingers and he almost dropped it. He snapped his hand over, caught it, and brought it up between his thumb and forefinger.

As gently as he could, his shaking hand placed the ring at the very center of the exhaust port strip. Seeing it start to slide off, he brought it back, held it, the huge ruby facing astern. It held, the jewel shimmying with the ship's vibration. Slowly, tentatively, he released his fingers.

With a furious uncoiling of his every nerve, he pushed back and away from the aircraft. He twisted momentarily in space, and then he was in the water. Scrambling around crazily, like a man on a steep roof, he started swimming furiously back toward the beach.

He sensed something huge in the water near him and heard the faint, chirping grunt of a shark. He couldn't see it, but he bellowed a blast of air and felt the shark swirl off. On he swam, whinnying with tension deep in his throat.

His outburst, though, had depleted almost all of his oxygen. Already his chest was beginning to ache. He angled upward. Just below the surface, he rolled onto his back and let his face break through. He gulped air once, cleared, gulped another lungful. Through the thin film of water he could see the sky, blue as chicory blossoms.

And then it was bisected by a tiny beam of light, thin as a needle yet green, phosphorescent, as bright as the sun's core. Its brilliance burned its image on his retinas. With it came a crackling, thunderous rending as it split the air.

He let loose a garbled cry of fear, arched his back, and tried to pull himself back down. One-millionth of a second later, there was a violent explosion. He felt it jar through the water as he drove for the bottom. The dark coral came up to meet him. It was dappled with a crazy quilt of shadows from the surface, which had been shattered into a thousand tiny prisms.

Then objects started falling through the sheet of prisms. Chunks of metal the size of truck tires, shafts and pieces of struts, minute bits sizzled past him like bullets. In the same instant the rolling concussion wave caught up to him and hurled him violently forward. Balling his body, feeling everything around him vibrating and roaring and echoing, he rode it like a wave.

Something ricocheted off his hip. He felt no pain, yet the jarring blow seemed to change the contour of his body. He glanced back. A thick fume of blood was coming off his side.

Gradually the turbulence and sound began to dissipate. An echo of it riffled far off in deep water as the concussion thrust rode the contour bottom, fading and surging. And then it was swallowed up, just like that, as if a gigantic door had been slammed shut against it. All that was left was a deep hissing sound and the roaring still inside his head.

He kept swimming, eyes closed, going full out. An endless amount of time seemed to pass, but finally his stroking hands touched bottom. He lunged to his feet and headed through the shallows, going toward the beach. He looked back. Where the Saber had been, there was now only smoking debris and a twisted, shapeless black metal bulk forming steam clouds that distorted the air like mirages.

He fell down on the sand and in that instant, as if turned on by a switch, pain shot through his body with scalding ferocity. He gritted his teeth and rolled over. His right buttocks had been sliced open, and blood was pumping out onto the sand. Grabbing the wound, he felt raw flesh that was spongy and hot. He clamped down hard on it.

But where was Kiri?

He turned and looked up through the line of palms. The atoll looked as if it had been strafed by a fighter. Several of the stunted Samoan palm trees had been torn out of the ground, and small grass fires dotted the crest. Chunks of the aircraft, still burning, were littered all over.

Kiri was dead. She had not quite made it back to the sanctuary of the wash trench before the force of the exploding aircraft had hurled her across forty feet of beach into a tree trunk, instantly breaking her neck. She lay curled over, her head nearly touching her thigh. Her eyes were open, but they reflected only the faint, washed blueness of the sky.

Numb, Cas sat down and stared at her. Her body was not torn open, not even bleeding. It was as if her life force had simply slipped away, that sharp, flashing energy of laughter and anger and passion, dissipated like a whisper in the night.

Obscenities and tender phrases bunched chaotically in his mind, touched searingly at his heart. He sighed, aching. Finally he reached out and closed her eyes with his thumb and forefinger. Then he lifted her and straightened her body out on the sand and proceeded to cover her with a blanket of sea grass.

He touched her for one final time: the soft sheen of her hair, the maple-colored smoothness of her skin. Then he rose and walked away. He gathered more sea grass to stanch the flow of his own blood. Holding it, he sat down in the cool, moist sand near the water's edge and looked out at the sea, waiting, silently and motionlessly, for those who would come to find him.